John Macpherson

Life and Labors of Duncan Matheson

The Scottish Evangelist

John Macpherson

Life and Labors of Duncan Matheson
The Scottish Evangelist

ISBN/EAN: 9783337238896

Printed in Europe, USA, Canada, Australia, Japan

Cover: Foto ©Raphael Reischuk / pixelio.de

More available books at **www.hansebooks.com**

LIFE AND LABORS

OF

DUNCAN MATHESON,

The Scottish Evangelist.

BY THE
REV. JOHN MACPHERSON.

"REALITY IS THE GREAT THING: I HAVE ALWAYS SOUGHT REALITY."

NEW YORK:

ROBERT CARTER AND BROTHERS,

530 BROADWAY.

1876.

CAMBRIDGE :
PRESS OF
JOHN WILSON & SON.

ST. JOHNLAND
STEREOTYPE FOUNDRY,
SUFFOLK CO., N. Y.

PREFACE.

DURING his last days on earth Duncan Matheson, in accordance with the wishes of his friends, set himself to write an account of his own life. The effort proved too much for his enfeebled health, and his autobiographic notes, stopping short at the beginning of his evangelistic course, were left in no fit state for publication. The facts recorded by his own hand have, however, been embodied in the present memoir; and the narrative of his conversion, by far the most valuable portion of his hastily written notes, has been given in his own words.

The cases of conversion described in illustration of the work of grace and the success of our evangelist are matters of fact of which I have the fullest knowledge, most of the individuals concerned being personally known to me; but I have deemed it best not to give their names. On similar grounds I have also in several instances withheld the names of localities.

Many of the incidents narrated I learned from the lips of my lamented friend; in fact, a great part of the volume has been derived from my recollection of the man and the work.

The best narrative of his evangelistic labors, I have reason to believe, was contained in his letters to his wife; but these have been destroyed. Vexed at the too hasty and too loud trumpeting of results on the part of some, and convinced that thereby the Holy Spirit was grieved and discredit cast upon the work, he set his face against even the appearance of what he regarded as a great evil, and for several years wrote at the foot of every letter giving account of his labors, "Destroy this." The stern decree was only too faithfully obeyed. In this way, doubtless, he preserved a full consciousness of the purity of his motives—no light matter truly to a servant of Jesus Christ; and however we may regret the loss of the letters, we cannot but admire the self-denying spirit of the man who thus deliberately sacrificed his own name at the shrine of his Master's glory.

This tribute to the memory of my truly noble friend I humbly commend to the Holy Spirit; at the same time earnestly entreating my Christian readers to pray that the book, as an echo of the evangelist's voice, may prolong his extraordinary ministry, and be the means of saving many souls.

CONTENTS.

LIFE AND LABORS

OF

DUNCAN MATHESON.

———··———

CHAPTER I.

BIRTH AND BOYHOOD.

Duncan Matheson was born at Huntly, in Aberdeenshire, on the 22d day of November, 1824. This little inland town, some of my readers may not know, is the capital of Strathbogie, a district now famous in the ecclesiastical history of Scotland as the scene of a fierce conflict, some thirty years ago, between the church and the civil power. The fame of that struggle has sounded far beyond the shores of Scotland, and its issues are constantly growing more momentous with the revolving years.

Neither the village nor the adjacent country presents features very striking or interesting. The soil is not of a generous nature; but its sons have developed the sturdiest manhood in its subjugation and culture. The climate, rigorously stern, is often in winter of arctic severity; but the keen biting winds

seem only to have sharpened the people's wits; the
gloomy sky if it has made them *dour* has helped to
make them sober-minded, and battling with storms
and drifting snows has proved a good training for
the battle of life. Bannocks of oatmeal and bickers
of porridge, together with early and successful con-
tendings with that great army of strong truths
whose leader presents to every young Scot this
memorable challenge, "What is the chief end of
man?" have contributed not a little in raising up
generations of strong, free men, able to push their
way and hold their own anywhere in the world. In
fact, hard work, coarse but wholesome fare, a severe
climate, the Bible, the church, the school, and the
catechism, have conspired to develop in them the
tougher elements of the Scottish character. The
inhabitants of that north-eastern province are as
hard as their native granite, as stern as their own
winter, and of a spirit as independent as the winds
that play on the summit of their lofty Benachee.
In short, the people of Huntly are Aberdonians of
the most Aberdonian type. Shrewd, hard-headed,
rough-grained, having ever a keen eye to the main
chance, and not to be overcome by force or over-
reached by fraud, they are a people pre-eminently
canny and Scotch.

In one of the plain homely dwellings, of which the
Huntly of that day was almost entirely composed,
the subject of this memoir first saw the light. His
parents belonged to that better class of the common

people whose intelligence, industry, thrift, God-fearing uprightness, and honest pride, have contributed
so much to the prosperity and glory of their country.
From his father, a Ross-shire man, connected with a
family of some note in that county, young Matheson
inherited the Celtic fire which fused all his powers
into one great passion; whilst from his mother he
seemed to derive the strong good sense, the irrepressible wit, and boundless generosity, that were
among his chief characteristics. To his mother, indeed, as in the case of many other men who in their
day have been powerful workers of good and uncompromising enemies of evil, the boy, the man, and the
Christian, owed more than pen and ink can set forth.
Her loving and fervent spirit, her wise and gracious
ways, impressed and captivated the warm-hearted
and ingenuous boy; her prayers issued in his conversion after her gentle head had been pillowed among
the clods; and her lovely memory glowing in his
fancy became a force, not the less mighty for its gen-
tleness, throughout his life. So true-hearted mothers
often live in their strong sons, the little quiet rivulet
somehow begetting the great broad river. Strong-
willed and even wayward as was the boy, he loved
and reverenced his mother with singular devotion.

The father, who for nearly thirty years occupied
the humble but honorable post of mail-runner between Huntly and Banff, enjoyed but a slender income; and it needed all the diligence and thrift of
the mother to keep the house and five little children

above want. They had their pinching times; but pinching times have done much, under God, to develop the real strength of Scottish character. In after years, when Duncan Matheson had taken up his father Colin's business of mail-runner, with this difference, that the son carried letters for another King, even Christ, and ran upon a longer line than the Banff and Huntly road, often did he remember how "his poor dear mother used to sit till midnight mending and making their clothes, and yet the beggar was never sent empty from the door." Sometimes the brave little heart gave way, and the child covering his face with the bedclothes would sob, and long for the time when he should be able to aid his mother in the struggles of life. One day coming into possession of a small piece of money, earned by running a message for a neighbor, he took his stand at the window of a little shop, which seemed to embrace in its contents all that was desirable on earth, and there meditated a purchase. The ginger-bread men riding on ginger-bread horses did not much tempt him; nor was he overcome by the little shining clasp-knife, so dear to the heart of boys. Remembering his mother, he invested his money in tea. Hastening home, he secretly deposited his purchase in the cupboard, and watched till he obtained a full reward in the glad surprise of his parent on finding her empty store thus unexpectedly and mysteriously replenished.

The lad was sent early to school, where he made

rapid progress, his love of books being fostered by
frequent contact with the teacher, who lodged in
the house of the Mathesons. In those days there
were two schools in Huntly, the parish school and
an adventure school, between which there was a
perpetual feud. Almost daily the boys met in battle, and young Matheson, whose martial spirit was
thus early stirred, took an eager part in the fray.
The school of that time wore an air of awful stern-
ness and solemnity. The thong was real master.
The impression made by the opening prayer was
too often sadly undone by impression of the *leather*,
as it fell with unmitigated severity on the tortured
fingers of some little rebel. Strange scenes, the result probably of that undue severity of government,
were sometimes witnessed in the school of those
days. A stream of water having been turned one
day from a neighboring lane into the schoolroom, the
master proceeded as a matter of course to find out
the author of the mischief. Young Matheson was
unjustly charged, the real criminal having turned
false witness; and loud protestations of innocence
notwithstanding, Duncan must be flogged. Here
the authority of the master failed. The lad's sense
of innocence, stimulated by some other feeling not
quite akin to innocence, roused him to self-defence;
and amidst the cheers of the whole school the scholar
beat the master, and reduced him to the necessity
of a truce.

The master, who was an earnest Christian and a

preacher of the Gospel, did his duty faithfully and well; and Duncan Matheson never ceased to speak of him with feelings of deepest gratitude and esteem. The pains taken by the teacher to polish that rough but genuine Cairngorm were not thrown away.

In the matter of religion it was not a good time in those northern parts. *Moderatism,* which means a religion without earnestness, a form without life, and a Gospel without grace, cast its deadly shadow over many a parish. Light, indeed, was beginning to dawn, the spirit that moved Chalmers was abroad, and when rare opportunity afforded men were listening to the ancient story of the cross as if it were a new thing. As yet, however, it was only dim dawn. Strange doctrines were given forth from the pulpit of many a parish church. One taught the people that if they paid their debts and lived a quiet life they were sure of reaching heaven. His brother in the neighboring parish declared, on the other hand, that nobody can attain to assurance of salvation until the day of judgment, and that the children of God generally die under a cloud—a doctrine he clenched with the scripture, "Whom the Lord loveth He chasteneth." A third publicly stigmatized praying people as hypocrites. A fourth acknowledged his dislike of preaching by calling Sabbath "the hanging day." Another apologized to his audience for having once used "that offensive and unpolite expression *hell.*" Several of these pastors were famous for their skill in agriculture; but while they kept a well-stocked farm-yard, their scanty supply of sermons grew more dry and mouldy year by year. The preaching was no more likely to awaken a slumbering congregation, than was the chirping of sparrows in the hedge to arouse the still, sad sleepers in the neighboring kirkyard. A clear, full statement of "the finished work" of Jesus, as the one only and all-sufficient substitute and sin-bearer, was seldom heard. As for the grace of the Holy Spirit the people were no more taught to ex-pect comfort from His fellowship than from the wind howling among the forest trees. In a certain parish contiguous to the district in which our missionary labored, the minister was one day catechising the people, and put to a woman, noted for the then rare qualities of earnestness and zeal, the question, "How many persons are there in the Godhead?" To the astonishment of all present she replied, "There are *two* persons in the Godhead, the Father and the Son." Again the minister put the question, and this time with a caution. The same answer was given. "You see," said the parson, turning pompously to his elders, and glancing round upon the people, "you see what comes of high-flown zeal and hyp-ocritical pretence. This woman thinks to teach others, and herself is more ignorant than a child. What gross ignorance! Woman, don't you know that the correct answer is, 'There are *three* persons in the Godhead, the Father, the Son, and the Holy Ghost,'" etc. "Sir," replied the woman, "I ken verra

weel that the catechism says sae. But whether am
I to believe, the catechism or yersel'? We hear you
name the Father, an' somtimes, but nae aften ye
mak mention o' the Son; but wha ever heerd you
speak aboot the Holy Ghost? 'Deed, sir, ye never
sae muckle as tauld us whether there be ony Holy
Ghost, let alane oor need o' his grace." The minister stood rebuked; and the people went away home
to discuss and think.

The Lord's flock was scattered on the dark mountains. Some were wandering in a wilderness of
perplexity; some were sticking fast in the quag-
mire of earthliness; some were ready to perish in
deep pits of deadly error; and sad were the bleat-
ings of the sheep and the lambs as they pined away
in want. Meanwhile the description of unfaithful
shepherds given by the prophet Isaiah was realized
to the letter. "His watchmen are blind; they are
all ignorant, they are all dumb dogs, they cannot
bark; sleeping, lying down, loving to slumber.
Yea, they are greedy dogs which can never have
enough, and they are shepherds that cannot understand: they all look to their own way, every one
for his gain, from his quarter. Come ye, say they,
I will fetch wine, and we will fill ourselves with
strong drink; and to-morrow shall be as this day,
and much more abundant" (Isaiah lvi. 10–12).

But amidst the Egyptian darkness there was a
people who had light in their dwellings. These
were chiefly Seceders and Independents. Amongst

the godly Dissenters there arose at this time a
notable preacher, Mr. George Cowie, grand-uncle of
Duncan Matheson. He was a man of rare humor,
great force of character, and unbounded zeal; qualities in which his relative, the subject of this memoir,
strikingly resembled him. Cowie was both pastor
and evangelist. When he began his work in Huntly,
where he was ordained as pastor of the Secession
Church, he received a baptism of reproach and persecution. The haters of evangelical truth mobbed
and pelted him; but he took all meekly, and though
well-nigh blinded by showers of dirt and rotten
eggs, he turned to his little band of followers and
bravely said, "Courage, friends, courage! Pray on;
the devil is losing ground."

Many who thirsted for the Gospel came from distant parishes to hear this bold witness for the truth.
On Sabbath morning you could see them gather on
their way to Huntly; one from yonder turf cot in
the midst of a wilderness of peat moss, where the
only sign of life is the smoke curling to the sky;
another from a little farm recently reclaimed from
a marshy waste which anywhere out of Scotland
would be regarded as an eternal morass ; and a
third from down a lonely glen where silence is seldom broken save by the cry of the wild bird. Thus
they gather from their native mists in search of
light—broad-shouldered men with blue bonnet and
plaid, thoughtful matrons with Bible and Psalm-
book wrapt in clean white handkerchief, and neatly-

dressed maidens, light-stepping but modest; and as
they journey together they talk of the things that
concern the King. Reaching a little well at the wayside they sit down and refresh themselves. They
need this rest, for they have come a long journey,
some five miles, some ten, and some even fifteen.
A drink from the well is followed by a draught of
the pure water of life. With the blue heavens for
a canopy, the green earth for a carpet, and the little
birds for a choir, they worship God in that great
temple of nature in which the religion of Scotland
has oftentimes been baptized with the blood of her
children. They sing the twenty-third Psalm. In
grave, sweet melody their hearts go up to heaven
in mingled exercise of faith, hope, and charity, as
they repeat the most familiar of Scottish household
words:

> "The Lord's my shepherd ; I'll not want :
>   He makes me down to lie
> In pastures green ; He leadeth me
>   The quiet waters by."

To some of those God-fearers the song is a matter of faith rather than of feeling. To others it is
a spring of hope and expectation, whilst in some
hearts it stirs joy and love. There are those too
who as yet knowing not conscious faith, or hope, or
love, or joy, dimly discern the beauty of this holy,
blessed, childlike worship, and secretly desire, almost without perceiving in themselves the desire,

to know the happiness of that people whose God is
the Lord.

When the Psalm is sung all heads are bent and
a prayer follows—such a prayer as we have heard
among the heather on a hill-side: "O God, oor souls
are jist as dry as the heather: oor herts are as hard
as the granite stane: but Thou that gi'est the draps
o' dew to the heather, gie us the drappins o' thy
grace this day, and let thy ain love licht upon oor
hard herts like the birdie sittin' singin' on the rock
yonner; an' fill the souls o' thy fowk this day wi'
peace and joy till they're rinnin' o'er like the water-
spout on the brae. Lord, it'll be nae loss to you,
an' it'll be a grand bargain for us, an' we'll mind ye
on't tae a' eternity. Amen."

The Haldanes were at this time engaged in their
noble evangelistic labors. Mr. Cowie permitted
James Haldane to occupy his pulpit, whilst himself remained at the door to listen. At the close of
the service the minister, convinced that God was
with the lay-preacher, rushed into the church and
invited the people to return in the evening and again
hear the stranger. For this encouragement given
to an evangelist manifestly heaven-sent, Cowie was
thrust out of the Secession. But he was not the
man to be silenced. His faith and zeal rose to the
occasion: he went on preaching and laboring for
souls as he had never done before, and the result
was the formation of an Independent Church. The
light spread. The torch was rudely shaken, but the

flame rose upon the night, and many afar off wondered and came to see. In barns and out-of-the-
way places meetings were held; and often in the
open air the manly voice of George Cowie was heard
calling sinners to the Saviour in terms he loved to
repeat—"There is life for a look! there is life for a
look!"

This faithful servant of God was consumed with
zeal. He was sometimes so overpowered with a
sense of the value of souls that he needed to be
supported by the elders as he went from the vestry
to the pulpit. Blessed, surely, are such ministers,
and highly favored the people who enjoy their ministry! Speaking of preaching, Mr. Cowie used to
say, "Go direct to conscience, and in every sermon
take your hearers to the judgment-seat." One day
a preacher, who occupied his place, spoke as if the
Holy Spirit was not needed by either saint or sinner.
At the close of the service, Cowie stood up on the
pulpit steps, and solemnly said, "Sirs, haud in wi'
your auld freen, the Holy Ghost, for if ye ance grieve
Him awa, ye'll nae get Him back sae easy."

Here Mr. Rowland Hill used to preach with all
his wonted dash and power. At a diet of catechising, a method of teaching to which some of the most
valuable and characteristic elements of the old Scottish religion were due, the English evangelist was
present and put a few simple questions. The answers were promptly and correctly given with the
superadded request of an old man, "Gang deeper,

sir, gang deeper." Mr. Hill having expressed his satisfaction with the results of the examination, the aged inquirer asked and obtained permission to put a question. "Sir," said he to Mr. Hill, "can ye reconcile the universal call o' the Gospel wi' the doctrine o' a particler eleck?" In reply Mr. Hill frankly admitted that while he held both the doctrine of election and the universal call, he was unable to solve the theological problem proposed by the gray-headed inquirer.

Mr. Cowie exhibited fine tact in dealing with men. "One of his attached hearers was the wife of a wealthy farmer, who, after weeping and praying in vain for her ungodly husband, brought her grief before her pastor, whose preaching she could by no persuasion induce him to hear. After listening to the case, which seemed quite inaccessible, he inquired, 'Is there any thing your good man has a liking to?' 'He heeds for nothing in this world,' was the reply, 'forbye his beasts and his siller, an' it be na his fiddle.' The hint was enough: the minister soon found his way to the farm-house, where after a dry reception, and kindly inquiries about cattle and corn, he awoke the farmer's feelings on the subject of his favorite pastime. The fiddle was produced, and the man of earth was astonished and charmed with the sweet music it gave forth in the hands of the feared and hated man of God. The minister next induced him to promise to return his call, by the offered treat of a finer in-

2

strument in his own house, where he was delighted
with the swelling tones of a large violin, and needed
then but slight persuasion from his wife to accom-
pany her and hear his friend preach. The word
took effect in conviction and salvation; and the
grovelling earth-worm was transformed into a free-
hearted son of God, full of the lively hope of the
great inheritance above."*

This good and faithful servant of Jesus Christ,
loved and honored over a wide extent of country,
died and left behind him the precious legacy of
many spiritual children bearing the likeness of his
own hearty, thorough, downright Christian character. Thousands followed his body to the grave, and
on his tombstone were inscribed the words of the
prophet Daniel, "They that be wise shall shine as
the brightness of the firmament; and they that
turn many to righteousness, as the stars forever
and ever." In after years his grand-nephew, Duncan Matheson, when newly ushered into the mar-
velous light of the Gospel, used to kneel beside the
grave in the silence and solitude of night, and cry
mightily to heaven, praying that the mantle of his
venerated relative might fall upon him, and that
the words of the prophet might be illustrated in
him also. That prayer was abundantly answered.

We are strangely linked to the past; its traditions, especially such as come to us through the

* Life and Letters of Elizabeth, last Duchess of Gordon. By
the Rev. A. Moody Stuart.

channel of flesh and blood, go far to make us what we are. Though the Matheson family were connected with the Established Church, they had strong leanings to the godly Dissenters; and in his early life Duncan drank in the story and teaching of his uncle from his mother's lips. The banner which dropped from the hands of George Cowie was taken up and nobly sustained by Mr. Hill, the pastor of the Independent Church, and Mr. Millar, the minister of the Secession, faithful servants of Jesus Christ, whose indefatigable labors prepared the ground for the wider sowing and richer harvest of our time. One day the worthy pastor of the Independent Church laid his hand upon the head of the boisterously frank and manly boy as he romped on the street, and bestowed upon him a prayerful blessing. Did the man of God see in young Matheson a second George Cowie, and even then separate the lad unto the Gospel of Christ by the laying on of believing hands? There are foretokens of a man's future that find no place in our philosophy. At any rate the susceptible heart of the boy was thus impressed, and he used to follow the godly minister upon the street with a curious and wondering reverence. Throughout life he never forgot the gentle hand laid upon his head—the blessing and the prayer.

From infancy up through boyhood the good angel of conviction never ceased to follow Duncan Matheson. Sometimes there is a lull of unholy peace; then comes a disturbed period when the gracious Spirit strives with the rebel heart. Now he seems near the kingdom of God; suddenly a back-wave of temptation carries him anew into the deep. Frequently he is all but overcome by drawings of invisible love; but as yet young flesh and blood prove too strong for these gentle touches of grace. One evening he is passing along the street and hears the sound of praise issuing from a cottage where a prayer-meeting is in progress. A good impulse carries him to the window. Peering in at a chink, he sees the faces of the company brightened up by no ordinary radiance, and as he listens he hears their glad voices singing,

> "O greatly bless'd the people are
> The joyful sound that know;
> In brightness of thy face, O Lord,
> They ever on shall go."

His heart is touched; he wishes he were amongst them to share their joy; but like one who would purchase a pearl were it not for the greatness of the price, he goes away with nothing but vague longings and hesitating resolves. These feelings do not last long; they are but the morning cloud and early dew. Next day he is a very ringleader in persecuting the children of the saints, whom he mocks and calls by opprobrious names.

A special interest was taken in young Matheson's spiritual welfare by James Maitland, an aged Chris-

tian and a convert of Mr. Cowie's. This old disciple
was always ready in his own quaint and homely way
to testify to the truth and grace of God. When a
shallow theorist one day attempted to make the way
into the kingdom of heaven easy to the flesh, James
said, "I ken verra weel that a human faith can receive a human testimony; but, man, dinna ye ken it
needs a divine faith to receive a divine testimony."
To another who paid him a compliment for his Christian worth, he replied, "I sometimes wonner if I'm
a Christian at a'; for ye ken we ocht to lay doon our
lives for the brithren, but I can hardly bring mysel'
to like the cross-grained anes." He kept an eye on
the young people of the place, and his wise, loving
counsels were not in vain. To a lad about to leave
the town he said, "Young man, you are like a ship
going to sea without compass or helm." These words
led to his conversion. Maitland's heart was much
drawn to Duncan Matheson, in whom he could discern not a little of the natural character of his minister and spiritual father. Duncan strove hard to
keep out of the old man's way, but being sent on an
errand one day to Maitland's house he was fairly
caught. James shut the door on himself and the
boy, and began to tell him the story of Mr. Cowie's
conversion. This done he brought the conversation
to a practical bearing by asking the lad about his
soul's case. The answer was unsatisfactory.

Then followed homely, tender words about "God's
wonderfu' love to sinners," and "the warm hert o'

Jesus yirnin' to save," and "the kind Spirit strivin' wi'
a' his micht," with solemn remonstrance as well as
touching appeal, not without effect, since conscience
was all on James's side.   Duncan went away very
unhappy.   The hour of decision had not yet arrived;
but one gun on the rampart of unbelief had been
spiked.   The impression made by Maitland's faithful
words and tender dealings was never wholly lost.

Speaking of this period he says, "My conscience
often pricked me, and if the thunder rolled I went
to prayer.   I knew only the Lord's prayer, and used it
as an incantation to ward off evil.   If I saw a funeral
I trembled, and thoughts of judgment pressed hard
upon me."   One evening his mother, who instead of
always speaking directly to her children about salvation, wisely followed the method of reading aloud
from some interesting book, had fallen upon a well-
known illustration of the endlessness of eternity.
Suppose a little bird comes once in a thousand
years and carries away a particle of dust from yon
lofty mountain, how vast a number of years must
elapse ere the huge mass has been entirely removed!
And yet when those countless myriads of years have
come and gone, eternity will be no nearer an end
than it was at first.   What, then, will be the misery
of the lost in the place where their worm dieth not,
and the fire is not quenched?   Such was the impression made upon the boy's mind that he could not
sleep, and spent a great part of the night in weeping.   The germ of truth thus lodged by a mother's

hand in the heart of her son was not lost. It did not indeed result in his immediate conversion, but it took hold of his spirit, and by the blessing of God became a great power in his soul; for throughout his entire Christian course one thought was never absent from his view, one motive never ceased to work mightily in his heart, one argument never failed to drop from his lips with amazing power on the ears of thousands, and that was *the endlessness of eternity.* Little did that mother dream of the great work she was doing as she read the simple illustration in the hearing of her boy. Little did she imagine the vast harvest to be reaped from that seedling, and the mighty forces that were being set in motion by so gentle a touch.

The dread of future punishment held him in check, even in his most lawless days. "The eternity of it," he says, "more than any thing else, awed me, and if I could have persuaded myself that after thousands of years the torments of hell should cease, I would have given full swing to my evil heart, and more madly than I was even then doing would have rushed on to eternal death."

The death of his sister Ann, "a sweet, holy child, who talked of Jesus with her latest breath," drew the furrows of conviction fresh and deep in his already well-ploughed heart; and as he stood by the grave, "the dull, muffled sound of the clods dropping upon the coffin-lid seemed to ring into his conscience this one word, Eternity."

Sickness followed: it was another gentle messenger from Him whose name is Love. Many thorns now vexed his pillow; it was sovereign grace arousing him from his dangerous sleep. A host of evils seemed to surround him; it was a host of angels sent to shut him in and chase the wanderer home. As yet he saw not the Saviour; he saw only the clouds that are about his throne. The darkness which he imagined revealed the Avenger concealed his Redeemer, and the sounds that seemed to his awakened conscience to be the roll of the chariot wheels of death, were but the echoes of approaching salvation. Sometimes he would bury his fears in the grave of good resolution, and write upon the tombstone, " By and by ; " but from the dead his convictions would arise with ghastly horror, and then his wretchedness, overflowing its banks, would pour itself out in wrathful torrents, making the whole house unhappy and even afraid. They knew not the terrible conflict that raged in his breast; they saw not the misery of the maddened spirit wrestling with the Almighty, and heard not the despairing cry, " Would God I had never been born? "

Before his mind's eye one great truth now began to appear in hazy outline. The absolute necessity of being born again was beginning to take hold of his thoughts. It was a point gained—one step towards the light. Not seldom did he pray God to convert him, though, like Augustine, he was fain

to add "not yet." Some friends perceiving his
talents advised him to enter the University, and
offered him a bursary on condition of his studying
for the ministry—a course which his parents earnestly desired him to follow; but he refused, saying
with characteristic frankness, "A minister ought
to be a converted and a holy man. I am not that.
I cannot do it." When he and two companions
were urged to become members of the church,
straightforward as usual, he replied, "I am not converted, and you know it. G—— is not converted,
nor is D——. We are on the brink, and you would
push us over. You would have us go to the Lord's
table in our sins, and then on Sabbath evening you
would pray for the unworthy communicants." Turning to his companions he said, "Come away;" and
as he went out of the minister's presence he said to
himself, "The whole thing is a sham. I may as
well be an infidel." In all this there may have
been a lack of courtesy, and a little pride; but he
had noticed the unfaithfulness of certain pastors in
the admission of young communicants, and the sad
effect on the communicants themselves, who made
a pillow of the Lord's table for their deadly slumbers, and his honest spirit rebelled against what he
believed to be an unholy sham.

The disruption of the Church of Scotland with its
stirring events drew near. Patronage was doing
its evil works. The conflict between the Church
and the civil power was becoming more fierce and

uncompromising. A minister was thrust into the
parish of Marnoch against the will of the people.
Duncan Matheson was present at the forced settle-
ment, and, young though he was, warmly sympathized with the Christian flock, whose rights were
thus trampled under foot. The scene made a deep
impression on his heart. But not until he submit-
ted himself to the Lord Jesus did he rightly understand the great question of the time—the independence of the Church, and the Crown rights of the
Saviour as her sole King and Head. At this time
able and faithful ministers of the Gospel were sent
down to Strathbogie, the scene of conflict. The
word was with great power. On one occasion Mr.
Moody Stuart preached a sermon on the strait gate,
which Duncan Matheson says was blessed to many
souls. On another occasion the Lord's Supper was
dispensed by Mr. Cumming, of Dunbarney, and Mr.
M'Cheyne, Dundee. The people met in the open
air and sat upon the grass listening to the word.
In the afternoon the sky darkened, and the thunder
pealing overhead added an awful solemnity to the
service. In the evening Robert M'Cheyne preached
with "Eternity stamped upon his brow." "I think
I can yet see his seraphic countenance," says Matheson, "and hear his sweet and tender voice. I was
spell-bound, and could not keep my eyes off him for
a moment. He announced his text—Paul's thorn
in the flesh. What a sermon! I trembled, and
never felt God so near. His appeals went to my

heart, and as he spoke of the last great day in the
darkening twilight, for once I began to pray. At the
close he invited all those who were anxious to retire to the chapel. Here began a tremendous struggle in my heart, a struggle I can recall as if it had
been but yesterday. I looked to see if my special
friend D. McP—— was going in, but I could see
him nowhere. He afterwards told me he was looking for me with a like desire. Were he to go in, I
would. Were he to be a Christian, I would. Slowly I went through the darkness, and reached the
chapel, with the words, 'Quench not the Spirit,'
ringing in my ears. I looked in at the window and
saw many there I knew. I hesitated: I approached
the door and looked in. Hastily I turned back.
The die was cast. The tempter whispered, 'Another time.' Alas! alas!

    'I chose the world and an endless shroud.'

Oh the long-suffering of God! Then and there how
justly might God have said, 'Let him alone.' I deserved it. I was near the kingdom: I stood trembling on the threshold: I did not enter in. My case
should lead no one to presume, not one in thousands,
perhaps, in such a state as mine was—trifling with
God—is ever saved. It is a solemn thing to say *to-
morrow* when God says *to-day;* for man's to-morrow
and God's to-day never meet. The word that comes
from the eternal throne is *now*, and it is a man's own
choice that fixes his doom."

After this grieving of the Holy Ghost, Duncan Matheson tried hard "to forget all about eternity, and took to novel-reading." For a season he seemed to be too successful: he was intoxicated with the vanities of fiction, and plunged into all but utter oblivion of God. It was probably owing to this sad experience that he never ceased to deplore the injurious effect of novel-reading on the minds and hearts of the young, and to denounce in no measured terms the conduct of Christians and ministers who give too great encouragement to indulgence in the sensational literature of our day. He once found a trashy work of fiction on the pillow of a dying person. No marvel, then, if he spoke strongly of the evil. From Dreamland into Eternity—what a transition!

CHAPTER II.

HIS YOUTH AND CONVERSION.

The time had arrived when Duncan Matheson, now sixteen years of age, must decide as to his future calling. His education was good for his years, his talents were of a superior order, and he might have entered the University with the fairest prospects. But fond as he was of learning, and ambitious of rising in the world, the conditions

attached to his enjoyment of a college education
were such as he could not accept. He was unconverted, and he would not be a minister because he
could not be a hypocrite. His novel-reading had
set him a dreaming; he would become a sculptor.
The mallet and chisel were his fascination; Rome
and the ancient masters rose before the eye of fancy;
and visions of success and glory dazzled his view.
But how is he to climb so lofty a steep? He boldly
resolves to plant his foot on the lowest possible round
of the ladder: he will begin his career of fame as a
stone-cutter. His general talents, and in particular
his turn for mechanics, seemed to mark him out for
the occupation of a builder. Accordingly he was
apprenticed to a master, and sent to hew his native
sandstone at Kildrummie, where he wrote his first
letter to his friends at Huntly. Here, as he tells,
romance is quickly changed for reality. At the
end of six months the stone-hewing is exhausted,
and his master sends him to the quarry. This is
going down the ladder, not up; and here his apprenticeship ends. From Kildrummie he goes to
Banff, where his quick parts procure him employment in the building of a bank. He saves all he
can of his wages; and although his mother needs
not his aid, his affectionate heart finds an unspeakable joy in sending her all his savings.

Whilst he is hewing stones the Divine Worker is
busy with mallet and chisel of sharp conviction and
providential dealing upon his rough granite nature.

He would be a sculptor, a builder, a worker of great works. The Master of all masters had another design, a better way, and was even now rough-hewing this proud spirit, and training the young tradesman to be a sculptor of souls and a builder of God's temple. There is no rest in the young man's spirit; he will not have religion, and yet he cannot do without it. He goes to hear the late estimable minister of Banff, Mr. Grant. The subject of discourse is "A good man." Matheson is convinced by a clear statement of the truth that no man can be really good, good in the sight of God, who is not regenerate. He next goes to hear the venerable John Murker, minister of the Independent Church in the same town. The preacher is that day reasoning, like Paul, on temperance, righteousness, and judgment to come. Trembling under the word, the young stone-cutter goes away resolved to hear the faithful preacher no more. He then turns his steps to the neighboring town of Macduff, and listens for a season to Mr. Leslie, the late earnest and devoted minister of the Free Church; but in vain. What he really sought for, though he did not know it, was a Gospel that would give him rest without repentance, and salvation without a sacrifice of self.

Work failing he returned home, bade farewell to his father's house, and carrying with him the counsels and prayers of his mother, who was then in declining health, he went to Edinburgh. Here he lodged with a godly couple, who he says did all they could for his soul. The providential hammer and chisel were again at work, and the Spirit of grace plied him in various ways. He must needs sit under the most faithful ministry he can find, and accordingly goes to hear Mr. Moody Stuart. No sooner is he seated than a lady enters the same pew, and leaning her head on the book-board engages in secret prayer. Matheson is self-condemned; conscience upbraids him for his prayerlessness. He is now at the preacher's mercy; the truth spoken with faithful plainness and holy fervor deepens his unrest into anguish, and he goes away saying to himself, "I cannot bear this; if I am to come here, I must be converted." The evil spirit of unbelief triumphed; he resolved to return to that church no more. During the rest of the summer he entered no place of worship, but spent his Sabbaths in walking abroad and in novel-reading. He dared not open the Bible; the very sight of it pierced his heart with an indescribable pang. He tried hard to avoid every thing suggestive of eternity. Daily did he flee from the presence of the Lord; and often did he rebelliously banish from his mind the thoughts by which the Holy Spirit was striving to draw him to the Saviour.

His fellow-workmen were for the most part Godless, drunken, and dissipated in the extreme. But he was preserved from joining in their follies; he never once could be induced to enter a public-house; and he was often shocked and saddened at the terrible miseries which these free-thinkers and free-livers were constantly bringing on themselves. If the fear of God did not restrain him, he remembered the prayers, the counsels, and the tears of his mother. When about to err, her gentle reproof sounded in his ear. In his sleep he seemed to see her beckoning him to the way of righteousness; and when all else failed, one monitor never failed effectually to warn him away from the gates of evil; that monitor was the remembrance of his mother's hollow and ominous cough. It is told of Simon Peter that throughout his life the hearing of a cock crow at any hour, and under all circumstances, caused him to burst into tears. Such was the power of that one look of love that melted the sinning disciple's heart and re-claimed the wanderer. By how little a thing can God hold fast a strong man, and accomplish a great work! From the day he parted with his mother till the day of his death, Duncan Matheson, manly and brave-hearted though he was, could never hear the cough of the consumptive without being deeply moved. The cords of love twined by a parent's hand around his heart he could not undo; and it may be safely asserted that except the grace of God nothing is more powerful than the wise affection of a mother.

One night he was induced by his fellow-workmen to go to an infidel meeting; but just as he was about to enter the room he remembered that the . eye of God was upon him, he seemed to hear his mother's counsel, and her dying cough. It was enough. He suddenly stopped, turned back, fled from the place, and went home.

When, many years afterwards, he sought for his former companions in toil, he found that "most of them filled a drunkard's grave; not one of them was known to have turned to God." Well might he exclaim, as he did, "Oh, the wondrous grace of God to me!"

Although careful of his morals, he hated all close dealing about his soul. This was the sore part which could not bear to be touched. On one occasion he met a faithful Baptist minister, who put the "one thing needful" plainly before him; but young Matheson adroitly shifted the ground by raising the question of Infant Baptism, which proved a too successful diversion from the great question.

In October, 1845, he was called home to see his mother die. The last year of her life was the brightest; she had reached Pisgah and could see the Land of Promise. She spoke to her son of Christ; entreated him to follow the Saviour; and charged him to meet her in heaven. Taking his hand in hers she bade him farewell, and then gently fell asleep in Jesus. Again, in the hour of grief divine love assailed the stubborn heart, but as yet the only result was a resolution to arise and seek the Lord. The noblest affections of our nature, and the bitterest sorrow of life, alike and unitedly fail to bring sinners to the Saviour.

3

After building a house for his father and the family, he returned to Edinburgh with a strange impression, of which he spake to his friends, that either he should die or be converted there. Thus the all-wise and gracious Spirit condescends to seek admission into our evil hearts by the lowest door. By putting before us the alternative of death or life, he appeals to our self-interest and our fears, if by any means He may obtain a footing within us for the furtherance of his merciful design.

In Edinburgh he strove to forget his good resolutions, and went on much as before, guarding his morals, shutting out conviction, and making no surrender to the Lord Jesus. Bent on professional success, he gave himself to the study of drawing and the acquisition of useful knowledge, with praiseworthy diligence improving his mind. To keep his thoughts occupied, and his heart quiet, he resorted to Freemasonry, which, as he acknowledged, did his conscience no good; for he found the freedom not such as he needed, and the secret no substitute for the mysteries of the kingdom of God.

One day a discussion on the evidences of the truth of Christianity arose among the stone-cutters. Duncan Matheson was the champion of the Bible. The leading sceptic, beaten in argument, assailed religion through the inconsistencies of its friends, declaring that Matheson was the only consistent Christian he had ever met. This compliment to his external morality, instead of pleasing his vanity, aroused his conscience, and he secretly charged himself with sheer hypocrisy in defending the truth, to whose divine power he felt in his heart he was an utter stranger. Another day, seeing a fellow-workman look sad, he expressed his sympathy, and found the man was distressed about his sins. Matheson took him aside, and although himself ignorant of the righteousness of God, and justification by faith in the Lord Jesus, directed him as best he could to the path of life. But this act recoiled on himself, and his conscience, now constantly awake, began to upbraid him. "You're a hypocrite," said he to himself. "You point others to Christ, and all the while you are treading the way to hell yourself." Then followed a fierce struggle between light and darkness; his soul was tortured almost to madness—a crisis was at hand.

His state at this time is by no means uncommon. On the one hand his conscience enlightened by the law of God suffered him not to plunge into the pleasures of the world, whilst on the other hand he knew not the peace of God. He could not forget God, and when he remembered God he was troubled. Poised between heaven and earth, as it were, he had religion enough to make him careful and sad, but not enough to make him holy and happy. Into infidelity he dared not plunge. Two convictions, like two unseen hands, held him fast. The one, firm belief in regeneration as a great fact essential to salvation; the other, an undoubted consciousness that he was not born again. As yet, however, re-generation, if an acknowledged necessity, seemed a dark and uninviting mystery. Thorns and briars of the wilderness were now to be his teachers. He was to learn the way of salvation in a fire that consumes every thing but truth. Let us hear his own story.

"On Thursday, 25th Oct., 1846, being the fast-day before communion, I attended Lady Glenorchy's church, where I heard Mr. A. Bonar, biographer of M'Cheyne, preach on the portion of the wicked in Psalm xi., 'Upon the wicked He shall rain snares, fire, and brimstone, and an horrible tempest: this shall be the portion of their cup.' I felt as he proceeded as if all were to myself. I dreaded the portion I was about to receive. I knew I deserved it. I left the church weeping, but tried to hush my fears by fostering in my mind a purpose of being converted that day twelve months. I had the notion that I could be converted when I liked: I had only to begin praying, and reading, etc., and then all would come right. Fatal delusion! There are gales of mercy, there are tides of grace, which do not always wait for us. It will always be man's inconvenient season when it is God's convenient time. I was afraid to return to the church in the evening. Satan furnished me with a pillow on which to sleep. It was this: 'If you are to be converted you will be converted; If not, you cannot help it.' I took the opiate greedily, and was rocked to sleep in the devil's cradle.

"Many strike on this rock; many a noble ship has been dashed to pieces here. This is not Calvinism, but fatalism. Can the husbandman expect to reap if he does not sow, or the sailor reach the port if he does not spread the sail to catch the breeze? What sick man would say, 'If I am to get well I shall, no matter though a physician be not called or medicine taken.' Of all preachers of election, Satan is the worst. He distorts that glorious truth, the first link in the golden chain of man's salvation. He hides the blood of Christ through which sinners should behold it. He keeps out of sight the only decree with which sinners have to do, viz., 'He that believeth not shall be damned.' 'You are not elect,' said the adversary to a sorely-tried Christian. 'Elect!' replied the man of God. 'Have you seen the book of God? Liar, get you hence; I have had more than ye ever had—an offer of Jesus Christ, and I have taken Him.'

"Next day I was sad, and unable to smile; but I tried to conceal my state. Sermon after sermon rose to mind, and my dying mother's counsels flashed into my heart. When the church bells began to ring on Saturday, two fellow-workmen, G. T. and M. T., infidels, began to curse and swear, blaspheming especially the Lord's Supper. Shocked, I could have fled from the place; and the prayer came into my heart, 'Father, forgive them; for they know not what they

do.' Then a voice seemed to say, 'How do you take
the name of Father into your lips, seeing you reject
Christ? Your hell will be deeper than theirs; for
you know, and do not. God is not your Father:
Satan is.'

"I could work no more, and I went home to ponder and weep. The arrow was driven home; and
this time I did not seek to withdraw it. On Sabbath
morning I was early astir, and, Bible in hand, was
the first at church. In serving a table, Mr. Bonar
said, 'This is a feast of love, the deepest love.' A
voice seemed to ask me, 'Why are you not at it?'
My heart was thrilled. I looked round, and saw
no one. The question drove me from the church,
and I rushed home. Even in this solemn hour I
dared dally with my convictions, and went to see
a friend, resolved to shun the church lest I should be
tormented afresh. My heart was too full to conceal my thoughts, and I began to speak about religion. The topic being manifestly disagreeable,
I left the house with feelings of wounded pride.
Reaching the Calton Hill, I looked down upon the
city, with its thousands of gleaming lights, and
upward to the stars, which seemed to shine most
sweetly upon me. I felt inwardly urged to go to
church. I went with reluctance, and almost not
knowing what I was doing, or whither I was going.
I became desperate and passed the church door,
but returned as if some invisible power moved me
against my will. Again, when I was about to en-

ter, I tore myself away. Two powers seemed to be lugging me hither and thither. Again I returned, and with a bound crossed the threshold, and mounting the gallery stairs took my seat in the passage. I felt I was a poor, miserable castaway. The sermon was nearly finished. One showed me the text: 'The Lord, the Lord God, merciful and gracious, long-suffering, and abundant in goodness and truth, keeping mercy for thousands, forgiving iniquity and transgression and sin, and that will by no means clear the guilty' (Ex. xxxiv. 6, 7). Mr. A. Bonar was preacher, and had come to the words, 'will by no means clear the guilty.' In a moment I felt the burning, piercing eye of God upon me. A mountain of wrath seemed to crush me down; and hell was opened beneath me. All round about me seemed to be on fire. Louder than the loudest thunder came the words: 'By no means clear the guilty;' and, 'Cursed is every one that continueth not in all things that are written in the book of the law to do them.' The congregation was dismissed; the people departed; but I remained fixed to the spot. Some as they passed gave me a look of pity. At last I rose and reeled home to my lodgings, realizing with awful vividness God, heaven, hell, judgment, and eternity. Falling on my knees I uttered my first real prayer, 'God be merciful to me, a sinner.' I was now thoroughly awakened, but I was not saved.

"When the eyes are opened by the Holy Ghost,

how differently are all things seen: they stand forth then in their true light. I saw the mass around me hurrying unsaved to eternity. I wondered they could laugh. It seemed to me like the condemned dancing on the scaffold. The heavens seemed as if clothed in sackcloth. Wherever I went I felt the burning eye of God upon me; and the threatenings of the Word came like peals of artillery in quick succession. I feared I should drop into hell at every step, and, like most other awakened sinners, I began to work for life. The language of my heart was, 'Have patience with me, and I will pay Thee all.' How I did pray, and agonize, and suffer! I was on the wrong track, and did not know that

"'Doing is a deadly thing,
Doing ends in death.'

I began to read many chapters, thinking that would do me good. I prayed all day long, but I was no better. If a tear started to my eye I felt proud of it, and thought surely now Jesus will regard my case. I had a long stair of seventy steps to climb to my room: at every step I uttered a prayer. Like Luther as he ascended the steps in the church at Rome, I groaned out a petition for deliverance; but no voice came to me saying, 'The just shall live by faith.' I labored to make of my works a ladder to heaven. I put my anxiety in place of Christ; and instead of seeking the One to be believed in, I set out in search of faith. Many a weary hour I spent trying to discover what faith is. I read all the books I could find, and searched the Word of God. Faith! faith! faith! was still my cry. Oh, if I had faith! The Star of Bethlehem was shining brightly before me. Jesus was standing near. He was uttering his voice, 'Look unto Me, and be ye saved.' But I passed Him by.

"I went to a minister in Edinburgh, who began to tell me how good a thing it was to be awakened, and with a view to my being comforted applied passages of Scripture that belong only to the people of God. He urged me to hope, instead of bidding me believe. Thus many are led to hope they may be saved, and rest there, instead of obeying the command of God to 'believe on Him whom He hath sent.' The effect was, I became proud of my convictions; my fears were hushed; for some days I felt great self-satisfaction; and, thinking that He who had begun a good work would carry it on, went smoothly.

"Some days after this I was startled by finding my heart beginning to love things I had forsaken, and then came the terrible question, What if this is false peace? I felt I had not taken hold of Christ, and something said, Now or never! now or never! Make sure work for eternity!

"How few can deal with anxious souls! Here was a good man settling me on my lees, taking the children's bread and giving it to a dog. He had no right to give me any promise addressed to the children of God. The promises are all yea and amen, but only in Christ Jesus. From Genesis to Revelation the promises belong to the Christian: they are his in Christ. Many have gone down to hell, pillowing their head on a promise, but not taking Christ. The good man was wrong in applying to me the text, 'Being confident of this very thing, that He which hath begun a good work in you will perform it until the day of Jesus Christ' (Phil. i. 6); for it refers to the work of sanctification, and as yet I was not justified.

"Mr. Cowie used to say, 'Some get such a fright at Sinai that they are in danger of running past Jerusalem;' that is to say, the very depth of their convictions may prevent them from entering the kingdom, for fear their peace may not be right. So it was with me. Fearing lest I should come short of eternal life, I cared not what happened if only I might be really saved.

"I sought my old friend John Cameron, who wept in his sympathy with me, and took me to his minister, Christopher Anderson (Baptist), author of the 'Annals of the English Bible.' This devoted man listened to my story, told in a romantic style; for I spoke of my sufferings as if I was passing through purgatorial fires. He saw I was lifted up, and said, 'Young man, were I to say I am pleased with you, you would go down that stair in a happy frame, but you are yet far from the kingdom of God. You have never yet dealt with the justice of God. His justice in condemning you for breaking

his law has never yet entered your thoughts. I see
you are angry with God for not giving you salvation as the reward of works. But it must be grace
from first to last.' After a few words he told me to
go. I thought it very harsh. I seemed cut off
from all hope. I reeled to the door, and when I
reached the street I felt shut up to God and alone
with him, and exclaimed, 'O God, it shall henceforth be Thee, and Thee alone.' After this I desired
that every thing might be settled between God and
myself, and I prayed that every truth might be
burnt into my heart by the Holy Ghost.

"Wearied and anxious, I left for home. A great
change was seen in me. My fierce temper was
checked: the lion had thus far become a lamb. All
the town heard of it, and pitied the poor lad who
had, as they thought, gone mad. Old companions
who I feared would hinder me never came near me.
Faith was still the prevailing question. The doctrine of the imputation of Adam's sin I could not
see, and I rebelled against the sovereignty of God,
and thought He dealt hardly with me. Slowly the truth in regard to imputation was opened
up. Dimly I began to see that I had nothing
but unholy thoughts, words, or deeds, and that for
these I must die. I saw that Jesus only had holy
thoughts, words, and deeds, and that these were
placed to my account the moment I believed. I
wanted a righteousness in which I could appear
before God, and slowly Jehovah-Tsidkenu, the Lord

Himself our Righteousness, shone forth in all his glory.

"I was standing on the 10th December, 1846, at the end of my father's house, and meditating on that precious word which has brought peace to countless weary ones; 'God so loved the world, that He gave His only begotten Son, that whosoever believeth in Him should not perish, but have everlasting life' (John iii. 16). I saw that God loved me, for I was one of the world. I saw the proof of His love in the giving of His Son Jesus. I saw that 'whosoever' meant any body and every body, and therefore *me, even me.* I saw the result of believing—that I would not perish, but have everlasting life. I was enabled to take God at his word. I saw no one, but Jesus only, all in all in redemption. My burden fell from my back, and I was saved. Yes, saved! That hour angels rejoiced over one more sinner brought to the Saviour, and new songs rang through the courts of that city to which I had now got a title, and of which I had now become an heir. Bunyan describes his pilgrim as giving three leaps for joy as his burden rolled into the open sepulchre of Christ. I could not contain myself for joy. I sang the new song, salvation through the blood of the Lamb. The very heavens appeared as if covered with glory. I felt the calm of a pardoned sinner; yet I had no thought about my safety. I saw only the person of Jesus. I wept for my sin that had nailed Him to the cross, and they were tears of true repentance. Formerly I had set up repentance as a toll between me and the cross; now it came freely as the tear that faith wept. I felt I had passed from death unto life—that old things had passed away, and all things had become new.

"I wondered I had stumbled at the simplicity of the way. I saw every thing so plain that I longed to go and tell all the world. I felt as if I could at once convince the most sceptical and the most hardened; and that if I met a thousand Manassehs I could say, 'Yet there is room.' I went everywhere, telling my glad story. Some even of the saints looked incredulous. Others, like the elder brother in the parable, did not like the music and the dancing. They had never left their Father's dwelling; they had never been sin-sick, and knew not what it is to be healed; no fatted calf had been killed for them. These warned me against enthusiasm, and exhorted me to be sober-minded. One old man told me I was on the mount, but would soon be down again. Another said I needed great humility; but I went on singing my song. Prayer had given place to praise, and night and day for more than three days I continued to thank God for 'his unspeakable gift.' I longed to die that I might sin no more, and discover more fully the height and the depth, the length and the breadth of that love which I now knew 'passeth knowledge.'"

CHAPTER III.

SPIRITUAL DISCIPLINE.

"He knoweth the way that I take ; when He hath tried me, I shall come
forth as gold."—Job xxiii. 10.

"I asked the Lord that I might grow
In faith, and love, and every grace;
Might more of His salvation know,
And seek more earnestly His face.

" 'Twas He who taught me thus to pray.
And He I trust has answered prayer;
But it has been in such a way
As almost drove me to despair."

You have seen a bright week of too early spring.
The sun has suddenly poured down an unusual
warmth. The brooks and streams emancipated from
the frost begin to babble afresh. The little birds are
full of joy, and warble a welcome to the genial year.
The buds are swelling, here and there a flower peeps
out, and the first tint of greenness is upon the earth.
Unexpectedly the sun, as if he had but mocked, with-
draws his smiling favors; frost, as if he had lain in
ambush, returns with his cruel bonds; the more ad-
venturous flowers are ruthlessly slain; the birds are
dumb with amazement and sorrow; and all the
voices of nature are again hushed. Life and death
are now fiercely struggling; but the former, though
for a while overborne, at length wins.

To this the spiritual world is not without its parallel. So it fell out in the experience of Duncan Matheson. His few days of enlargement and joy were followed by a weary season of bondage and misery. His song of triumph was quickly followed by the burning thirst of unsatisfied spiritual desire, the bitter waters of a Marah experience, and all the anguish and travail of the wilderness. It was as when the sun has just arisen upon some benighted traveller, and he is making his escape from fearful dangers amidst dazzling floods of light. Suddenly again it becomes pitch dark, and night without a star overshadows his path. During those years the young Christian's joy, if not also his faith, suffered an eclipse. Like a lamb bleating for its lost mother, he went about during those weary months bemoaning himself with piteous lamentations and sorrow. But a fighting faith is as precious as a resting faith, though not so pleasant; and stern battle is the way to victory.

"Gradually," he says, "my joy began to abate. I had been soaring on the eagle wings of praise, but now my song failed. At any rate, I thought, I am free of sin; but, alas, I soon discovered that in my flesh dwelleth no good thing. I could see two distinct principles at work in me—the flesh and the Spirit. To an old Christian of experience I complained that I was dead.

"'Dead!' said he, with a curious twinkle in his eye; 'you are a curiosity. I never heard a dead man speak before. There comes nae a sigh frae a coffin, and they never cry feich in the grave. Ye're nae dead, but feelin' deadness. After having been dandled on the knees of consolation you must be weaned, and go and fecht the battles of the Lord.' This gave me a little comfort, but only a little.

" Young converts live more by sense than faith, and they must be taught that Jesus Himself, and not the comforts He gives, is their life. The weaning time is a critical period; then it is a man's Christian character is stamped. Skilful teachers are needed to show the workings of nature and grace, to separate the precious from the vile, so that he who begins in the Spirit may not be led away to seek perfection in the flesh. I was now in a wilderness, sorely tempted of the devil. The fountains of the great deep were broken up, Satan came down on my soul like a sweeping avalanche, and I was tempted to curse God and die. I staggered beneath my burden day and night for nearly two years. Terrible were the fiery darts with which I was assailed. Horrible and unutterable thoughts of God, of the Holy Ghost, and of Jesus, were injected into my mind. If I began to sing, the very note seemed to be changed into a blasphemy on the tip of my tongue, and many a time have I had to put my fingers in my ears and my hand on my mouth. These bolts of hell caused me indescribable anguish and sorrow, and never till I saw they were not mine but Satan's did I get deliverance from them.

"Sometimes he tortured me about election; sometimes he suggested that my former joy was only the joy of the stony ground hearers; sometimes that I had fallen away, and that according to the Word of God in the Epistle to the Hebrews, chap. vi. 4–6, it was impossible for me to be renewed unto repentance. The dread of apostasy hung over me like a sword from which I could not escape. The journal of my spiritual life I burned, that there might be no record of my apostasy left behind me. Above all, I was tempted to believe I had committed the unpardonable sin—the sin against the Holy Ghost. 'You have blasphemed,' said the tempter one day. 'Go and take your fill of the world; mercy is not for you.' I left the house, but had only gone a little way when I was compelled to return. Taking up the 'Pilgrim's Progress,' I read a note, which said, 'If you have any desire to be saved, if you wish you had not sinned against the Holy Ghost, you have not done it.' I was somewhat relieved, and began afresh.

"When I struggled, Satan said it was of no use; when I rested, he taunted me with sloth, and said, 'How can you get the blessing when you are sleeping?' Sometimes he said, 'Where is your joy? Are not wisdom's ways ways of pleasantness? Her paths are paths of peace.' I was tempted to Atheism, to Unitarianism, and was continually urged to take life away. Oh the agony of those months! I suf-

4

fered till my frame was sadly reduced. Often did
hurry to the hill-side, and oftener to the banks of the
river, and my weary wail, 'Oh that I knew where I
might find Him!' mingled with the flow of the dark
waters. But never was I desirous of giving up.
Eternity was stamped on my eyeballs. I had seen
a sight which dimmed the glory of all else.

> " 'The cross, the cross ! the Christian's only glory,
>   I see the standard rise;
>   March on, march on ! the cross of Christ before thee;
>   That cross all hell defies.

> " ' The cross, the cross ! redemption's standard raising,
>   I see the banner wave;
>   Sing on the march, salvation's Captain praising;
>   'Tis Christ alone can save.

> " ' The crown, the crown ! Oh, who at last shall gain it?
>   That cross a crown affords;
>   Press on, press on with courage to obtain it;
>   The battle is the Lord's.'

"I had now and again sweet, short tastes of coming glory. I felt as if I could have struggled cen-
turies to reach the goal at last. 'I was persecuted,
but not forsaken; cast down, but not destroyed.'
Though for the most part I groaned out, 'O wretched man that I am! who shall deliver me from the
body of this death?' yet there were moments when
I could say, 'I thank God through Jesus Christ our
Lord.' Dark indeed was the night, and starless the
sky, but hope bore me up, and I felt an unseen hand
supporting me; and when the dark vail was for

a little drawn aside, I could realize the verse of
Cowper—

 " 'God moves in a mysterious way,
  His wonders to perform;
  He plants his footsteps on the sea,
  And rides upon the storm.'

A portion of the diary mentioned above escaped
the fire. A few extracts from it will serve to illustrate his state of mind, and the fiery conflicts through
which he was then passing. Perhaps it will encourage some poor struggler to hold on his way
through fire and water till he gets into the "wealthy
place."

"January 2d, 1847. When I awoke in the morning, all my thoughts were evil and good mixed;
evil thoughts preponderating. Alas! what are my
thoughts but evil? what my prayers but sin? what
my desires but mixed with self? Were I left to my
own heart I would perish. Throughout the day I
have thought awful thoughts, hard, wicked, unbe-
lieving thoughts of God. Satan has been raging
like a lion, seeking to devour me, my own heart
helping him. When I think of these thoughts I
can well say that God for one of them could justly
cast me off. Prayed much for the Holy Spirit, without whose aid I can see and do nothing. Tried to
rest all my thoughts on Jesus, but it is hard to do
so. I am always running after something of my
own. More settled just now (evening). Very much

in need of a humble heart; clearer views of Jesus; a heart to acknowledge God in all things. May the Holy Spirit open the eyes of my understanding, lead me and guide me aright; for left to my own heart I would go astray. Enable me to cast my care and burden on Jesus, who can save me.

"January 3d. Sabbath morning. Very much tormented with awful thoughts which I shudder at. I have a fearful heart that would dictate to the Creator of the universe. Very much tormented by Satan, who fills my tongue and imagination with curses and blasphemies. May God for Jesus' sake, on whom I would rely, disappoint him.

"Went to church, my thoughts wandering, and very wicked thoughts rising up. Heard a discourse from Ps. xix. Set my secret faults before my face. Mr. Millar spoke well on presumptuous sin. Alas! how many have I committed even since the Spirit awakened me. It is of mercy I am not cast off. Truly God is long-suffering.

"Prayer-meeting in the afternoon. Thoughts away, but rather better staid than in the forenoon.

"Evening. Mr. Hill on Psalm xvii. The poor commit their way to God. Very good discourse. I would commit my way, guilty, weak, and unworthy as I am, to God through Jesus. O guide me, and give me grace to support me under every trial. Give me thy Spirit. Impart thy love, dear Lord Jesus, to my heart.

"January 4th. When I awoke, my mind confused, my imagination going after every evil. Truly the thoughts of the heart are only evil, and that continually. My mind throughout the day was a chaos of evil and good. How terribly fallen I am, for my mind is enmity against God. Awful thoughts were in my heart against Him. A great conflict going on in my mind, and I am unable in myself to submit my will to God. Oh that He would in mercy give me a humble heart, to see and acknowledge Him in all my ways, and to submit my will to his! I find it a very difficult matter to subdue self, my mind even taking pleasure in confessions. Give me, O Lord, the heart to ascribe glory, honor, and praise to Thee; for I have a heart that would say or think every evil. I would, guilty as I am, put my trust in Jesus. May his love shine into my heart, that I may be humbled and have true sorrow for sin.

"A few moments this evening of awful interest. Satan or my own heart is always putting much to my prayers, thus dictating to God. What a heart! how rebellious! Teach me humility, O Lord. Give me a meek and lowly heart.

"January 5th. Confused thoughts, wicked in the extreme. Yet self-sufficiency. I cannot check my wicked thoughts, and my heart is very unwilling to acknowledge God. No human reason, no learning on earth can give me peace. Alas, my wisdom is a stumbling-block to me; my thoughts are so wicked, that at times they overwhelm me. Trying to trust all in Jesus, but I see it must be a divine faith, for a human faith can give no peace. Went to prayer-meeting, but found no good; yet resolved to follow on to know God. O Lord, give me thy Holy Spirit to reveal thy dear Son to my soul. Give me a humble, broken heart.

> " ' O may thy Spirit seal my soul,
>   And mould me to thy will,
>   That my weak heart no more may stray,
>   But keep thy precepts still.'

"30th. The worst day I have ever had with the suggestions of Satan. Yet God has saved me. I need to be humbled at the foot of the cross. I have resolved in the strength of Jesus to be his. . . . Eternal life is worth struggling for. Lord, make me thine; bend my proud heart by thy Holy Spirit.

"31st. Sabbath. Thoughts mixed — good and evil. . . . Temptations and suggestions of Satan. Heard a sermon on the joys of heaven; was benefited, and quickened to go forward. Temptations are my grievous lot, but what are they all compared with the joys laid up for those that are tried and faithful?

"February 4th. Seeing more and more of my heart every day. Oh that I had faith to lean on Jesus.

"7th. Went to church; but oh, what corruption— what sin! How many idle thoughts. Nothing but sin in my heart. Meditation on the words of Jesus, ' Father, if it be possible, let this cup pass from me.' This should strip us of all self-righteousness. O Lord, give me a heart to love Thee above all earthly things."

Thus far the journal of the conflict. During this dreary period Duncan Matheson was learning the most difficult of lessons—"the just shall live by faith." Mark the goodness of God. He was refreshed at the well before he began to ascend the Hill Difficulty. Ere he entered that dark Valley of Humiliation and engaged in fierce conflict with Apollyon, he was girded with truth and clad in mail. In his worst times he could remember the Lord from "the land of Jordan and of the Hermonites, from the hill Mizar;" the memory of his three happy, triumphant days, sustained him, and although deep was calling unto deep, he could still hope in God. Sometimes, indeed, the tried saint is kept from utter apostasy and atheism by the memory of a sweet experience on the Mount of Communion.

As yet it was only the dawn of grace. Night was passing and the day was coming in, though slowly and with clouds. In rude but majestic outline, invisible things were coming to view. He sees God; God is real. He is dealing with God, but God in his holiness rather than God in his love. He sees Jesus; but it is not so much Jesus revealed in the glass of the Word that he sees, as the image of Jesus faintly reflected on the troubled waters of his own heart. The Holy Ghost is real; but he marks his own grieving of the Spirit, rather than the Spirit's graciousness to him. Satan has become real, near, and terrible; but he is not yet seen as vanquished in the cross. Sin in its guilt and power is now to him a gigantic Upas, on whose branch his harp is hanging, and under whose shadow he seems doomed to sit, and weep, and die. Mark how the valiant struggler divides his charges between the devil and his own heart, giving to each a fair portion of the blame. He who knows sin knows also the devil; fools, knowing neither, make a mock of both. When a man is passing through this stage of religious experience, an awful, eternal importance attaches to the minutest element of his existence. He weighs his thoughts in a balance. He measures his feelings, affections, and motives by the broad standard of divine perfection. His words are not mere empty sounds, but winged messengers going before to judgment; and all his steps leave their impress on conscience one by one.

Those two years were spent on the hardest bench in Christ's school. That lowly seat of spiritual discipline has been occupied in turns by all the most distinguished servants of God. During the years preceding his conversion, he had been taught the mad and desperate opposition of the natural man to the grace of God. Now he learned how the flesh lusts against the Spirit; how legalism counterworks grace in the believer's heart; how it fetters the liber ty, mars the joy, hinders the progress, disfigures the character, and lessens or even destroys the usefulness of the Christian. To one who was to teach multitudes the true way, all that painful experience was of prime importance. His mistakes should save many from similar errors; his miseries should diminish the misery of others. Our bitterest trials are our best lessons. Joseph studied statesmanship in prison. Moses found a Divinity Hall in the back side of the desert. Forty years in the wilderness made Joshua one of God's greatest soldiers, one of his bravest heroes. Saul's persecution did more to make David the king he was than Samuel's sacred oil. Elijah learned the Gospel in its "still small voice" in a cave. Jonah graduated in the whale's belly. Peter got his best lesson in evangelistic theology when he went out in the dark night to weep bitterly for his great sin. Paul was not conferring with flesh and blood during the time spent in Arabia. John went to the highest class in Patmos. The long agony of Luther has lessened the sorrows of millions. John Bunyan called more pilgrims into the King's highway from his dungeon than ever he did from his pulpit. And so of thousands more.

To the Christian and the preacher of Christ, a thorough knowledge of sin is of the highest importance. This knowledge, bitter but wholesome, Duncan Matheson was now learning. "I have found original sin in the Bible," said a student to Haldane. "Well," replied the latter: "but have you found it in your own heart?" Few know what it is to see all the terrible hell of man's depraved nature. To be

let down into that abyss with the candle of the Lord
in your hand, to see its bottomless depths of pride
and passion, its tumultuous risings against law and
holiness, its desperate rage against God, its Satanic
challenges of the Divine Sovereignty, its insane athe-
isms, its blasphemous horrors, its cloud-covered delusions, its ambushed hosts of armed iniquities, and
its infinite capability of engendering evils enough
to waste the fairest world of God, and people many
hells—to see all this and far more than words can
convey, is not merely to learn the *doctrine*, but to
know *the reality of sin*, so that the sense and memory
of its nature, criminality, power, and destiny, are
branded as with a red-hot iron upon the soul forever. This knowledge is beyond the ken of short-
sighted professors and stone-blind hypocrites.

When such an one, like Luther, goes about for
weary months or years bemoaning himself and cry-
·ing piteously, "Oh, my sin! my sin!" shallow Christians and evil-doers ask, "What great crime has he
committed? Surely he is living in gross sin." All
the while the man is living a holy life, waging war
against the very thought and possibility of evil; but
"a sword is in his bones," and his "soul dwells
among lions."

The young convert was pursuing holiness as a
man runs for his life, but he was partly in error.
'I can see," he says, "looking back on that period
of my history, where exactly I stood. I had begun
in the Spirit, and I wanted to be made perfect in

he flesh. My spirit was most legal; I prayed continually, and if I lost a moment I tried to make it up as a man pays a debt. I had a scrupulous conscience, which brought me great torment. My eyes were fixed within myself, and my comfort was drawn from my frames. The Spirit's work in me was the ground of my peace and hope, rather than the work of Christ in our room. I did not see Jesus as my sanctification as well as my justification. I did not then know the meaning of this word as describing the secret of progressive holiness: 'We all, with open face beholding as in a glass the glory of the Lord, are changed into the same image from glory to glory, as by the Spirit of the Lord.' Although I drew comfort from the person and work of Jesus, I did not live on Him. I was continually analyzing my feelings, drawing comfort from what I thought was divine, and rejecting what was natural. Hence my hope rose and fell like a barometer. I remember one day going out to the Castle Park, expecting I should audibly hear a voice from heaven assuring me that all my sins were forgiven. When in this attitude, the word came with power to my heart, 'Except ye see signs and wonders, ye will not believe.' Indescribable pangs tore my heart at that moment, and I almost felt I had rather be lost than go on in the way of believing. Immediately another passage of Scripture took forcible hold of me: 'See that ye refuse not Him that speaketh: for if they escaped not who refused Him that

spake on earth, much more shall not we escape,
if we turn away from Him that speaketh from
heaven '" (Heb. xii. 25).

From Huntly he went to Edinburgh, and wandered from church to church saying, "Saw ye Him
whom my soul loveth?"—"They have taken away
my Lord, and I know not where they have laid
Him." In vain his search. Back again to Huntly
he took his way for the purpose of celebrating the
Lord's Supper, and showing forth the death of Jesus;
but no relief came. "Never did criminal stand on
the scaffold with more rueful countenance," he says,
"than mine was as I sat at the Lord's table that day."
He trembled lest his "blood should be mingled with
his sacrifice." This "service was the service of the
slave, not of the free." By and by, however, he
came to know that justification realized is the great
vantage ground in striving after personal holiness,
and that a happy consciousness of acceptance in the
Beloved is the great incentive to true obedience.
He who joys in God his Saviour cannot fight against
his divine Friend. The blood of Jesus brings purity
in bringing peace. Grasping pardon you grasp holiness. He who receives Jesus receives his Spirit.
Love springs from faith; and he who realizes most
assuredly his standing in grace, walks most steadily
in fellowship, works most cheerfully in obedience,
and lives most freely in the liberties of holy joy.
This lesson Matheson now learned. The two years'
tempest shook the tree but did not uproot it. If the

storm damaged the branches it strengthened the roots. The young Christian unlearned frames and learned faith. He learned to lean on the word of God, the bare word, and nothing but the word. He was taught to trust not in the Christ of his heart, but Christ in the Word. He was taught to "be strong" not in the grace in himself, but "in the grace that is in Christ Jesus." At length realizing that God was his salvation through his oneness with Jesus he could say:

"So nigh, so very nigh to God,
  More near I cannot be;
For in the person of His Son
  I am as near as He.
So dear, so very dear to God,
  More dear I cannot be:
The love wherewith He loves His Son,
  Such is His love to me."

Having been brought clearly to see the standing of the believer in Christ, he quickly attained a well-grounded assurance of salvation. He had given diligence to make his calling and election sure; but he had sought assurance in vain because he had sought it mainly by searching himself. This priceless jewel he found where all good is to be found, at the foot of the cross. Henceforth, although he did not cease to work out his own salvation with fear and trembling, he could always say, "I know whom I have believed, and am persuaded that He is able to keep that which I have committed unto

Him against that day." This happy confidence in
the Lord fitted him for the work of an evangelist,
and sustained him amidst many labors and trials.
The joy of the Lord was his strength, and true of
him were these lines:

> " There are in this loud and stunning tide
>   Of human care and crime,
>   With whom the melodies abide
>   Of the everlasting chime;
>   Who carry music in their heart
>   Through dusky lane and wrangling mart,
> Plying their daily task with busier feet,
> Because their secret souls a holy strain repeat."

During this period, in his insatiable hunger for
the truth, he read incessantly, and devoured large
and substantial meals of the good old Puritanic theology. Owen, Baxter, Howe, and the other divines
of that age were his delight. Thus he laid in a
good store for days to come, and treasured much
precious seed to be afterwards scattered broadcast
over Scotland. In the course of his reading, he
stumbled on the writings of Huntington, and for a
season was led away into the dreary wilderness of
hyper-Calvinism, where some poor souls seem doomed
to wander all their days, perhaps as a punishment
for their hair-splitting or their spiritual pride. For
a time he was bound in the strait jacket of this form
of fatalism. He dared not speak to every one of the
love of God, lest he should give encouragement to
one who was not elect. After a while he discov-

ered his error, and was led to see that to close the
door of the universal call of the Gospel is to close
the door of salvation against the elect themselves,
since the only warrant to believe is simply the general invitations addressed to sinners of mankind.
He noticed that these ultra-Calvinists are generally
unpractical, and much given to preaching in their
prayers. When one of this class was leading the
devotion by an elaborate theological discussion, some
one, as Matheson used to tell, probably enough
himself, touched the sleeve of the pious theorist,
saying, "Ask something from Him." With brusque,
quaint irony he was wont to say, "Ah! I see you
have taken the divine sovereignty under your special patronage and care, but I have no time for
chopping logic with you; I want to win souls."

The insight he obtained into the subtle workings
of the human heart during his long conflict prepared him for the work of an evangelist. He could
discover at a glance the whereabouts of an inquirer.
He was taught to distinguish between mere blind
alarm and genuine conviction. If the inquirer was
seeking more conviction, instead of seeking Christ,
he could point out the error in a word. Pride,
pretence, legalism, fear of man, and unbelief in
its varied forms, he could clearly expose, and so
remove stumbling-blocks out of the way. To the
despairing he could say, "I was once where you
are now;" and from his own experience he could
speak wisely and lovingly to those deeply afflicted.

ones who think they have sinned the unpardonable sin.

During this period of discipline he learned to pray without ceasing. In company, on the street, in the railway train, in the bustle of business, amidst the solemn fervors of his preaching, and in the very torrent of his own quaint, racy, picturesque talk in social life—in short, everywhere and in all things, his faith went up to heaven in quick, pointed, battle-like cries. When others were preaching we have often heard him praying thus, "Help, Lord, help! Give the blessing, and save many!"

Such, then, were some of the lessons taught him by the Holy Spirit during those two hard and bitter years. A thorough knowledge of sin, of the workings of the human heart, and of the devices of the devil; a clear view of the ground of the believer's standing before God, victory over his adversaries, assurance of salvation, and the habit of praying always—these were precious fruits in his own experience and through his work as an evangelist seeds of blessing to others, which he scattered far and wide.

CHAPTER IV.

HIS EVANGELISTIC APPRENTICESHIP.

"Son, go work to-day in my vineyard."—MATT. xxi. 28.

"Why stand ye here all the day idle?" This question could not have been appropriately addressed to Duncan Matheson at any period of his Christian life. Immediately on his conversion he began to labor for the salvation of souls. At first his light was small; but he kept trimming his lamp both for his own and others' good, and the flame increased. Every effort of faith and sacrifice of love seemed to add live coals to his altar of fire. For twenty years the flame of zeal was never suffered to expire; no, not for a single day. Night and day, in season and out of season, he strove with all his might to win souls.

His first attempt was at Burntisland, where the minister of the Free Church kindly gave him the use of the school, and otherwise encouraged him. He began by wisely conjoining the temporal with the spiritual, making the former subservient to the latter. Having acquired proficiency in drawing, he offered gratuitously to teach his fellow-workmen. The class was opened and closed with prayer and reading of the Word. His interest in the temporal well-being of the workmen was genuine; but he cared chiefly for their souls. While they were learning to draw sketches, he was striving to save

5

sinners; while they studied architectural plans, he
was brooding over plans for their salvation. Here
he reaped one of the less pleasant fruits of doing
good. One of the class obtaining the use of Matheson's drawing instruments, disappeared with the ill-
gotten spoil, and the benevolent teacher was left at
a great loss. He was vexed, but nothing daunted.
Throughout his life he invariably set himself to promote in every possible way the earthly welfare of
his fellow-men; and this he did not merely as a
means to the highest end, the saving of souls, but
because it was his duty and his joy. Frequently,
when he had spent all his earnings in charity, did
he go about and solicit aid for the poor. Sometimes
he was known to go amongst the neighbors and beg
a scuttleful of coals, carry them to the cheerless
home of the destitute sick, with his own hands
make a fire, and then prepare the " cup that cheers
but not inebriates," procured at the expense of his
own last shilling. Only after the poor, forlorn, bed-
ridden, solitary one was refreshed did he take his
Bible from his pocket to read, and pray, and speak
of Jesus and salvation. " I never believed," he says,
" in speaking sweet words and honeyed counsels to
starving people. If you want to do them good, go
to them with a loaf in one hand and the Bible in the
other. Actions speak louder than words."

About this time he succeeded in preventing a
strike. His sympathy with the men, his manly
frankness, his judicious counsel and weight of char-

acter, were, by the blessing of God sought for in prayer, entirely successful. He felt he obtained his reward in the evils thus averted and in the harmony restored between masters and men. He found the Gospel to be the true remedy of every woe. Jesus is indeed Jehovah-rophi.

Returning to Huntly, he began with all his energy and enthusiasm to make known the Saviour he had found. Every hour was spent in visiting the sick and distributing tracts. His efforts were not confined to his native town. Everywhere in the neighboring parishes he sought his way with more or less success. Hitherto he had confined his evangelistic services to prayer, reading the word and conversation; but the time had arrived when he must take a step in advance. One day Miss Macpherson, a devoted Christian, who had been his friend, counsellor, and good angel throughout the period of his protracted spiritual conflict, requested him to address a company of aged women whom she had gathered together. Matheson declined the invitation. He "could not preach." Miss M. reasoned, urged, and entreated; but all in vain. Finally, demanding what he would answer at the great tribunal for a neglected talent, she charged him not to refuse lest souls should perish in consequence. This was more than he could bear. He went to the meeting, though with the greatest hesitancy and fear. Opening the Bible at Isaiah xxxii. 11, "Tremble, ye women that are at ease; be troubled, ye careless ones," he spoke with great freedom and power. Both the text and matter of his address seemed to be laid to his hand; and such were the results that he felt assured the Lord was calling him to this work. The Christian lady, who by her wisdom and faithfulness was instrumental in calling into exercise a gift of inestimable value, little knew at that time the greatness of the service she was rendering to the Church and the world.

From this time onwards to the end of his days he found at once his greatest labor and his chief joy in preaching Christ. In a short space of time he established a great many cottage meetings, which he carried on with uncommon vigor and success. Solemn events occurred. One night our evangelist addressed a meeting on the parable of the ten virgins. A woman deeply impressed, went home, and spent a night of sleepless anxiety. Early in the morning she called her neighbor to go and fetch Duncan Matheson. As the messenger left the house a great crash was heard: the anxious inquirer had dropped dead. "While they went to buy, the Bridegroom came."

A man, in whose house Matheson held a meeting, taking offence at the word, informed the evangelist that the next meeting would be the last under his roof. The young servant of Christ was deeply grieved, and prayed much for an appropriate subject of final address. One text took hold of his mind, and he could not get rid of it. Accordingly he

preached on the solemn and touching words of the
Lord Jesus: " If thou hadst known, even thou, at
least in this thy day, the things which belong unto
thy peace? but now they are hid from thine eyes."
At the close the evangelist shook hands with the
master of the house, and said, " Prepare to meet thy
God." The ark of the Lord was thrust out, and the
ark-bearer with it. Next day the man, when drinking with his companions in the public-house, suddenly fell dead. These providential visitations served
to deepen the impression made by the word. Great
power accompanied the preaching, the people were
seen running home from the place of meeting in a
state of great alarm.

The Duchess of Gordon, hearing of young Matheson's zealous and successful labors, sent for him and
offered to employ him as missionary at a salary of
forty pounds a year. Hitherto he had maintained
himself; but his means were now exhausted. His
worldly prospects were indeed bright. His skill as
a builder, his energy, enterprising spirit, business
talents, and moral integrity, held out the promise of
position and wealth; but he cheerfully turned his
back on honor and gain, and betook himself amidst
opposition and scorn to build the walls of Jerusalem.
Being now fully possessed by the great passion of
his life, the saving of souls, worldly considerations
were with him of small account. The offer of the
Duchess was accepted. He went to work with all
his might. Although he never received more than

the small salary named he spent a large proportion of it in the purchase of tracts, and in the relief of the poor; and this noble and generous practice he followed whilst he lived.

His strength was great, and he often worked sixteen hours a day. Sinners were converted, and he was filled with joy. Often, however, no success attended his labors; but although cast down and led to humble himself at the sight of souls perishing in their wilful rejection of Christ, he learned many a useful lesson. Some men, he observed, concealed a hard heart beneath " a thick coat of evangelical varnish." They assented to all he said, but repented not. He watched them at the last hour of life, and saw them die without giving one sign of grace. There were no bands in their death; their strength was firm. He concluded that there is no more dangerous delusion than the confidence begotten by a mere "head knowledge," or intellectual faith.

He frequently visited the old Christians who had been disciples of Mr. Cowie, and in his intercourse with them learned several useful lessons. One of these pilgrims was Isobel Chrystie, then upwards of ninety years of age. "Come awa, my son David," said Isobel to the missionary one day as he entered her humble cot. "Perhaps," was his reply, "the hands are the hands of Esau, but the voice is Jacob's. How do you know that I am not a hypocrite?" "Ah," said she, "d'ye think I dinna ken the breath o' a true Christian?" The Rose of Sharon may lie hid in the believer's bosom, but its fragrance cannot be concealed from others. "We ocht to lay down our lives for the brithren; an' hoo could we dee for them if we dinna ken them?" So thought Isobel Chrystie. When in the course of conversation allusion was made to the salvation of the dying thief, she rattled her little staff on the floor and said, "That was a gey trophy to gang throw the gowden gates o' heaven. I'm thinkin' there was a gey steer amo' the angels; but nane o' them would try to pit him oot. Na, na; Christ brocht him ben." When Isobel lay dying she was unable to recognize minister, missionary, friend, or neighbor. To each inquiry she still replied, "I dinna ken you." At last the question was put to her, "Isobel, d'ye ken Christ?" The countenance of the dying saint brightened at the sound of her Saviour's name. Looking up with a smile she promptly replied, "That I do, but nae sae muckle as I would like, and will do by an' by." That night the aged believer went to be with Him whom she remembered and knew when all others were forgotten and unknown.

A dying saint of the same generation gave him this pithy advice: "Haud in wi' Christ; whatever happens, aye think weel o' God; and tak' care o' yersel'; for, ye ken, a breath dims a polished shaft."

Another Christian, ere passing away, charged him to warn the believers against "razing the foundations." "I often did it," she said; "I rashly denied the Spirit's work in my soul, and I have paid dearly for it." This she said in reference to the excessive and morbid retrospection in which some Christians indulge, to the hurt of their souls and the discredit of the Gospel. They pull up faith by the roots to see if it is growing. They pluck out their eyes to see if those eyes are genuine. Peace and joy depart from them. Dark suspicions of God, as if He watched for their halting, overshadow their hearts, and they are plunged into misery. Growth in grace becomes impossible; for, as one has said, "kindly thoughts of God lie at the root of sanctification." Self-examination is important; but surely not less important is faith. Looking into the heart and looking out to Christ should go together. The pilot at once keeps his eye upon the compass and his hand upon the helm: if he neglected either he would speedily lose his course. "Keeping the heart" must be coupled with "holding the Head." "Examine thyself" should never be separated from "looking unto Jesus." The best way of testing the pitcher of our faith is by dipping it often in the Well of Life and drawing its fill for constant use.

In the journal of his missionary labors he kept a minutely detailed account of every visit and conversation, and his impressions of the people. This record, large enough to fill a volume, was written with perfect accuracy and fastidious care, and serves to illustrate the *thoroughness* that always characterized the man and his work. Plainly too it appears

from this diary that in simplicity and godly sincerity did he bring before every man, woman, and child,
the things of their peace. As usual, he found two
classes, viz., the few that are open to conviction,
and the many that entrench themselves behind their
own righteousness. One refuses to make any sign
in regard to personal religion, and he is silenced by
silence. The candle will not burn for want of air.
Another agrees with every thing the missionary
says, and in that panoply of perfect formalism no
joint is found. The candle burns, but it is in the
presence of the dead. A third "will not speak of
his religion to any man, because it is a matter between himself and God;" to which the missionary
bluntly replies that if he had true religion it would
make him speak, for he would seek communion
with men of like mind, and out of the abundance
of the heart the mouth speaketh. Some men conceal their religion as they would a scab. Eloquent
about the merest trifle, they have nothing to say
for Christ. These are the devil's dummies. Another, a middle-aged matron, receives him kindly, but
is at first shy and reserved. His quaint, ingenuous,
spirit-stirring talk quickly unlocks the good woman's heart, and she begins to tell him that she "fears
she is mair o' a hypocrite than a Christian, for she
canna see hoo a child o' God could hae sae muckle
indwallin' sin as she has: but still she daurna deny
that she canna do without prayer, that she has a gey
likin' to God's Word, an a warm hert to God's chil-

dren, and a terrible fear o' sin, though she is some-
hoo aye sinnin' an' sinnin' for a' that." The missionary takes up the case, and by the help of his own
experience so sets forth the truth of the Gospel, that
the inquirer enters into light, freedom and joy: and
ever afterwards he is to her as an angel of God, and
she is to him a "daughter of the King."

Sometimes he held as many as seventy prayer-
meetings in three months. In his reports he com-
plains of scanty fruit in the fewness of conversions.
At one time he feels nothing but "formalism" and
"leanness of soul" in discussing solemn truths.
Again, he goes to the meeting in great fear, and
finds the stone rolled away from the mouth of the
sepulchre; instead of "darkness, guilt, confusion
arising from self-sufficiency," he enjoys enlargement
and blessing. "I have seen impressions made, yet
soon after I have seen the last trace of them effaced.
I have been helped to set a gracious soul a step up
the ladder, yet on going back I have found them ten
steps down. What I have longed, and prayed, and
sought for has been conversion unto God, and any
hope or comfort I have had in seeking this has arisen
from this very truth, that He works as seemeth good
in his sight, and calleth whom He will."

Not satisfied with the efforts of his voice, he devised means for the circulation of tracts on the
widest scale. Means failing him, for he had spent
his last penny in the work, he began to cry to God for
aid. One night in prayer, the thought came into his

mind, "If I could get a printing-press I could make as many tracts as I could use." On this he began to pray for a printing-press, and for several months continued to supplicate this gift from his God. The prayer was unexpectedly answered. Accidentally discovering that an old printing-press was for sale, he made inquiries as to the terms, although he did not possess the means of purchase. Much to his astonishment, the person whose property it was let him have it, with a set of old worn types, at a merely nominal price. Never did warrior bear away the trophies of victory with deeper joy than he felt in carrying the old printing machinery to his father's house. On reaching home, he wrote upon it,

FOR GOD AND ETERNITY;

and then, hastening to his closet, "fell upon his knees, and asked the needed skill to work it." Nothing daunted by his ignorance of printing, he set himself to learn "the divine art," his only instructors the two great teachers of all heroic souls and successful workers, to wit, Failure and Perseverance. Apprentice and master, printer and publisher, missionary and philanthropist, all in one, he ascended by the slow and painful steps of experience struck out of repeated failure, like fire flashing from the smitten eye of him who runneth in the dark, till at length he reached the summit of his fondest wish, and unaided could send forth thousands of tracts like leaves from the tree of life.

His first attempts at printing ended in failure and chagrin. Whole nights were spent in ineffectual efforts; but never despairing, he cried to God for help, and went to work again. Often for hours the work of "composing" goes on, till at length his eye rests with complacence on a page of type, when suddenly the whole falls down into what printers call "pi," and his mortification is complete. Falling again upon his knees, he prays for patience and help. The sight of his own inscription, "For God and Eternity," inspires him with fresh zeal, and although oftentimes "the lumbering press goes all wrong," he perseveres till at length success comes to him, as Jesus came to the disciples upon the sea at the latest watch of the night. "I went on," he says, "till I managed to print two thousand four-page tracts a day. How I did toil, and sweat, and pray at it! Some nights I never slept at all, but went on composing. My constitution was strong, and night after night was spent at the work."

The tracts brought him no money, and his own slender means were speedily exhausted. His benevolent labors excited little sympathy in his native town; the only contribution to his tract enterprise he ever received in Huntly was half-a-crown, brought him by a poor widow. Falling short of paper and money, what was he to do? Give up the unprofitable business, and leave an ungrateful people to themselves? Never. Not in that way are souls won for Christ, and the glory of God advanced.

Again he betook himself to prayer, and the same gracious Master who provided the printing-press provided the paper also. Certain Christians in Lincolnshire, whom he had never seen, fell in with one of his tracts, and pleased with its spirit and contents wrote for a supply. He could not supply them for want of paper. This led to further correspondence, and the supply of means to procure paper from time to time.

One tract, entitled "The Lord's Supper Profaned," called forth not a little opposition. After printing it, he went round and with his own hand left a copy in every house in his native town. For the professors who have but a name to live it was too searching; hence it gave deadly offence. It was blessed of God, however, in the conversion of several persons, and is still in circulation in the Stirling Series of tracts. Mr. Drummond, who has done so noble a work of the same kind, reissued the faithful tract, and several others also of Mr. Matheson's. Another tract, entitled "The Origin of the Chinese Bible Fund," intended to further the circulation of the Scriptures in China, found its way into the Royal Palace, and thus afforded an illustration of Solomon's saying. "Seest thou a man diligent in his business? he shall stand before kings; he shall not stand before mean men."

In addition to original matter, our evangelist took extracts from Boston, Edwards, Flavel, and other favorite authors, and went on printing, till at length in an incredibly short space of time he had by his own unaided efforts thrown off and put into circulation a hundred thousand little Gospel messengers, the voice of whose quiet but powerful testimony cannot have been in vain. He was now sowing what many years afterwards he was destined to reap.

That young man, with his immense capacities for earthly promotion and enjoyment, turning his back on all the ambitions and pleasures of the world, and after a long day of sorest toil, spending the silent watches of night in so great a labor of disinterested love, was surely a pleasing sight to the angels of God. Toil, privation, ingratitude, opposition, scorn, disappointment and failure, neither weakened his hands nor discouraged his heart. He endured as seeing Him who is invisible; and bravely did he march forward in his lofty mission of self-sacrificing love to souls, ever affording practical illustration of his own motto, "For God and Eternity."

Feeling that his work would soon be done in Huntly, he labored night and day to win souls; and ere he left his native place for other fields, he could say in truth he had warned every sinner and testified the grace of God to every soul. Of all the rare privileges enjoyed by Huntly during a day of merciful visitation extending over the last thirty years, not the least has been the faithful testimony and apostolic labors of her own brave and much-enduring son

Duncan Matheson, whose name will be an honor to his native town whilst Christianity lives within her borders, and whose example of untiring energy, heroic perseverance, and Christ-like love of souls will stir the hearts of the ingenuous youth in future generations, and kindle noble aspirations in the bosoms of many yet unborn.

At this time the perishing millions of China lay heavy on his heart, and he longed to go forth and preach the Gospel in the land of Sinim. Much did he "sigh and cry" about the heathen, and often did he say in his inmost heart, "Lord, here am I; send me." During the last months he spent in Huntly, as he went from house to house pleading with men to receive Christ, the words of Heber's hymn were constantly sounding in his ear:

"Shall we, whose souls are lighted
    With wisdom from on high,
Shall we to men benighted
    The lamp of life deny?
Salvation, O salvation,
    The glorious sound proclaim,
Till earth's remotest nation
    Hath learnt Messiah's name."

CHAPTER V.

HIS MISSION TO THE CRIMEA.

"Also I heard the voice of the Lord, saying, Whom shall I send, and who will go for us? Then said I, Here am I : send me."—ISA. vi. 8.

His evangelistic apprenticeship was now at a close. He had obtained "a good degree, and great boldness in the faith which is in Christ Jesus." Even if he had accomplished little he had learned much. By constant and prayerful study of the Scriptures and the best divines, he had greatly increased his intellectual and spiritual stores. His mind was braced by severe discipline, his judgment matured by deep reflection, and his gift of utterance developed by exercise. His knowledge of the truth kept pace with his growing insight into human nature; and the frequent rebuffs he met taught him to add tact to straightforwardness in dealing with men. His faith, like his person, was sturdy, stalwart, and full of robust health; his assurance was as clear and calm as a summer morning; and his consecration to God was entire. In his consuming zeal for the salvation of men he was willing to go anywhere or do any thing at the Master's call. Born a soldier, every inch of him a man of war, he was not the less fitted for camps and the rougher scenes of life, now that he stood clad in the whole armor of God, "a good soldier of Jesus Christ." The man of prayers and tears, and love to souls, had his humble part to play in the gathering of the armies of the nations; and though that part nobly performed finds no place in the annals of the Crimean struggle, the record of the missionary's campaign is on high, and its results, when disclosed in the last great assembly of the human race, will doubtless receive a nobler reward than the perishing laurels of earthly fame.

Our evangelist happening to witness the departure of soldiers for the Crimea in 1854 was deeply moved by the sad farewells. This changed the current of his thoughts and sympathies; and although he did not cease to pray for the perishing millions of China, his heart went with the soldiers, and he began to lay the matter before the Lord. The more he thought of the peculiar circumstances of a soldier's life, its hardships, its snares, its constant risk and peril, its need of counsel and of the cross, the more he prayed and longed to go as a herald of mercy to the camp, the field, and the hospital, in the distant East, to share his joy with the weary, the wounded and the dying. How this could be brought about he had no idea. His desire was known only to God; but he believed in the Hearer of prayer, and continued to wait at the throne of grace.

The call for which he was praying came from an unexpected quarter, and it came stamped with the broad seal of a special providence. It happened in this way. One day he received a letter, which in substance ran thus: "If you are still in the mind to

6

go to the East, reply by return of post, and please
say when you could start." The letter was from the
Rev. J. Bonar, convener of the Colonial Committee of
the Free Church—a gentleman whom Duncan Matheson had never seen, and did not know. Surely he
thought as he read Mr. Bonar's note, there is some
mistake here. Yet he felt as if the hand and voice
of God were in it, calling him to the scene of conflict. He went and told the Duchess, saying that
there was clearly a mistake, but that he was willing to go. " How strange!" exclaimed her Grace;
" I have been praying that God would incline you
to go, and others have been praying also. If there
is a mistake, I will send you myself." He wrote to
Mr. Bonar, and ascertained that the letter was intended for another of the same name, a Gaelic-speak-
ing licentiate of the Free Church, who had been
employed for some time among the navvies. The
Countess of Effingham desirous of sending a missionary to the Highland Brigade, had requested Mr.
Bonar to find a suitable agent for the work. Mr.
Bonar wrote to the Rev. D. Matheson; but the letter going astray, a clerk in the post-office had written on it, " Try Huntly," and so it came into the
hands of the wrong D. Matheson, according to the
proposing of man, but the right D. Matheson, according to the disposing of God. Mr. Bonar, glad
to find a fit man ready to undertake so arduous a mission, requested him to come up to Edinburgh and
arrange for taking his departure for the East, in

connection with the British and Foreign Soldier's Friend Society. He whose "kingdom ruleth over all," and who "holdeth the seven stars in His right hand," overruled the mistake of the post-office for the accomplishment of a great purpose.

With characteristic decision he went up to Edinburgh the day after he received Mr. Bonar's letter, and without an hour's delay, entered into engagements with the Society to go to the East as a Scripture-reader. At the same time he received a commission from the Free Church Colonial Committee, and a recommendation "to their brethren at Constantinople or other places where Providence may cast his lot."

The following scrap was found in his room after his departure; " I surrender father, sister, brothers, myself—all, all that concerns me, into thy hands, O my God. For the past, I bless Thee. For the present, I praise Thee. For the future, I trust Thee. My feet shall stand within thy gates, O Jerusalem. Nights end. Partings close. I am thine, O Lord, wholly thine.—Nov. 8th, 1854." This was counting the cost.

At the quiet rectory at Beckenham, a green spot to him ever after, he was received with unbounded kindness; and the parting blessing of the venerable servant of Christ, Dr. Marsh, was fresh on his heart to his dying day. In contrast to this was the discouraging language of certain ministers of the Gospel, who, meeting him at another stage of his journey, warned him against speaking to the soldiers about *conversion.* " You will be expelled from the camp, if you do," said they. He replied, that he was going to the Crimea for the very purpose of telling the unconverted soldiers that they needed to be born again, and by the grace of God he would do it, be the consequences what they might. In this way he experienced light and shade.

TO HIS SISTER.

" London, 11th Nov., 1854.

" I have met with kindness such as I never felt on earth, and have met with some of the Lord's dear family in the highest ranks of life. Surely goodness and mercy follow me. I feel it—I know it. My heart is stayed on the Lord; it is truly humbling and cheering. Letters come daily from persons I have never seen. My destination is in the meantime Scutari. My whole energies will be devoted to my dear countrymen. . . . . I long to get to my work. I feel no shrinking. I commit my way to the Lord. I go his errand. I seek his glory; it is enough. Do seek to rejoice that He counts me worthy to go. I am calmly resting on his arm. I feel no fears. Truly I am not alone. He bears me up. Clouds, trials, darkness may come; yet all works for good. Dear father and sister, be of good courage, for I am forever the Lord's."

" London, 15th Nov., 1854.

" I long for my work. I see the need great and

pressing. I seek no rest till I get it on high. I know to his own God will be a Shepherd, gently leading and guiding them. Never did I feel so much as now the power, the deep sustaining power of grace. Ah, dear sister, it is sweet to be passive in the Lord's hand; to know his grace, to enjoy his smile. I offer myself to the Lord. I may meet rough tossing, billows heaving, seas swelling; yet the throne, the crown, the kingdom on high—that is our goal—that is enough for me."

"Off Cape St. Vincent, 22d Nov., 1854.
"MY DEAR, DEAR JESSIE.—How I shall write you just now I know not, the motion of the steamer is so great. Still I am anxious to send you a few lines as we expect to be in Gibraltar to-morrow. . . . . It seems as if the Lord were giving me such displays of His goodness as to compel me to say, 'This God is my God forever and ever; He will be my guide even unto death.' On getting aboard the steamer, I saw my luggage safely put away, and was then conducted to my berth by the steward. I knelt down in it, and committed myself, you, father, friends, and all on board to the Lord. Felt deeply and calmly reposed. And here I mark his hand—I got a cabin to myself, whilst the other passengers were placed two and two together. The scene as we steamed down the Mersey was truly exciting to most; to me it was not. My thoughts were on my work, home, the need of

close walking with God; all these pressed on me. I walked the deck alone, yet not alone. I write a note to you. The pilot left us. The wind freshened and we sped onward. Night settled on us, and still I was on deck. Oh, it was strange, passing strange to me; and most of all to watch the phosphorous light dancing on the crest of every wave far behind. I went below as night stole on, and committing all to the Lord, fell calmly asleep.

"Sabbath morning dawned, and with it a raging sea, rolling mountains high; each wave as it broke on the vessel's side made her quiver from one end to the other; but the wind was favorable and on we sped. I felt that there was no Sabbath on board. All was bustle and confusion. The light-hearted gaiety of souls without God. I had tracts and Bibles with me; these I went and gave the poor sailors, who had none. Never did I see such gratitude expressed; it saddened my inmost heart. Once and again I have asked to be the means of saving souls in this vessel, and it may be the Lord's will to do it. How solemn a matter to be saved! How deeply momentous the issues that hang on *not being saved*. Not saved, though the Bible is read, the Spirit strives, sermons are preached, providences are sent—solemn thought! Shutting myself in my cabin, I hope I had something of the real Sabbath-keeping spirit. Yea, I dare not question it, for I felt borne up and calmly stayed upon the Lord.

"We had one fearful day going through the Bay

of Biscay. Most of the passengers were sick. I felt rather qualmish; but kept on deck, for I was anxious to see the ocean in all its fury—and certainly the Bay of Biscay is the place to see this. Now and then as a wave broke on the vessel, the noise resembled thunder, but I felt no fear; for 'He holdeth the sea in the hollow of his hand,' 'His ways are in the sea' was forcibly opened up to me. Who would look for a path in the sea? And yet so strange are his dealings (and to me they have been so) as to look like the opening of a way in the sea.

"My one grand desire is to go and tell of Christ and Him crucified, looking for the descent of the Holy Ghost to own the word for the conversion of souls. I am compassed about with a great cloud of witnesses. The eye of Israel's Shepherd is upon me. Months, years, glide on; eternity seems at hand. For a while, earth has been losing much of its attractions for me; and heaven with its undimmed purity, its endless pleasures, its streams of bliss, its unwithering crown, and its blessed God, grows sweeter and sweeter."

At Constantinople he was received with much kindness by Messrs. Thomson, Turner, and McKutcheon, of the Free Church Mission to the Jews. Bitter was his disappointment on finding that military law strictly forbade his going to the Crimea, and it only remained for him to return home, as other missionary agents had done. That night was spent in prayer;

towards dawn, as he tells, he felt in his heart as if
God had heard his cry, and would open up his way.
Next day accompanied by Mr. (now Dr.) Thomson,
he applied to Admiral Boxer for permission to go to
the scene of strife; and contrary to all expectation
that officer at once granted him his request. Great
was his joy and gratitude, and cordially did he praise
God for "having touched the Admiral's heart."

Losing no time, he embarked on board a transport
conveying soldiers, and quickly found himself steam-
ing up the Bosphorus, and entering the Black sea.
By order of the Admiral, he was entitled to share
cabin accommodation with two chaplains; but when
night came these gentlemen, forgetting the law of
love, thrust him out. A kind-hearted engineer gave
him his berth in the forecastle, but he could not
sleep. The conduct of the soldiers and sailors was
more than he could endure; it was like "hell let
loose," and he was glad to escape on deck, where
under the starry vault of heaven he spent the night,
thinking of heaven and home, praying for needed
grace, and feeling assured that the unslumbering
eye of Israel's Shepherd would watch over him,
and all would be well. At break of day on 5th December they sighted the Crimea, and when they
reached Balaklava, the troops were ordered on shore
at once, as an attack was expected from the army
of Liprandi. "All was mirth and excitement. We
could distinctly hear the booming of the cannon,
not in mere holiday salute, but in deadly earnest.

What a tide of feeling rushed through my mind, as
I thought of mothers weeping for their sons, wives
for their husbands, and sisters for their brothers,
whom they should see no more, and of the brave
men fallen in battle, their bodies buried in the common pit near the field of strife, and their spirits passing from the roar of battle into the immediate presence of God. Turning to my text for the day, I
was cheered when I found it was, 'The Lord pre-
serveth those that love Him.' I felt I was nerved
for whatever might befall me; and stranger though
I was—knowing no one, as a messenger of peace,
with a lion heart I stepped on Crimean soil.

"Alma had been fought, and Inkermann won.
The thin red line had been formed on the plains of
Balaklava, and the grand death-charge had been
made. But the very elements had risen in arms
against us. It would be impossible to describe the
state of the army at this time. The hospitals were
crowded; many were dying. Day after day, ship
after ship with its load of suffering was despatched
to Scutari. Many of those you met were in rags.
Most were emaciated and smitten with hunger.
Some were almost shoeless; many had biscuit-bags
instead of trousers, whilst others had newspapers
tied round their legs; and often such was the wretchedness that you could not distinguish officer from
man, or recognize the best known."

Matheson, with characteristic generosity, immediately gave away all the clothes he could spare,

and then began to distribute his spiritual stores in
the shape of tracts and Bibles, of which latter there
was a great scarcity in the camp. The books and
especially the Bibles were received with the greatest eagerness, and read with wonderful earnestness.
Some 25,000 tracts, selected by the Tract Society,
by Mr. Drummond, of Stirling, and by Miss Marsh,
were quickly put into circulation.

"January 25th, 1855. How shall I describe the
scenes I hourly see. I shrink from it; they are truly
appalling. The condition of our army is sad. Yesterday 600 were brought sick from Sebastopol, and
conveyed on board ship. I took my stand in the
midst of them, and spoke to them of the only all-
sufficient Saviour. Many listened with interest, and
at last the gushing tears told a way had been found
to the heart. My heart was like to break. Oh, I
have often felt since coming here that the one thing
needed is the Holy Ghost. All looked haggard and
worn. Death is thought nothing of. I had a long
conversation with an officer yesterday. He speaks
of the demoralization of the army as truly awful,
and says swearing and ungodliness are increasing.
Since I came here I have not gone ten paces without hearing profane swearing. And yet there are
hopeful appearances. . . . The taking of Sebastopol is no easy task. There seems as yet no recog-
nition of the Lord's giving the victory. The men
are greatly dispirited; yet, strange to say, long for
nothing so much as a battle. I can, and do at this

moment, hear the roll of the cannon. At every shot my heart leaps, for usually some one is hurried into eternity. O happy people whose God is the Lord. Truly I feel it, and can really say thoughts of heaven are growing sweeter and sweeter every hour. I long for rest, yet am resigned to his will. O how fondly my affections twine around home and friends! Huntly! I cannot, I will not forget it. I see other scenes; I possess other friends; but the dear saints in Huntly and in Scotland have the largest place. . . . I feel there is nothing I more need than the prayers of all who love the Lord. I cannot tell what I may have to undergo. All is in the Lord's hands. I need a close, calm, and holy walk with him. One needs to be always ready here, for it is a death-stricken scene. My comfort in my work is, 'He shall see of the travail of his soul, and shall be satisfied.' Come, Lord Jesus: come quickly. Amen."

Mr. Matheson was not slow in seeking out men of his own spirit in the army. His first acquaintance was Hector Macpherson, drum-major, Ninety-third Highlanders, a soldier both of his country and of the cross, of whom our missionary used to tell the following story: One day a chaplain, newly arrived, called on the sergeant, and asked his advice as to the best method of conducting his work. "Come with me," said Hector, "to the hill-top. Now, look around you. See yonder the pickets of Liprandi's army. See yon batteries on the right, and the men

at the guns. Mark yon trains of ammunition. Hear
the roar of that cannon. Look where you may, it
is all earnest here. There is not a man but feels it
is a death struggle. If we don't conquer the Russians, the Russians will conquer us. We are all in
earnest, sir; we are not playing at soldiers here. If
you would do good *you* must be in earnest too. An
earnest man will always win his way." Such was
the advice of Queen Victoria's servant to the servant of Jesus Christ.

Hector and Duncan on the first Sabbath after the
arrival of the latter retired to a ravine, and there
amid the deafening roar of cannon, which the missionary thought was always worse on the Lord's
day, they read, and prayed, and sang together the
old battle-song of David and Luther:

> "God is our refuge and our strength,
>   In straits a present aid ;
> Therefore, although the earth remove,
>   We will not be afraid."

Here making intercession for their friends at
home, for their country, and for the army, they
found a Bethel; and for a moment almost forgot
that they were in the presence of one of the greatest woes of earth. "Thus we had many a pleasant
hour together," says our missionary; "and the only
strife we ever had was about the soldiers' scanty
meal which we divided between us, each insisting
that the other should have the larger share. Our

watchword without which we never met or parted, was 'The Lord reigneth.'"

Mr. H. Macpherson, writing of his friend says, "Our first interview took place on a ridge within the entrenchments of the 93d Highlanders, which ran along the north side of the plain of Balaklava, opposite the harbor, and about a mile from the village, and which formed the key of the base of the siege operations of the British army. I was standing watching the movements of the Russian forces, who appeared as if designing to threaten our position, when I noticed a stranger in the attire of a civilian approaching, who from his clean white breast and respectable dress, contrasting with our rags, I concluded was a minister or lay-missionary, newly arrived. This supposition led me to resolve on exercising caution as to committing myself to him, feeling that unless he was a man of God, and had thoroughly counted the cost, resolving in dependence on promised grace to throw his whole soul into the work, he would neither gain the attention nor win the heart's affection of British soldiers; for carrying their life in their hand, they are above every class of men prejudiced against and opposed to mere official piety and ecclesiastical hirelingism. As these thoughts were passing through my mind, the stranger advanced, and in his own unreservedly frank and manly way introduced himself, saying with real feeling, 'Oh, Hector, man I am glad to see you. How are you?' Suspicions quickly vanished, and

I felt grateful to the Disposer of every event that in
the thick of deadly strife on the plain of Balaklava,
I first met Duncan Matheson, who became my fond,
fast friend for life. The report I had received from
a worthy minister of the Gospel in Scotland, of Mr.
Matheson's character, I found to be in no degree
exaggerated, and I reckon it one of my most highly-
prized privileges on earth that ever I became ac-
quainted with such a man. Since that day many
a happy and profitable hour have I spent in his
company; and it has been my rare privilege to be
associated with him in evangelistic labors in many
towns, villages, and rural parishes of Scotland. I
could not fail to respect him for his great ability; I
admired his sterling worth; his unwearied, self-denying devotedness in the cause and service of God,
his manly frankness and unflinching courage, and
his large-hearted sympathy with distress, all tended
to endear him to me in the bonds of closest friendship. Never had the British soldier a more true,
loving, and devoted friend than Duncan Matheson. I believe there is not a British soldier now
alive, who served in the Crimea, but would heartily
subscribe to my testimony in his favor; for all, both
officers and men, knew, and loved, and respected
him. As to the fruit of his labors in the Crimea,
the day of God will declare. My own conviction is
that he labored more abundantly, and accomplished
more real good among the troops, than all the others,
with the exception of the Rev. J. W. Hayward, a

noble minister of the Church of England, who devoted his time, his talents, and his fortune, to the
promotion of the temporal and spiritual benefit of
the soldier. With this zealous and faithful servant
of Christ, Mr. Matheson was most intimately associated; they were daily together, and went hand in
hand in all labors of love.

"Happening to mention to my friend, just after
we made each other's acquaintance, that the first
clause of the first verse of the 93d Psalm had been
a comfort to my soul, Mr. Matheson, feeling the
power of the truth in his own heart, and realizing
its appropriateness in the circumstances in which
we were placed, seized it as a watchword; and ever
after, wherever and whenever we met, 'The Lord
reigneth' became the password between us.

" Wherever I met my dear friend I was sure to
find him, like his Master, going about doing good;
sometimes laden with Bibles, sometimes with tracts
and other suitable books, and seldom without some
temporal comforts for the sick and wounded. Many
of the sick, wounded, and worn-out soldiers, was he
the means of relieving, and who, but for his devoted,
kind, and sympathizing efforts, would have sunk
into the cold embrace of death. He was the trusted
friend of all, French, Turks, and Italians, as well as
his own countrymen. Soldiers of every grade and
nationality looked on him as their special friend.
How he managed to procure in a time of famine so
many comforts for the starving soldiers was a mys-

tery; but none knew better than he, 'Where there is a will there is a way.' His tact and genial frankness made him a favorite with the captains of the mercantile steamers employed by the Government, some of whom were truly Christian men. By the graphic and touching descriptions of the destitution and sufferings of the soldiers in the entrenchments, backed by his own evident sympathy, he reached the warm hearts of the seamen; and the never-failing result was a thorough searching of the vessels for every thing that could be spared for the benefit of the suffering soldiers.

"Entering the encampment of the 93d Highlanders one icy cold winter day, he observed our destitution of fuel either to cook our rations or warm our persons. The great majority of us were clothed in rags; some without shoes; others without a cap to cover their heads from the pelting of the pitiless storm; and some of us with more mud than clothing attached to our bodies. After a few words of loving sympathy he said, 'Hector, I must try and help you.' But what could he do in such a case? Why, next day he returned, and informed me that he had made an effort and succeeded in procuring several tons of coals from the different steamers in the harbor of Balaklava, which were conveyed to the camp as soon as possible. This is one instalment of many noble acts of kindness done to the sufferers in that terrible winter. For the relief of the men who were exposed not only to the hail of the enemy's fire, but to the fierce blasts of winter, almost without a rag to cover them, he labored incessantly, and unweariedly, until his gigantic efforts broke his constitution down.

"But what he chiefly aimed at was the spiritual and eternal welfare of his fellow-men. The soldiers understood this; and whenever he spoke to them of salvation they listened with respectful attention. They knew he was no mere official hireling, but a man who loved their souls; and not a few through his instrumentality, by God's almighty and distinguishing grace, have been prevented from going down to an unblest eternity. In his love to souls he forgot himself. Often have I had to make a cup of coffee to relieve his fainting frame, after a weary day's tramping through the mud, laden with provisions for the benefit of others, whom he deemed in more absolute need than himself. A more unselfish man I never knew. With the exception of the late Rev. W. C. Burns, I never knew one so entirely devoted to the good of others. The amount of mental and physical labor he went through in the Crimea was truly marvellous, and was enough to break down the most robust constitution. However wet or cold, or however violent the storm, he was always on the move, and always with a special and important purpose. On one of the most tempestuous and piercingly cold nights I ever experienced in the Crimea my regiment received orders to move eight or ten miles to the south of our entrenched position,

7

under cover of the darkness of the night, to dislodge a body of the enemy from a threatening position they held under the covert of a high ridge. We were absent till mid-day following. Matheson was informed of this expedition, and such was his sympathy with others, that although, had he chosen to consult his own ease and comfort, he could have secured protection from the inclemency of the weather, he remained exposed in our original position until our return. I shall never forget the joy he manifested when he saw us all safely return without a single casualty, with the exception of some of the men's ears having been bit by the frosty wind.

"Mr. Matheson was well fitted by personal experience, and much owned by God, in encouraging, comforting, and strengthening the Christian soldier in the Crimea, both officers and men. It was a special evidence of his own living Christianity that he was a sincere lover of all in whose spirit, temper, and deportment he could discover the impress of Christ's image, without distinction as to sect or creed."

For a time he lodged on board ship; afterwards he took up his abode on shore. There he found a wretched lodging in an old stable, of which he took possession with right good cheer, remembering that his Master was born and cradled in as mean a place. It was too well ventilated, for the fierce wind blew in at a hundred crevices in wall and roof, and often as it whistled through the crannies overhead it seemed to mock the shivering missionary. In an unoccupied corner he erected a rude and comfortless bed, on which at the close of each day's overwhelming labor he laid him down to rest, but more frequently to pray than sleep. To increase his discomfort the stable was infested with rats, and not a night passed but whole armies invaded his couch and rendered him sleepless and miserable. But "necessity is the mother of invention;" our missionary, whose wits often began where other people's end, found means of relief. Amongst the stores lying in one end of the stable he discovered an immense quantity of lucifer matches, which the British Commissariat in its wisdom had laid up here. Taking a large supply to his bedside our Scripture-reader drops asleep with a box in one hand and a bundle of matches in the other. By and by, in the silence and under cover of night, the hungry Russian hordes stealthily issue from their entrenchments, and attack the person of the hapless foreigner. The not unexpected sortie awakens the slumbering Scotchman, who instantly fires his rare artillery; and amidst the horrid noise, the phosphorescent blaze, and the sulphureous stench, enough to put the Cossacks to flight, the enemy scamper off in all directions, leaving the missionary, for the present, master of the field.

Yet in this rude dwelling he was contented and thankful; and even feared it was too good to last long. "My room," he says, "is quite a sight. I

have paper for glass in the windows; in some of
them not even that. My furniture consists of a bed,
which also serves for a chair, a Russian chest of
drawers, and the hay for Mr. W——'s cow. A jelly
jar, a brown earthen basin, and a Turkish jar are my
dishes. I have a sort of lamp for making my coffee.
My pocket knife cuts my bread, and it also serves for
eating my egg with; a stick serves as a spoon to stir
the sugar with; and a bottle serves for a candlestick.
I rise early, light my lamp, make my coffee, clean
my boots, sweep my room with a few Turkish feathers, and I can tell you I was never happier in my
life. I have a perfect palace, and I have decorated
the walls with copies of the 'Illustrated London
News.' I fear it is too good to last, but it is in the
Lord's hand. How contented I feel with all, and
how well it is that I learned when young to help
myself. I am happy as a king, yea ten thousand-
fold more so than one without grace."

From his journals and letters it is not difficult to
form some conception of his daily life in the Crimea.
Rising early he prepares his breakfast, and seeks
refreshment to his spirit in meditation and prayer.
Whilst he intercedes for all, the Sardinian army lies
upon his heart like a prophet's burden. Having thus
renewed his strength, he carefully selects tracts and
books for distribution. His next step is to visit the
harbor, where his loud, hearty voice wakens the
echoes in many a bluff, kind response on board ship.
Humor and pathos are keys to open the heart of

Jack, and the missionary is master of both. A sick soldier is in the crisis of disease, and he succeeds in procuring some delicacy for the prostrate warrior. Another whom he met the day before suffers from a threatening cough ; an old woollen shirt may save the poor fellow's life. Away he goes with his cargo of stores, temporal and spiritual, and trudges through unfathomable mud till he reaches the camp. In the hospitals he ministers to the sick and wounded with the skill and tenderness of a woman; and when by gentle touches of humanity he has smoothed the sufferer's pillow, he tries to point to Jesus, and allure to heaven.

As he passes through the camp he hails every body, and is hailed in turn; for his is the peculiar gift of knowing every one, and making himself known to all. Now you hear him talking in his broadest Doric to some countryman, and anon he is jabbering in broken French or Italian. Under cover of a cool, easy, off-hand exterior he conceals an intense desire to say some good, strong thing bearing on *eternity;* and rarely is the opportunity missed of making the home-thrust right under the fifth rib. Sometimes he is repulsed, but he knows conscience is on his side. Sometimes he is answered with a smile, and "Ah, sir, that is all very well, but it won't do here." This is a good opening for the missionary's heaviest shot. "But death is here, and how are you going to meet God?" Occasionally he is met with a raking fire of profanity, and is put to grief and silence. He tries all his keys into the locked heart. Perhaps the man was once at the Sabbath-school; perhaps he has a mother, the traces of whose love even sin can hardly obliterate. He finds an opening at length, and the man who met him with swearing and laughter goes away in tears. Onward amidst the tents the missionary holds his way, a strong sower scattering good wheat upon the waters—the folly of reason, and the wisdom of faith. Sometimes his heart faints within him; but he quickly renews his strength in fellowship with some one of his godly friends.

After a hard day's work he makes his way to the market at Kadi Keni, to "forage" for dinner. Here too he often does some business for his Master. Frequently, indeed, he stands for hours amidst a crowd gathered out of many nations, and endeavors to find an entrance for the word of life. On returning home, he cooks his meal only to find that his appetite is gone. But dinner or no dinner his day's work is not yet done.

The last hours of the day are spent in writing his journal and in attending to a vast correspondence by letter. Many write him from all parts of the three kingdoms, inquiring about their relatives and friends in the army. Not one scrap is neglected, and an answer is duly sent. Commissioned by the sick and wounded, he writes on their behalf to wife, or mother, or sister, or affianced one, far away. Besides all that he must prepare his quarterly report, and not forget the claims upon his pen of his numer-

ous friends, whilst the public ear must be gratified
by stirring letters in the newspapers and religious
periodicals. His writing is not done in an easy
chair and slippers; it is subject to frequent interrup-
tion by visitors from the allied camps, for whom the
old stable begins to have rare attractions. Be he
soldier or navvy, Sardinian or Turk, officer or man,
the missionary is at his visitor's service. The pen
is laid aside for the employment of his most effective
weapon—frank, genial, copious, and forcible speech.
His words are often quaint in the extreme, but they
are as nails fastened in a sure place. The oddity
of his sayings may provoke a smile; but he is
a wise fisher of men, and knows how to bait his
hooks.

Such then is his daily life in the Crimea; and ere
the last sand of the glass has seen him rise from his
knees to creep into his corner for the night, it is no
more than truth to say that the work of two days
has been pressed into one.

A few extracts from his published journals may
be here given:

"April 10th. At Sebastopol. A sheet of fire as
it were encircled it; the engines of death poured
forth their deadly volleys—the sun shone forth
brightly, marking forth each embrasure in bold
relief in the devoted city. It was a trying sight,
and finding no opportunities of usefulness, owing to
the excitement prevalent, I retired early to my quarters, anxious that the day might soon arrive when

the alarm of war should be heard no more, and the din of battle be forever hushed.

"April 14th. Took farewell of the Hospital Ship, where for nine weeks I had been living. My work on board was pleasant and painful—far more pleasant than painful; for I sought to know amongst them nothing else 'save Jesus Christ, and Him crucified.' I had spoken to many of them about their souls— had prayed by their sick beds, and given them many tracts, and the result of all the judgment of the great day shall bring to light. May it be found that the arrow of conviction had reached some heart, and that souls there had been 'born again to God.'

"April 16th. On board Transport No. —— to visit the soldiers invalided for England. Many a poor sick man seemed to revive at the prospect of once again meeting those he loved in his native land. The scene could not be described; it was pleasure mingling with pain; they were going home, yet leaving many friends behind. They had high hopes yet many fears. I had known most of them during the winter, and the most devoted of all my friends and the best loved was amongst them. Gladly was I welcomed each day. I went on board ere they started, and the supply of tracts given for the voyage was highly valued. To each I gave a Testament for reading on the voyage, the gift of Colonel L——, and had, to remind them of the Crimea, to write my name in each. I parted with them with much sorrow, which I believe was mutual. As I saw the vessel leave the harbor a tumult of feelings filled my heart. These veteran sick soldiers were leaving the land where they had known so many trials— met so many difficulties—seen such deadly work. I could only commend them to the care of Him who holdeth the winds in the hollow of his hand, and who could guide them safely to their own father-land.

"April 18th. I am distributing tracts on the wharf—met a soldier who had been long confined to hospital. I had met him before, and had gained his confidence. He asked me to go aside and talk with him. I did so, and his first inquiry was for a Bible: he said he had never read it, or had one to read, being deeply opposed to it, now he felt the need of reading it for himself. I had much conversation with him about the need of spiritual religion, and commending the Lord Jesus to him and giving him my last Bible, bade him for the present farewell, as he had to go to his battery on the following day.

"April 20th. Spent the afternoon with Colonel ——, sick on board ship. Rarely, if ever, have I spent such a hallowing hour. He told me much of the Lord's kind dealings with him, and the marvel-lous way He had led him since called by his Spirit to be a partaker of the glorious Gospel of the ever-blessed God. He has done much for the spiritual welfare of his men, and returns to England beloved by all, yet his loss is deeply regretted. Before leav-ing he made me a present of several copies of the

Scriptures in all the languages of the East, and a goodly number of English and French Testaments.

"April 22d. In the evening with the Rev. Mr. G——, railway chaplain; held open-air service; the attendance was good, most being soldiers. It was sweet to sing songs of praise on the outskirts of Balaklava, and pleasant to hear the voice of prayer amidst the round of oaths and blasphemy from the huts around.

" In the front, at —— battery, met one of the most pleasing trophies of grace it has been my privilege to witness, in the case of bombardier ——. Truly the meeting was a joyous one to both. He has charge of the hospital attached to the battery, and every good influence he brings to bear on the invalids. It has been his custom, in case he should be taken prisoner, to carry his Bible in his breast with him to the trenches or on the march—as he remarked, 'if taken prisoner he should at least have one to speak to him.' Yes, and I believe he hears and follows the voice as few, very few soldiers are found to do. We walked long together, and next day he visited me, and we had prayer and reading the Word. A pleasing trait in his character is, he supports an aged father in the Highlands of Scotland, and that very day gave me seven sovereigns to transmit for him.

" A Russian officer, taken prisoner a few days ago, called on me, and through an interpreter asked for a Bible. I presented him with one, for which he seemed very grateful. An opportunity of giving the

Russian Testaments now and then presents itself, and it is embraced.

"April 29th. A good few were wounded last night in the trenches by a sortie made from Sebastopol. They were brought to hospital to-day, and to those not seriously hurt I gave a Testament. Poor fellows! they seemed much softened and melted. I was, and have often been, much struck by their calm endurance of pain, and their unwavering fortitude.

" A corporal of artillery called on me for tracts and books, for himself and a few comrades attached to the siege-train. They have not the same time many others have, and it was the more pleasing to see their desire for reading.

"Visited Main Guard, and presented each soldier on guard with a Bible. I found confined a soldier transported for life. In a fit of intoxication he had seized a musket and fired it, wounding a man. I spoke kindly to him of his condition as a sinner in the sight of a holy God, and tried to open up the heart-cheering, soul-comforting, soul-saving truth— ' It is a faithful saying, and worthy of all acceptation that Christ Jesus came into the world to save sinners—even the chief:' the strong man was unmanned and bowed to the dust. It seemed deeply to touch his heart—the message of mercy carried to him, and the kindness in visiting him. I presented him with a Bible, which in his solitary confinement he promised to read, and took farewell of him, to see him no more on earth—in the earnest hope that he might yet be a trophy of redeeming love—a diadem in Immanuel's crown, in the day when He maketh up his jewels. It seemed on leaving as if I could sing with a joyous heart:

> " 'There is a fountain filled with blood,
>   Drawn from Immanuel's veins,
> And sinners plunged beneath that flood,
>   Lose all their guilty stains.'

"Presenting a Testament to a sailor, he said, 'It's of no use to offer me that; I hate my work and every thing else; my life is a torment to me; and, alas, it's all one thing.' Argued with him, if this was so bad a world, would it not be wiser to seek a better one to come? and urged on him the necessity of doing so. He took the Testament with the promise of reading it.

"Visited by Quarter-master-sergeant. We spent the afternoon together in reading and prayer.

"Attended and took part with the Rev. G. G——, at the funeral of a man killed by accident; it was a heart-touching scene. In the evening, just as the sun had sunk, we moved beyond the lines; the grave was already made, and the busy hum of voices could be distinctly heard in the camp. As we stood in prayer around the grave, the gentle breeze bore the sound of the cannonade distinctly towards us. The company gathered were select and numerous, and I believe every one felt as we stood by the open grave, we were in the midst of strangers—far from

home, friends, and country. As the address proceeded, marked impressions were made, and I believe I am right in saying, the Lord was with us of
a truth.

" Visited by a sergeant of the —— at three o'clock
P.M., and by ten he was dead. Whilst with me I
could see symptoms of cholera on his countenance,
but little, ah, little did I think, when speaking to
him, he would be so soon in eternity. This terrible
scourge has again broken out in our army. We are
surrounded on all hands by death and disease, and
life is felt to be most uncertain. How solemn to
see the mighty mass hurrying to the grave—how
solemnizing to see such crowds marching to eternity. Even during my stay in this land I can look
back and see tents recrowded, but not by those I
had known; ranks filled, but not by those to whom
once and again it had been my privilege to address
the Gospel message of salvation. Thousands have
passed away, as the leaves in autumn or the snow-
flakes before the sun. Often when sinking, at
heart, have I wished I could cry in the ears of God-
taught souls at home, 'What meaneth thy sleep?
Are you girding yourselves for the conflict? Are
you wrestling with the God of Jacob and prevailing?' Ay, and it has come with deeper force, as I
have seen the Lord during the last few months
gathering home His children from the army, and
leaving it well-nigh forsaken of those who fear His
name.

"All things at present speak loudly, and urge to instant, deep, believing, persevering prayer for the descent of the Holy Ghost, that waters may break out in the wilderness, and streams in the desert:

> "'Then shall the earth yield her increase;
> God, our God, bless us shall.
> God shall us bless; and of the earth,
> The ends shall fear Him all.'"

In Mr. Hayward, an English chaplain and devoted minister of Christ, he found a true friend. In all his troubles Mr. Hayward came to his help. When about to be evicted from his humble dwelling, the good chaplain interfered, and he was allowed to remain. When the priest at Balaklava attempted to stop the distribution of tracts, his faithful friend withstood the priest, and the work went on. They labored much together. Laden with material and spiritual comforts, they often sallied forth in company to visit the sick, the wounded, and the dying. Sometimes they did their cooking together, the Rev. chaplain trying his culinary skill in making a pudding of biscuit, while the lay missionary washed a few potatoes which he had been fortunate enough to procure about the ships. At every juncture in the war they retired to a lonely spot to pray; and never could Matheson forget the impression made upon his heart when as they knelt Hayward would raise his noble countenance toward heaven, and amidst the thunder of the cannon plead with a voice full of emotion, "Lord, prepare those that are appointed to die." They organized a service in which, besides prayer, praise, and preaching, Hayward introduced the practice of reading all round. This gave additional interest to the meeting; and it was pleasing to see a general and a navvy reading each his verse in turn. The devoted chaplain spent his private means in promoting the good of the soldiers. At length, exhausted by his great labors, he fell ill, and was obliged to leave. In his last sermon—a memorable one—he told his audience he had changed his mind in regard to the apostolical succession; he now believed that all who brought souls to Jesus were of the true apostolical succession. His friend, our Scripture-reader, assisted in conveying him on board ship, and they laid him gently down upon the quarter deck beside other sick ones, to whom the afflicted chaplain began to speak of Christ. There Matheson and Hayward parted, with such pangs of sorrow as large and true hearts only feel. The two faithful soldiers of the cross now worship and serve where the din of war is hushed forever, and the weary are at rest.

Sad were the sights witnessed by the Scripture-reader every day. Hundreds of sick and wounded were brought down to Balaklava—famished, emaciated, clothed in rags, many a noble form, a total wreck from lack of timely aid. He wept at the sight. The sufferers fixed their eyes on him in touching appeal, and many uttered a piercing cry

for water. He did what he could. Some of them
he saw die on the wharf. On board many lay hud-
dled together under the open hatchway. Some lay
on bags of biscuit—anywhere, anywhere in the hurry and helplessness. "Scotland I'll never see again,"
was the heart-piercing lament of a poor Scotch soldier laddie. Ah, no! Poor boy, he never did see Scotland again. A Lincolnshire lad whom he sought and
found was unable to speak a word. "Your mother
bade me seek you," said the missionary. At this
word the dying soldier suddenly revived, and exclaimed, "My mother! O my mother!" It was the
last flicker of the candle. He said no more, and
died. The last tender throb of his heart was given
to her who had known its first gentle beat.

Suffering does not necessarily soften and refine.
Feelings and affections are tender plants: unless
care is taken, rough winds blight and kill them.
A heart-hardening process in the army was only
too apparent. One day the missionary, marking the
conduct of a burying party who had cast the dead
into a pit with no ordinary levity, admonished them
with much feeling and impressiveness. A party of
soldiers was one fine day seen playing at cards in
the trenches. A shot laid one of them low. Instantly they rose, and carrying the dead man away,
returned in a few minutes and resumed the game.
Despite all this callousness of heart, the missionary
often succeeded in making an impression even to
tears. In particular, he knew how to reach the

hearts of his countrymen, and not seldom did he unseal the fountains of emotion by an allusion to Auld Scotland, the scenes of boyhood, the parish school, a question in the Shorter Catechism, or the 23d Psalm, "The Lord's my Shepherd; I'll not want," learned at a mother's knee.

He was very careful in respect of the matter contained in the tracts he put into circulation. By whomsoever issued he cared not, provided only they contained the truth as it is in Jesus. A great heap of Popish trash, full of Mariolatry, coming into his possession, he was at a loss how to dispose of them. By the help of a party of soldiers, he dug a deep trench. "There," he says, "we gave them decent burial;" adding with grim humor, "We read no burial service over them, and dropped no tears; but quietly said in our hearts, 'Let the memory of the wicked rot.'" Such was the burial of dead tracts. Another heap, "all about schism, and not at all about Christ," he thrust into a Russian furnace, at which he and a friend warmed their toes. In all conscience they knew enough already about schism in the Crimea; what they needed was union with Christ and peace. A third parcel of rubbish he took out in a boat, and cast the dangerous lies into the sea. "We put poison out of the way of children," says he. This, verily, was soldier-like work.

One night, weary and sad, he was returning from· Sebastopol to his poor lodgings in the old stable at Balaklava. He had labored all day with unflag-

8

·ging energy, and now his strength was gone. He was sickened with the sights he had seen, and was depressed with the thought that the siege was no nearer an end than ever. As he trudged along in the mud knee-deep, he happened to look up and noticed the stars shining calmly in the clear sky. Instinctively his weary heart mounted heavenward in sweet thoughts of the "rest that remaineth for the people of God," and he began to sing aloud the well-known Scriptural verses:

"How bright these glorious spirits shine !
  Whence all their white array ?
How came they to the blissful seats
  Of everlasting day ?

"Lo ! these are they from sufferings great,
  Who came to realms of light,
And in the blood of Christ have washed
  Those robes which shine so bright."

Next day was wet and stormy, and when he went out to see what course to take, he came upon a soldier standing for shelter below the veranda of an old house. The poor fellow was in rags, and all that remained of shoes upon his feet were utterly insufficient to keep his naked toes from the mud. Altogether he looked miserable enough. The kind-hearted missionary spoke words of encouragement to the soldier, and gave him at the same time half a sovereign with which to purchase shoes, suggesting that he might be supplied by those who were

burying the dead. The soldier offered his warmest
thanks, and then said, "I am not what I was yesterday. Last night, as I was thinking of our miserable
condition, I grew tired of life, and said to myself,
Here we are not a bit nearer taking that place than
when we sat down before it. I can bear this no
longer, and may as well try and put an end to it.
So I took my musket and went down yonder in a
desperate state about eleven o'clock; but as I got
round the point, I heard some person singing 'How
bright these glorious spirits shine,' and I remembered
the old tune and the Sabbath-school where we used
to sing it. I felt ashamed of being so cowardly, and
said, Here is some one as badly off as myself, and
yet he is not giving in. I felt he had something to
make him happy of which I was ignorant, and I
began to hope I too might get the same happiness.
I returned to my tent, and to-day I am resolved to
seek the one thing." "Do you know who the singer
was?" asked the missionary. "No," was the reply.
"Well," said the other, "it was I;" on which the
tears rushed into the soldier's eyes, and he requested
the Scripture-reader to take back the half sovereign,
saying, "Never, sir, can I take it from you, after
what you have been the means of doing for me."

He says he did not find many real Christians in
the army. There were a few stars of the first magnitude, and they shone conspicuous in so dark a
sky. Our lay missionary was not long in discovering those who feared the Lord; and he found in them

true friends. The first time he entered the tent of Capt. Hedley Vicars, he observed that although the officer was absent at the time, his Bible lay opened upon a sort of table made of an old box. Thus the godly Vicars showed his colors, the open Bible intimating to all who entered on what terms they might have his fellowship. "His manliness and whole-heartedness," says Mr. Matheson, "struck you at once. There was nothing morose or gloomy about him; nothing to repel. He retained the freshness of boyhood with wisdom above his years. At our first meeting my heart was glued to him at once." In his journal he writes: "March 19th. At Sebastopol. Met with Dr. Cay and Major Ingram in Vicars' tent. We had prayer and reading the Word together. It was to us all a well in the desert, a bright spot amidst surrounding gloom. We blessed God on hearing that a day of national humiliation and prayer was appointed. Cay and Vicars accompanied me on my way. After Cay left us Vicars and I stood on the plateau above Sebastopol, the doomed city, as it was often called, lying in its beauty before us. The sky was without a cloud; the sea was as calm as a pond. It was on one of those sweet evenings you never can forget. Our conversation was on the purity, blessedness and endless peace of heaven, where the din of battle shall never be heard, nor the strifes of earth be known. We expressed to one another much longing to reach it. Speaking of some who had gone,

we remembered Peden at the grave of Cameron exclaiming, 'O to be wi' Ritchie!' and our
feeling was the same. We could hardly part. He
agreed to meet and spend a day with me at Balaklava."

On the day fixed for the meeting Hedley Vicars
was taken home to his God. Matheson was over-
whelmed with grief, and could only exclaim, 'Dear,
dear Vicars!" As he stood beside the grave on the
day of burial he felt in his inmost heart as if "another link had been snapped on earth, and another
bond formed in heaven."

One of his best friends was Bombardier M'L., a
warm-hearted Highlander and a Christian. Just as
the alarm was sounded and the men were called to
arms, Mr. Matheson on entering the bombardier's
tent found him buckling himself for the fight and
putting his Bible into his bosom, saying, "If I fall,
it will be there: and if I am taken prisoner, it will
speak to me, and I can never be weary with such a
companion." One day when they had retired to a
quiet spot for prayer and reading of the Word of God,
a shell dropped at their feet. On this they went a
little further off; but again the exercises were disturbed by another terrible invader which fell beside them, shaking the very ground beneath them.
"Never mind," said the soldier, "it is only the devil
trying to spoil our enjoyment: let us go on." They
had just resumed when whiz, whiz, with a loud fall
a thirty-two pound shot lay beside them. The mis-

sionary was alarmed, but the soldier calmed his fear by quietly saying,

> "Not a shaft can hit
> Till the God of love sees fit."

This brave man Matheson used to tell, once stood alone by his gun in the midst of an assailing Russian host, and in a hand-to-hand encounter maintained his ground till the enemy was driven back, one of the Russians with whom he grappled falling dead at his feet.

The missionary, peaceful though his part of the business was, occasionally experienced danger, and had his narrow escapes. One day, when conversing with a godly officer in a retired spot, the latter said, "We have been long enough here, let us move away." No sooner had they removed than a 13-inch shell dropped and burst on the very spot where they had been standing. "God had cared for us," he says, "and we were safe."

"At Sebastopol during the unsuccessful attack on the Mamelon. It was a fearful night. Thousands were hurried into eternity, and yet our soldiers marched cheering to the trenches, and seemed totally unconcerned. The mail had arrived just ere they marched, and you could see them reading the letters from home. Two hours after, they were dead or dying. There seemed to reign an utter recklessness of life, and I could hear the wild oaths as they marched bandied about in the ranks. I had an opportunity of speaking a few words to some of them, and during part of the night remained with the outlying sentries, in one of whom I felt special interest. At midnight went to the tent of Bombardier ——, and had prayer with him. In the morning all was calm, save now and then shot from some heavy gun, and the wounded were carried away in great numbers. It is in such scenes as these one can truly appreciate the reign of righteousness yet to arise on this benighted world, and long and pray for its speedy advent."

One day, 17th June, we find him speaking about the "one thing needful" to "a large draft for the Rifles, mostly boys," newly arrived. On landing they are drawn up and ranged, before "marching to the front;" and as he slips out and in among them, giving them Testaments and speaking in his own hearty, affectionate way about home, and battle, and death, and eternity, he is pleased to mark unwonted signs of emotion, and remarks that "it seemed as if their hearts had got tender when brought so near the seat of conflict." These boys were going to be butchered on the morrow at the Redan. "Next day," he adds, "I was at Sebastopol, and some of these very men were carried past wounded, whilst others had been killed in the fight."

"Attended and took part in the meeting, specially with reference to the expected assault on the morrow. The worthy chaplain's address was most solemn, affecting, and impressive. It was indeed a night of deepest feeling, and much of the Lord's presence was enjoyed."

In reference to the disastrous attack on the Redan, he writes in his journal: "June 18th. Early in the morning went to Sebastopol. I trust higher and holier motives than those of mere curiosity led me. Was eye-witness to all the proceedings of the fatal morning. It produced feelings that cannot be expressed; to hear and see the deadly conflict, and be witness to the dead and dying carried past, enduring their sufferings with calm fortitude and unmurmuring silence. Spoke words of kindness to a few; and sought, as able, to tell others the lesson to be learned, viz., to seek the Lord, who only could grant victory, and put no confidence in an arm of flesh. When the fury of the storm had passed, and something of a depressing calm was felt, looked in at —— Hospital, but could not stand the sight. Some had limbs amputated; others hands off; and many were suffering from unextracted bullets. There are events in every man's history he can hardly forget, and through grace, I should like to retain the many lessons taught me on the 18th of June, before Sebastopol."

He was well received by the sailors in the harbor of Balaklava. When not admitted on board he left a parcel of carefully selected tracts to be distributed among the men. One day a soldier refusing a tract, a sailor with the wonted frankness and good humor of Jack stepped up and said, "If he won't, I will," adding for the encouragement of the missionary, "Thank ye, sir; I like a good yarn." Captain T——, master of a transport, used to hoist the Bethel flag on his ship, and Matheson held service on board.

He was also called to minister to the navvies of the Army Works Corps, among whom cholera had broken out. As early as five in the morning he was astir with his Bible and his medicine. His counsel and aid were in great demand, for the navvies had taken it into their heads that no medicines were so effective as his. Something, no doubt, was due to "the effectual fervent prayer" which "availeth much." This opportunity of usefulness was seized with his usual promptitude and good sense; but the work sometimes proved more than even his strong frame could bear.

Mr. Gymgell, chaplain of the Army Works Corps, being taken ill of cholera, our missionary watched him till he died. Through the long weary hours of his last night on earth, Matheson sat by his bedside ministering to him, till at length, as it drew towards the dawn, the faithful chaplain, breathing out faith and hope, peacefully fell asleep in Jesus. On the Scripture-reader devolved the last offices of friendship, and keen were his feelings in transmitting the sad tidings to the widow and children far away. Just as the sun was setting they buried him in a quiet spot near the grave of Admiral Boxer, and Matheson addressed all those present with more than ordinary impressiveness and power. He felt as if the disease had fastened on himself, and he spoke with the light of a near eternity in his soul.

Utterly prostrate, he reeled home to the old stable, and crept into his comfortless bed, where he lay sick, helpless, and alone for three days and three nights. Growing worse hour by hour, he was at length no longer able to rise for his only comfort—a drink of water; and despairing of life he turned his face to the wall to die. This the hour of his extremity was God's opportunity. The Lord sent an angel to minister to him in the person of Mr. Medley, a gentleman in the Commissariat, who had formerly been a London city missionary. Happening to come to the door, he discovered the forlorn condition of the Scripture-reader, ran to his relief, and never left him till he began to recover. "It was the sound of Mr. Medley's voice singing psalms," said our missionary, "that first brought me to myself, and from that moment I began to get better."

For the benefit of his health he took a trip to Trebizond, of which he speaks in a letter to his sister. "I wrote you that I was going to Trebizond. I did go, and was absent a week. I cannot tell you how much better I was for the trip. It was in the 'City of Aberdeen' I went, and the passage was beautiful. It would be impossible for me to describe the beauty of Trebizond and the adjacent country. I hardly thought such gorgeous scenery was to be seen on earth. Should I be spared to return I may be able to convey some idea of it to you. I was most taken up about its spiritual condition, which is sad in the extreme. Of 60,000 inhabitants there is only one Englishman, the British Consul. The Americans have a missionary there doing a good work; but as he had gone to Constantinople I did not see him. I left a letter for him and some books. Some of the converts I saw and was much pleased with them. I felt, O how deeply! the want of knowing their language; for as I walked through the city given up to idolatry, I wished I had been able to preach 'Christ and Him crucified.' The sight of so many thousands believing a lie gives one an interest in missions such as many speeches could not give.

The Turks in Trebizond I found to be most inveterate against Christianity; but their days are numbered. . . . Although only a week absent I had many friends wearying for me, and once again I was glad to see them and enter on my work. All friends here, however, must be held very loosely, for they soon remove or are taken away."

The market-place, Kadi Keni, situated about a mile from Balaklava, was a stirring spot. English, French, Italians, Turks, Jews, Maltese, and others, assembled here. The Jews were extremely debased, but the Maltese, if possible, were more wicked still; for they were sometimes caught in the act of spoiling the dead. The market was just the place for our Scripture-reader: here he did much business for his Master. No Jew was more bent on making gain than he was on winning souls; his constant cry was, "Who will buy the truth?"

At Kadi Keni he met officers and soldiers of the Sardinian army, and made their acquaintance. "From the day that the compact, brave, accomplished, and well-behaved Sardinian army set foot on Crimean soil," he writes, "my heart was set on doing them good, and I prayed that God would enable me to spread the Word among them. Knowing that God could bless one text as well as a thousand, I committed to memory from the Italian New Testament that Gospel in miniature in John iii. 16: 'For God so loved the world, that He gave His only begotten Son, that whosoever believeth in Him should not perish, but have everlasting life.' I went out, and standing amongst them repeated the passage, and then passed from group to group with my little Gospel message. Then I took the New Testament and went out reading it as best I could, till a deep interest to possess it was called forth, and the time had come for its distribution."

Cholera, too, came to clear the way for the servant of the Lord Jesus. Many soldiers of the Sardinian army were taken ill: there was a lively demand for the medicines, of which Mr. Matheson had a large store, and very soon his services were held in as high repute by the Italians as by the English navvies. He saw the door of access opening; he felt assured the Lord was answering his prayers; and so incessantly and lovingly did he labor among

them, that he came to be named, "The Sardinians
Friend." His kindness won a way into their hearts;
prejudices gave way; he became a universal favorite, and many of the Italians received the Word of
God at his hands, when they would have rejected it
at the hands of any others.

In his journal of June 1st he writes: "Began the
distribution of Italian New Testaments in fear and
much trembling. Opening after opening presented
itself, and the avidity with which many received
them was remarkable, whilst others sternly refused
them. One officer asked for a copy, and assisted
me to supply all his company, remarking, 'A better
book they could not possess.'" Again, June 2d,
"Took a large bag full of Italian New Testaments
to market-place, Kadi Keni. Met many Sardinians,
and on presenting them with the Word was offered
by nine tenths payment for them. Some sternly refused. The joy of others was great."

Day after day the interest increased. One walked
five miles in the darkness of night to knock at the
old stable door and get the Word of God. Another
came begging the whole Bible, because he had found
the New Testament so good. "I have a great treas-
ure now," said another, as he put the book in his
bosom, and went away. At five in the morning
the missionary is aroused by Sardinian soldiers seeking the Word of God. They were going to join the
advance, and feared losing their only opportunity of
procuring a copy. A Waldensian corporal lying ill

at this time, in answer to the kind inquiries of the
Scripture-reader, said, "The source of all true courage is, whilst the body is on earth, the soul is in
heaven,"—a truly Waldensian and martyr-like view
of the matter. "Spoke to the Sardinian guard,"
Matheson writes in his journal, "and told them of
the only Saviour of sinners, and gave each of them a
New Testament. They said they would take them
home to Italy. Visited by seven Sardinian officers,
who wished to have Bibles. As an army of reserve,
they said they had much time for reading, and
would take their Bibles home as a memorial of English affection and of the Crimea." Two Tuscans,
burning with zeal for liberty and Italy, enlightened
and able to speak English fluently, visited the stable, and heard the good old story of freedom through
Jesus Christ. A Tyrolese, of noble countenance,
who had fought under Garibaldi at Rome, and shared
the perils of his flight, received a copy of the Word,
and became attached to the missionary. Thus the
work went on day by day, despite all the efforts of
the priests, who did their utmost to stop it.

Duncan's frank, genial disposition, and intense
sympathy with the Italians in their aspirations for
national liberty and unity, were largely instrumental in opening the door for the Word of God
among the Sardinian troops. God gave him favor
with the officers. Dr. S——, who could speak English, became his friend. That gentleman had been
led to embrace Protestantism by reading the Bible,

and comparing the religion of Rome with the truth.
He introduced Mr. Matheson to other officers, who
invited him to dinner. The missionary made a
speech, Dr. S. being interpreter. After depicting
in glowing colors what he firmly believed would be
the future of a free and united Italy, whose flag
should one day be unfurled on the Capitol of Rome,
he proceeded to speak of the Gospel as the greatest
glory of a nation, and Jesus Christ as the only true
liberator of men. His sincerity and enthusiasm
carried all their hearts as by storm, and thenceforth
"The Sardinians' Friend" enjoyed all but unbounded
liberty and respect in carrying on the work of the
Lord in the Italian army.

Thus his field of labor was constantly widening,
and knowing that the day of opportunity would
soon close, he pressed into every breach with in-
domitable courage and unquenchable zeal, till at
length in the capture of Sebastopol he saw a certain
indication of the end of his mission. His account of
the final bombardment and assault deserves a page.

"Balaklava, 10th September, 1855.

"The din of battle has been hushed for a time,
and I have found a little leisure to write. I hardly
know where to begin, and I do not for a moment
conceive I shall be able to give you any right idea
of the transactions of the last few days. My last
told you of the mighty preparations going silently
and mechanically on for the final assault. For days

and days nothing was seen but the transit of ammunition, and the transport of gabions, etc., for the front. The fire for some time back every night had been truly terrific. It seemed the Russians well knew how our works were coiling themselves around their devoted city, and if they could not prevent this, they seemed determined to annoy us. What was often thought to be the reopening of the bombardment was only meant to allow the French at the Malakoff and us at the Redan to finish the works under cover of it. On the morning of the 6th it seemed as if all batteries had opened. Gun after gun sent forth its deadly charges, and during the whole day nothing else was heard but the whiz of shells as they flew through the air. The accuracy of our aim was remarkable. In one minute you could count nine shells bursting upon the parapet of the Redan, and the Malakoff seemed entirely shrouded in a sable covering of smoke and dust. Thus it continued during the day, and as evening had settled on us, one of the Russian ships in the harbor was seen to be on fire. Slowly the flames flew up the rigging, and soon the burning fragments were scattered around. It was a brilliant sight. The dark night—the horizon lighted up for miles—the city seen as if by day—the sound of the rifles, as they went off, pop, pop, in the advanced works—the heavy cannonade—and the star-like fuses of the shells, as they rolled through the air, made it all awfully imposing. For hours the ship burned, and when morning broke you could see the hulk burned to the water's edge, and the other vessels lying lazily in the spot where they have so long been.

"If the fire of the 6th was heavy, it was as nothing to the fire which opened on the 7th. Every spot seemed to possess a gun, and from every side the smoke, fire, and noise were terrific. It seemed as if all the guns and mortars in the French left went off at one moment. Volley after volley shook the air, and the whole seemed as made of living fire. For a short time it seemed as if they had spent their fury, and as if the work were done. The guns were only cooling. In a little while they burst forth with greater fury than before. Thus during the whole day it continued. There seemed no slackening, no flagging, no wearying. Now and then the Russians replied, but it was feeble and faint—not one shot for the thousand given. Thousands of spectators, chiefly, yea, almost all, soldiers, crowded the heights, where a passing glimpse could be had as the smoke cleared away. It was touching to see them in little groups discussing the probability of an attack, and their remarks were often of a mellowing cast. Gray-haired soldiers felt certain of it, though all was kept profoundly silent, and it sent a strange thrill through the heart to see some of the young, only joined a few days before, gambolling to the sound. During the night there was no cessation, and the rockets flew at intervals, kindling the city in various places.

Sleep was far from our eyes. The night seemed long and dreary, and the sighing of the wind on the fierce blast seemed to sound in the ears like sighs deep and loud from a sepulchre. At length morning broke, cold and cheerless. The sun now and then seemed ready to shoot forth, but kept back, as if afraid of shining on the work of the bloody day. The wind was strong, and carried the dust in whirling eddies through the camp. It blew well-nigh a hurricane, and seemed ready to carry all before it. We approached Cathcart's Hill and found the whole line guarded by our dragoons. One could scarcely stand for the cold, and yet the interest of the moment absorbed every thought. The cannonade seemed still fierce, and now and then through the strange mingling of smoke, fire, and dust, you could catch a glimpse of the two spots of interest—the Malakoff and the Redan—greatly battered, and only now and then firing a solitary shot, as tokens of being yet unsubdued.

"By seven a.m. the Light Division had marched. By eleven the other divisions had assembled, and marched to their respective posts. They wound down the various ravines in good order, and seemingly knowing the desperate nature of the work they were to do. I saw several soldiers' wives weeping after them as they went. Each man carried forty-eight hours' provisions. Their advance could not be seen, for the wind carried the dust and smoke in darkening columns, shrouding all well-nigh in midnight darkness. It was blowing into our works, and straight away from the Russians. A large building burned in Sebastopol, and yet it was scarcely noticed, so eagerly did all look for twelve o'clock. It came. We heard the crack of musketry at the Malakoff, and the cannonade still went on. In a few minutes the report, 'The Malakoff is taken,' reached the camp. The 3d Division in reserve gave three hearty cheers, which could be distinctly heard through the camp above the din of all. The opposition at the Malakoff was faint. In ten minutes the eagles of France floated on it. It seemed unexpected. The French works were so near it—one bound, and it had fallen. All eyes turned to the Redan. Here, in a moment, the battle raged. Such hot musketry has rarely been seen. Our men mounted its parapets, and were hurled into the ditch below. Man after man ascended, and one officer, mounting the parapet, waved his sword and cheered them forward. He was soon laid in the dust. Mass after mass pressed forward, and, over the dead bodies of their comrades, got within. They had gained it, but the dense mass of Russian infantry poured in countless thousands upon them, and one battery within, unseen, played hard. The Russian force, in leaving the Malakoff, poured into the Redan, determined to make it the final settling-ground. The few of our soldiers that got a footing made a noble stand, but they were as a drop in the sea, or a leaf in the forest, compared with the dense masses that

came against them. They had to retire, and yet
time after time they rushed to the assault, and kept
the enemy from gaining one inch of ground. Between the Malakoff and Redan the contest fiercely
raged. Victory seemed to hang tremblingly in the
balance, and moments passed as hours—so deep
was the suspense. At three o'clock the wounded
began to be carried up. It was a sad and melancholy procession. The Woronzoff road was one con-
tinuous stream—officers and men all alike. Some
walked themselves, limping, whilst the blood oozed
from their wounds, and now and then, as the wind
threw the cloak or covering a little aside, you saw
the pale cold face of some one who had gone from
the battle to the judgment-seat. As I stood marking the sickening sights, three soldiers' wives rushed
down the ravine, asking after their husbands, and
presenting a dreadful spectacle of misery and grief.
A ball from some of the Russian batteries fell close
beside them, and they had to run with all speed to
the rear. The wind still blew, and the cold continued intense. Now and then it lulled for a moment,
and the sun burst brightly forth. All was silent
along the French right, and only our batteries and
the French left kept up the fire. The mark was
still the Redan. It was evident the Russians were
losing heart.

"Night closed on the scene, and the wind died
away. The reserves were marched off for the work
of the coming day. The town was on fire in sev-

eral places, and the shipping seemed without a gun.
Explosion after explosion took place. At two o'clock
—one louder than the rest. Part of the Redan had
been sprung. The Highlanders, who behaved nobly,
held in reserve for the next assault, entered, and
found it evacuated. The Russians had fled, and,
whatever else may be said, made a masterly retreat,
displaying the most consummate generalship. As
they went, they fired all behind them, and our men
were not allowed to follow, which was well, for yesterday explosions were taking place the whole day.
In the night they had sunk their shipping, so long
the terror of the Allies, and the cause of so many
deaths. The eye had got so long accustomed to the
sight of these mighty vessels, and now it is cheerless to see the waves gently cresting over the spot
where they were, and to glance at the large bay
without a speck, save a few harmless steamers cow-
ering under the guns of the opposite shore.

"Yesterday, we had our first quiet Sabbath in the
Crimea. How pleasant, how calm, how refreshing
it dawned upon us! Before, all used to be bustle,
and the cannonade kept no Sabbath, and had respect to no commands. Not a gun was now heard.
The stillness of death seemed to reign, and the deepest interest to be felt in knowing who had or had
not survived. Many a sad blank was found, and I
had to weep specially over one friend who had only
arrived from England two days before, and who fell
at the first attack. He was an officer of the Rifles,

and if honored with a tombstone, the epitaph truly may be, 'He walked with God.' Only a few entered the town yesterday, and our troops moved cautiously, there being so many mines springing. It is all mined. Not a building remains uninjured. Shot and fragments of shell pave every spot. Buildings have been scattered in ruins, and what has been left the flames have devoured. It has a desolate, dreary aspect, and the wind howls hideously through its deserted streets. The dead lie all around, and heap upon heap meets the eye at the various points of sharpest contest. Yesterday and to-day, the last offices are performing for the dead, laying them in graves on the spot where many of them fell. The stern tide of war has mercilessly swept them away, and left many to deplore their loss. Friend and foe lie together, and Sebastopol is in the possession of our army.

"It has been got at a dear rate, and the price of it has been much blood. How many thousands, yea, tens of thousands, have found their graves before it, there to await till the trump of God shall summon the sleepers to arise! When I think of the mingled joy and weeping the sound of this victory shall produce at home, my soul is filled with deepest feeling. I feel greatly it will be laid to the bravery of our army, and to the skill of our commanders; but those whose hearts are filled with divine light, and who know any thing of the tremendous difficulties overcome, and the magnitude of the struggle, will give all the glory to the Lord, to whom it belongs."

The following letter to Mr. P. Drummond, Stirling, will furnish some idea of his work, and the free course of the word of God in the Crimea:

"Balaklava, Sept. 20th, 1855.

"My Dear Mr. Drummond: Now that the town of Sebastopol has fallen, and the din of battle for a time has ceased, I have found a little leisure to write to you. And first I desire to thank you very sincerely, in my own name and that of others, for the many kind grants of tracts you have sent from time to time, since December last, and to assure you all have been widely scattered, and in many cases gratefully received. I also enclose you a thank-offering from a few friends of £7 10s., to help you forward in your work. The silver and the gold are the Lord's, and as such we cast it into His treasury.

"I hardly knew from what point to start to let you know of my work since entering this field of death and bloodshed. It has been an eventful, thrilling, soul-trying time; and yet in the midst of all, much of the seed of the kingdom has been scattered—seeing since the fourth of December last I have given away—tracts, 52,000; Bibles, 622; Testaments, 1,477; French Testaments, 770; Bibles, 32; Italian Testaments, 4,300; Bibles, 200; Welsh, Russian, and German Testaments, 173; books for officers, 450.

"The work has now and then been pleasant, yet seldom has a joyous heart been known, seeing so much abounding iniquity and such an utter recklessness to the things of eternity. You cannot think what a vast wilderness of ungodliness our army is. You cannot move a step without hearing that name, dearer to you than all others, continually blasphemed. Gambling has been carried on in the hospital, the camp, the trenches, to an amazing degree; and the curse of our country, drunkenness, is widespread indeed. The sufferings of last winter were not overdrawn, nor was the lesson to be taught ever learned. Judgment hung heavy on us, and it passed away unheeded. The Lord had a few holy witnesses in our army, but most of these were taken away by death, the bullet, or removed to England. No widespread blessing has ever descended, and tens of thousands have passed to the judgment-seat. The sins of our nation were punished in our army: and a slumbering church started for a moment to sink into a deeper sleep than before. Often when ready to faint have I been sustained by the blessed truth, 'All that the Father hath given *shall* come;' and some measure of faith in the omnipotent power of the Holy Ghost has revived the drooping heart, and enabled me more urgently to present Christ and Him crucified to dying men. Few have cared for the soldier's soul; an exception here and there with joy may be made—but Popery and Puseyism have had it much their own way. The means to meet the wants have been totally inadequate, and every barrier has been thrust in the way of those that would. Evangelism has met with little favor, and Rome has plied her arts with untiring assiduity. What has tended much to demoralize our army has been the almost total extinction of the Sabbath. The Crimea has, I may say, known no Sabbaths. True it is, for a few minutes the form of parade-service has been gone through, and the men instantly hurried to fatigue. Let those who would like to see what Britain would be without Sabbaths visit the Crimea, and they will see the soul-destroying effects of it. The poor soldiers long for it to recruit their over-worked systems, but the demands of man cannot afford it, and the ceaseless toil must go on. I wish to draw a vail over much that I have seen in the Crimea these ten months. The scenes witnessed, and the dark pictures presented, often make the blood run cold, and draw tears from the eyes. Sure am I if it were really known at home by those who know the value of their own souls, they could not but cry, weep, pray, beseeching the Lord to open the windows of heaven and pour down a great and an abundant blessing. One cannot but admire the calm endurance of our army, and stand amazed at their contempt of danger, and the unflinching bravery ever manifested; and oh, how well it were if a real deep and abiding awakening took place! then it would be bravery drawn from a right source, and endurance of suffering the result of right principle.

Much prayer ought to be made for our neglected army, for it is high time to know the real spiritual state of it, and to awake out of sleep regarding it.

"You are aware, in the end of May, the Sardinian army landed here. Hearing of its coming I had sent for thousands of Italian Testaments, not knowing but the Lord would open a way for their distribution. I began the work with much prayer, yet in great fear and trembling. At first it went on slowly. Many prejudices had to be removed, and much wisdom to be evinced. Cholera broke out among them, and many hundreds died. It softened them much; soon group after group called on me for the Word, sometimes thirty in one day. Since the 1st of June it has continued; one brought his companion, and another his brother, till 1,500 have so visited me. I cannot give you any idea of their eagerness to possess the Word. I have known many come miles for it; and never have I seen such joy as they manifested while gazing on the precious gift. Had I time it would be pleasing to me to send you more details, for it has been a glorious, cheering work. Time after time I have gone through their camp, and seen some in little groups reading it, others in their tent; and in the hospital nothing else is read. Many officers have visited me, written me, or sent for Bibles; and in some regiments every officer, from the colonel downwards, has got a copy, while most of the medical staff have also been supplied. A spirit of earnest inquiry is at work

with some, and an apparently anxious desire to
know the truth by most. Wondrous are the ways
of God. Italy, long shut, is opening; Popery is
losing its power; the mask is being torn; light
thrown around; and who can tell the amount of
blessing the 4,700 copies of God's Word given to the
Sardinian army may be the means of accomplish-
ing? It is touching to hear them say often, ' My
father, my mother, or my sisters, possess not this,
and if I return they shall have it.' Those that have
been invalided and sent home carried it with them;
and, as they embarked, have held it up to me, saying, 'This is my memorial of the 'Crimea.' The
work is still going on, and I expect, if the door is
still open, to circulate 1,000 more. Opposition was
at one time greatly threatened. A Maynooth priest
in our army tried to stir the Sardinian priests against
the work, but ere his plans were fully mature he
fell sick, and had to leave. One thing is clear, Sar-
dinia is lost to the Pope, and every fresh bull ful-
minated is making the breach wider and wider.
Oh for living men for Italy to preach the everlasting Gospel, and for the descent of the Holy Ghost
from on high to call the dead to life! It presents a
glorious field. It is ripe for the harvest. Who
will enter in and raise the standard of the cross, so
long trampled in the dust; yea, buried under forms,
traditions, and soul-destroying ignorance?

"I cannot find time to tell you of the progress of
the truth in Turkey. The only ray of hope is in the

American Mission amongst the Armenians, which is greatly prospering. The Turk is what he was. There is no more opening of his mind to receive the truth. His enmity to Christianity is as deep as ever, and the effect produced by the presence of the Allies is bad indeed. As a nation they are dying out; evidently *doom* is written on Mahomedanism, and it is well. Gladly would I see the Crescent prostrate in the dust, and a Christian state raised on the ruins. The time is fast hastening on; the night is passing; the day breaketh. Soon the cry shall be heard throughout earth's millions—'Hallelujah! for the Lord God omnipotent reigneth.'

"Wishing you all success, and seeking for you much of the hallowing, humbling grace of the Eternal Spirit, I am, in much haste, your affectionate friend,

"DUNCAN MATHESON."

From September till the winter set in he continued his labors—not, however, without frequent interruptions from sickness and prostration. "Many say, rest; take things easier," he writes at this time. "I cannot rest, for it is a mighty graceless army, and needs most tremendous exertions. Oh that I might be the means of saving souls!" Much did he feel the loss of Christian friends. "Captains Craigie, Vicars, and Beaufort are gone. Lieut. Wemyss died on his way to England, and has his grave in the waters of the Bosphorus. I feel it much—keenly, deeply.

Oh how cheap is life here! You sorrow for one, for many, and next day you sorrow for more, till the mind gets quite hardened. Many talk of hundreds dying as if it were nothing. Most look not into eternity, and know not the value of souls. I often think it is well I counted the cost ere coming here. I have not been disappointed. It is useless to think of trials, if the Lord prosper you in your work. . . . You and others fear for me. I alone fear not for myself. Am I not in the Lord's work? Can any thing happen without his permission? If I live, let it be to his glory. If I die, may it be for his glory. I am not my own. I know there is victory through the blood of the Lamb; and what after all is death? The entrance to eternal rest—the door to God's right hand."

Again and again he is smitten down by the combined effects of fatigue, exposure, and want of material comforts. In a letter he says: "Since I last wrote you I have known what it is to be laid low. Indeed, when I wrote you I felt rather unwell, but thought I should rally, as I have often done. I was seized with violent diarrhœa, accompanied with fever, which continued nearly eight days, five of which I was totally confined to bed. A few days after I took ill my kind friends, Drs. Derriman and Brown, pitched a tent for me at their hospital, and their attention to me was unremitting. Through the mercy of God, I am restored again, and in my own house, and at my work. Many of the poor Sardinians called on me during my illness, and I had to hand them copies of the Word of God from my bed. Indeed every one was exceedingly kind. Most of those who sought to labor are now either dead or left. The doctors say I ought not to remain another winter here on any account, as those exertions I have through grace been enabled to make must recoil on the system. This is in the Lord's hands."

His privations were often well-nigh past endurance. Often had he suffered the gnawings of hunger, till at length he lost his appetite entirely. "How gracious the Lord is," he says in a letter to his sister; "the last two days I had the delicious pleasure of being hungry." Again, "I am getting sorely out of clothes. Last week I got a present of a new pair of boots sent from England. Next day they were stolen. I had my last shirt on. I could not find another; but a staff doctor called, and made me a present of one yesterday. So the Lord provides."

At length his failing health compelled him to leave the Crimea, and return to Scotland, where he arrived about the end of the year.

After spending six weeks at home, he set out again for the East, rejoicing, and counting himself more highly honored than if he were the ambassador of a king. His connection with the Soldiers' Friend Society had ceased on his return home; but, liberally aided by the Countess of Effingham and others, he went forth absolutely his own master, and with

an eye single and full of light. Feeling assured that
he was called by the great Master to seize an opportunity such as might never recur, he girt up his loins,
and at once prayerful as well as self-reliant, cautious
as well as enthusiastic, he took his way to the scene
of his former labors and sorrows.

His stores of Christian literature for gratuitous
distribution were immense, varied, and judiciously
selected. Besides Bibles, tracts, and other books in
the several languages of the East, he carried with
him a considerable number of copies of the Shorter
Catechism with proofs, in Italian, under the title of
"Compendium of Christian Doctrine," and also Pa-
leario's "Benefits of Christ's Death," in the same
language. His own countrymen were not forgotten.
At Gibraltar, Malta, and almost everywhere a slow
lumbering voice would be heard asking, "Hae ye
ony Bibles wi' Psaums?" Knowing and sympathizing with the likings of his countrymen, he was fully
prepared to supply honest Sandy's want.

It may be worth while to notice that his services
were eagerly sought at this time by more than one
Missionary Society or Committee. The "Jews' Conversion Committee" offered to "employ him as an
assistant missionary of the Committee at Constantinople, at a salary of £150 a year." At the same
time the Free Church Colonial Committee desired to
secure his services for the East; but fearing lest he
should be trammelled in his work, he declined every
offer, in order that he might be free to carry out his

own peculiar mission in his own way. Dr. John
Bonar, Convener of the Colonial Committee, again
wrote him in noble, generous words of encouragement. "You go," he writes, "to unfurl the Lord's
banner in the sight of assembled nations. You go
to breathe words of peace from the Prince of peace
amid the din of war. You go to sow the incorrupt-
ible seed of the Word, which liveth and abideth forever, amid the very things which beyond all others
show the vanity and uncertainty of all earthly and
human things. You go to speak to men of their
souls and of eternity, in the midst of the very things
which may summon them to that eternity while you
yet speak. You go to give the word of life to those
to whom it is a sealed fountain at home; and, in a
word, to do good to *all* as you have opportunity.
Going on such an errand, and called to fulfil so important a mission, we bid you God speed."

LETTERS TO HIS SISTER.

"London, March 6th.

"I long much to get away. I have got every
thing for my mission I could desire. To-day I have
been at Beckenham. I have got forty copies of Captain Vicars' Life. Mr. Moody Stuart went to the
Edinburgh Bible Society, and got £25 for me for
French Bibles. Mr. Learmouth has paid for 1,000
Bibles for me."

"March 14th.

"At sea, off the Spanish coast. We are nearing

Gibraltar, and on getting ashore I expect to post this letter for you, that it may relieve any anxiety you may feel. . . . To be united to Jesus is the one great thing. What is all else beside? A dream —a shadow—nothing. To-day I was led to think of my awakening and after-life. What a miracle of mercy it has all appeared. To be used at all by the Lord is truly wonderful. Yea, it is all His grace— His own peculiar dealing. I long for nothing more than spiritual life. It seems to me, looking at the work to be done and the greatness of eternal things, as if I had not yet really begun to live. What an amount of time have I lost. How little it has been really occupied for the Lord. How little accomplished. Life, life, the endless life of grace, is all I need, and all I want. . . . . . It is difficult to write with the motion of the vessel. We speed on our voyage. Such is life. Yes, we are passing along. How soon shall it be all done here."

After touching at Malta, where his soul was vexed at the sight of the Popish mummeries of Good Friday, he reached Constantinople on the 31st March. Here he began the work of Scripture distribution at the Sardinian Hospital at Yenikoi, where there is a great rush on the part of the Italian soldiers to obtain copies of the Word of God. Doctors, officers, and men are waiting for him, and their joy is great on seeing their old friend with his precious stores. Day after day he passes, and the work seems to grow.

10

He again proceeds to the Crimea.

"Crimea, June 16th.

"I do not anticipate staying long in the Crimea. All will depend on my entrance amongst the Russian soldiers. In all my previous journeys the Lord has graciously prospered me, and I hope in this I shall be able to sing the same song, and talk of the same goodness. Since my arrival it has been an incessant whirl. I would I could get rest! But it cannot be. The doors are too open, and the readiness to receive so great, that it must be "now or never." I expect a thousand French Bibles soon from London. I have already given above five thousand copies of the Word in all languages. Oh for the breath from on high! My heart is set on the Lord. I love his service. I seek grace to glorify Him. Soon all will be done. It is passing away."

In the arduous work of Scripture distribution in the Sardinian army he received no small help from an Italian priest, who had been favorably impressed by the dying testimony of his nephew Paolo, a young soldier converted by reading a copy of the New Testament given him by Mr. Matheson. When counselled by his uncle to confess, Paolo replied that he had confessed his sins to Jesus Christ, and having received forgiveness, he needed not to confess to man. His beautiful death touched the heart of the priest, who appears to have been a quiet, kindhearted man.

Early in 1856 some of the Sardinian officers had written to the principal newspaper in Turin, and challenged the priests to come to the Crimea, if they dared, and stop the circulation of the Scriptures. On this an accomplished Jesuit was sent, who on his arrival threatened to have the fellow hanged who was, contrary to all law and order, spreading heresy and Bibles among the good soldiers of Italy, and the children of the Pope. Matheson providentially discovered the Jesuit and his scheme, and informed certain officers (his friends), who outwitted the priest and he was obliged to sneak away as he came.

One day he found his spiritual stores exhausted. A ship with a fresh stock of books was seen for days in the offing; but stormy weather prevented all access to the vessel. Becoming impatient he got a boat, manned by several stout Aberdonians, and taking the tiller himself, he put off to the ship. In the face of a tremendous sea they endeavored to make way to the vessel; and when all but baffled, the missionary, in his bluff, hearty style, cheered them on saying, "Row, boys, row; I'll, may be, tell this yet on the Castle-gate of Aberdeen." They succeeded in reaching the vessel, got the books, and returned to the harbor in safety.

In the report of the Society for Promoting Christian Knowledge, Mr. Matheson, in reference to his work among the Sardinian soldiers, says: "My house at Terrikoi was literally besieged, and day after day I had to return to Constantinople for fresh supplies.

On the return of the steamer many were awaiting me on the quay, and sometimes all my books were gone before I could reach the Locanda. Many fresh invalids, scarcely able to walk, applied to me there; and instead of any opposition being thrown in my way by those in command, I was greatly aided by them; indeed they were the first to ask for Bibles. . . . . . . In six days I had given away 500 Bibles—46 of these to officers. At Terrikoi I did not offer one copy; all were asked for; and pleasing indeed it was to bestow it on one and another and another, who remarked, 'I was robbed of mine at Milan;' or, 'I have long desired one to take home, seeing that in my distant village it cannot be found.'

"The work being completed there, I hastened to the Crimea; and if the interest at Terrikoi was great, it was far transcended by that manifested on my arrival here. Soon the object of my mission ran like wildfire through the camp, and singly, in couples, in groups, yea, in masses, I was visited. In one day seven hundred thus came to me, and were supplied. Officers of all grades called for Bibles; and I have in my possession very many letters sent me by some of them in high standing for the Word. It was perfectly agonizing to have to send away hundreds without it; and I have known soldiers walk six miles, four or five times in succession, for Bibles. Now and then small supplies arrived, and many, in the very act of embarking, came running breath-

lessly for that which to them had now become 'more
precious than gold.' The new edition was indeed
the more highly valued; and many were the expressions of gratitude sent to friends in England for the
noble gift. Had I had ten times the number they
could have been distributed, as over and over again,
when all were gone, many, I hear, offered all they
had for a copy. And surely it is pleasing to think
of 1,000 Testaments and 674 Bibles of this edition
being amongst them, and now in Piedmont. Of
the 674 Bibles distributed, 250 were given to officers
who called for them.

"A nobler army than that of the Sardinians cannot be found. Many, very many of them, are men
of great intellect; and it is no unusual thing to meet
with men in the ranks who are classical scholars,
and who would adorn any society in any country
in the world. They have left this land for the land
to which they so fondly cling—and whose emancipation from spiritual thraldom they long to see fully
consummated—loved by all, and with an affection
deep-seated and sincere. What most gladdens the
heart is, that few return home without the book of
God, the record of eternal life, the Gospel of Christ,
In faith we look for mighty results. Piedmont is
rising among the nations. She has taken a noble
stand. Let but the Word of God be scattered there
in rich abundance, in copies of the faithful version
of Diodati, the only translation, save in a few instances, I have ever been asked for; nor let it ever

be forgotten that they, and they only, are free whom
the truth makes free."

At length his work was finished in the Crimea.
One result was that eighteen thousand copies of the
Word of God were carried into priest-ridden Italy
in the knapsacks of the soldiers.   He was sent to
read the Scriptures to his own countrymen, which
he did, and at the same time sent a host of Scripture-
readers into the dominions of the Pope.

After the proclamation of peace, the Russian soldiers came freely into the camp of the Allies.   Our
missionary's heart was stirred anew: a fresh field presented itself; he was not slow to embrace the opportunity; and he met with no small encouragement
among the Russians.   Sometimes he was awakened
at the dawn of day by a Cossack on his shaggy
steed, come to beg a copy of the New Testament.
"My friends the Cossacks," he says in a letter,
"showed me much kindness, and I had to submit
once and again to the embrace of Russian soldiers,
smelling strongly of onions!"   The beautiful mon-
astery of St. George, situated on a high perpendic-
ular rock on the sea-side between Balaklava and
Kamiesch, he found occupied by seventeen monks,
with their superior.   Thither he repaired with a bag
of Russian New Testaments, and, with the assistance
of his friend Dr. C——, presented each of the monks
with a copy, which they received most gratefully,
and with earnest request for the entire Bible.   The
missionary, as he passed from cell to cell, offered

fervent prayer that God would bless each and all of those peace-loving dwellers in St. George with the saving knowledge of His glorious name.

It was a touching sight to behold, as our missionary did, the former dwellers returning to seek in vain their once happy homes. So changed was every thing by the desolation of war, that often did the poor people, on looking around upon the scene of their former habitations, lift up their voices and weep; and my reader will not marvel when I tell him that the tender-hearted man of God wept with them.

The allied armies took their way back to the setting sun. Our missionary waited till almost the last man had embarked. "Going to the top of a hill, I looked abroad upon the desolate scene. Miles of huts were left standing without a solitary occupant. Not a human voice was to be heard. Here and there a Russian might be seen prowling through the deserted camp. On my right lay Inkermann and the beautiful valley of the Tchernaya, with the Russian cavalry grazing on its field of battle. A little beyond, in sweet repose, was spread out the plain of Balaklava, scene of heroic daring unsurpassed in the world's history. Sebastopol reposed in calm beauty, rendered more touching by its ruins. Further off the Black Sea looked in the rays of the setting sun like a mirror of glory. Wherever I turned my eye the hill-sides were covered with graves, and every ravine was like a charnel-house. With bursting heart and streaming eyes I thought of the many friends I had lost, and the myriads of broken hearts and bereaved homes far away. All alone I went to take my farewell look of Vicars' and Hammond's graves. Thought upon thought, quicker than the lightning, flashed through my mind as I said to myself, What an army shall arise from these graves on that great day! Each spot will be instinct with life. What a different scene from that once witnessed here, when man girt on his armor to meet man, then fought and conquered, or laid them down to die! These men will rise from the dust of death to face not man but God. At the blast of the archangel's trump the sleeping warriors shall awake. But what an awaking to those who were wrapped in a Christ-less shroud and laid in a hopeless grave! And how shall the dead in Christ arise with joyous songs of triumph as they shout, 'O death, where is thy sting? O grave where is thy victory?' They shall mount up 'to meet the Lord in the air; and so shall they ever be with the Lord.'"

Returning to Constantinople in June, he plunged into the work of Bible distribution among the French and Turks.

"Constantinople, 3d July.
"Since my last I have been exceedingly busy. My labors have been entirely amongst the French and Turks. I gave 190 Bibles in one day to the French, besides a large number of tracts and books.

I wish much silence kept regarding my work among
the Turks, though in some cases it has oozed out.
Scarcely a day passes without some Turkish officers
calling for the Bible. With Mr. M'Kutcheon I have
given 300 copies already. Since my arrival here
6,600 copies of the Scriptures, in all languages, have
been distributed. . . . . What a picture our
poor countrymen give of Christianity here. You
hardly see any one drunk but an Englishman or a
Scotchman; and English oaths are the first thing
many learn here. The cursed drink, how it ruins
the soul, how it hinders the Lord's work. The
Church at home countenances it, and the ruin of
thousands must lie at the door of professed Christians who support it and lend it their influence."

In the midst of his incessant and absorbing labors
his own vineyard was not neglected; nor was the
spiritual welfare of his friends and native place forgotten, as the following letter will show:—

"Constantinople, 5th July, 1856.

"My Dear Christian Friend: How quickly the
time rolls past. Its tide is ceaseless. Its current is
often unmarked. Its filling up as it drifts along
presents a solemn history. Done with it all, how
soon! Yes, done with it to enter eternity. The
prospect is often solemn, and well-nigh makes, in
view of it, the heart cease to beat and the soul to be
still. I am a deathless being; I am marching to the
world of spirits; I shall soon be unclothed. Of that

world I know but little. The certainty of its being
mine to spend my forever with Jesus is my only
concern. Lord, more grace! more grace! more
grace! that the thought of this may swallow up
all others. Make me to feel the gilded things of
earth nothing, and lead me to see a glory in the
things of holiness surpassing in brightness, splen-
dor, and endurance all else besides.

"Five months have passed since I took farewell
of Huntly, the scene of many a sorrow, the field of
many a conflict, the spot of glimpses and of sweet-
est communion. When, oh when, shall the day of
visitation appear? When shall the clouds break?
When shall the pall of death that has hung so long
above them be rolled away? Lord, soon! soon!
soon! In memory I look at the blanks that have
been made—sad blanks for us certainly. One saint
after another has been called away. Our little company has been lessened, and Death seems to say to
the rest of us in no doubtful voice, ' Be ready! be
ready! be ready!'

"Since leaving I have been preserved in deaths
oft. Twice have I visited the Crimea, and endured
misery enough to crush the stoutest. That dark
scene I have bidden likely a last farewell. I cannot tell you my feelings as I gazed from the vessel's deck on the sun setting behind its hills, and
casting its retiring rays on its rugged shore. I had
escaped. His word had had free course. I was safe.
I longed for some one to help me to praise, for I

could not. Alas! I still carried a diseased soul, a
corrupt heart; and hour by hour well may I say,
'If I had only hope in this life, I were of all men
the most miserable.' I need no uncommon trials to
keep me lowly. I need much grace to keep me at
his feet. Daily do I get deeper and deeper discov-
eries of my own heart, and the past seems to have
only been a mere touching of the edge—a mere
glance at the surface. I would often seek to hide
in some desolate wilderness, and there seek to cry
for the only thing I need—mercy! mercy! mercy!
I hope it is better with you. How well to be at his
feet. How well to be soured of earth. How well *to
be shut up* to salvation through Jesus. Weak as this
hope of mine often is, I cannot yield it. It has out-
lived many a storm; it has upheld me in furious
tempests; it has twinkled in solemn, trying hours.
A religion of *reality* how rare. Far clearer than before I see the current religion hollow and insecure.
It is the fruit of no trial, the result of no divine fire,
the product of no omnipotent power. The spark
shall go out at last. Thy searching, O God, give
me. Thy work let it be mine. I would seek to
find my all in Thee. To find our all in God, how
high the thought! how exalting the prospect! how
humbling the immense distance from its possession! One day it may come. The night shall
cease. What is impossible with God? Alas! that
this fickle heart of mine should ever wander away.
Alas! that it should ever seek at the cisterns what

it can only find in the fountain. Pray for me. You can have no conception of the state of this city. I never walk its crowded streets or look on the dark cypresses marking the place of sepulture, but I sigh and am sad. It lies heavy on me. One day it shall be the Lord's. Little is doing, and things seen personally are very different from what is seen through reports at a distance.

"To all the friends I send my Christian love and affection. Mrs. F—— seems often as if with me. Is poor M——, or I——, or B—— yet fleeing from the wrath to come? H——, M——, C——, all, I hope, remember me. How precious time is here. I often long for the rest of one hour, but I cannot find it. May the grace of the Lord Jesus rest on you. Uprightness of heart and integrity of soul I feel I need much. What a place *integrity* has in the Word! Divine leading and integrity go together. Surely, one day we shall sing in the heights of Zion. What hinders it? We deal with an unchanging God. I hope to hear soon from you. In much haste.

"Yours in Christian bonds,

"DUNCAN MATHESON."

"Constantinople, 16th July, 1856.

"I have very lately bidden the Crimea and all its many scenes and trials farewell. Scarcely one soldier, English, French, or Sardinian, is left in it. A few connected with the commissariat may be; of the line not one. The winding up was a scene of constant bustle and much hilarity. All were glad to be off, and the cheers of the soldiers were much heartier on leaving than on entering.

"I was witness of many touching scenes, but the saddest of all was the exodus of the Tartars. Such a scene I never witnessed. The old men raised their hands and wept as they took their last look from the vessel's deck, and the poor women buried their faces in their hands, scarce daring to cast a look upward. Many of our soldiers I saw deeply affected; and yet the great mass of the Tartars thanked God that they had the prospect of getting from under Russian oppression, and smoked, laughed and chatted as if nothing was wrong. They are a poor race, and strong in their affection for Mahomedanism, much stronger than many of the Turks are. I fear a strange tale may yet have to be told of them under Turkish rule, and breathing the air, the deadly tainted air, of the Dobrudscha.

"My object in going to the Crimea was accomplished. I had been asked to come, carrying the Word of Life to the Sardinians. My arrival was known to a few, and soon it ran as wildfire through the camp. In one day seven hundred soldiers and officers visited me, asking for Bibles; and ere the last soldier had left the scene of their trials and triumphs I had given 2,347 Italian Bibles, 1,230 Italian Testaments, and upwards of 3,400 books and tracts. I did not offer one copy, I did not present one tract.

All were asked; and 250 officers of all ranks either called or wrote for Bibles. It was all done in open day. It was known to thousands. There was no disguise, and no efforts to proselytize. They asked for God's Word—who would withhold it? They had it; and pleasing is the fact, that 18,000 copies of it have entered Piedmont during the last twelve months. Noble men, they deserve well at Britain's hand! They entered the struggle when all looked dark and gloomy. They have fought well, and sustained the honor of Italy; and their conduct has been such as to call forth universal admiration. I never met a republican in their army. All love their king and country, and long—how evidently long no other can tell—for the emancipation of fair yet down-trodden Italy.

"A story once appeared in our leading journal, copied into all the other papers, of a complaint and prohibition being made against the giving of the Bible. We believe the then correspondent (not Mr. Russell, whose accounts I have ever seen truthful and correct) was deceived. No prohibition was ever uttered; and if complaints were made, they were not heard of. The whole army were implicated. What could be done? Generously they were left to their own convictions, and General Della Marmora and our own generals deserve the thanks of all who love and value the Bible. To the friends in and around Huntly I send my hearty thanks for generously helping me in this work.

"I am no politician; but I cannot but feel that a solemn time is at hand regarding Italy. It is impossible to keep such a noble people long in slavery, or under the iron heel of despotism; and I know there is not one man in the Sardinian army but has felt anxious for the time when he shall be called to the field to unfurl the banner, and strike the blow. They have learned much in this struggle. They have been inured to hardship, and trained to the vicissitudes of a camp; and in the next war of Italian independence, we believe Piedmont shall be the rallying-point round which all will cluster. Statesmen stand aghast at the wrongs of Italy, and know not how to interfere. Its regeneration is a question surrounded by many difficulties; yet the solving will one day come. Naples has her crowded prisons; the fair plains of Lombardy are trodden by the Austrian vassal; Tuscany seeks to stifle the truth; Rome is kept by the soldiery of France. The question of Italy is closely connected with the East. If war should arise there, the nations of Europe will be more or less involved. Then comes the time for Russia to strike; for no one here believes her pretensions are finally laid aside, and are led to feel that Turkey, drained and inert, can form no bulwark against either Russian diplomacy or arms, if left alone in the conflict.

"No one can credit the hatred existing between the Muscovite and Turk. Their enmity to us will soon subside; for in the Crimea I had much intercourse with the Russian soldiery, having had the privilege of giving them 480 copies of the Scriptures. These I found them very ready to receive, and many were the expressions of their gratitude. In few countries is the censorship of the press so strict as in Southern Russia, and there is well-nigh a total lack of literature of any kind. In the city of Simpheropol, there is not one bookseller's shop, and not a page of literature is sold. For years not a copy of the Russian Scriptures has entered Odessa, and the Russian prisoners who had received them were deprived of them on landing. From all quarters they came visiting ruined Sebastopol, and it was often painful to see them looking in blank astonishment and sorrow over the place where their houses had been, and trying to fix the boundary of their lot. There seems a servility in the Russian soldier not to be found in the English or French. What may be done, now the Crimea is their own again, no one can tell. It is supposed tourists will have no liberty of inspecting, and the terms of the treaty may not be carried strictly out.

"As to Turkey, its real condition is not known. Its exchequer is exhausted—its resources unexplored —its army much wasted—its progress just where it was. They are generally far from grateful for the help we have rendered, and feel the same contempt for the Giaour as before. The prejudices of some of the higher classes are exploded, and some have got the length of thinking attempts at reformation are necessary. At home things regarding Turkey have been much exaggerated. The promulgation of the new law has excited high hopes, and been hailed with joy, as well it may. But who is to carry it out? Turkey makes laws and then is powerless in putting them into effect. With many it is a question if she really means it; but we believe the time is drawing on for great reforms, and sweeping changes cannot be made in any nation in a day. Good laws may be made, but a people needs to be created to value them, or carry them out. Christianity for Turkey is only what can save her, and give her a place among the nations of Europe far greater than she can ever have under the reign and rule of the Koran. Serious disturbances are apprehended, but they may come to nothing; and Britain will, we hope, demand the carrying out of those reforms to obtain which the flower of our army have found graves in a foreign soil, many of our homes have been left desolate, and our resources drained.

"I have had much intercourse with the French since March here and in the Crimea, having along with a friend given them 2,000 copies of the Scriptures, in very many cases asked. In some cases they came for miles for them. Glad are they to get home. The East has lost its attractions, and in their real character they look and long for something new. They have extended their influence immensely in the East, and one would often think it is dominant. No effort has been spared for its becoming so, and

11

the study of the French language in the Turkish colleges has greatly helped it forward. A little time will be necessary ere the bearing of things can be clearly seen. Every thing at present is at a standstill, and of trade there is little. On Saturday the English sovereign was less in value than it has been for years.

"I had intended to give you an account of the missionary operations here, but I have not time at present. Doors are opening on every hand. A spirit of inquiry is abroad. The sleep of many years has been broken by the stirring events of the war. Every thing is in motion. Now is the time for the Word to be scattered, and to let the nations that have so long been in darkness have the sound of the glorious Gospel, whose message is 'Peace on earth, and good will to men.'

"DUNCAN MATHESON."

In Constantinople he devoted much of his time and attention to the French, by whom he was treated with the greatest consideration and kindness. When he went to Sweet Waters, where a French division was stationed, the officer in command ordered out his men, and when they had fallen into rank, the missionary was permitted to go the round and present each man with a New Testament, tract, or book.

His heart was set on doing something for the Turks. In the ancient temple of Mahomedanism chinks were opening through which silvery rays of Gospel truth were quietly stealing. Matheson, having picked up a little Turkish, used to frequent the burial-places, and wait there for hours, praying that God would open some Mahomedan mourner's heart to hear the truth concerning one Jesus. Never did the prayer remain unanswered. Some sorrowing one, standing or sitting by the grave of their dearly-beloved, would listen to the stranger telling in his few blundering words about Him who is the resurrection and the life.

This indiscriminate distribution of the holy Scriptures was not unattended by the evils of waste and abuse. Yet there were not wanting instances of good springing out of this very evil. A Turkish lady one day received from her grocer a parcel wrapped in a leaf of the Bible. The leaf was read, an interest in the strange book was awakened, and the lady sent a member of her household to inquire if the merchant could send her another leaf of the same kind. All that remained of the precious volume was carried home, and who can tell but the interest awakened may have deepened, under the Spirit's teaching, into faith and salvation?

An intense longing to put a copy of God's Word into the hands of a pasha or some other Turk of influence was gratified in a curious way. One day, when distributing the Scriptures at Sweet Waters, he was attacked by an infuriated mob of Greeks, whose religious antipathies had been thoroughly

aroused.   To escape their wrath he took refuge in
a ship.   Next day a gentleman, brother of a certain pasha, called at his lodgings to convey the re-
grets of the great man at the ill-treatment the missionary had received from the Greeks, at the same
time requesting for the pasha's use a copy of the
Word of God.   My readers will not forget that at
this time an Englishman was held in peculiar honor
by the Turks, hence the pasha's apology.   The missionary, of course, did not fail to send the book of
God to the pasha, nor did he forget to praise God
for this answer to his prayer.   On the Greeks he
sought revenge by endeavors to disseminate among
them the glad tidings of great joy that are for all
people; but his success was small.   One family of
Greeks appeared to derive benefit from his labors;
but for the most part the way was not prepared for
the entrance of the Word of God among them.

As winter drew near he prosecuted his enterprise
with redoubled energy.   Daily did he take his stand
at the Golden Horn, and distribute his books to the
thousands crossing to the other side on their way to
all parts of Asia.   "The work gets harder," he writes.
"The Turks and Greeks get more prejudiced.   Yet
the Lord reigneth, and all his purposes shall be accomplished.   .   .   .   How soon all wanderings here
shall close.   Life's sand is running fast.   We hear
the summons daily.   Oh to hear it indeed, and prepare to meet God!   I look daily forward to this, to
be with Him and like Him."

"Constantinople, Nov. 5th.

"Since I last wrote you I have been very ill and confined, but I am better, and at work again. I was so weak that one day when I tried to rise I fell, and have got one eye bruised. I suppose I must have fainted."

"Constantinople. Nov. 18th.

"I feel weak indeed, and have had medical advice. There is no danger, but I must cease work, and when called to do so I am like a chained lion. The total lack of any comfort has been much against me. Many a day almost without food, and have had to be contented with food of any kind. . . . Since March I have been enabled to distribute nearly 10,000 copies of the Scriptures—1,000 of them to Turks—and 60,000 tracts and books in all languages. The value of all has been about £1,000, and truly I may say the Lord has provided. . . . I had a letter from Piedmont lately. The work is going on nobly there. Perhaps I may get 'The Knowledge of Sin,' by William Burns, translated into Armenian. Dr. Dwight is examining it at present. Truly he is a godly man."

Entirely prostrated, he lay for some time at the point of death. During this period he was tenderly watched by his friend Mr. M'Kutcheon, of the Jewish Mission, and to him, under God, he believed he owed his life. As soon as he was able to rise, he settled his affairs and left Constantinople for Egypt.

From Egypt he sailed for Italy, where he visited his friends:

"L——, Italy, 1857.

"My Dear Sir: In my last I gave you some account of matters in the East, which I hope you duly received. Since leaving Constantinople I have visited Egypt, ascended its pyramids, drunk of its river, and gazed with deepest horror on the spiritual state of its inhabitants. I have heard the groans of the oppressed Sicilians, and seen the gloomy prisons of Naples, its blinded devotion and its down-trodden condition. I have walked the streets of Rome, admired its palaces, entered its catacombs, once the refuge of oppressed Christianity, and talked amidst its ruins to its enslaved people, and every day has convinced me we know little of Popery at home, and deal far too lightly with such a soul-destroying system. As it is in Italy no one can portray, no mind can fully conceive, and no language can express. Every eye is turned towards it, and every Christian heart utters the cry, 'How long, O Lord?' In Sicily the people sigh for freedom, but still cling to the system that has chained them. It is a fair and lovely land, but it is blighted. The number of priests in it is incredible, and the education of the young is wholly in their power. I saw here a brazen head of John the Baptist in a charger carried from door to door, every one placing money in the charger; and in many streets you meet a man demanding money, having on a box carried for the purpose the words, 'For the souls in purgatory.'

"At Naples it is worse. On every church you read, 'Indulgences granted;' and you see at every step men and women prostrated before the picture of the Virgin; and at one column raised in her honor it is written, 'An indulgence of fifty days granted to all praying here.' I saw on the Grand Square more than one thousand people prostrate before the Host, and asked one what it was. To which he replied, 'It is Jesus Christ.' Terrible is the condition of Naples. Terror is marked on every face; and I could hardly get one to speak to me, because every third person in the streets is a spy. Many shops are shut, and you feel the very atmosphere oppressive; whilst cannon is to be seen pointing down its principal thoroughfares. Naples is a land where few Bibles have yet entered, and the people are deeply sunk in ignorance, and bound to Romanism more than any other people in Italy. Political and spiritual freedom are the results of Protestantism, and go linked together. Naples knows neither. . . . Bibles! there are no Bibles in Rome. I entered every bookseller's shop in it, and could only find two—one in Latin, the other in Italian. Preaching! there is none in Rome. The glory of the cross is darkened, and the way of salvation through it is never proclaimed. You have relics—Madonnas, holy altars, indulgences, by thousands, and masses for living and dead; but no pointing to the Lamb,

no inviting of weary sinners; no justification by
faith. Christian literature! truly you may say there
is none. You have heaps of lying legends of lives
of saints, of flimsy novels; but the Index Expurga-
torius excludes all works worth the reading; and
sprinkling with holy water is considered more safe
than unloosing the mind and giving scope to the
intellect. Freedom! ah, it is not in Rome. Ask
the inquisitors, and they will tell the price of seeking it, and as you ask, listen to the music coming
from the Pope's dragoons. Commerce, trade, agriculture—alas! a withering blight is on the land, and
the fairest portion of God's earth is left untilled. So
true is it, that wherever Popery has most potently
maintained herself, there life has become extinct,
and prosperity and morality have disappeared, as if
under the influence of some mysterious malediction.
The worship of Italy is the worship of Mary—pictures of Mary—statues of Mary—churches to Mary
—columns to Mary—songs to Mary—prayers to
Mary, in every spot. Idolatry! where is it, if you
see it not in Rome? Go to the church of Ara Coeli,
and there you will see a small image of Jesus, with
many kissing its feet, and crossing themselves before
it. Wait for a little. The priests take it up, enter
a coach, and drive—that the sight of it may cure
some dying person! Yes. Startle not. The priests
told us it had performed many miracles; and the
people prostrating themselves before it is a proof
that they believe it. Common is it to see written

over many altars—'Specially privileged;' 'For the dead;' 'Every mass said at this altar frees a soul from purgatory.' And in large gilded letters you often read—'Plenary indulgences granted by special favor of the Pope.' Where is the Luther to cry with trumpet-tongue, and proclaim the vicious nature of such Pagan Christianity to its blinded devotees, pointing them only to Him who is the Way, the Truth, the Life? Sadly deserted are the churches of Rome, and most of the educated have become infidels. They asked for bread, but got a stone. The craving for something better could not be met; for the Gospel was buried, and Christ was not named. It is the natural result of such training, and sad is the account to be rendered by the authors of it. Pleasing was it to go from all this to the gloomy catacombs, and see engraved tombs of the early Christians—the calm, sublime hopes which they enjoyed! Simple are the inscriptions, yet what so cheering?—'In Peace;' 'In Christ.' Rome has nothing there to favor one of her doctrines. They knew them not.

"Need I tell you, Italy knows no Sabbaths. Feast-days have more authority; and the people look astonished when you tell them God has commanded all His day to be kept holy. It is their day of greatest enjoyment. Every theatre is opened in Rome; and if any one had witnessed the Sabbaths of the Carnivals now ended, they would go home resolved to keep it inviolate, and be led to bless God they lived in a land where in great measure the keeping of the Sabbath is known. In this matter —and it is well it should be known—the Protestants on the Continent—ministers and people, are very lax. They do not look on it with the same sacredness that we do. The evil effects of such views daily appear, and almost universally our own countrymen leave keeping of Sabbaths at home. One fact is worth mentioning: I have never yet seen one in Italy drunk, and during the days of the Carnival thousands met every day.

"And now you will be ready to ask, What is doing in Italy for the spread of the truth, and how does the work succeed? The question, for many reasons, is difficult to answer. I can say nothing of Rome, but that I believe many of the people would hail the Bible, if it were put within their reach. Throughout all Italy there is a preparation in the people's minds for this, and in many instances far, far more. They desire to see the Book which is kept from them. Tens of thousands of them have their eyes open to the evil of Papacy. This is well, but it goes no farther. In the case of thousands—yea, millions, attachment to the Romish religion, if not to Pope and priests, is as strong as ever. Even in Piedmont this is the case; and in the case of others, here and there saving conversion has followed the reading of the Word through the divine blessing. This is especially true of Tuscany, where every effort is made to keep it from them, and where the surveillance is stricter—much stricter than ever it was before. Tuscany is the tool of Austria, and yet the work goes on the more it is tried to crush it, and souls are born to God. Here and there small companies meet for worship, and in wondrous ways the truth finds entrance. Many are Protestants in name, though not apparently savingly converted; but there are undoubted trophies of grace, and much, very much, to cheer and encourage to prayer. I have no hesitation in saying, if liberty were granted, thousands, many thousands, would hail the Gospel, and the demand for the Word would be so great it could hardly be supplied. In Piedmont—the only free country in Italy, and on which the hearts and affections of so many are set—the work goes on in some places rapidly. We must now separate the political from the spiritual. One party—the greatest—seek political freedom, and others seek to know the truth. A remarkable advance has been made. The Word is finding entrance by thousands, and is read. Men here and there, knowing the truth themselves, are boldly declaring it, and the Lord is giving testimony to the Word of his grace. One case has reached us of the Bible given in the Crimea having been blessed. A soldier brought one home, and gave it to a farmer near A——. He began to read it with his wife and family, and all became deeply interested. His neighbors also came to hear it read, and joined with the farmer and his family in sending for a Waldensian Evangelist; and thus a small church is formed in the midst of a dark corner of Piedmont, which may yet extend wider and wider, till many be embraced in its fold. I do not know what may be the future of Italy. I cannot say how soon revolution may shake it from one end to another. I believe it is not far distant. Endurance has its limits, and men may be made slaves only for a time. The light is beginning again to rise on it. Its progress we should watch with fear and trembling, being neither too sanguine nor depressed. We cannot estimate the value of one soul. God has lighted a light—shaded for a time it may be—but out it cannot be put, neither by popes nor princes—neither by the fires of martyrdom nor the bolts of a prison. Our duty is clear, our path open, our command plain. Prayer, much prayer, must be made, and specially for God to raise up men fitted to carry on his work, and in their devoted, earnest, holy lives to exemplify the doctrines they teach. We know his truth shall triumph, and triumph gloriously, and that even now the first streaks of light on the horizon are but the prelude of the full flood of light which shall yet arise on this sin-blighted world.

" Ever your affectionate friend,

"DUNCAN MATHESON.

"Mr. P. Drummond."

"Turin, March 13th.

" I have not had a minute to write you till now, for I have been intensely occupied. I arrived at Genoa on the 6th, and remained three days. I could hardly walk a step without soldiers running and saluting me, etc. I had much joy in the presence of some of them, and on meeting some English friends. On Sabbath I addressed a meeting in the Free Church, and felt greatly assisted. On Monday I came here, and immediately started for the Waldensian valleys. Yes, I have seen them, and truly every spot is full of interest. At La Tor I visited the college, church, and schools. What a simple, intelligent people! How can I tell you of the scenes here! It is like the march of a conqueror. I cannot move a step without being accosted. Sixty soldiers have been round me in a circle at once. Hundreds have shaken hands with me. Poor fellows! they are deeply, deeply grateful. I feel a deep, very deep, interest in them. To-day I have been in the Parliament House with Mr. Milan, the Vaudois deputy, and was much and deeply interested. Truly freedom is here. Do forgive my brevity. Every moment is occupied. I was in Florence since writing you, and escaped, though carrying eight copies of the Word into it. This is a wonderful field, and I expect much to be done here. The Lord has helped me to set many things in motion since my arrival. To Him be the praise."

In March, 1857, he brought his stay in Italy to a close. This visit was in reality the accomplishment of a great Christian work. He had been enabled to make his mark on a vast number of the Italian officers and soldiers. "The Sardinians' Friend" is not yet forgotten; and, while his memory is treasured in many a brave heart, there can hardly be a doubt that he was the divinely-chosen instrument of enshrining the Word of God in the affections of thousands who, but for his gigantic exertions, would have returned to their native land to live and die in worse than Egyptian darkness. That the fruit of this wide and prayerful sowing of the seed, at the first blush of Italy's spring, will be glory to God in the salvation of many souls we cannot but believe.

Passing rapidly through France, he reached home ere yet the sun of the northern summer had waxed hot. To rest, to tell his story, and prepare for new labors, needed a breathing-time.

CHAPTER VI.

DAYS OF REVIVAL.

His native air speedily restored his health. Not one day was wasted in needless rest. Often at this period did he at public meetings tell his Crimean story amidst torrents of tears; but he always took care, when the fountains of emotion were stirred, to cast the bread of truth upon the waters, in the hope of finding it after many days. Invited by the minister of the Free Church at Insch, he occupied the pulpit for the first time. Here he held the first inquirers' meeting, which was attended by a few, and among the rest an old man who said, "I've come that ye may search me weel. Oh, dinna scruple to try me, as it wad be a fearfu' thing to be deceived for eternity. Noo, sir, begin." "John," said the evangelist, "do you love the Lord Jesus?" "I dinna doot that," was the reply, "but I wad like mair." The old disciple was still inquiring. During his three months' labor at Insch several persons were awakened. One of these afterwards became an elder in a Free Church, and another, a young woman, became the wife of a missionary, and was instrumental in winning souls.

In October, 1857, he went to labor as an evangelist in Whitehaven, at the request of a minister of the Church of England, who was desirous of promoting the spiritual welfare of his native place. He found the soil of Cumberland stiff; but his labors were not wholly in vain. It was a sowing-time rather than a harvest. Then he began to preach every day, a practice he followed throughout the rest of his active ministry. "To this place," he says in a letter, "I have almost done my duty. Surely, if I go home I shall get a little rest. *Rest* did I say? Nay, truly, whilst health is granted. The days pass swiftly. Soon all will be gone. Since I came here I have not got half an hour to take my dinner at a time, and the door is widening on every hand."

Here he resorted again to the press. When lying at the point of death in the East, he had prayed that

ten years might be added to his life, and vowed that
if spared he would publish a testimony for Christ.
The prayer was answered, and the vow duly performed. The testimony for Jesus took the form of
a little monthly periodical, which he entitled, "The
Herald of Mercy." After much prayer he issued the
first number at the close of 1857. "I had no money
to advertise it with," he tells, " but I trusted in God,
and cried to Him to spread and bless it for his own
glory." Under his editorship it held on its way till
it reached a circulation of 32,000 a month. It was
declared by many to have been the herald of mercy
to their souls. Its aim was the awakening and conversion of sinners. It was not designed or specially
adapted for the edification of saints, excepting so
far as it kept before the eye of believers the worth
of souls and the realities of the eternal world. Never
did the trumpet give a more certain sound than in
the mouth of "The Herald of Mercy." It recognized
nothing on earth but *souls:* souls in sin, and souls in
Christ: souls going to heaven, and souls going to
hell. Every article, paragraph, and sentence, original or selected, bore directly and plainly on the
great truths—ruin, regeneration, and redemption.
The little messenger was owned of God, as a few
facts will show.

A stranger came to Mr. Matheson one day in Crieff,
and asked him if he remembered a " Herald of Mercy " with an article headed, " Quench not the Spirit."
"That," said he, " was the means of my conversion."

An English lady, resident in Constantinople, for whose spiritual welfare much had been done in vain, received from a friend a copy of the "Herald." The reading of it resulted in her conversion.

A tradesman in Berwickshire one day finding a fragment of paper on the floor, picked it up, and as a matter of curiosity, began to read. It proved to be part of the "Herald of Mercy," being a brief article, headed, "Are you converted?" It was an arrow from the King's own bow. Conversion followed.

Two young men stood side by side at an open-air meeting. One of them held in his hand a copy of "Special Herald," with hymns; but while they sang the eye of his companion wandered from the verses to a little paragraph put in to fill a vacant corner. It was enough: both eye and heart were fixed. The little article spoke with divine power, and brought him to Jesus' feet. The young man is now a minister of the Gospel.

A herd-boy was sitting at the wayside, when some one passing put a "Herald of Mercy" into his hand. As he tended the cattle he read, was awakened, and brought to Christ. He is now known as a devoted follower of Christ.

Invited by Lady Pirrie, he went to Malvern in the autumn of 1858, and labored there for a short time. Here on the hill-side he held his first open-air meeting, and felt he received a special call to this kind of work in the blessing that attended the service. Henceforth he gave himself to preaching

12

in the open air. By day, by night, beneath the
summer sun, out in the drenching rain or piercing
cold of winter, in the remote glen amidst the bleating of the sheep, at the sea-side, where the singing
of David's psalms mingles with the still more ancient harmonies of the great ocean, on the crowded
street, in the noisy fair, beneath the shadow of the
scaffold, in the face of the raging mob—everywhere,
in short, as far as in him lay, he strove to preach
Christ to perishing men. In this way his voice
reached many who otherwise would never have
heard the glad tidings of salvation.

From Malvern he retraced his steps to Cumberland, and for a while labored at Workington. Here
by invitation of the people he occupied the pulpit of
the Presbyterian Church, and combined the offices
of pastor and evangelist. His preaching excited no
ordinary interest. Crowds flocked to hear him, and
not a few were impressed.

On February 2d, 1859, he was married at Weston-
super-Mare to Miss Mary Milne, a Christian lady
whom he ever regarded as an invaluable gift bestowed upon him in answer to prayer. Not one day
was withdrawn from labor. Exuberantly social and
tenderly affectionate though he was, the winning
of souls was to him infinitely more than the most
endearing relationship or the most hallowed earthly
joy. " We'll get settled up yonder in the Father's
house," he said; "meanwhile let us work and win
souls."

In the spring of 1859 Mr. Matheson returned to
Scotland, and took up his residence in the city of
Aberdeen. The great religious awakening of that
period was just beginning. Tidings of the work of
grace in America and Ireland stirred the hearts of
Christians, and many were in expectation of a similar blessing. The spirit of grace and supplication
was poured down, and many a blessed scene was now
witnessed. The winter was indeed past, and the
time of the singing of birds come. The beginning
and progress of the work were everywhere characterized by a real faith in the efficacy of prayer,
and the power that attended the testimony of Christians to Christ. In answer to prayer the treasured
petitions of years seemed to be granted in one day.
The simplest utterances of even babes in Christ were
instrumental in converting sinners. In fact, the testifying of believers and its effect was a marked feature of the work. In teaching, the truth is set forth
simply on its own merits. In preaching, there is an
authoritative, herald-like proclamation of the Gospel
in the King's name. In testifying, the speaker bears
witness to matters of fact of which he is personally
cognizant. The best preacher, doubtless, is teacher,
herald, and witness, all in one. But testifying has
its place and power. Many were saying, "Christ is
dead; Christianity is dead," when suddenly thousands arose, and with one voice declared, "Christ is
not dead. He lives, and the proof is this, He has
saved us: He has raised to a new life us who were

dead in trespasses and sins." "The Lord gave the word, and great was the company of those that published it."

It is worthy of remark that the work began, at least in its more striking manifestations, in the fishing village of Ferryden, and quickly extended to the numerous little towns that dot the north-eastern coast. It reminded many of the beginning of the Lord's ministry in the fishing villages of Galilee; and the recent gracious visit of the Lord Jesus to our own Galilean regions seemed to some like the return of an old love.

In Aberdeen Mr. Matheson occupied the pulpit of Blackfriars Street Independent Chapel. Joining his friends, Mr. Radcliffe and Mr. Campbell (minister of Free North Church), he threw himself heartily into the work. Not satisfied with ordinary effort, they set themselves to carry the war into the very camp of the enemy by open-air services in the streets and elsewhere. In writing to a friend, he says:

"I have only time for a few words, and my object in writing is specially to ask your prayers that at this time the Lord may greatly bless me in the ingathering of souls. Yesterday was one of the most remarkable days I have spent in my life. Mr. F——, the godly man who brought me to Aberdeen, was well yesterday morning. He went at two o'clock to the meeting in the County Buildings; read 16th of John, sang a psalm, engaged in prayer for the outpouring of the Spirit, sat down, cast his eyes to

heaven, gave a deep sigh, and in a moment his spirit
was with Jesus whom he loved. At eight o'clock
Mr. Campbell and I preached to thousands in the
open air. What a night! We had over and over
again to preach. The crowds had to be divided, for
they were too large. We could not till nearly eleven
o'clock get away from the awakened. Mr. Radcliffe
was unable to speak. Pray, pray for us. The Lord
is doing great things. I believe almost every time
one speaks souls are brought to Christ. Pray for me
—for humility. The Lord bless you. I am weary.
" Yours in Him,
"DUNCAN MATHESON."

Speaking of the work of grace in Aberdeen, in a
letter of date 17th August, 1859, he says:

"After a residence of nearly five months in this
city, and having come in contact with the work in
all its phases, I have no hesitation in saying that a
great and glorious work of grace has been felt here,
and that it is still going on. It is impossible to estimate its extent, or gather up one half of the results.
More, far more, has been done than is apparent; and
yet it is a fact that numbers have been more or less
influenced by the truth, and that many, very many,
manifestly have been brought to Christ. There can
be no doubt of this, and as yet I have not met one
case of any truly awakened returning to the world.
The Lord has given a visible stamp to not a few, and
the zeal, love, affection, prayerfulness, and humility

of many of the young converts is remarkable. I never during my life saw more deep concern for souls than I have seen here, and the close clinging to each other, though in different churches, is refreshing—most refreshing. Groups of the young are to be found here and there throughout the whole city meeting for prayer; and one thing has struck me almost more than any thing—the holy boldness in confessing Christ, and acknowledging what He has done for their souls. Another striking thing is this, that few have found Christ themselves, but they have been instrumental in the awakening of others. Many instances of this have come under my notice. A leading feature in the prayers of the young converts is the prayer offered up for the Christian ministry. One would often think they were burdened with the care of the ministry; and a high, deep respect for the ministers of the Gospel, in so far as they are owned of God and devoted to His work, is manifest. We have had the revival, and the fruits are apparent to all who have mingled in the work. Often has it pained us, many going away and saying, 'I saw none.' Nay, and how could they, if they did not go where it was, and if they did not ask those who do know it?

"The grace of God has been much displayed in not a few instances that have come under our notice, of parties coming to spend a Sabbath in the city, going away to their homes deeply awakened, or rejoicing in Jesus, and becoming centres of blessing

where they lived. I have passed through many
parishes in the country, and found here and there
anxious souls; and one thing is undeniable, that
never was there a time when so many were thirst-
ing for the Word, and that where ministers have
taken advantage of this, and entered with intensity
into this new state of things, there a blessing has
descended. At Chapel of Garioch, Banchory, etc.,
the Lord has been working, but with much power
at Chapel of Garioch; and I believe that there is not
a parish around it but has its awakened ones. The
truth that above all others seems to be owned is—
'You are lost. A Saviour has been provided. It is
your duty to accept Him *now*.' Ruin by the fall,
righteousness by Christ, and regeneration only by
the Holy Ghost, are the leading truths of every address. They are uttered in much simplicity, from
loving hearts (I speak of Mr. Radcliffe and the ministers well known engaged in the work), and in
much dependence on the Holy Ghost, and the blessing does descend. We can convince no one if they
will not believe. Hearts leap for joy, and songs of
holy triumph are sung. The Spirit is breathing; the
Holy Ghost is working; the gale is blowing; the
tide has risen and is still rising. Blessed they that
take advantage of it, and girding themselves for the
battles of the Lord, go forth to preach Christ,

> " 'As dying men unto dying men.'

But how sad to awake and find the opportunity

gone, and hear, in the looks of hardened sinners, powerless sermons, and unheeded warnings, the voice, deep and solemn—' *Thou hadst a day.*' God bless you evermore."

From Aberdeen he went frequently to the country, and found many of the rural parishes awakening as out of a deep sleep. Let us follow him to two or three places of interest. An awakening took place in the Free Church of Garioch in August, 1859. Mr. Matheson was present when the work began. "The prominent characteristic which ever attracted most our love for Mr. Matheson," writes Mrs. Bain, wife of the esteemed minister, "was his devoted and continual watching and working for the salvation of souls. I noticed this at my first meeting with him, which occurred in a stage-coach about 1848, on which occasion I was greatly refreshed while listening to a conversation in which I found my two fellow-travellers engaged when I entered the coach. One, an elderly man, was making objections to the doctrine of sovereign grace. The other, a young man, although evidently suffering under severe toothache, was using the opportunity to plead for truth wisely and lovingly. I felt so interested as to be constrained to inquire on reaching our journey's end after his name, and found it was Duncan Matheson, then said to be a stone-cutter, but evidently being prepared to use skilfully the hammer of the Word of God in polishing living stones for the great temple. Some years afterwards, being employed in missionary work in and around Huntly, he was asked to address a meeting here, which, I think, was almost the first of his evangelistic labors beyond his native district. From that occasion onward to his last visit, after his illness was far advanced, many were his kind and stirring visits to us and among us, and many have cause to bless God for them.

"Mr. Matheson was engaged to preach here on the evening of August 4th, 1859, Mr. Bain being then in Ireland, drawn over by the great revival there. Some days before I received an intimation from Mr. Radcliffe of his willingness to come and address our people, and spend some time here, which being accepted, Mr. Matheson's previous engagement proved a very gracious arrangement in providence for leading him to be present, and giving his most valuable assistance on that remarkable night of the outpouring of the Holy Ghost on the people gathered from the surrounding district, his previous knowledge of not a few of them giving him an advantage in dealing with the many souls awakened on that memorable occasion.

"After the market-preaching began, Mr. Matheson came to us for several years on the Sabbath nearest the Whit-sunday and Martinmas terms. These visits were looked forward to with desire, and much prized by our people. On one of these Sabbaths the power of God was manifest upon the souls of many, especially in the afternoon. Mr. Bain being absent, I was called out of church after the close of the first service, and while a prolonged meeting was being held on account of the agitated state of some young persons. I found at the church door a lad who had long been in my Sabbath Bible-class, and who up to the morning of that day had been, as far as I could see, entirely hard and careless, answering questions with perfect ease and indifference, so that I found it necessary, in order to keep him in his own place, to frame questions of some difficulty for him. My amazement was great to see his usually hard face pale, his whole frame trembling. And when I asked the cause, he could only gasp, 'My sins! my sins!' I brought him and his sister, also awakened, to the Manse, and advised them, after other efforts to help them, to cry to God. 'I cannot pray,' he said, in great distress. I left them a little, and then returned, when I found him wrestling in an agonizing way to find the words which were gradually coming out of his lips. Mr. Matheson took much interest in this case, which, after some time of deep distress, appeared to isssue in a new birth and consistent profession. The young man having left this neighborhood, I have not seen him for several years.

"Mr. Matheson's influence over the people here was great, as may be judged from the fact that, after the revival in 1859–60, he one day threw out while preaching a suggestion that the young men of our congregation should agree to support a native Chinese evangelist under Mr. Wm. Burns. A few took up the idea, and ever since the yearly salary has been gathered, although he who suggested and some who began the work now rest from their labors.

"Mr. Matheson's preaching was wonderfully attractive in most places to some whose position and previous training would not have led one to expect a Scottish lay-evangelist to be listened to with pleasure. But I believe the secret of his power lay in his deep heart-yearning over souls, and dealing with God in secret for them in connection with the sanctified wisdom and tact with which the Master gifted him as a fisher of men.

"He was engaged in this work in season and out of season, in secret and in public. On one occasion, while walking alone in this neighborhood, a lady passed on horseback, whose general bearing and talents had led him to feel interested in her while yet a stranger to saving grace. He retired into a wood, then and there knelt down, and cried to God for her conversion; and I doubt not this was one of the links in the appointed chain of circumstances by which ere long she was drawn by the cords of divine love to God, and became for a few years, till called to the home above, a bright Christian."

Towards the close of 1859 he began to extend his evangelistic itineracy to Banffshire, preaching for the most part in the towns and villages along the coast. His labors were specially blessed in the burgh and seaport of Cullen. This little town is situated on the brow of a hill looking full in the face the blue waters of the Northern Sea, where it begins to narrow into the beautiful Frith of Moray, whose ample tide is bounded on the southern shore by wild, picturesque, and caverned rocks; whilst the lofty mountains of Sutherland and Caithness rise far upon the deep, like giant warders of the northern coast. Beneath the burgh proper lies the fishing village in a tumult of houses upon the beach, where the storm often breaks with Arctic fury, casting clouds of spray high into the air, and sometimes invading the cottages that line the shore.

Early in 1860 the whole place was moved as by an earthquake. Fear took hold on the sinners in Zion; trembling seized the hypocrites. Careless ones, whose shadow had not darkened the door of God's house for many years, found their way to church or chapel; and even worldly men talked to one another about the great question upon the streets. At first the awful shadow of an angry God coming to judgment fell on many, and it seemed as if there was one dead in every house. Awakening was followed by conversion. The thunder of Sinai gave way to the peaceful sunshine of Calvary. Christians who had never known the liberty of the Gospel were suddenly delivered from the spirit of bondage, and ushered into the joyful assurance of acceptance in the Beloved.

Our evangelist visited Cullen just as the work of grace was becoming manifest, and preached frequently in the Free and Independent churches, re-

ceiving from the pastors a cordial welcome. On one
memorable night he preached to a crowded congregation in the Free Church. The subject of his discourse was "The Barren Fig-tree." From the beginning of the service a deep solemnity rested on
the people, and the minds of many were in a state
of strange expectancy. Unveiling the truth, the
preacher describes a community favored with the
light and privileges of the Gospel. Privilege after
privilege is enjoyed. Sabbath follows Sabbath in
peaceful succession. Opportunity after opportunity
occurs, and sermon on sermon. Mercy presses on
the heels of mercy, like the bright days of summer
chasing time to its wintry close. The sharp dispen-
sations of the providential pruning-knife come again
and again. But all is in vain. The sunshine and
the rain have been to no purpose; the digging and
the dunging have been in vain. The Father's love
has been to them as nought. The blood of the Son
has been despised. The grace of the Spirit has
brought forth no fruit in them. Forbearance and
intercession have yielded no result but failure. After
the resources of the Godhead in the Gospel of Christ,
what then? The people know that He is drawing
their portrait with unmistakable resemblance. Feeling they are found out among the trees of the garden, they tremble and listen with breathless attention. The sonorous voice of the preacher grows
thrillingly solemn and tender as he proceeds, till at
length he pours out his last warning in a torrent of

compassionate feeling. His eye glances with an awful light, as if he is looking into eternity, while he lifts his hands and pronounces the sentence with a mighty and judgment-like voice, "Cut it down; why cumbereth it any longer the ground?" Never did woodman aim a better stroke. God is in the Word. Old rotten trunks are crashing beneath the blow. One and another are saying with irrepressible alarm, "It is I! it is I! God be merciful to my soul!" The results are with Him who knoweth all things; but there is reason to believe that some of the audience will remember that night and the felling of the barren fig-tree amidst the songs and joys of eternity.

On another memorable occasion he preached in the Independent Chapel. The little meeting-house is crowded to the door. The night is intensely cold and dark. The frost having rendered the ordinary lights unavailable, the darkness is made visible by a single candle which the preacher holds in his hand. His text is "Remember Lot's wife." The narrative receives a graphic handling. The clear sky of early morn suddenly darkens, a cloud of appalling blackness throws the shadow of approaching judgment upon the cities of the plain. Then a gleam of more than lightning vividness kindles all the air, a whirlwind of fire sweeps down upon Sodom and wraps its four corners, its every street and suburb, its every house and chamber, its every man and woman, in the very winding-sheet of hell. Ah! now

the inhabitants of the doomed city wake to find that
their damnation slumbereth not. But a little band
of four escapes. An angelic saviour leads them on.
Well may they hasten, for the devouring fire sweeps
fast along the plain. One of the four lingers, only
a little; but a little is at this awful moment decisive
of much. God's wrath is abroad. Is this a time to
trifle? The fiery tempest suddenly closes her round,
and there she stands under an eternal arrest, a pillar
of salt. Some such picture is before the eye of the
people's imagination as the preacher proceeds to the
more important part of his discourse—its application
to the consciences of the hearers. God enters by little, lowly doors into men's hearts. The Spirit uses
little things to make and deepen impressions of the
unseen and the eternal. The darkness of the place;
the solitary candle throwing a dim, pale light on the
preacher's countenance, and giving it a strange weird
look; the deep silence, broken only by a sigh or a
sob, and the solemn tones of a voice speaking, as it
were, out of the invisible, and warning every trifler
with the soul and with God to "remember Lot's wife,"
conspired, in the hand of the Holy Spirit, to bring
about one of those supreme moments of crisis when
souls must and do decide their destiny for eternal
weal or eternal woe.

Our evangelist made his mark on the young men
of the town. His broad, free, genial manners captivated their hearts; his talents, magnanimity, and uprightness commanded their respect. Many of them

were converted at this time; and it was pleasing to
see the finest youths of the place sitting in a company round about their father in the faith, and receiving his counsels as from an angel of God. For
the young men he had a peculiar love: they were
his joy, and as his very life. He cared for their interests as a father for his children, and cherished
them as a nurse cherishes a babe. He guided them
with skill, warning them against the errors of his
own early Christian days; and having won their
confidence, he strove to lead them to the highest
idea of the life of faith. In particular, he ever urged
upon them entire consecration. "Be out and out
for Christ," he would say; "nail your colors to the
mast; labor for God, and live for eternity." In this
way he succeeded in stamping upon them the impress of his own decided and energetic character,
and through the grace given him inspired them with
an intense longing to win souls. One of them is now
an ordained missionary in China; another labors in
Turkey; a third preaches the Gospel at home; a
fourth is preparing to take the field as a medical
missionary; and others are occupying their talent
in the quiet corners of the vineyard.

An instance of the way in which the fire was then
spreading may be here given. James Wilson, a native of Cullen, and an accomplished classical scholar,
was at that time master of a school at Aberfeldy, in
Perthshire. Hearing of the work of grace in his
native town, he was deeply moved. Previous to

this he had regarded earnestness in religion as a mere extravagance; but now "the name to live whilst dead" satisfied him no longer. The work of God began in the village, and the minister of the Free Church was frequently assisted by Mr. Matheson. The teacher was led to take a decided stand for Christ, and thenceforth all his learning and influence were given to the work of the Lord. His school became a nursery for the church and the divinity hall. Remarkable success attended his labors among the youths, some of whom, after a brilliant academic career, have entered on the work of the ministry with much promise of usefulness. The course of the devoted teacher was terminated by an early translation to glory.

Cullen lay much on the heart of the evangelist. For years he continued to visit it, laboring to win its inhabitants to Christ. On his way thither many a weary mile did he trudge, often amidst the rains and snows of winter, receiving no pay and seeking no reward but "souls." Divining his motives, the shrewd fishermen said, "That man fishes by the cran;" that is to say, he is no mere hireling: he labors not for a comfortable living, but finds his reward in the number of souls saved. Often was his stentorian voice heard ringing from the centre of the town to its circumference in the quiet of the evening, when the deepening shades added solemnity to the preacher's word; and strong men were known to tremble at their own fireside as the question fell

13

upon their unwilling ears, "Who shall stand before this holy Lord God?"

In most of the villages that stud the Banffshire coast, a stranger in those days had but to signify his willingness to preach the Gospel, when suddenly, as if by magic, the whole population, men, women, and children, would assemble to hear the Word of God. To see the great crowd kneeling reverently on the grass amidst the deepest silence broken only by a groan, a sob, a loud cry for mercy, to be followed by fond, enthusiastic demonstrations of love and hearty songs of praise, characteristic of these impulsive children of the sea, was a sight impressive beyond description, and never to be forgotten. From such scenes Duncan Matheson, like one refreshed with the new wine of the kingdom, was wont to come away singing his favorite Psalm—

> " When Zion's bondage God turned back,
>   Like men that dreamed were we;
> Then filled with laughter was our mouth,
>   Our tongue with melody."

The landward parishes were not overlooked by the great Redeemer as He marched along the sea-coast in glorious majesty: from His bountiful hand the blessings of His grace were now being scattered far and wide. The reapers on the field, from the master to the gleaner, were known to lay aside at noonday the urgent labors of the harvest to attend to the more pressing business of the soul. Jesus was

gathering golden sheaves into his garner. Matheson at this period, strong to reap rather than patient
to sow, lent his powerful aid in every place. Few
in all that region missed hearing the jubilant voice
of our sturdy reaper, and seeing the gleam of his
sharp sickle among the yellow corn. Prompt in
word and deed, skilful above most men to strike the
iron while it was hot, brooking no restraints of mere
policy or empty form, and impetuous almost beyond
measure, he was in his proper character an Arab in
the service of the King. Hungering after great results, having capacity for work and fatigue enough
for two men, and withal possessing that rare and
dangerous power of will by which strong souls can
indefinitely postpone the season of rest, the unwearied spirit keeping the wearied flesh up to its
own high mark, our evangelist moved from one
place to another with the rapidity of a courier in
the crisis of battle. Seizing the opportunities that
will not tarry for the timid or the too cautious, he
launched on the full tide when others were laying
down canons for discussing the conditions of its ebb
and flow. The very air seemed full of elements
deeply solemn and heart-touching. A divine presence rested everywhere, and men were compelled
for a time to breathe the atmosphere of eternity.
Doors that might soon close were opening on every
side, and the energetic lay-preacher was not slow to
enter in. Pushing along the coast as far north as
Moray and Nairn, he bent his steps into the inte-

rior, and visited Dufftown, Tomintoul, and Braemar.
Sweeping southward to the counties of Forfar and
Perth, he gradually extended his circuit until it
embraced the whole country from John o' Groat's
to the English border. To follow him into every
town and parish is impossible: we can only seize on
a few points.

In the gracious visitations of this period Dundee
was not passed by. In the many evangelistic services then held in this town Mr. Matheson lent frequent and effective aid. He preached in churches
of various denominations, and his voice was often
heard in the open air. One winter he remained
here three months, every day and night of which
was spent in exhausting but fruitful toil. One Sabbath evening early in 1860, he addressed a crowded
congregation in Hilltown Church. An unwonted
solemnity, deepening as the service proceeded into
a feeling of awe, seemed to rest on the audience.
The preacher discoursed from Matthew xxv. ·46:
"And these shall go away into everlasting punishment: but the righteous into life eternal." In words
most telling and pictures most vivid he described the
sinner's going away—away from the fair scenes of
nature, from the warbling of the birds and the murmur of the brooks, from the smiling of the summer
sun and the rich glow of autumn—away from every
lovely sight and every pleasant sound—away from
friends and home and social joys, of every thing dear
to the heart of man upon the earth—away from the

peaceful Sabbath, with its hallowed services and its heavenly calm, to hear the sound of the Sabbath bell and the song of praise no more forever—away from the affectionate efforts and touching appeals of the faithful preacher, and from the sympathies and prayers of Christian friends—away from the Bible, with its beautiful stories, its comforting promises, and its heavenly truths, like God's windows, letting down light upon a dark world—away from all the peace and purity and hope of the Gospel—away from God, whose mercy they reject, forever—away from Jesus, whose blood they trample beneath their feet—away from the gracious Spirit to whom they have done so great despite—away from all joy and blessing and good, for evermore. To render the truths more vivid, he described a heart-melting scene he had witnessed in the East in the departure of a weeping crowd of Circassian exiles, whose loud and agonizing wail told the love they bore to their fatherland, from which they were being driven by the scourge of war. As he went on in his own pathetic manner, with a certain grandly plaintive music as of eternity in his voice, to describe the departure of the woe-stricken exiles of sin and despair into the blackness of darkness forever, speaking as feelingly as if he saw them disappearing in that dismal and unknown night, the heavy sigh, the stifled sob, and the pallor on many a face, revealed the all but uncontrollable emotion of the people. At the close of the service the session and vestry were crowded with the awakened. The place was a Bochim. The first person that obtained deliverance started up, saying, "I have found Him! I have found Him! I never saw the way before!" and began to praise and glorify God. This only pierced the hearts of the others with a keener sorrow. Fearing lest they should be left in their sins, they began to charge themselves with unpardonable hardness of heart, and to prostrate themselves before God in the most affecting manner. To one after another came peace and joy in believing, and quickly, the weeping was changed into songs of praise. Such scenes as these were afterwards renewed with blessed frequency; and the gracious character of the work came out in holy lives, patient sufferings, and triumphant deaths.

In the autumn of the same year open-air meetings were held in the Barrack Park in this town. On the second day several of the ministers and others, fearing lest there should be no blessing, retired, on the suggestion of Matheson, in great heaviness of spirit to pray. Kneeling on the grass, we continued in intercession for nearly two hours. It was one of those seasons of agonizing prayer which seem ever to precede a remarkable display of divine grace. It was the slumbering spouse arousing herself with painful effort at the call of her Lord; the laborious undoing of the bars of the everlasting gates to let the King of glory in. By the end of the praying the darkened sky began to pour down torrents of rain, and the mass of the people, with most of the speakers, were dispersed. The voice of Duncan Matheson was heard calling aloud, " Perhaps God is trying us by the rain; let us wait a little." Gideon's three hundred remained, and continued in prayer and praise. Mr. Campbell (Aberdeen), whose labors were so signally owned amongst us at that time, together with his friend our evangelist, and another, leading the services amidst descending torrents. Just as the sun was beginning to shine out again and the rain was ceasing, an extraordinary sense of the Divine Presence fell upon the whole assembly. Suddenly the Christians were filled with great joy. Simultaneously many of the anxious found the Lord, and began to break forth in songs of praise. Every one began to speak to his neighbor of the Saviour he was seeking or the Saviour he had found. On passing through the whole company, we did not find one who was not either rejoicing in Christ or seeking Him with intense earnestness. The cloud of glory rested there for a season; and no visible signs or miraculous gifts could have added to the blessed consciousness and most veritable certainty of the immediate presence and gracious working of God. Till memory fails or the more "excellent glory" of the unveiled face of Immanuel obliterates the remembrance of faith's brightest visions on earth, it is impossible for us to forget the awful nearness of God at that time, the overpowering sense of blended majesty, love, and holiness, the solemn gladness, and the soft, pure radiance of a Redeemer's face that chased the dark shadows of doubt and sin away from many a soul. "We beheld his glory, the glory as of the only begotten of the Father, full of grace and truth; . . . and of His fulness have all we received, and grace for grace." Many of the believers, if not all, were then sealed anew, and they began henceforth to testify to the grace of God with great freedom and boldness. Some Christians who had never known assurance were then ushered into the full light of the Gospel; their bonds were loosed, and they entered into the liberty of the Sons of God. Many sought and found the Lord upon the spot. The door of salvation then seemed to be peculiarly near, easy of entrance, and inviting. Whilst you were praying with an inquirer, he would break out, "Oh, I have found Him!" or "I see! I see!" And then followed the new song. Often, as we sung the opening verses of the fortieth Psalm, the light broke in upon the distressed soul, and peace followed.

After this the work went on prosperously; numbers were found awakened at the close of every meeting. Many thousands attended the open-air services, and great power accompanied the word. The way in which many were converted, stamp the movement as the work of the Holy Spirit. A young man entered a church from sheer curiosity, and stood near the door in order that he might the more conveniently retire if aught should offend his ear,

He heard the text, and heard no more. That led
to his conversion. Another young man was returning from business one evening, when a serious
thought took hold of him. Entering his room, he
opened the New Testament at the tenth chapter of
the Gospel according to John. "Seeing the open
door," he said, "I slipped in, and now I find Jesus
to be the Way." "When I saw that my sister was
so changed and so happy," said another, "I was
afraid lest I should be left, and in my alarm I sought
the Lord and found Him." "One shall be taken,
and another shall be left," was a preacher's text at
an open-air meeting. A woman whose husband had
been recently converted hearing that word was
pierced to the heart, and thus brought out of darkness into the "marvellous light." Another was
carelessly passing by, and hearing the preacher solemnly repeat the question, "How shall we escape,
if we neglect so great salvation?" was arrested and
brought to the Lord. A man was sitting at his fireside, when his wife returned from a meeting. Something in her manner cut him to the heart; the result was his conversion. A young woman scoffed
and swore she would never attend revival meetings.
Her wicked vow recoiled upon her. She feared she
had sold herself to the devil. After a season of
mental anguish, she obtained forgiveness, and led a
new life. A young man came with his companion
to an open-air service for the purpose of scoffing.
He was awakened and enabled to receive Christ,

at which his friend went away in a rage. "I wondered why they were so happy," said another, in
reference to the joy of the Christians. "I was resolved to get at the bottom of it, and had no rest
till I found out the secret for myself." One day,
about the time the work began, a piercing cry for
mercy was heard in a church. That cry was the
voice of God to several persons, who dated either
their first conviction or their conversion from that
day. It was thus, they said, things unseen and
eternal were made real to them.

A company of men were one night carousing in
a public-house in the outskirts of Dundee, when the
sound of voices was heard singing a spiritual song.
It was a little band of Christian young women on
their way home from a religious meeting, and they
were giving expression to their joy in the Lord by
singing—

> "One is kind above all others,
> Oh, how He loves!"

The words of the hymn fell with a strange power
upon the ear of a young man sitting at the tavern
table. The others seemed not to hear the voice of
the singers as they passed: to him it was the voice
of God. He was arrested by the Holy Spirit, and
became dumb with silence. His companions were
astonished. They thought he had suddenly gone
mad. In vain they questioned him, in vain they
jeered. He rose and left the house. As he paced
the street in the darkness of night, the words of the

hymn kept ringing in his ears. He thought of the love of that Saviour whom he had hitherto rejected. The thought pierced his heart, and he burst into tears. I shall never forget his subdued and grieved look as he made his way into my study and told me how God had smitten his heart in the public-house, and turned his pleasures into wormwood and gall. He seemed to see his sins in the light of Christ's love. In answer to his eager inquiries about the way of salvation, I did not fail to preach Christ to him, and not in vain, I trust, as he entered at once on a new course of life.

As contrasting with this case and illustrative of the variety of means employed by the Holy Spirit to awaken sinners, the following instance may be given. A young man, well known to the writer, was living without God and without hope in the world. He was not conscious of a single thought respecting a future state, and did not so much as believe in the being of a God. His Sabbaths were spent in worldly recreation and pleasure. One Lord's day in summer he was rambling in the fields. The sun was shining brightly, and nature was clad in her most beautiful array. As he looked on the smiling landscape, suddenly and for the first time the thought arose in his mind, All this must have had a beginning: whence and how did it begin? A long train of thought led him to the conclusion that the world must have had a Maker. Then came the question, Who is He? What is He? Again he launched out on a sea of speculation, and once more reached firm ground in the belief that the world's Maker must be a living, personal Being, very great and very glorious. By this time he had lost sight of the beauties of the landscape, and felt as if he was alone with the Creator. Now another question arose: What am I to this glorious Being, and what is He to me? On this line of thought he entered with great reluctance, for he felt a misgiving as to the result, and feared He would discover things fitted to render him unhappy. But he dared not, he could not turn back. He felt he was like a man waking up in a dark cave with a solitary ray of light coming from afar. If he is to emerge under the open heavens he must follow the light. He tries, he stumbles, he is stunned, but he rises, and again spying the glimmer of distant day, he holds on his doubtful course. He now said to himself, If there be such an one as God it concerns me to know as much as possible about him. He then and there resolves to use all means to find out about God. He went home and betook himself to reading, meditating and reasoning. The next stage arrived at was the painful conviction that he had never acknowledged this God, or done his duty to Him, and had in fact poured contempt upon Him by his negligence. As soon as a sense of guilt thus fastened on him, he felt he could ramble no more on the Lord's day. Thenceforth he began to pursue his inquiries by prayer as well as reading and thinking. The light grew; his trouble increased. He would now see what Christians had to say in the matter; and accordingly began to attend the ordinary and special services of religion at a time when remarkable power accompanied the preaching of the Word. Here he found God. He found Him in Christ. He found Him at the cross. Now, this young man's religious experience has always seemed to me to be a good practical illustration of the text, "We shall know, if we follow on to know the Lord," and also of Christ's word, "If any man will do his will, he shall know of the doctrine whether it be of God, or whether I speak of myself." He seemed to act up to his light, yielding to the force of truth, truth in its own native energy with the superadded force of the Holy Spirit, in whose light alone we can see light. The logical faculty is strongly developed in him; and by that door the Holy Spirit saw fit to enter into his heart. He still goes on reasoning out every thing. The other day I found he had just proved to himself on logical grounds these two things; first, that a Christian ought to be filled with *humility and love;* and, secondly, that no religion but the religion of Christ can make a man *truly humble and loving.* After his conversion, he found recreation on the Lord's day in teaching a class in the Sabbath-school. He is now prosecuting a course of study preparatory to the ministry of the Gospel.

Listen to a dying man. "Five years ago I was a drunkard, a profane swearer, an infidel, and little better than a beast. I heard the Gospel in the street. The Lord arrested me and turned me to Himself. He has kept me ever since, and I am saved. I am going to be with Christ, which is far better. Help me to praise Him." So saying, he began to sing,

"Rock of Ages, cleft for me,
Let me hide myself in Thee ;"

and he literally sang out his last breath and died.

Look at yon gray-haired mother, whose heart is beginning to know joy for the first time these many years, as she clasps to her bosom her only daughter recovered from a life of folly and sin. "O my Annie! my Annie! my ain lost Annie! I never thocht I wad hae seen you mair. But the gude God has been better to me than a' my fears. Are we ever gaun to pairt again, Annie?" "Never, mither, never! Jesus has saved me Himsel', an' He has promised to keep me, an' He will never brak His word. We'll never pairt, mither; na, by His grace, never, never?" Nor did they ever part till the Lord Jesus came and took Annie away. I saw her depart, and in the truth she went home as a bride adorned for her marriage. The daughter's recovery led to the mother's salvation.

A young man was one night awakened at a meeting, and began to inquire the way of life. Night after night passed; he was constantly present, but no peace came to his heart, and he grew worse. One evening Duncan Matheson took him aside into the anteroom of the hall, and said to him, "Now, are you really willing to have this awful business settled? Christ is willing, are you?" The young man replied that he was willing. They knelt to pray. As they prayed light and peace suddenly dawned, and the young man started to his feet in a tumult of joy and praise. Several of us, and among the rest the father of the young man, who was greatly alarmed at the son's despair, entered the room at that moment. Addressing the father, a Christian man, the evangelist introduced the son, saying, "Sir, this thy son was dead, and is alive again; was lost, and is found." As the son rushed into the arms of his affectionate and overjoyed father, the heart of every one present was deeply moved.

A woman, mother of a large family, was one day awakened, and so heavily did the terrors of the Lord press upon her spirit, that she fled the house of God. She could bear preaching to sinners, she said, but when the people of God were addressed, it was too much for her. Some can hear the law who will not hear the Gospel. She became worse and worse, till at length reason seemed to be giving way. She dreaded to enter a place of worship because she was so wicked. At this juncture Mr. Matheson, who had frequently spoken to her, as a sort of last resource, said, "Well, I can say no more to you than this: do you as one poor soul did, who said, 'I will just lie doon here till the Lord lift me up.'" Curiously enough this proved to be the grand turning-point.

She said to herself, "I will just do so." In short, she ceased from her vain efforts of self-help, and cast herself on the Lord. Great was her joy. She was a wonder to her neighbors, who had witnessed her previous "madness," and, better still, she has these many years maintained a thoroughly Christian profession, and one after another of her family has through her instrumentality been turned to the Lord.

One evening a young lady of great intelligence and personal beauty, who was perfectly thoughtless and gay, was induced, as a matter of curiosity, to enter a certain place of worship. There was nothing new or striking in the service, she thought; "It is just the old thing," she said to herself. One thing, however, struck her as the service proceeded, and that was the *solemnity of the preacher.* "The thing is evidently *real* to him," she said to herself; and she could not but listen to him, although she imagined she knew all he had to say. The solemnity of the preacher impressed her. This impression was the opening of her heart, and by this gate the King of glory entered in. Her subsequent life was singularly beautiful. She seemed to walk beneath an unclouded sky. Always trusting, always hopeful, always rejoicing, always ready for every good work —a most rare instance of childlike, progressive blessed discipleship. Her bright career was short. After a few years she took ill and died. A sharp conflict with the great adversary befell her in her last days; but she came up from that valley of humiliation "more than conqueror through Him that loved us," and she felt assured, she said, Satan would never assail her any more. In her communion, which was singularly close and elevated, she seemed to speak to her Lord face to face. Her path from first to last was indeed as the shining light, that shineth more and more unto the perfect day.

"I was fairly in the devil's grip," said a working man, in his homely, graphic way, as he told me the story of the Lord's merciful dealings with his soul. "But Christ cam' to me when I was little expectin' Him, an' took a hand o' me. Syne the deevil pulled me ae way, an' Christ He pulled the ither way, an' I had a sair time o't. But I cam' to ken that Christ is far stronger than Satan, an' that was weel for me." I was witness so far to this pulling, which seemed well-nigh to rend the poor soul in pieces. It was, doubtless, the tug of war—Immanuel laying siege to the city of Mansoul.

Let a different sort of witness speak—a gentleman of the most accomplished type. "Several years ago I was, I regret to confess, a Pharisee of the Pharisees. From my infancy I was taught to respect religion, and despise every thing vulgar and coarse. Accordingly I attended the house of God, maintained a fair reputation, fancied I was a good man, and had the best chance for heaven. Unexpectedly God opened my eyes. This he did by means of the merest trifle—a petty act of meanness done to a friend, which somehow took posses-

14

sion of my thoughts, tormented me, put me off sleep, and led me to look deeper into my heart than I had ever done. Thus I was led to discover what I had never really seen before—my native depravity, and proud hostility to God. I saw that my own righteousness, to use the common phrase, was only filthy rags. I saw that my very religion was full of sin, and that, in fact, I had been going to church and to the Lord's table just to patronize the Almighty and honor myself. I was now in a measure humbled, and was not ashamed to make my appearance at the revival meetings, where fresh light awaited me. You know the rest. I became indeed a new creature. So completely was my mind revolutionized, that the very hymns I used to hate as being exaggerated, Methodistic, and ranting, now expressed the deepest feelings of my heart. But the change was more than one of mere sentiment. Had I previously died I should certainly have perished."

"Sir," said a woman to me one day whom I happened to meet, "I am happier than I was on my marriage day." Some time previous to this she had been brought to Christ at one of the evangelistic meetings when Mr. Matheson was assisting us. Her husband, a drunkard and scoffer, was maddened by her conversion, and gave her no peace night or day. Her godly ways were intolerable to him. He beat her till her life was in danger; but she bore this brutal treatment with true Christian fortitude and meekness, rendering good for evil, and praying for his conversion without ceasing. "I am happier than I was on my marriage day. God has heard my prayer; my poor husband is converted. He is like a lamb, and thinks he cannot do enough to please me. Oh, sir, if you had but seen him the other night holding family worship for the first time! It was like heaven upon earth! There wasn't a dry eye in the house; and our little lassie looked up in his face and said, 'Father, ye'll win to heaven noo. An' I'll gang wi' you; an' we'll a' be there. I never thocht I wad like to gang to heaven afore.'" Grace, mercy, and peace seem since that day to have rested on the house.

Yonder, at the corner of Ann Street, early on Sabbath mornings, you can see a fierce, tiger-like young man going about among the loungers, and begging a few pence to procure the drunkard's indispensable dram. A few years pass, and the same young man is seen at the same street corner at the same hour on Sabbath mornings; but what a change! With his Bible in one hand, whilst the other is stretched out towards his hearers, he beseeches them with tears to believe on that Saviour who has delivered his soul from the lowest hell. The preaching may be poor enough, but the man himself is a sign and a wonder. "I knew *the two Robert Annans*," said one to me; "and when I remembered the wild profligate begging a dram, and saw him now so meek and Christian-like, nothing ever impressed me so much, and I began to feel for the first time there must be a reality in religion." *

There were many striking answers to prayer. One of the most remarkable I may here give. A young woman who had found the Saviour at one of the meetings when Mr. Matheson was with us, requested special prayer one night on behalf of her brother, a sailor, who had not been heard of for a long while. Prayer was offered for the conversion of the wanderer. Some three months afterwards the young woman appeared at a meeting, and introduced her brother in a state of religious concern. Strange as it may appear, he had been awakened at sea on the very night on which prayer had been offered on his behalf. His own account of the matter was this: He was pacing the deck in the stillness of the night, when a thought about his soul took hold of him, and the more he strove to put it away from him the worse he grew. He had no peace until he returned home. We, of course, preached Christ to him. Why should we reckon such things incredibly strange? Does not our Father in heaven answer the prayers of his children every day? Has he promised, and will he not perform? Where is our faith?

In many ways our evangelist rendered important service to the cause and work of God in this town. When the movement had nearly reached its limit,

* See "The Christian Hero: the Life of Robert Annan." Same author.

and it seemed as if the hand of the Lord was being withdrawn, Mr. Matheson, ever fertile in resources, and panting after greater things, suggested that a whole night should be set apart for humiliation and prayer. With his wonted energy and promptitude he arranged the details, and cleared the obstacles away. Accordingly a goodly company of praying men assembled in Euclid Street Chapel, and spent the night, from nine or ten o'clock till six next morning, in intercession. That night was to many present one of the most memorable seasons of their life. The sense of the majesty and immediate presence of Jehovah rested on every soul. In the awful stillness of the night watches we realized eternity. The fact that thousands of our fellow-citizens were sleeping on the verge of hell seized our minds with overwhelming vividness, and the whole company were bathed in tears. O Dundee! Dundee! how hast thou been exalted unto heaven in the compassionate cries and anguished pleadings of those that loved thee even when they were hated by thee! May thy repentance turn away from thee the judgment of Capernaum! That night of prayer was followed by most striking displays of saving power. Instances of conversion sufficient to fill a volume could be here given; but I must forbear.

Of the converts, some are now in the ministry, some are missionaries, evangelists, Scripture-readers, elders, deacons, students, Sabbath-school teachers, and district visitors; while a still greater number are embraced in the less known, but hardly less useful, rank and file of the King's army. Some of all those classes were converted through the instrumentality of Duncan Matheson. To his sword, indeed, which seemed seldom to return empty, ever fell a full share of the spoils of this glorious war.

-------◆-------

CHAPTER VII.

THE DIOCESE OF OPEN AIR.

The Huntly meetings played an important part in connection with the work of grace in the north of Scotland. They had their origin in a thought of Duncan Matheson's, and to him under God they owed no small part of their success. One day, pondering the best means of promoting the good work, the thought of gathering the people from the surrounding country for a great field-day of the Gospel in the Castle Park flashed across his mind. After prayerful consideration of the scheme, he mentioned it to his fellow-laborers, Mr. Williamson and Mr. Bain, as they were all three returning from Cullen feeing market, where they had been preaching. They resolved to lay the matter before the Lord. There and then, wearied though they were, they betook themselves to the throne of grace, and as the train was speeding on its way, they cried to God for light to guide them. Light was not withheld: the scheme was settled at the mercy-seat. The use of the Castle Park, with suitable aid in other respects, was freely accorded by the Duchess of Gordon, and preparations were made, the burden of which mainly rested on Mr. Matheson and his pastor. The labor thus entailed was extremely great, and our evangelist was well-nigh crushed beneath the load of responsibility and care. After a sleepless and prayerful night on the eve of the Huntly meetings, he said to me, "I feel as if I were breaking down. I have been putting up blood, and feel very ill. Sometimes Satan tempts me to take it easier, and do less for souls: he whispers when I am speaking in the open air, 'You had better take it easier, or you'll burst a blood-vessel.' But I just reply, 'Never mind if I do; I could not die in a better cause.'"

The object of these meetings was stated in a printed request for special prayer. "We do not believe," said the pastor and the evangelist, "in any special virtue in meetings in the open air. We put no confidence in any peculiar form of address, neither in any instrument. But we do believe in the power of prayer: we believe 'the hour is coming and *now* is, when the dead shall hear the voice of the Son of God; and they that hear shall live.' We believe it a good thing and ground of hope to see a number of the Lord's people met together 'with one accord in one place.' And we most firmly believe that the God of all grace may be expected to honor such

meetings and efforts, when preceded and accompanied by earnest and united prayer for the outpouring of his Spirit.

" We, therefore, most earnestly ask secret, social,
and united prayer, that the arm of the Lord may be
revealed; that Jesus may be lifted up, and draw all
men unto Him; and that throughout eternity many
may have cause to bless God that they were present
at these meetings and found salvation."

The first meetings were held on the 25th and
26th July, 1860, and were renewed for three successive summers. Many thousands assembled year by
year in the Castle Park, with its hoary ruins tow-
ering amid the softest scenes of sylvan beauty. Here
of old the Gordon clan were wont to gather in preparation for some distant and bloody raid. Now
another clan assembles for very different ends. The
children of Zion gather themselves together to meet
their King; the soldiers of the cross rally around the
standard of Christ. The coming and going of the
people to serve God amidst the loveliest retreats of
nature reminded one of the conventicles of the Covenanters in some remote glen or dewy hollow, and
of the still more memorable scenes when multitudes
gathered round the Prince of open-air preachers by
the shores of the Sea of Galilee. Here nature and
grace embrace each other in true fellowship, and
the works of God throw a peculiar charm around
his word and worship. The lofty canopy of heaven
reminds you of the true tabernacle which God hath

pitched, and not man. The fair landscapes on every side picture heavenly things to the sense, and shadow forth in natural form and hue the invisible glories of the spirit-world. The grassy plains suggest the green pastures where the Good Shepherd feeds his flock, and makes them rest at noon. The sighing of the wind among the trees, and the warbling of the birds, seem like the rustling of angels' wings, and the stir of ministering spirits sent forth to minister to the heirs of salvation. The pure air comes to wearied pilgrims like deep, refreshing draughts from the Creator's wine-cup. The sweet sunshine is to faith but the visible radiance of the Redeemer's face; and the alternations of light and shade are like the mysterious comings and goings of our God in his sanctuary. The very sound and shock of the falling rain carry into the believer's heart symboled thoughts of grace far more true to nature than the peal of organs or the swell of pompous choirs. Altogether there is a naturalness, a simplicity, and a freedom more akin to the spirit and privilege of new-covenant service than is often realized in those dull artificial caverns in which custom and the rigors of climate compel us to worship. Sitting under the shadow of cumbrous roofs and dingy walls, and too oft fettered by form, truth, love, joy, and praise, pine away like caged birds; but out in the open, unbounded expanse, where form is simplest and sense is purest, worship is the more free and unrestrained.

It was pleasing to witness the assembling of the

people in the Castle Park; old and young, rich and
poor, master and man are there. Yonder the honest cotter, with his wife and bairns in the rude cart
consecrated to the service of God, it may be for the
first time, jogs cheerfully along not far behind the
gig of the well-to-do farmer, whose wife and daughters are looking forward to the ongoings of the day
with deeper and stronger feelings than any they
ever felt on their way to kirk or market. Some
are trudging on foot, and all are talking with more
or less personal interest in the great event of the
time—the Revival. Listen to yon knot of ploughmen and farm-lads. One wonders "what it's gaun
to come tae." Another "kens weel aneuch what it's
gaun to come tae, for he has fan't in his ain heart;
it has brocht him to Christ, an' it'll bring him to
heaven." A third admits that "a wonderfu' change
has come o'er Jake Tamson; for there was na a rocher
chiel in a' the country side, an' noo he's as hairmless
as a stirk, an' sings an' prays instead o' swearin' an'
fechtin' as he used to do." "Eh, mon," says a half-
grown lad, "gin ye only heard my brither Jock!
he prays like a minister; in fack, his prayer is ilka
bit as gude as the pairish minister's prayer on the
Sacrament Sunday."

"Do you ever take God's name in vain?" asks a
minister of the Gospel of one of these herd laddies.

"Na, na, sir; God's children never sweer."

"You are one of his children, then? When did
that come about?"

"Weel, sir," says the lad, "it was at the Mertimiss term last year, when I gaed hame to see my
father's fouk. I wonnert when I saw a' things sae
sair changed. My father was changed, an' the hoose
was changed-like. An' my father, he prayed afore
the supper an' after the supper, an' he never used
to say a grace at a'. An' syne he said, 'Fesh ben
the buik;' an' he read, an' he sang, an' syne they a'
gaed doon upon their knees, an' I never saw that
afore. An' my father he prayed, an' I grat, an' we
a' grat, an' I was convertit that nicht. That was
Mertimiss last year, ye ken, an' I never could sweer
sin' syne."

The full meaning of all this can be comprehended
only by those who know what a northern bothy used
to be. There, if anywhere on earth, Satan was wont
to have his seat; now, however, to some extent the
"strong man" has been displaced by a stronger than
he.

The greater number came by rail, which, in this
way serving God as well as man, seemed to anticipate the day when "holiness to the Lord" shall be
upon the bells of the horses, and doubtless also on
the whistles of the engines. In one carriage prayer
is being offered for a special blessing on the meetings. In another the Word is read with comments,
homely enough, but well seasoned with a devout
spirit and a gracious experience. In a third a distressed soul is being lovingly dealt with; difficulties
are cleared away, and the cross lifted up before the

eye of the afflicted sinner.   High over all, and above
even the din of the train, is heard the voice of holy
song.   One group is singing "Rock of Ages, cleft
for me;" in another part of the train you can hear
the splendid burst of the ancient church,

> "All people that on earth do dwell,
>   Sing to the Lord with cheerful voice."

A traveller who has left his religion at home—perhaps because it was scarcely worth the carriage—
is to be pitied, for in escaping from one compartment
to another he finds that he is only out of the pan and
into the fire.   It would be a curious turning of the
tables if some day this poor foolish world should be
so filled with purity, goodness, and the love of God,
that the few remaining sinners, to escape the gentle
persecution of light and grace, should flee for refuge
to dens and caves of the earth.   Then, indeed, the
church would be "fair as the moon, clear as the sun,
and terrible as an army with banners."

The services were characterized by the fervor and
simplicity of the prayers, the heartiness and jubilance of the praises, and the variety, directness, and
power of the addresses, full as these were of the
richest truths of the Gospel, and fragrant with the
perfumes of *the one great Name.*   In love, joy, and
unanimity, the believers seemed to anticipate the
general assembly of the Church of the first-born in
heaven, and the triumphant services before the
throne.   On the other hand, the deep shadows of

eternal verities seemed to rest on the minds of the
unconverted, not a few of whom found Him whom
they sought after, and sometimes, ere the tears were
dry on their cheeks, were beginning to "rejoice
with joy unspeakable and full of glory."

The testimony of an eye-witness, a venerable minister of Christ, may be here given.   "During each
day," he writes, "numbers were personally spoken
with and specially prayed for, in every stage of religious concern.   Not a few were awakened for the
first time during the time of the meetings, princi-
pally by witnessing the great earnestness manifested
in prayer in behalf of the unconverted, as well as by
listening to the pointed and soul-searching appeals
addressed to the various classes.   Others, who had
previously been under great spiritual distress, had
come some of them twenty and even thirty miles,
as well as lesser distances, seeking relief to a conscience ill at ease.   In the case of others who came
under our notice, former convictions that had well-
nigh died out were revived with double power.
The superficial observer could form no correct estimate of the amount of impression by merely looking at the appearance of the assembly; for there
was comparatively little manifestation of emotional
excitement; nor by simply looking at those in the
tent and marquee, who professedly took their place
among other inquirers.   We found numbers of the
most interesting cases of this class at a distance
from the crowd, either holding intercourse with God

alone, and breathing into his ear their noiseless
grief; or in some by-corner holding close conversation with some godly friend who sympathized with
them; or in the midst of little groups among the
trees, where spiritual things were freely talked over
by those with open Bibles in their hand, following
up conversation with prayer. We conversed with
several persons, some of them considerably advanced
in years, upon whose minds something like the dark
shadow of despair had been brooding for months.
They could distinctly tell what was the matter with
them, and what they needed; but somehow they
stumbled at the simplicity of entering upon the way
of life as sketched in the charter of human salvation. Of the above-mentioned cases a considerable
number, before they left the meetings, were enabled
to leave their sins and their sorrows within the
shadow of the mercy-seat at the foot of the cross,
and went home in possession of a good hope through
grace. All who took pains to make themselves ac-
quainted with what we have stated are firmly persuaded, and on good grounds, that in connection
with these meetings, 'to Satan many captives were
lost, and to Christ many subjects were born.'"

The meetings were held for two successive days
every summer, from 1860 to 1863 inclusive. Duncan Matheson was the presiding genius of the arrangements: he was everywhere and in every thing.
Here speaking to an afflicted soul, there encouraging a young Christian; now pouring out his quaint,

spirit-stirring speech amidst a group of youths, and a moment after gravely settling some deep experimental question with an aged pilgrim. Almost at the same point of time he is providing lodgings for his friends, and making suggestions of the most sagacious character as to the programme of religious services. Now he is leading the devotions of the great assembly in his own impressive and Elijah-like manner, and in less than five minutes he is in the outskirts of the crowd, endeavoring by wise, kind words to hush some rising controversy. At every juncture he knows what to do. When the people were hurrying away on account of a thunder-storm, he stopped them by reminding them that the Covenanters could stand a shower of bullets, and that God can stay the rain in answer to prayer. Prayer was offered, and the rain ceased. "Look!" exclaimed the evangelist. "Behold the bow of promise spanning the heavens! emblem of God's good-will to earth." All eyes were turned to look on the rainbow, "like unto an emerald around the throne of God." Revealing itself just as the thunder-torrent swept over the horizon of the distant hill, as if chased away by the sudden outburst of sunshine, it symbolized to many the glory of God in the face of Jesus Christ, in whose cross mercy and truth are met together, righteousness and peace have kissed each other. Many who have forgotten the preaching, remember the lesson of the evangelist, who, with hand uplifted to heaven, bade the vast multitude read the Gospel in the sky, and see the beauty of Jesus in the bow with its matchless hues.

It was a good work to bring together so many thousands of Christians to sing the same song, to mingle faith, hope, and charity in the same prayer, and to encourage one another in the common Lord. It was the gathering of all the live coals into one great fire, whose flames were bright enough to illuminate no small part of Scotland. In this way the evils of sectarianism were mitigated, and the bonds of Christian brotherhood strengthened. Young converts, suffering from isolation and the lack of fellowship, were refreshed and sent on their way rejoicing. The poor starved sheep of Christ's flock were fed on green pastures and strengthened to endure. Persecuted believers, reproached by friends, scorned by neighbors, cast off by companions, and frowned upon by carnal pastors, were emboldened to fight the good fight of faith. Many who were halting between two opinions, being uncertain as to the nature and tendencies of the great movement of the time, had their doubts and fears cleared away. Many earnest and faithful ministers of the Gospel went home from those happy scenes to labor in their own quiet vineyards with a still holier zeal, livelier hope, and deeper joy. Many saints returned to walk more closely with their God; and some whom we knew received at the Huntly meetings a double meal, like Elijah in the wilderness, in the strength of which they went, and came even to the mount of God. To many it was the starting-point of their pilgrimage to Zion, and the sweet memories of those gracious espousals and first loves will merit and inspire "nobler songs above." In short, thousands live to praise God for the open-air meetings in the Castle Park, and similar meetings elsewhere, of which the gathering at Huntly was at once the parent and the broad, distinct pattern.

Thus the little germ of thought arising in the mind of our evangelist bore choicest fruits in marvellous abundance. It was part of the arduous and honorable work assigned him by his Master. A double grace was bestowed upon him in it— grace to do the work faithfully and well, and the grace of abounding success. For this kind of work he was pre-eminently well qualified. His powerful physique, his cheerful countenance, his exultant voice, his overflowing humor, his innocent, and childlike egotism which carried in it something of the charm of genius, his practical sagacity and swift decision, his fertility of resource and power to grasp a multitude of details, his keen-eyed intuition of human character, his ability to inspire and command, his invincible ardor in the presence of difficulties, his great faith, largeness of heart, and Christian self-sacrifice, combined to fit him in an extraordinary degree for the masterly and successful management of a great undertaking such as this really was. There were many witnesses to the grace and truth of Christ at the Huntly meetings, minis-

15

ters of every name, learned professors, eloquent divines, lawyers, physicians, lords, land-owners, mer-
chants, officers of the army and navy, and many
others down to the fisherman and the butcher, who
said, "I canna write my ain name, but it has been
written by the finger o' Anither—written in blood
in the Lamb's book o' life," one of the truest and
noblest of them all was the old stone-cutter, Duncan Matheson. His it was not merely to speak for
Christ, but to gather up this great united testimony,
which illustrated the unity of the true faith as it has
seldom been illustrated in our own day or in our
fathers. His it was to concentrate as in a focus the
scattered rays of the glorious sun that was then
pouring his golden floods upon our favored land,
alike on hill and dale, on barren moorland and fruitful field.

At a "conference on the subject of the present
religious awakening," held in the Free South Church,
Aberdeen, on August 15th, 1861, we find our evangelist saying: "Revival is an established fact. It is
a great fact. Thousands, many thousands, have felt
the power of God in their own souls. I do not, perhaps, know of one place in the county of Aberdeen
where there are not living witnesses to the power
of God's grace and the might of his Spirit. There
is one thing that has always struck me with wonder: it is this—Why should we think it a strange
thing to see a work like this work of revival? If
we believe God's Word at all, we must believe that

He is able, willing, and mighty to save. Why wonder, then, that He is saving so many? Might we
not rather expect that He will do far greater things?
A man said to me, 'Are you in the revival?' 'No,
sir,' I replied, 'the revival is in me; it is in my heart.'
I believe that many of God's people feel this. We
never did feel so much joy, and blessedness, and
gladness, as since these blessed days when the Lord
has been pouring out his Spirit—planting flowers
in his garden that will bloom through an endless
eternity. I could hardly tell you where I have not
seen God's work. I have been wandering for nearly
four years—north, south, east, and west—and the
Lord is doing great things everywhere. We see the
sheaves being gathered to God's harvest-home; and
what can we do but say, 'Our God reigns; verily
we have seen the salvation of Israel; verily we have
seen answered the prayers of the men whose blood
was shed in defence of our faith—the witnesses
whose souls have been crying under the altar.'
And we have only seen the beginning; the end is
at hand. Why, I ask again, should this be thought
a strange thing? What is the great end of the Christian ministry? There is no antagonism between us
and the ministry; we go as breakers-up of the way
and God has been pleased to own us. We do not
interfere in the least with the constituted ministry;
for I believe, as solemnly as I do in any part of God's
Word, that He has appointed a ministry for the conversion of souls, and the upbuilding of his people;

and the cry of our heart day by day is, 'Oh, would that all the Lord's people were prophets!' We look and see day by day souls going down to perdition; and if we believe in a heaven and hell, in an unending eternity, we will go forth like men going to quell fire, saying, 'Stop, poor sinner! come with us, and we will do thee good; for the Lord hath spoken good concerning Israel.' I might tell in this meeting what I have seen in many places. I might speak of what I witnessed in S—— during the last few days; of the awful solemnity upon our spirits, when it seemed as if we felt the immediate power of God in our hearts; and we were almost afraid to speak, as if one felt very near the gates of heaven. Some of us felt so at S——. And when we saw the Lord working and the slain so many, we lifted up our hearts and sang, "Hallelujah! for the Lord God omnipotent reigneth.'

"One thing I have seen, and I have thanked the Lord for it; it has done immense good; it is the deliverance of the last Free General Assembly on this great and glorious work. The results from that deliverance, the good it has done, we cannot estimate. I have seen members of the Free Church lifted up in their souls, and thanking God for that noble testimony. Since it was issued it has given a great impetus to the work. It has been true, and always will be true to the end, 'Them that honor Me I will honor.' I have seen the objections of many scattered to the winds since it was given. And since it was read from the pulpits of the churches, I have seen a manifest blessing upon the ministry and the people. Let me remark this other thing—that some people always find fault. Well, we cannot help it; and we admit that there are very many things that we ourselves cannot prevent, that yet we do not desire. A great many things have been said about inquiry meetings. I look upon these as the most solemn part of the work—just dealing with souls face to face. It is of great importance that all who thus speak to the anxious should be known—that their real state and character before God should be tested. We should know also that they have something of that wisdom that cometh down from above. I believe there are many of God's people who fail in this work. I have seen them giving the comforts of God's children to the anxious. I have heard godly persons saying to such, 'Wait God's time;' and, 'You are in a very hopeful state,' just strangling their convictions. Oh, if there is one part of the work in which we need more than in another the aid of the Holy Spirit, it is in dealing with anxious souls.

"Mr. Ross has spoken about the coast. I know a great deal about the coast, and upon this coast no one has been more honored than Mr. Turner, of Peterhead. That man's footsteps, speaking after the manner of men, I have been able to trace all round the coast. Look at Banff—what a work he has done there; and at Portknockie, Buckie, Portgordon. You see the Lord taking that instrument and using him;

he was used for a time, and then put aside. It is a solemn thing when God uses a man for a time, and then puts him aside. It is not the opposition of man we fear. I was never able to do any thing till I was opposed, and so it has been with others. I would remark, in closing, that I have always seen the work produce greatest fruits under the soundest teaching. An old Highland minister said, 'It is a dangerous thing for a child to get bad milk;' and you generally see where there is not sound teaching they are like the young thrushes, ready to eat mud if given to them. They have no discernment. But where there is sound teaching they grow up like calves in the stall; the grace of God is in them, and we see it shining. There is just this in it—the good old doctrines will stand the test, for they are built upon the Rock of Ages. Oh, may we hold them fast; and when we depart hence, leave behind us 'footprints on the sands of time,' or, rather, on the shores of eternity."

Not content with scouring his native country, he sometimes crossed the border, and everywhere the strong voice and steady hand were raised to point men to the cross. In the autumn of 1862 he visited his old friends, the soldiers, at Aldershot, and described his visit in the following letter, which appeared in *The Revival:**

"My Dear Friend: Swiftly has the time passed

* A weekly periodical now incorporated with " *The Christian.*"

since I came here, and never throughout eternity shall I forget my visit to this place. There is not a spot in Britain around which such interest clings, and for which more prayer has been offered up.

"My heart thrilled as I saw a camp once more, heard the strains of martial music, and gazed on the red coats, either singly, or in groups, or regiments marching along. The past was brought vividly before me, but the contrast could hardly be realized. In the Crimea, day and night, nothing was heard but the roar of the cannon, or the din of battle; and during a long dreary winter, nothing seen but misery, that made the heart bleed, borne with calm endurance and heroic valor, giving English history a page it never had. It is true that at Aldershot the bugle sounds, but it calls only to parade, or to take part in mimic fights. Regiments march, but not to battle. The gun fires, but only to mark the hours as they pass along. The scene is bustling but peaceful, and order reigns in the camp supreme.

"I have met few old friends, for death has done his work, and the heroes of Alma, Inkermann, Sebastopol, have passed away—yes, away like the snow-flakes before the summer's sun, or the leaves of the forest before the wintry blast. In the lone graveyard here, on the bleak moor side, lie many who escaped unscathed amidst the iron showers and the deadly pestilence. With constitutions impaired, they returned to die, leaving as an heir-loom in many a home the medal and its bars of glory, worn but for a little, and then laid aside forever. *Sic transit gloria mundi.*

"It is estimated that during the summer from 15,000 to 18,000 men are stationed here, and the influence of such a mass on the town of Aldershot is of the most ruinous kind. Much has been written about it, and yet it is impossible to make the picture too dark, or to bring out in relief its degrading aspects. Just think of upwards of seventy public-houses outside the camp, and you will realize in some measure the seething mass of iniquity behind. The camp has made the town what it is, and the town sends back to the camp the curse intensified it has given. Many a daughter comes here to die, over whom a mother, it may be in the far north of Scotland, is weeping day and night. One was asked lately if she had a mother; and, as if stung by a serpent, she fled out of sight. Another says she is dying fast, but asks what she can do. A third laughs; but it is hollow, coming from a heart torn with anguish, from burning fires within, fed by the memory of home and days gone—never more to come back again.

"Blessed be God, all is not dark. The cloud has a silver lining! There is much to quicken and cheer; for the great God is visiting the camp, and drops of blessing have descended. Witness after witness is being raised, and the prayers, so long lying on the altar, are being answered. Hardly a week passes but there is an accession to the little army, and twelve prayer-meetings are held weekly by the men themselves. At some of these I have seen sixty men and a few officers present. What songs from yours 'Hymns of Prayer and Praise' they sang! With what a heart did they peal out 'Rest for the weary,' and with what holy pleading did they cry for their comrades drifting to perdition! The leaven is working; the seed is springing up; and many are halting —lingering at the gate.

"Mrs. Daniell, so well known for her labors in the cause of Christ, has founded a mission for Aldershot, and forty officers and men have come forward as volunteers to help her on. The United Presbyterian Church is organizing a congregation, and will, I doubt not, succeed. May God speed them, and may their church be the birth-place of many a soul. May He also bless the labors of the chaplains and Scripture-readers, whose work is so arduous, and who need more than common wisdom and zeal. Night after night I preached outside the camp in the open air, with a body-guard of Christian soldiers around me, some of whom, with much feeling, have addressed their comrades passing by.

"What noble missionaries these soldiers, if converted, would make! How would their influence tell amongst the heathen abroad! What a sight to see Britain sending forth an army of living men displaying a banner for the truth!

"I feel assured there is many a Hedley Vicars,

Hammond, Vandeleur, Marjouram amongst them, and that God, by His Spirit, will soon bring them out. Aldershot is the cradle of the British army. The fire here is kindled. The work has begun. The Prince of Peace is saving souls, and God is calling on his people to bestir themselves. England, Scotland, Ireland, your sons need help. Will you cry for the army, and forget not Aldershot?

"Yours in the Lord,

"DUNCAN MATHESON,

"Late Soldiers' Missionary in the Crimea."

The Rev. H. M. Williamson, Belfast, who was at once the pastor and fellow-evangelist of Mr. Matheson, writes:

"Confining myself to what I have witnessed, I would like to give you a brief sketch of his labors in the north of Scotland. He used to map out a district, and arrange for an evangelistic tour, extending over six or eight days. I frequently accompanied him on such expeditions. Starting perhaps on a Monday, we were accustomed to preach generally twice each day, holding meetings in all conceivable places—in barns, on the squares and streets of villages, under the trees of the woods, sometimes in various churches placed at our disposal. He thoroughly knew the feelings, habits, and prejudices of his countrymen, and with singular sagacity he employed that knowledge to gain the attention of his hearers and a favorable hearing for the Gospel. He was never at a loss, and full of hope; he had a remedy for every difficulty, and was ready for every emergency. Let me give you as an illustration a scene which occurred on one of our preaching expeditions. We had arranged to hold a meeting in the streets of a certain village. The place was drowned in drink, and consequently spiritually dead above most places. At the appointed hour we made our appearance, and having made our way to the square of the village, and having borrowed a chair for a pulpit, we were prepared to proceed; but audience there was none, save two or three ragged children, who gathered round and stared at us as a curiosity. It was certainly a situation exceedingly trying to flesh and blood, and one that gave ample room for the exercise of faith. Matheson by the grace of God, was equal to the occasion. I think I hear his cheery words, as he said to me, speaking in his broadest Doric, 'Haud on, haud on, Mr. Williamson, for a wee bit as weel as ye can, an' I'll fetch out the folk wi' the help o' God.' He started off, leaving me on the chair—no envied position, I assure you—with the children for my audience. He started off, and beginning at the extreme end of the village, he knocked at every door, and cried aloud *as he could cry*, 'Come awa' out, come awa' out; the Gospel is come to the town;' and using at the same time, with his usual sagacity, the children he met as his agents, he said, 'Rin, laddie rin; and tell yer mither to come awa' to the square, and hear the preaching.' We had a meeting—a successful meeting—we adjourned in the evening to a church in the village; and I have good reason to believe that redeemed souls in eternity will bless God for that meeting.

"There are few parishes in Aberdeenshire and Banffshire in which the name of Duncan Matheson is not known and loved, and very few in which he has not preached the Gospel. The extent of the blessing which rested upon his labors shall only be known on that day when the secrets of all hearts are made manifest. I regret exceedingly that the account of all these labors is now lost forever. Had he been spared to give it, it would have been a record of the Lord's doings of thrilling interest, and well fitted to strengthen every laborer in the Lord's vineyard. Many incidents attending his work were of a very remarkable nature, and if they had been recorded would have been pregnant with instruction and encouragement. I remember while holding a meeting one night in a certain place an occurrence which made a deep impression upon me at the time, and which I had occasion to mark afterwards. The meeting was crowded, and better still, it was full of spiritual power. Many souls were deeply wounded under the sharp strokes of the Holy Ghost. Some smitten ones were crying out, 'What must we do to be saved?'

" While we were going about among the anxious, seeking as we were enabled to point them to the Lamb of God, the individual who had control over the place of meeting began to urge the people to go home, and to crown his advice he proceeded to put out the lights. I think I hear Matheson as turning to me he said, 'Mr. Williamson, mark my words, you will see something happen to that man—the Lord will put out his candle!' Matheson, though pretending to no spirit of prophecy, knew how dangerous it is to meddle with the work of the Holy Spirit. And so it came to pass. Matheson lived to see that man disgraced and dishonored, and driven from his position. But if I persevere in calling up the events of these years of blessing my letter will swell into a volume.

"The great gatherings for Christian fellowship and for preaching the everlasting Gospel with which Scotland, and especially in the northern parts, was favored in past years are closely connected with Duncan Matheson.

"Shortly after the work of the Spirit began to be manifest in the awakening and conversion of sinners in Aberdeenshire in the years 1858–9, a conference of ministers was held at Huntly Lodge, under the auspices of the late Duchess of Gordon. That conference brought out the fact, that the work of God was much more extensive and thorough than any one had supposed. The work still made progress under opposition of various kinds and from all sources. Matheson traversed almost every parish of Aberdeenshire and the district around, everywhere preaching the Gospel, and much blessing was added.

"Returning from one of these preaching expeditions, he proposed to me the idea of a grand gathering at Huntly, seeking the aid of men of all churches, both lay and clerical, whom God had honored in the work of revival. The proposal took shape. It was approved of by the Duchess of Gordon, and by others whose good judgment, spirituality of mind, and zeal for the cause of God we could trust. The whole arrangements of the meetings were put into Matheson's hands, and the results were great and blessed. Multitudes of believers from every corner of the land were refreshed and strengthened, and multitudes of the unsaved brought to Jesus.

"He had a singular gift for organizing such meetings. He thoroughly knew the people, as I have stated,—their mode of life, their habits, their prejudices on religious subjects, their wants, and their religious position. And with all this knowledge, when the meetings were assembled, he arranged accordingly with wonderful tact—he put the right man in the right place. He aimed at the conversion of sinners as the great end of the meetings, and in carrying out this end he exhibited marvellous spiritual instinct in selecting the right speaker at the right time to give, under the Holy Spirit, the message which would bring about the blessed end. He knew too the men that were mighty in prayer, and endeavored to keep them, with praying companions, lifting up holy hands

without wrath and doubting. And in this matter
he suffered no respect for persons to interfere. The
men he believed were likely to be the instruments
in the hands of the Spirit to do the work needed at
any particular time in the services, these he brought
forward.

" You and I have seen, in other cases and at similar gatherings, the whole work marred, and the
fruit almost completely lost, because those who conducted such meetings deemed themselves bound to
put forward speakers in a prescribed order, because
of their social position or ministerial standing in
church connection.

"Matheson never for a moment allowed such
considerations to influence him. The result corre-
sponded. As he sought to honor the Holy Spirit,
and keep a single eye on the great end, the salvation of souls, much fruit appeared.

" His efforts in preaching the Gospel in the feeing
markets of Aberdeenshire were also attended with
a very abundant blessing. It is a question upon
which, perhaps, Christian men form different opinions. I think it admits of no controversy with all
who are taught of God, that whenever men are
willing to hear the Gospel, then the Gospel should
be preached to them. Now, it is also a fact beyond
dispute, that for some years the Lord poured such
a spirit of hearing upon the people that they were
willing to hear; and this also I may add, I have seen
as marked and manifest fruits of the Spirit's presence

and power attending these market-preachings as I have ever witnessed on the Sabbath and in the most solemn assembly. This market-preaching was a department of labor for which Matheson was in many ways singularly fitted. Ready for every emergency, and with a tact which usually disarmed opposition, with a courage that never faltered, and with a voice like the tongue of a trumpet, he labored in this field most laboriously, and in it I feel persuaded reaped many sheaves of the harvest of the Lord. I have met many in later years who have testified that they would have cause to bless God forever for these market-preachings.

"Alas, the band of laborers in that field are now widely scattered! What sweet and solemn memories of these days and of the beloved fellow-laborers who wrought in this work with us! The saintly Macgregor and the good soldiers of Jesus Christ, Colonel Ramsey and Major Gibson, and the fearless Matheson—a prince of evangelists—all gone to their rest and their reward. The devoted pastors, Bain and Forbes, and Fullarton and Campbell (tried and true helpers), Tytler, and Macpherson, and Anderson still with us, and many other beloved brethren who have never been ashamed of the Gospel of Christ.

"But this letter is drawn out far beyond what I intended, and yet I feel as if I had said almost nothing concerning the labors of our departed friend. Let me add, he was one of the most unselfish of men; he would and often did share his last shilling with a poor saint. He was ever ready to commend the Gospel to the careless and the scoffer by deeds of generosity and liberality. What the Church owes to Matheson has never been acknowledged. His share in elevating the standard of religious profession in the land, and especially in the northern part, has never been justly estimated. But his reward is on high. 'They that be wise shall shine as the brightness of the firmament, and they that turn many to righteousness as the stars forever and ever.'"

An important part of our evangelist's mission was the preaching of the Gospel in village fairs. The feeing market, at which farmers engage their servants from one half year to another, is a long-established institution in the northern counties of Scotland. It is usually held in the street or neighborhood of some little town or village. Early in the morning of the market-day there is a wonderful stir in the erection of refreshment-tents, booths for the sale of sweets, trinkets, and all things dear to a ploughboy's heart, shows, and all the other paraphernalia of a village fair. Soon after breakfast the market is crowded by farmers and their wives, ploughmen, female servants, and all who have business to do. Besides these there is a general assembly of all the idlers and *ne'er-do-weels* in the country-side; tramps, tinkers, ballad-singers, fiddlers, rogues, beggar-women with starving babies, the man who is "out of employment" because he will not work, the shipwrecked sailor who never was at sea, the veteran soldier who has seen no service but the devil's—in short all the scoundrels within a radius of thirty miles.

No time is lost; the whole machinery of the market is set a-going. All the animal spirits of half-a-score parishes and villages are now crowded into one place. There is no restraint; universal freedom reigns. Wild hilarity, roaring frankness, outrageous demonstrations of friendship, characterize the scene, and a tumult of varied sounds fills the air. Underneath all this, however, there is an eye to business. Yonder in the open air, at the end of a tent, a fat, red-faced dame is piling up a blazing fire of peat, over which a huge pot is boiling with the farmers' broth. Close by a master is higgling with a ploughman about five shillings more or less of half-yearly wages; and the bargain, after an immense deal of manœuvring as if both were perfectly indifferent to the matter, is settled in the good old Scotch way of "splitting the difference." Then follows the indispensable dram. A young swain has just spent his "arles" in treating his sweetheart with rude demonstrations of attachment. Another, already drunk, is dancing and capering to the wretched strains of a fiddle. Sailor Jack moves along with a curious limp as he sings his favorite ditty. The showman is doing his best to entertain the people and obtain their pence. Cheap John, with incredible generosity, insists on enriching the public to his own certain ruin, mixing his jokes and lies in due measures to meet the tastes of the gullible portion of market-goers. A recruiting sergeant is describing to a knot of young men the glory and blessedness of a soldier's life. On the outskirts of the fair a crew of drunken carters are bargaining with an unscrupulous horse-dealer for an old nag, which is being trotted up and down at the utmost speed possible to his wooden limbs. A tall, villainous, one-legged speculator in human simplicity tempts to a game of chance, which is yet no chance to himself; whilst his one-armed brother offers to teach the young idea how to shoot by means of bow and arrows which Tell himself could not have shot straight. A hundred voices are crying their wares. As the day advances men and matters become more and more lively. Suddenly the crowd begins to surge to and fro, everybody knocking into his neighbor, no one knowing why. There is a fight; strong drink is master of the situation. A score of voices are raised with a score of hands; hard blows are dealt; but the greatest sufferer is the poor old woman whose "sweetie stand" is overturned in the scuffle, all her gingerbread cakes and colored sweets are scattered in the mud. The same commander-in-chief is marshalling his hosts in a neighboring tent, where a fierce conflict rages around the rude board. You can see the whole affair from without by the moving of hostile heads and arms against the canvas, which at length gives way, and the entire tabernacle of Satan, with a loud crash of bottles and

glasses, rolls over upon the ground. Still the business of the fair goes on as before, its very life being
in noise, excitement, and uproar. Towards evening
the more respectable people take their way home-
wards, carrying with them all sorts of useful household articles purchased at the fair. Among the remaining portion the drinking and quarrelling go on
apace; coarseness, profanity, and violence increase,
till at length the deepening shades, not a moment
too soon, cast the mantle of God over a very hell of
riot, charged with all the elements of misery and
ruin.

It was a bold idea to introduce the Gospel here.
It was like David's attempt to save the lamb by
attacking the lion and the bear. For men of fine
feelings to stand upon a box or barrel, occupying
as it were the same platform with all that is coarse,
sordid, and villainous, and amidst the bawling, the
laughing, the blaspheming, the singing, the fiddling,
the fighting, the ribaldry of mockers, the rage of
the ungodly, and in the very atmosphere of black-
guardism, to raise the "still small voice" of the Gospel and speak to men heated with every passion, of
"righteousness, temperance, and judgment to come,"
was a work of the most trying kind. Sometimes
they were made to feel that it were easier to face an
armed host than bear the calumny and the shame.
Often were they threatened, often assailed, and sometimes well-nigh put to silence; but they trusted in
Him who hath all power in heaven and on earth;

and sometimes, when they thought the Word was only like water spilt upon the ground, they were amazed and overjoyed to discover rough, burly ploughmen breaking down under the truth, weeping like children, and asking what they must do to be saved. All over the north-eastern counties you come upon strong, hard-headed, tender-hearted, God-fearing men, who tell you that they were "brocht tae the Lord" at such and such a market, giving you place and date of their second birth. Besides that, the general improvement in morals, particularly in the matter of sobriety, decency, and order, at some of the feeing markets, was so marked as to draw forth expressions of wonder and admiration from even men of the world. If a sufficient number of suitable laborers were found for this work, a thorough reformation should be effected, as the experiment proved; but men possessing the necessary courage and zeal appear to be few, and such gigantic labors exhaust or kill them.

Nature and grace conspired to make Duncan Matheson a prince of market-preachers. His handsome, well-knit form impressed the sons of the soil with a sense of his great strength; his frank, straightforward manner commanded their respect; his ready wit captivated a people whose genuine humor is proverbial; his voice, rising above the din, summoned them as with a trumpet to listen; his manifest superiority to all fear made him a hero in their eyes; and the grace of the Holy Ghost with the truth as it is in

Christ Jesus, did the rest. In this rough, self-denying work he was nobly assisted by several ministers
of the Gospel and other right-hearted servants of
Jesus Christ.

Sometimes when a hearing could not be obtained,
and further prosecution of the work seemed an utter
waste of energy and time, Duncan would start up
and begin thus—" I will tell you a thing that happened when I was in the Crimea." Immediately
there is a respectful silence; the audience seem as
if spell-bound while the preacher proceeds to tell
his story, which is only an introduction to the
Gospel.

In a certain town a gentleman well known in the
place came up to him as he was preaching in the
market, and mockingly said, " Well, what is the
word of the Lord to-day?" Our preacher turned
with a piercing glance of his eye, and promptly replied, " O earth, earth, earth, hear the word of the
Lord!" Shortly afterwards that same scoffer lay at
the point of death in a room right over the corner
where he had assailed the servant of God. He had
been suddenly seized with what he believed were
the pains of death; and in his alarm he cried, " I am
dying—run, run for Mr. ——; get a Bible—quick,
quick!" But ere human aid was procured, or the
Bible brought from the shelf where it lay neglected,
the accomplished scoffer had passed to his final account. This incident, with others of a similar character, tended to lessen the hostility at first shown to

preaching in the market, and to pave the way for a respectful hearing of the Gospel.

In another town the preachers were one day furiously assailed and subjected to much personal indignity and violence by a mob, led on by paid agents of tavern-keepers, whose profits were diminished by the effective preaching of the Gospel. For hours the preachers maintained their position in the outskirts of the market; towards the close of the day, led on by Matheson, they pushed their way into the centre of the fair. Here they were set on by the entire rascality, hired and unhired, of the town; but a shower happening at that crisis, the stentorian voice of our evangelist was heard high above the clamor shouting, "Off hats, men, and let us thank our Father in heaven, who sendeth rain on the just and on the unjust, for this refreshing shower, instead of fire and brimstone to consume us." The effect of this appeal was striking. Every voice was hushed, and every head uncovered, and one who was present describes the prayer of the evangelist as overwhelmingly touching and solemn. The battle was now turned to the gate, and the preachers carried all before them.

On another occasion the showman of a penny theatre, finding that his sarcastic merriment did not shame the preachers into silence, challenged them to come up to his platform, and see if they could speak there. The challenge, contrary to the expectations of the showman, was accepted, and our evangelist accompanied by Mr. Hector Macpherson took possession of the stage, to the astonishment of the whole market. Mr. Matheson began; the showman was put to silence, and went away, leaving the evangelists in possession of his platform, from, which they addressed an immense crowd with remarkable effect.

Prudence and tact were needed as well as courage. Sometimes he deemed it right to buy up the showmen; by giving them a fair day's custom he procured their silence.

In a "Special Call for Prayer," he says: "These markets are fields of deepest trial. For long they have been left in the power of the wicked one, and thousands of souls have been ruined for eternity. Surely, we shall not ask for prayer in vain; and when the banner of Christ is unfurled shall there be one living soul found shrinking from the fight, or refusing to cry from the depths of their hearts, 'Awake, awake, put on strength, O arm of the Lord'?"

The "special call for prayer" was accompanied by the use of other means, such as the following advertisement in a newspaper:

"MARKET PREACHING.

"If the Lord permit, the Everlasting Gospel will be preached at Longside, Ellon, Aberdeen, Turriff, Inverury, and other feeing markets.

"A SOLEMN QUESTION.

"How long do you think it would take you to count a billion? A billion is a million of millions;

and if you were to count at the rate of two hundred a minute, it would require more than nine thousand years to finish it. Now, you must live a billion of years either in heaven or hell, and when that billion of years is past, you must live another billion of years, and then another; and another; and even then your life will only be, as it were, beginning. *You must live forever, whether you will or no.* Is it not an awful thought that you are an immortal being, and that there is no escape into nothingness? Dear friend, you are making an awful blunder if you are living for this world only; and, if you die unsaved, it is a blunder that can never be remedied. Jesus offers to save you now. He died to save; and if you come to Him as you are—no matter how great a sinner you may be—He will save you; for He says, 'Him that cometh to Me, I will in no wise cast out.' The time is short, your soul is precious, and eternity is near.

"D. M."

Mr. Matheson frequently assisted his friends in preaching at the Dundee annual fair. In those days this fair was held in a quarry-pit in the centre of the town, and for crowds, excitement, dissipation, and ruin to the souls of the gay and thoughtless revellers, was equal to forty country markets. Here, as we too well know, many of the young tasted for the first time the devil's sweets. Here receiving their first great impulse hellward, they went bounding down the steep of dissipation until they disappeared amidst the darkness of a living death, or were wrapped in the deep shades of a premature grave. Here I have known the girl of fourteen disappear; and no tongue could tell the father and the mother's agony as they prosecuted for days and nights the saddest search on earth, in the hope of plucking from the jaws of ruin some fragments of their lost child's humanity.

In this very place, where Folly was scattering wide the seeds of death, handfuls of the good Word of God were cast in, not without yielding fruit. To preach here seemed mad enough to many, and useless enough to most. Amid such sounds and scenes it was hard to sustain the voice and maintain composure of spirit; but exhaustion, loss of voice, violent opposition, occasional peltings with stones and other missiles, mockery and scorn, only served to inflame zeal, deepen compassion, and rouse every energy in the interests of the divine glory and of the souls of men. The pains thus taken were amply rewarded in the snatching of brands from the fire. "Let us raise the banner once more," our evangelist used to say. Accordingly, after much prayer, we sallied forth with joyful hearts, and, surrounded by a little band of singers, we continued preaching, praising God, and praying till the latest hour of night. We were often assailed by "lewd fellows of the baser sort;" but in the most tumultuous moment of danger prayer never failed, and frequently at the worst a sense of the Lord's presence suddenly filled our hearts with joy, so that we spake the word with boldness.

On one occasion a burly Yorkshireman attempted to stop the preaching by driving his horses and caravan in amongst us. Matheson, who was speaking at that moment, turned his face to the adversary, and in his solemn way, thundered out these words, "Prepare to meet thy God!" The showman drew up his horses, listened for a few minutes, and then turning deadly pale, quickly beat a retreat.

One night a showman, thinking we had taken our stand in too close proximity to his tabernacle, fetched his magic bottle, and with a significant glance in our direction, said, "Talk of revivals! Here is something that will revive you!" Shouts of derisive laughter followed. We paused a moment, then began to sing the twenty-third Psalm. As we sung, the people began to leave the showman, and come to our side: there was a charm for them in King David's song. Prayer was offered: more of the people came over. A simple exposition of the Psalm followed: the larger portion of the showman's audience left him to hear about the green pastures and the still waters. Ere we finished the show was well-nigh deserted, and we could see the tears trickling down the cheeks of some as they listened to the story of the Good Shepherd coming into the wilderness of this world to seek and to save the lost.

Patience and love always prevailed. One Sabbath

evening, at the time of the fair, we were resting ourselves in the house after a service in the open air. Suddenly four young men, maddened with strong drink, rushed into the room, and furiously assailed us, while a fierce and numerous reserve remained at the door. The object of their wrath was the person of the writer, who had reproved them in the street for scoffing. A violent struggle followed. Matheson interposed, and seizing the ringleader by the arm, said, "Let us pray." We both dropped upon our knees, and fervently entreated God to bless and save the young men. For a moment they were paralyzed by astonishment or fear. Again and again, for nearly two hours, the battle was renewed; again and again we resorted to prayer, striking no blows but those of faith and love. At last the victory remained with us; the young men became as quiet as lambs. We preached the Gospel to them, and ere they went away we formed an alliance of peace and friendship that has never been broken. Such incidents were not infrequent, and the result often illustrated in a striking manner the sovereignty of the grace of God. Men who were at one time leaders of the mob in their most violent attacks on us in the open-air meetings are now, as the writer can testify, ranked among the peaceful disciples of Jesus, and distinguished for their zeal in the cause of the Gospel.

One night at Perth, while we preached in the street we were set on by an infuriated crowd. We

sang the hymn, "There is rest for the weary;" but
as we sang matters grew worse and worse. Not
contented with hooting and yelling, they rushed
upon us, and gathering the dirt of the street, be-
spattered us freely. Matheson, who never lost his
self-possession, frequently whispered in my ear,
"Never mind; perhaps a soul will be saved." We
continued to sing until we reached the door of the
hall where a meeting was being held. Our strength
exhausted, our pride in the dust, we turned to address a word of affectionate entreaty to our victori-
ous assailants, when suddenly the Spirit of God fell
upon us and upon all those people. Our hearts were
filled with a new and wonderful joy, heaven seemed
to be opened above us, the awful verities of eternity
were disclosed with soul-piercing vividness, and
with bleeding hearts we besought them all to re-
pent and believe the Gospel. At the same moment
the great crowd ceased its fiendish rage and mock-
ing; the stillness of death followed; and as we urged
them to flee to Jesus from the wrath to come, many
burst into tears. The people seemed ready to cast
themselves at our feet as we preached Christ to
them. It was a memorable night, the issues of
which are with the Lord. Thus we learned that
Satan rages when his kingdom shakes and his victims are about to escape.

One night at the fair in Dundee a young man bent
on folly stopped for a little to hear the preaching.
Stung by the truth, and angry lest he should lose

his pleasures, he tore himself away, and rushed into the next street, saying, "Now I've got rid of them." Scarcely had he turned the corner, however, when he came upon another preacher, was arrested, and brought to the Saviour. A policeman on his rounds stood for a moment to hear "what in all the world those preachers could have to say in the fair," when suddenly a ray of light shot through the darkness, and he too was converted. Two young women, bent on pleasure, stopped as they pressed through the crowd to hear the singing of the hymn—

"O happy day that fixed my choice
On Thee, my Saviour and my God!
Well may this glowing heart rejoice,
And tell its raptures all abroad."

"Come away," said the one to the other; "we'll be too late." "I dare na gang," was the reply.

They strove, and parted; the one going to the pleasures of death, the other remaining to seek the protection of Jesus, and to join the society of His people.

A poor woman, a drunkard's wife, steeped in poverty and clothed in rags, was coming along the street with a babe in her arms. Happiness had forsaken her long ago; desperate struggles with want made her weary of life; hope, that most patient of angels, had disappeared in the clouds; and all her days and nights seemed but steps to deeper woe. A voice strange to her fell upon her ear. The one utterance that fell like dew upon her weary heart

was the word of the Lord—"Come unto Me, all ye
that labor and are heavy laden, and I will give you
rest." She stood still upon the pavement, far off
from the preacher; and as she listened, the voice
seemed to come nearer and nearer to the heart.
"Rest!" she said to herself, as the preacher went
on to explain rest in the Lord Jesus—"rest! that is
what I want." Jesus heard the groaning of that
oppressed spirit, and came to her relief. There and
then she believed on Christ; there and then she entered on the rest of the Gospel. Peace and joy, like
birds of Paradise, began to sing in her soul. She
carried the blessing home, and the light that filled
that mother's heart illuminated the drunkard's house,
and transformed it into a Bethel. Years have passed;
she still hearkens to Jesus, and still hears Him saying, "Come unto Me, and rest."

> "I hear the voice of Jesus say,
>   'Come unto Me, and rest;
> Lay down, thou weary one, lay down
> Thy head upon my breast.'
>
> "I came to Jesus as I was,
>   Weary, and worn, and sad;
> I found in Him a resting-place,
> And He has made me glad."

These are a few instances out of many; the day
alone will declare all the results. To the wise and
prudent the preachers might appear to be fools; but
the Gospel was preached to the poor, evil was prevented, good was done, souls were saved, and God

was glorified. From strange quarters, and in ways too strange to find an explanation in the philosophy of the rigidly systematic Christian, God gathers his elect. It does seem meet, that from amidst those scenes where Satan has his seat, and those on-goings where the destroyer of souls enjoys his proudest triumphs, the Redeemer should gather the trophies of his matchless grace. When in glory the ransomed shall tell each his strange story of a Saviour's love; and one shall say, " He found me in the nursery;" and another, " He found me in the school;" while others tell how they were found in the house of prayer, the sick bed, the workshop, or the field; one will say, " He found me mad upon my idols, amidst the revels of the fair—there He cast the charm of his love around me, and thence He drew me to Himself."

Several of the Christian helpers in this work have gone to be with the Lord. Mr. Johnstone, pastor of a Methodist Church, fell like a true soldier at his post, and passed from the hallowed services of the Lord's day on earth to the joys of the everlasting Sabbath in heaven. He was mighty in prayer, and it was the practice of our evangelist to ask at the commencement of his meetings, " Is Johnstone here to pray?" Robert Annan, the stoutest of street-preachers, is also at his rest. Dan Collison, a young man of remarkable faith, said one night as he left the fair, " I am gaun' hame to tell my Faither," meaning that he was going to spend the midnight hour in prayer. In a few hours afterwards he reached the Father's house of many mansions. When charged, like Paul, with madness, Dan was wont to say, "If I'm mad, I'll get heaven for an asylum." "The Lucknow Hero," a Christian soldier of gigantic stature, who had fought in the Indian mutiny, used to assist in these services by marching in front to clear the way. He could not preach, but he could help in his own way. Drawing himself up to his full height between the preachers and their opponents, he seemed to say, "If you dare meddle with these men, you see what you have to encounter." He also has received the palm of victory. Mr. Nairn, merchant, an unwearied helper in the work of the Lord, is also numbered with those who have crossed the flood. Amidst the ravings of the fever that closed his earthly career, he spoke only of the Saviour whom he loved. Others, whose chief part was not to speak or act, but to watch and pray, we have accompanied to the border-land, and have seen them depart, leaning on the arm of their Redeemer.

Dr. W. P. Mackay, pastor of the Presbyterian Church, Hull, who accompanied Mr. Matheson to the feeing markets and assisted in the work, writes as follows: "Among the very first times I spoke with him was at a railway station. We had been speaking of entire consecration to the Lord, and the noble work of preaching Christ and getting souls saved. My mind was not very clear as to my own

17

path. I was seeking light as to my future course
—whether I should give myself entirely up to preach
the Gospel or enter a professional course. Many
young men are similarly placed, and often require
an encouraging word when all around seems doubtful or dark. We had to go in different directions,
He crossed over to the other side of the platform,
and his last words before our trains came up were
in his manly accents, 'Go and read George Muller,
of Ashley Down.' I had never heard the name before, but I put it down in my memory. On the first
opportunity I read his history, and for the first
time in my life saw the meaning of practical every-
day faith. I had known about faith to save my soul,
but this opened up quite a new aspect of God's
glorious truth.

"Time wore on. I was often in his company,
and always felt in his presence, There is a man in
real earnest, and his one word is 'Eternity.' He
used to say to me, 'Stick by what God has blessed
to your own soul. Every evangelist has a something that God has given him as a great reality,
and God uses the evangelist to carry home that
truth to do his own work. One, for instance, has
this word, *God is love;* another is used to impress
on his audience, *It is written;* a third has to preach
Oneness with Christ; and a fourth, *Believe and live;*
and so on, just as God has burned the truth into
their own souls.' 'Well, Duncan,' I said, 'What is
yours?' 'Ah mine is plain, *Death, Judgment, and*

Eternity; and by God's grace I mean to hold by it.'
And so he did.

"Well do I remember my first introduction to
the feeing market campaign under his guidance.
It was in May, 1862. On the 13th we went to
Ellon, in Aberdeenshire. Here, supported by a
number of earnest pastors, we preached till night-
fall the words of eternal life, Duncan's voice reaching well over the whole fair in an earnestness all his
own. Next day we went to Potarch market, up Dee-
side, and there we met with strong opposition. A
goodly number of laborers, pastors, and evangelists
—several of whom, as Major Gibson and Colonel
Ramsay, are now with the Lord—drove down to the
fair. This was about as hard a battle-field as we
were on in all the campaign. We had had much
prayer about it, but the opposition, or rather indifference, was very marked. We could hardly get a
dozen at a time to listen. But Duncan was determined they should hear. 'Come,' said he, 'let us
blow the rams' horns outside the city.' We all went
to the outskirts of the crowd, and knelt round in a
circle, and began to pray to God, as we felt we had
no power with men. Many of the men inflamed
with drink came round and looked at the rare spectacle. There were more than a dozen uncovered
heads of kneeling men, who were entreating God
to have mercy on those who had no mercy on themselves. As the spare gray locks of several of the
veterans waved in the summer breeze, and the tones

of entreaty went up to the throne, there was something that seemed calculated to calm the wildest opposer; but Satan appeared let loose. They danced, and whooped, and yelled round the circle of prayer like so many fiends. One coarse fellow deliberately came beside Major Gibson and spat in his face while he was praying. The gallant soldier merely took out his handkerchief, wiped his face, and prayed for the poor sinner. We rose from our knees. 'Now,' said Duncan, 'let us again unfurl the banner,' and turning to me, he said, 'Strike up "Rest for the weary," and let us in to the centre of the camp.' Then we got an audience indeed, and the word seemed to be with power. I spoke at least to two who were stricken with great conviction of sin. Duncan would not stop preaching even when the horses were being yoked to drive us from the fair, but from the conveyance preached, exhorted, and entreated sinners to come to Christ.

On Friday, the 16th, we went to Insch, where there seemed many attentive hearers, several of those who had been converted under Duncan and other laborers rallying round us. On the Monday following we were at Alford, where constant preaching went on all day, many dear brethren from Aberdeen and elsewhere taking part. I have letters in my possession from those who profess to have been benefited for eternity from this day's work, besides having seen several who had been brought to the truth at former preachings there. On Wednesday

we went on to Huntly, where such wonderful
things had been seen in years gone by, when
Duncan, Radcliffe, and others, gathered by the
Duchess of Gordon, were so owned of God in the
market. Here, assisted by other brethren, the Gospel was proclaimed, and there were many attentive listeners.

"On the following Friday we went to Elgin. In
the train, as Duncan and I took our seats, a man
sat down beside us, whom we recognized as a very
prominent Cheap John in the fairs, and who we
supposed was going to Elgin. He recognized us
also, and said, in a very hoarse voice, 'Are you going to Elgin?' 'Yes,' said Duncan. 'Like ourselves,
you seem to be very hoarse; here is a lozenge for
you. But, man, if you would use that splendid
voice of yours in the service of our Master instead
of the service of Satan, it would be worth living
for.' He was about the smartest in the whole of
the markets, and he smiled at us as he took out a
handful of pound notes and shook them before us,
saying, 'Ay, but you could not bring me that with
your preaching.' 'No,' said Duncan; 'but what
shall it profit you, if you gain the whole world, and
lose your soul? Ah, Jack, perhaps you had a praying mother, who took you to her side as she knelt
and taught you "Our Father," and who prayed that
she might meet you in heaven. Shall we not see
you preaching in the markets yet? When God
converts you, send for me, and I'll join you, wher-

ever it is.' The poor fellow seemed quite solemnized, and took it all in the spirit in which it was
given; but the Searcher of hearts knows if Duncan's
desire was realized.

"A week after this we went to a fair in the south,
upwards of a hundred miles from where we parted
with Jack, and no sooner had we taken our stand
than the first man we saw was our railway friend.
He immediately recognized us. He had his large
hand-bell ready to begin operations, when Duncan
said, 'Let us pray.' The man stopped his bell,
bowed his head until the prayer was done, and
then began to scatter coppers to draw a crowd.
Coppers were, of course, more attractive than the
Gospel of eternal life, and so he gathered the large
crowd, and we the small; but Jack, noticing this,
and, as if not to interfere with our work, wheeled
his platform away to the furthest end of the fair,
and left us undisturbed.

"Duncan had a rare gift of getting respect from
even the unconverted by his manly, open-faced
manner. The lame sailors, with their shipwreck
picture before them, and other itinerant beggars,
lifted their hats to him as he gave them a word of
warning and Gospel.

"From Elgin we went to Turiff, and met with
considerable opposition, but also considerable attention to the Gospel preached. In private we had a
meeting on our knees here, that brought us so
closely into the presence of the Master, and showed

us the worthlessness of all flesh, that it will never be forgotten by many of us.

"These scenes happened eight years ago, and it is difficult to recall particulars; but many will have to thank God through eternity for having raised up Duncan Matheson, who with living voice and his *Special Herald* carried salvation home to their souls. It is a noble and fruitful work. One man came to us saying, 'I at least hear the Gospel once a year, and that is at the fair.' Another said, rather from sarcasm than any thing else, 'Your sermons here seem to have nothing in them but Christ. It seems to me that you can speak of nothing else but Christ —Christ from beginning to end. Ye let us hear more about Christ than we get in a whole year.'

"Duncan used often to say, 'Keep the Word at them;' and when he could scarcely be heard in a continued discourse he launched out short, pithy, telling texts of Scripture. As a man would be pushing his merchandise, he would sound in the ears of buyer and seller, who were thinking of profits, 'What shall a man give in exchange for his soul?' He would come in front of a man being weighed for a penny, and in his solemn tones and earnest manner, making the man tremble all over, he would say, 'Thou art weighed in the balances, and art found wanting.'

"Many other places we visited in company during the happy years I had the privilege to labor with him; but I have no doubt you have fuller in-

formation than I can give. His warfare was no easy
warfare. He never thought of rest. 'Rest!' said
he, 'no, I can't. Eternity! eternity! I'll rest there;
and you can gather the northern converts, and over
my grave sing, " *Rest for the weary.*"' Often he got
the opposite of a kind reception, of course, as did his
Master. At one place we were going to get our tea
at a temperance hotel. A woman came after us,
saying, 'You shall not go there as long as I have a
house;' and she did give us a hearty reception. He
was too independent of men's smiles or frowns to be
universally acceptable. He rejoiced to do God's
work in God's way. The water of life flows as a
river, not as a canal; and many men quench the
Spirit by determining the exact shape, depth, and
width of the canal, instead of taking the winding,
irregular river as God sends it.

"The life of Duncan Matheson may well stir us
all up to live more in the light of eternity, working
to please but One, working to gather souls to that
glorious One, and build them up in the knowledge
of Him who is the light of eternity."

For two or three years—from 1862 to 1865—there
was a slight and natural reaction in many places
where a real work of grace has been wrought. This
lull was not pleasant, but it was profitable. Heaps
of stones having been gathered from the quarry, the
work of selection and rejection, polishing and building, had to be carried on. Reaping, with its sun-

shine and its songs, is delightful work; but after it comes the work of the barn, with its din, its dust, and its stern process of separating the chaff from the wheat. At the same time new fields were opening to the indefatigable evangelist; slumbering communities here and there were moved by the voice of the awakening Spirit. During those years his labors were without ceasing. "We must not lower the standard" was his constant saying. If the field was ever widening, his power for work seemed to grow in equal measure. Wherever a religious interest was awakening he hastened to render help. Where no work was wrought and no testimony raised, true captain of the forlorn hope as he was, thither he bent his steps, and there to use his own martial style, he "unfurled the banner." He was seldom at home. One evening, before a meeting, he said to his wife, "Mary, this is a royal night with you. How long is it since you took tea with me on a Sabbath evening?" "Just three times the last three years," was her reply. Solemnly and tenderly he said, "There will be plenty of opportunity in eternity to speak together." At another time he said, "Wife and children must be nailed to the cross; I must go and preach the Gospel."

In carrying on the work he was opposed on various grounds. A minister of the Gospel in a certain town was accustomed to offer prayer for a revival of religion. The great awakening in America took place; but it was "too American," and the minister went on praying as before. The work of grace in Ireland followed; but it was "too Irish," and he went on praying as before. Remarkable movements occurred in various parts of Scotland; but it was "wild-fire, and he would have none of it." The Spirit of God began to work in his own town, very much through the instrumentality of our evangelist; but in the opinion of the minister the instruments were contemptible, and the whole thing of doubtful tendency, and he now began to pray for a *true* revival. At length members of his own congregation were converted under the preaching of Mr. Matheson, who said to them, "Go and tell your minister what the Lord has done for your souls; it will cheer his heart, and do him good." They went; some to ask direction, and some to acknowledge grace received. The minister was angry. Next Sabbath he said it was all excitement and delusion, and he stamped with his foot as if he would stamp out the spiritual rinderpest. The excitement and delusion seemed to be all his own. His prayer had been answered; but he would not accept the answer in God's way. The work of grace stood before him, but he knew it not. Jesus came to his own, but his own received Him not, because his visage was so marred. The Holy Spirit came to the minister, but the minister disowned and rejected Him because He came in a garb of humiliation offensive to human pride. A work of grace without a flaw must be an impossibility so long as God is pleased to work by means

of imperfect tools on the corrupt material of human
hearts and lives. The minister would accept no revival but one according to his own ideal. What a
pity that ministers should go a-dreaming when the
world is perishing!

Some opposed the work because they had no scruples of conscience, and others because they had too
many. Certain religious people have more scruples
in their conscience than conscience in their scruples.
To those who in effect said, "Sermons, sermons are
our business," his reply was, "Souls, souls are mine."
His constant cry, "Eternity! eternity! souls are perishing!" was a cutting rebuke to mere sermon-mak-
ers and sermon-hearers. He did not practise trum-
pet-blowing for a bit of bread. His was not the soft
serenading of lovers, but the sounding of shrill battle
blasts. He refused to say, "Peace! peace!" when he
ought to cry, "Fire! fire!" To gratify carnal tastes,
he would not put the devil's butter on God's bread.
In this way he offended both the lullaby players and
the lullaby lovers. Moreover, his zeal sometimes carried him beyond the bounds of prudence; and Mr.
Perfectly Small—the same who is denounced in an
ancient prophet for making a man an offender for a
word—could not tolerate the evangelist on account
of his blunders. Does he never blunder himself?
No; no more than a periwinkle blunders. Small,
heartless men do not usually blunder so much as
men of much feeling and soul. Heartless people
keep to the arithmetic of every thing. But love,

zeal, courage, feeling, heart, soul, rise above vulgar-fraction rules of mere carnal policy. Some men can gauge the tear of penitence, and weigh as in a balance the breath of a dying saint. There is a crow's nest in the great oak; therefore, hew down the tree. There is a cobweb in a cornice; rase the temple to its foundation. The watch-dog barks out of season; slay him. There is a crook in the furrow; hang the ploughman. Let a man live a holy life; let him toil for the good of others till life is shortened by his self-denying labors; and let the broad seal of heaven be stamped upon his work; yet one word amiss shall, in the estimate of some, outweigh the whole. Shall a single particle of dust outweigh and render of no value a hundred talents of fine gold? Well, shall the warrior stop the battle because the grasshopper is chirping? I trow not. So this soldier of the cross went on.

At this time a handsome offer was made him by the Presbyterian Church in New Zealand. They proposed to ordain him as their first missionary, with the status of a minister in the Presbytery, and offered him a suitable salary. This offer he declined. Ordination by the laying on of the hands of the Presbytery he did not despise; and although to a high spirited-man, such as he in the best sense was, with an increasing family, a stated income was to be preferred to his uncertain and precarious mode of living, with its inevitable humiliations, he could not leave his own country, where his labors were so much blessed, and over whose spiritual necessities his patriotic and Christian spirit brooded with a singular love. "So long as God is blessing my labors here in the conversion of sinners," he said, "I cannot on any account go away."

During the rest of his active ministry his work, both in its character and results, was very much of a piece. A few facts, therefore, in illustration will suffice. To gather the people in obscure and out of the way places, he procured a hand-bell, which he was not ashamed to ring up and down the streets, announcing to the astonished inhabitants that he, the bell-ringer, was going to preach at the cross or market-place. Curiosity brought many to hear him; and frequently those most unlikely, in man's estimate, to come under the power of the Gospel were awakened and saved. The bell-ringing and similar devices he felt to be a humiliation, and he sometimes said, "I never knew I had so little grace till I began to do that."

One summer evening the quiet little mining village of Stevenston, in Ayrshire, is startled from its centre to its circumference by a strange voice, whose loud sonorous tones waken the echoes and compel men to ask, What is this? The people rush to their doors; a hundred windows are thrown open, and the heads of eager listeners are thrust out. Even the public-house is emptied of the drunkards, who come out in stark amazement. The stranger, like Jonah in Nineveh, has come no one knows whence.

He stands alone, calm, bold, and solemn, as if he had just come out of eternity. With prophet-like authority, he cries, "Prepare to meet thy God!" As night falls, the voice waxes louder and louder, and many of those rough miners tremble. The service closes with an appeal to the great I Am, and the people somehow feel they are in the presence of God as they have never been. The preacher then takes his way along the street, and improves the awakening interest by speaking of Christ and eternity to every man, woman, and child, as they stand at their doors. Coming to the public-house, he goes up and says with great tenderness, "Ah, men, prepare to meet your God!" Words cannot describe the feelings of the villagers that night. The whole affair is so novel, so unexpected, so conscience-moving. It was as if God had suddenly come to the village, as He was then coming to many a village in the land. What was too little considered, He was come not to stay but to pass on.

In another mining village, known to the writer, he was violently opposed by a band of infidel mockers, who came to the meetings for the purpose of turning the evangelist and the work into ridicule. For a time, it seemed as if they should carry every thing their own way. Strong in the hardness of their hearts and their unholy league, they laughed and jeered. The evangelist marked their conduct, and having offered prayer for their conversion, drew his bow at a venture. One of the scoffers was arrested and turned to Christ. Henceforth he separated himself from his companions, who only seemed to grow more profane. Next night they returned to the meeting to scoff. Again one of those high-handed sinners was prostrated by grace, and the mocker began to pray. Again and again was this advanced guard of Satan thinned by the sword of the Spirit, till at length only one remained, and he the worst of all. It seemed as if he would hold out. At last, however, the thought took possession of him, "Am I to be left to go to hell alone?" That led to his conversion. This triumph of grace made a profound impression on the unconverted people of the district, and the work of God made remarkable progress at that time, the fruits of which are strikingly apparent at the present day.

He found his way into places where gates were barred against all evangelistic effort. " You need not attempt to go there," said his friends, speaking of a certain country town in the north. "The ministers have told the people that the revival is a delusion; nobody wants you, and you will get none to hear you." Not discouraged by the failure of attempts made by others, he resolved to go. After praying for a blessing, he went, hired a hall for a week, announced his meetings, and commenced at the appointed hour. Not a soul appeared: undisputed victory seemed to remain with spiritual apathy. Most men would have looked on the empty hall as an intimation of the will of God to depart and seek a more promising field; but our evangelist opened his book, and saying, " Let us praise God," sang one of David's psalms, with somewhat of David's spirit. Thereafter he said, " Let us pray," and proceeded to pray aloud, as if all the town were there. As the prayer was closing, a little boy dropped in, and sat down with all a child's wonder and simplicity. The Word was read, the text announced, and the sermon preached, the great voice ringing and reverberating strangely in the empty hall. Ere the close, two or three men came stealing in from sheer curiosity, to see "a man preaching to nobody," and sat as near the door as they could. The service ended, and the preacher announced that having made an engagement with the great God to meet Him for prayer, praise, and preaching of his Gospel in that hall on every night of the week, he would be there, God helping him, at the same hour on the following evening, come what might, come who may. Next night more came from curiosity, and ere the week closed the hall was crowded by an attentive, and in some instances awakened audience. Faith triumphed. Bolts and bars of triple steel gave way before the invisible artillery of believing prayer. Our evangelist once more realized our Saviour's words—"All things are possible to him that believeth."

In another part of the country, the name of which I forbear to mention, an extraordinary power attended the word one night. The distress of the

awakened was exceeding great, and the individual
who presided at the meeting, becoming alarmed, ordered the people to retire to their own homes. It
seemed a hard case for those weeping inquirers to
be sent away without an opportunity being afforded
them of stating their difficulties and hearing an answer to the great question then and there. The
meeting-house was cleared, and as the key turned
heavily in the lock, these unsophisticated children
of the soil stood about the door and wept. "Go
home," it was said to them. "Go home!" they exclaimed. "We are going down to hell; and what
are we to do?" Seizing the arm of the evangelist
and his companion, they begged them as servants
of Jesus Christ not to leave them. That night the
woods resounded with their cries to God for mercy
as they went away.

Duncan's labors were much blessed at Hillhead, a
mining district near Glasgow, where there was a
considerable movement in 1865. This place has
been singularly favored of the Lord. Here that
Christ-like missionary, David Sandeman, preached
- and prayed and wept for souls. Sometimes he tar-
ried at the throne of grace all night, and towards
dawn he could be heard saying, "The whole district,
Lord—the whole district! I cannot ask less." "He
made every body love him," say the people still.
Here too James Allen, who, like David Sandeman,
went to an early rest with Jesus, preached with
Baptist-like solemnity and power. Of him the peo-

18

ple say, "He brocht eternity doon about us." It was
Matheson's privilege largely to reap what these
faithful men and other earnest laborers still living
had sown in the unpromising soil of Hillhead.
Night after night he continued the services there
amidst striking displays of divine grace. At the
close of the meetings, often near the hour of midnight, when he tore himself away from the group of
men in the agony of conviction, he trudged his
weary way for miles through the deep snow to the
neighboring city of Glasgow, where necessity compelled him to lodge. Next night, however, invariably found him back at his loved work as cheery
as ever.

His circuit was now a very extensive one. At one
time—July, 1864—we find him preaching at Dover,
where several officers of the army are converted, and
ere the month is out he is in the extreme north laboring amongst the Highlanders at the herring-fishing
at Wick. Now he is raising his voice on Glasgow
Green, where during the last ten or twelve years
many a soul has been saved; by and by he is rang-
ing the lonely glens of Sutherland in search of the
lost sheep. Here the proclamation of free grace is
blessed. "I have heard that Mr. Matheson was riding very high, that he was preaching *assurance* to
the people of ——," said a pastor, who seemed to
think that the Christian is safe only under the
shadow of Doubting Castle. "Is it not a matter
about which we should be sure?" was the reply.

"Oh, you women!" was all the good man had to say in defence of his system of ultra-Calvinistic exclusiveness.

In 1856, when lying at the point of death on the scene of his exhausting labors among the soldiers in the East, he had asked from his God ten years more of life to preach the Gospel and win souls. He was now entering the tenth and last year; and as if conscious that his more active career was about to close, he inserted in a newspaper the following address:

1866.

NEW YEAR'S ADDRESS.

DEAR READER: The sand-glass is running out. Another year is *gone!* Three hundred and sixty-five days past! How silently—yet how quickly again—has grain after grain, particle after particle, hour after hour, dropped in this glass. Deathless hours they are; uncounted, unnoted, and forgotten it may be by man, but every falling grain has been noted by God. The busy pen of Heaven has been marking every moment. Ask thyself the searching question, "Has it been with me a *happy* year? It has brought me nearer Eternity; but has it brought me nearer God? Does it find me better fitted for Heaven, with more of the *pilgrim spirit* than I had when the year began!"

What a time for serious thought! Another new year summons thee to a Pisgah-Mount—from the top of one of life's memorable eminences solemnly to review time past—consider time present—and prepare for time to come. Cast, then, thine eye on the past year's journey, and how full of impressive recollection is the retrospect!

God has been dealing with *thee* individually, and speaking to thee surely, in language not to be misunderstood.

Hearest thou not the rustling wings of the Angel of Death? Have not his arrows been flying fast and thick, and thousands made his victims? Look back! Seest thou that crowd of fresh-made graves?—they are silent preachers to *thee!* and this is their silent text and sermon, "*be ye also ready.*"

Many of those who slumber underneath these sods were cut down without a note of preparation. One was busied in the market-place; the Angel of Judgment met him *there*, and before evening he was DEAD! Another was seated at his fireside, planning bright thoughts and schemes for the future—*he never saw the morrow's sun.* Another was in company, loud in godless merriment, and breathing out his blasphemies—a few hours more, and he was arraigned at *the bar of God!* Another flung himself prayerless on his nightly pillow—next morning he awoke—but it was—in ETERNITY!

And, reader, has He spared *thee?* What! cut down others and left *thee* to count in the review of a past year—fig-tree after fig-tree blighted and fallen—and yet *thyself*, the most "barren" of all—a fruitless cumberer—still "*spared!*"

Canst thou calculate on another year? Let these green graves answer. *Another* year? Thine own grave may be among the number of these silent preachers on another anniversary. Who can tell but the summons may even now be on the wing, "Get thee up and die!" *Thou* mayest this time next year be reading to others the solemn lesson now read to thyself, "The race is not to the swift, nor the battle to the strong."

Dear reader, if this be a *possible* thing, take one look *forward.* If the arrow of death were indeed during this coming year to mark *thee* out, how would it fare with thee? Couldst thou say with exulting Paul, when he had the prospect of death before him, "I am NOW ready?" (2 Tim. iv. 6.) Are you at peace with God? Are you resting your eternal

all on his dear Son? Are you in that blessed state of holy
weanedness from *this* world, and holy preparedness for
another and a better, that "living or dying" you can say
and feel that "you are Christ's"?

Would the angel summons, "Behold! the Bridegroom
cometh," find you exclaiming in joyous rapture, "Even so!
come Lord Jesus! come quickly"? Would you be ready
to pass from a death full of hope to a judgment divested of
all terror—a God reconciled—an immortality of endless
glory? These are solemn things and solemn thoughts!
Answer them on thy knees—with the solemnities of the
past year *behind* thee—an unseen God *above* thee—a great
eternity *before* thee. Answer them *speedily!*

And as ye begin to descend the mount and commence the
journey of a new year, let the feeble voice of the old one
whisper its dying accents in thine ear, "Seek ye the Lord
while He may be found: call ye upon Him *while* He is near;"
for He who testifieth these things saith, "*Behold I come
quickly!*"

> "Time is earnest, passing by;
> Death is earnest, drawing nigh:
> Sinner, wilt thou trifling be?
> Time and death appeal to thee!
> Christ is earnest, bids thee 'Come;'
> Paid for man a priceless sum!
> Wilt thou spurn the Saviour's love
> Pleading with thee from above?"

INSERTED BY D. MATHESON.

Perth, Jan. 1, 1866.

Early in the year we find him in the north-west
Highlands, whence he writes:

"Balmacara House, Lochalsh, January 5th, 1866.
I am here! What a place of beauty, yet of tempest
and storm! I left Dingwall yesterday in an open gig,

and came on here through a range of mountains covered all the way with snow. Now and then it was grand going along lake sides and then down mountain steeps. It was very cold, and we had at the end of our journey very heavy showers. I am none the worse. I think we came sixty-five miles in an open gig. When I reached, the thunder was rolling and lightning flashing. The rain fell in torrents. In summer it must be a glorious place. The people are scattered, and my work is laid out for next week. May the Lord guide! Captain O——, his wife, her sister, and daughter, are here. They are kind to me. He is a good, good man. My work will not be amongst large companies, for few understand English. Pray that the Lord may bless my efforts. I have a meeting to-night, and to-morrow, Sabbath, here.

"Balmacara House, January 8th. Yesterday Mr. Colville joined us. We drove to church—a most uncomfortable one. No plaster, no roof—only the bare boards, no flooring. The minister is a good man. It was a good sermon. We drove back, singing all the way till the very hills rang again. At five we dined, and at seven we met in a shed. It was packed with people, some having come six or eight miles. I preached first, and then Mr. Colville. The people were intensely interested, and about twenty waited after the meeting. At ten o'clock we left. We meet there to-night again. It is a poor, poor country, but very beautiful to look upon.

You see nothing but green mountains and mountains covered with snow. I am to be very busy. I wish you were here. I always like you to see any thing that is grand.

"January 9th. We are working away. The people seem very dead. It is a lovely spot; but how sad to see people going down to hell unmoved! I feel deeply for the people, but as yet have no power. . . . Oh for a blessing! Life is ebbing fast away. Eternity is near. Pray for me.

"January 10th. At 4 P.M. yesterday we started with the carriage over the hills. It was a grand drive. Now and then we had to come out and walk, as the hills were so steep. Coming to a ferry, we crossed, singing all the way in the boat. In a village on the other side we got a school, and held a meeting, Mr. C—— and Captain O—— with me. I preached; and, blessed be God, I had great freedom and power. The Lord helped me. I was happy in my soul. Mr. C—— followed. In the second meeting we saw awakened souls.

"January 13th. I have to go some six miles over the hills to Plockton, the place of my father's birth. I have seen some poor Highland girls here. It would be a good thing to get places for them; they are so faithful and trustworthy. Poor things, I feel for them. In the snow many of them have no shoes. I am glad I am come to this place. I have seen much of the country and people. It shows me the value of my work among the Highlanders." The

work to which he here refers was chiefly the religious books which he was getting translated into
Gaelic, and circulated freely, or sold at a mere nominal price, throughout the Highlands.

In course of the summer we find him in Nairn,
Inverness, Ross, Sutherland, and Caithness. Returning south, he preaches at the fair in Glasgow;
and from that city he proceeds to Laurencekirk,
Bervie, Kirriemuir, and other places in the eastern
and central counties.

On Aug. 4th he went to Forfar, whence he writes:
"I have only fifteen minutes, passing through. We
had good meetings last night, open-air and indoors.
I hope God blessed the word; but the place is hard,
and the people sadly indifferent. The whole land
seems at ease. Few are seeking God; few are car-
ing for God. I often feel it deeply. Cholera is
not apparently decreasing. The voice is loud and
solemn. Nothing, however, will do but the Holy
Ghost.

For Forfar he had often prayed. Frequently, as
he passed it by rail, he raised his voice in prayer
for the salvation of its people. "When I die," he
said, "you will find Forfar written on my heart."
"If God would only bless Forfar," he said, character-
istically, "I would be content to stand and hold Har-
rison Ord's hat while he preached." His prayers
were now to be answered, and his longings in
measure gratified. Early in September he went to
Forfar, took lodgings, obtained the use of a school-

room for his meetings, and commenced in the open
air and within doors. For paying the necessary expenses means were liberally furnished by Christian
gentlemen whose sole interest in this town was the
salvation of the lost.

"Forfar, Monday, September 10th, 1866. Praise
the Lord, He has begun his work. We commenced
at seven on the street on Saturday. A great crowd
gathered round. They listened breathlessly. It was
a blessed meeting. I have seldom seen such a solemn meeting on the streets. At eight we went to
the school. A good company were present. At close
some waited in anxiety to be spoken with. We did
not leave till ten.

"Yesterday Hopkins, Boswell and I went through
the streets giving tracts and speaking. We had solemn talk with the people. At six we met on the
green. About one thousand were present. God
helped us all wondrously. He gave a very solemn
address. The people hung on our lips. We then
went to church. About four hundred came. It was
a very solemn meeting. Rarely did I ever feel such
power at a meeting. About a hundred remained
to the second meeting. Some ten or twelve were
really anxious. We could hardly get the church
cleared. Mr. C——, who had been preaching in a
village, came and had a meeting for the anxious in
the street. Some one asked them in. He had to
speak till eleven o'clock. Some evidently found the
Lord. Is it not blessed? I praise the Lord. The

Lord send floods. It is sweet to see such fruit at first.

"September 13th. What a night we had last night. I shall never forget it. We met at one o'clock, and spoke in a small street; at seven H. Ord at the Cross, and Hopkins and I took another place. We then collected all into a school. It was packed. At close, going out, they laughed, swore, and mocked. Within we spoke to anxious souls, a few; and outside I tried to control the rabble. Oh, how obscene they were! It seemed as if the devil had entered into them. At ten o'clock we could hardly get the gate shut. We go to Mr. M'Phail's church to-night, as the school is too small. This is a fearful place. No tongue can tell its sin. I do pray that God may convert many. Nothing is too hard for Him.

"September 14th. The work goes on. God will work here yet, I do believe, wondrously. We wait, we long, we pray.

"September 18th. We had good meetings last night. We only want more power—more power from on high. A breath would fan much that is now smouldering into a flame. We had some anxious ones last night. Pray for me, and very specially for Forfar. The time is short. It is passing away. It will soon be done. Some thirty attend our daily prayer-meeting at noon.

"October 3d. We had a blessed meeting last night. I was very ill yesterday, but to-day am quite well. It was a very solemn meeting, and several were brought to peace at close. One, a farmer's daughter, was a very decided case. All yesterday I had much freedom. The work here is truly a very decided one. We find every night some new cases. It is a great thing to get something to cheer. Oh, rejoice in the blessing descending! We have trial, but we have many blessings. We shall have a kingdom yet and a crown of glory.

"October 15th. We had a very remarkable night at the Cross on Saturday. About one thousand came to hear. We went to the school at eight o'clock. Last night (Sabbath) was a great night in the church—great every way. I had much freedom. Truly the Lord spoke through me. *I never left a place with such regret, never in twenty years.* The work seems only beginning."

In November he went north to the feeing markets, and on his return visited Forfar, to find precious and abundant fruits of his trying labors there. The end of the year found him at home, making preparations for an evangelistic journey to the Orkneys.

CHAPTER VIII.

HIS MANNER OF LIVING AND MODE OF WORKING.

During the last years of his active life our evangelist prosecuted his work with unflagging zeal. He never rested save when he slept. He was often weary; but the more he was spent in the service of Jesus, the more he loved the work. Indecision never brought him to a stand-still. The silken cords of sloth never detained him. Every minute was an opportunity, and every opportunity was seized with an almost stern promptitude. Through the grace given him he could say, " I do not know that ten minutes of my life ever pass without thinking of the salvation of souls." His motto was, " Whatsoever thy hand findeth to do, do it with thy might; for there is no work, nor device, nor knowledge, nor wisdom, in the grave whither thou goest." Often, when exhausted and sick, did he say, " Ah, I know the deep meaning of those words, 'There remaineth therefore a rest to the people of God;'" and the hope of that rest roused him, weary and ill though he was, to fresh efforts in the work of the Lord. Let us see how he spent his days.

The first part of the morning was given to prayer and reading the Word. Thus he refreshed his own spirit, and found a portion for others. To Christians he happened to meet he was wont to say, " Here is a sweet morsel for you—I have been rolling it like candy-sugar in my mouth all the day." The portions of Scripture in which he found comfort were sometimes such as would not readily occur to others. For example, he would say, "I cannot tell you how much comfort I have found in this word, 'If the righteous *scarcely* be saved.' I find it so hard for me to be saved that I often fear I will never get into the kingdom; but then when I read that those who are saved are saved with difficulty, with just such a struggle as I have, I feel encouraged."

In the earlier years of his course he spent part of the morning in sketching or writing fully out his sermons and addresses. A specimen of his outlines may be given:

FOLLOWING AFAR OFF.

"But Peter followed Him afar off."—MATT. xxvi. 58.

I. Point out those that follow Christ afar off. 1. Those who have some love, but grace is weak. 2. Those who are ashamed to confess Christ before men. 3. Those who walk inconsistently. 4. Those who do not heartily promote Christ's cause.

II. The causes of following Christ afar off. 1. Weakness of faith. 2. Fear of man. 3. Attachment to earthly things. 4. Self-confidence.

III. The sin and danger of following Christ afar off. 1. It is not honorable. 2. It is not reasonable. 3. It is not comfortable. 4. It is not safe.

Part of his time was daily occupied in letter-writ-

ing. A benighted soul needs direction, a young convert needs warning, a persecuted Christian needs
encouragement, a backslider needs healing, a poor
saint needs money, a fellow-laborer needs succor:
short, incisive, business-like notes winged with light
are quickly on their way. In one letter he pleads
the case of a neglected and poverty-stricken sufferer
whom he has discovered in some out of the way
hovel. In another he offers to find means for building a bridge over a Highland stream far away in
the north, and as he urges the prosecution of the
work with the greatest earnestness, you would fancy, if you did not know the man, that the erection
was a matter of pecuniary interest to him, instead
of being, as it was, an affair of pure benevolence.
In all his letters he seems to breathe the air of eternity. "Oh, how near eternity seems!" is his constant exclamation. Death, judgment, heaven, and
hell are realities never lost sight of; and in the fore-
front of every epistle, however brief, stands the name
of the Master, too dear to be ever forgotten by the
fond disciple—JESUS CHRIST, Saviour of sinners. It
is not too much to say that by his letters, so prompt,
wise, affectionate, full of the Spirit and of eternity,
he was instrumental in conveying light and comfort
to thousands.

His publications, and the circulation of books and
tracts, formed part of his daily care and work, both
at home and in his evangelistic journeys. Whenever or wherever you met him, you found him bring-

ing out or putting into circulation some fresh tract
or book. He studied the signs of the times. None
knew better than he the tastes of his countrymen
and the wants of the day. For instance, he brought
out a cheap edition of Hoge's "Blind Bartimeus," and
got it circulated in many thousands during the widespread awakening of 1859-61. He took the pains,
and risk too, of getting it translated into Gaelic; and
"Blind Bartimeus" was sent up many a Highland
glen, and into many a sequestered nook, to tell of
Him who openeth the eyes of the blind, and saith
in his love to every needy child of man, "What wilt
thou that I should do unto thee?" His edition of
Brooks's "Cabinet of Choice Jewels" was seasona-
ble and useful. For example, it was instrumental in
the conversion of a young man who is now a zealous Sabbath-school teacher and elder in the Free
Church. At one time we find him printing and
circulating 300,000 tracts ringing with the genuine
truth of the Gospel. Of this kind of literature, in
fact, he circulated whole tons. He procured the
translation into Gaelic of many little books which
were gratuitously distributed, or sold at a merely
nominal price.

To bring the Gospel before the eyes of careless
men he frequently devised new methods. For instance, immense placards with "The Two Roads"
described, being the substance of a discourse on the
wide and strait gates, met your eye everywhere in
town and country. I have seen it on the wall of a

populous town in the strange company of quack advertisements and theatre bills, and have heard one passer-by say to another, "Stop, Jim, here's a new style o't." They stopped, and read the old Gospel in a new style. I have seen it hanging up in a saw-mill in the corner of a dense wood in a wild Highland glen, where all who trafficked in timber read its sharp, soul-piercing truths amidst the dust and noise. It found its way into the ploughman's bothy. "What are you doing?" said one to a couple of ploughmen in F——shire, who, with hoe in hand, were scraping the walls of their bothy. "Ou, sir," was the reply, "we're just scrapin' aff the deevil's sangs, and we're gaun to put up Christ's in their place." At this juncture the foreman making his appearance angrily forbade their proceeding further in the ornamentation of the walls, but the men stoutly made reply, "Deed, you never said a word again' oor swearin' and singin' coorse sangs, and surely you'll nae hinner's frae worshippin' and praisin' God! Na, na; we'll dae naething o' the sort as stop. We'll hae doon the deevil's sangs, and put up Christ's." "The Two Roads," with sundry hymns and spiritual songs were then pasted in the most conspicuous places.

He was watchful against the spread of error. Of all he ever published it would be difficult to find a sentence that could be fairly construed to mean error, or be held as likely to mislead a soul. Every little book had its mission; every tract was a messenger

sent in the name of God. One was to awaken and
alarm; another was to warn and reprove; a third
was to persuade and win; a fourth summoned to decision; a fifth was fitted to comfort and sanctify;
and all were sent forth in the name of Christ to seek
and save the lost. Taking into account the quality
and quantity of the seed, the breadth of deeply-fur-
rowed soil that was sown in those days, when God's
great ploughshare was running sharply through the
fallow ground and virgin soil of Scotland amidst
sweet April-like alternations of sunshine and shower
that then gladdened our happy land, it may be safely affirmed that the fruits could have been neither
few nor small.

All the profits of the publishing business went to
the gratuitous circulation of the particular tract or
book then in hand. Although the entire burden
lay on himself, his admirable business capacity and
methodic habits enabled him to keep his accounts
with perfect accuracy, and thus amidst a multitude
of affairs to avoid confusion, if not also loss. It was
but a subordinate part of his evangelistic work. The
risk, indeed, was considerable, and the labor immense; but he sought no recompense save the reward that shines afar, and shines only to the clear
eye of faith.

A portion of the day was invariably spent in visiting the sick, the aged, and the friendless. For this
kind of work he possessed a peculiar fitness, and in
it he found a peculiar joy. " You will miss your

19

friend Mr. Matheson," I said to a Christian couple of feeble health and straitened circumstances. "Deed, sir," was the reply, "we'll miss him sair. He had a gey traffic wi' us, an' he was aye sae cheery. An' mair than that, his hand was aye as ready wi' his ain siller as his tongue was wi' God's promises. Mony a time he cam' in an' got's greetin,' an' he was sure to leave's laughin." *He's* past the mournin' noo; he's weel hame, an' we a' maun try an' win hame tae. But 'deed, sir, we'll miss him sair." Into many a garret and cellar he carried the sunshine of an unclouded cheerfulness. His divinity was always served out with much humanity. Rare humors of fancy mingled with his spiritual sayings, and seemed no more out of place than children playing under the shadow of a great cathedral, or birds singing in a churchyard. As playful winds, seemingly of little use in nature, precede the genial rain, so his drolleries prepared the way for those tender touches of the deeper heart that call forth tears. Heavenly thoughts arrayed in symbols of the earth imparted interest to his talk. His conversation—proverbial, quaint, suggestive, always genial and often powerful—was scarcely less useful than his preaching.

To a timid young Christian he said, "Be what God meant you to be—a man." To one whom he deemed unpractical he said, "Be real." To a flighty one, "The Lord will clip your wings some day." To a newly-married couple, "Mind this; A man canna grow in grace unless his wife let him." To

students preparing for the ministry, "Lads, tak' a
guid grip o' God;" an advice which some of them
appear to have laid to heart. To warn them against
the deadening effect of classical studies he said,
"Mind, Christ was crucified between Greek and
Latin." To a student who seemed to him to be in
danger of intellectual pride he said, "W——, *intellect* is the rock you'll split on." If that student, now
in a high position in the church, has not made shipwreck, his safety may be in measure due to the advice of his outspoken friend. To a preacher who
had crotchets he said, "B——, preach *Christ.*" To
one who was becoming a separatist: "You are doing
the very thing Satan desires. If he cannot destroy
a child of God, he will cripple him and destroy his
usefulness." To a Baptist disposed to make too
much of the water he said, "Labor to bring sinners
to *the blood.*"

To a Christian complaining of coldness: "You
are cold because you are going away from the
fire: keep nearer to *Christ.*" To young converts he
would often say, "Keep about Christ's hand." "Few
Christians shine; be you a shining one." "If you
wish to get *far ben* in heaven, keep near Christ on
earth." "You'll aye get what you go in for," was
his homely way of stating an important principle
of the divine administration.

To a desponding believer he said, "What would
you sell your hope for?" "I would not sell my
hope for worlds," was the reply. "Well, then,"

said he, "you are very rich, and need not droop."
"Oh, but I am so dead!" said another. "I never
heard the dead complain in that way," was his
reply.

"A lady, an earnest Christian worker, whose
creed is summed up in these three articles, "I
believe in heaven, I believe in hell, and I believe
in the third chapter of the Gospel according to
John," said to him one day, "Ah, Mr. Matheson,
I have lost my peace and my hope; I fear I am
going to perish." His reply was characteristic:
"What! you perish? I tell you, woman, if you
went to hell, the devil would say, 'What is that
woman doing here, aye speaking aboot her Christ?
Put her out, put her out, put her out!'" Curiously
enough, that reply brought a relief to her mind
which much reading, prayer, and conference with
ministers and other godly friends had failed to
supply.

To young religious professors he said, with much
feeling and solemnity, "I often fear lest I turn out
at the judgment day to be nothing but a hypocrite."
That was his way of warning them, and in some
cases I know it took effect. More than one of
those young Christians, awe-stricken, went home
to search and abase themselves before God, and so
were saved from the perils of self-confidence, if not
also from delusions that ruin the soul. The fear of
being a hypocrite, I firmly believe, was the only
fear Duncan Matheson ever knew.

He had no idea of the uneducated lay-preacher affecting to be the fine gentleman or the clergyman. Meeting two young lay-evangelists, he said, "So you have become grand gentlemen," glancing at the same time at their new and finely-polished walking canes. "Away with these showy things, and be like your Master." To another he said, "L——, when did you become a minister?" "I am not a minister," was the reply. "Well, then," said he, "put away your white necktie, and just be what you are, no more, no less." Then thrusting a piece of gold into the young evangelist's hand, he said in his kindliest tone, "This is to help to pay your expenses. I am not able to preach, and I must be doing something for Jesus." These are little matters, but they serve to show with what godly jealousy he watched over his younger brethren, and how keen was his eye to discern the first step of pilgrims into Bye-path Meadow.

In a certain place where evangelistic meetings were being held, the lay-preachers, among whom was Mr. Matheson, were sumptuously entertained at the house of a Christian gentleman. After dinner they went to the meeting, not without some difference of opinion as to the best method of conducting the services of the evening. "The Spirit is grieved; He is not here at all, I feel it," said one of the younger, with a whine which somewhat contrasted with his previous unbounded enjoyment of the luxuries of the table. "Nonsense," replied

Matheson, who hated all whining and morbid spirituality; "nothing of the sort. You have just eaten too much dinner, and you feel heavy."

He had learned how to abound and how to suffer want; and he once said, "I have observed during all those years of evangelistic labor, that invariably when I have enjoyed most blessing in the work, I have suffered the greatest hardships; and, on the other hand, when I have been dined, and feasted, and carried shoulder high, there has been little good done." He who is to be instrumental in gathering in the elect of God must taste of Gethsemane and Calvary. Christ's tools are tempered in a hot furnace and sharpened on a hard grindstone. Luxury and ease are bad oils for the chariot wheels of the Gospel.

Speaking of the encouragement given by the Master to a young evangelist who was rejoicing in his first success, Matheson said, "The Lord gives these young soldiers victory without a wound; but when *we* are leaving a place we get a shot in the back to keep us humble and remind us that the glory belongs to Him." He was very tolerant of the faults of young converts. "The Lord winks at their blunders and foibles because they don't know better," he would say. "Let them sing away; God Himself will teach them other tunes."

"There is no use in your coming here," it was said to him in a certain place; "for the people won't come out to hear the ministers themselves."

"Well, then," was his reply, "if they will not come out to hear broadcloth, I will put on fustian." He was right.

Of pointless and unfaithful preaching, however pleasant to the ear or agreeable to the intellectual taste, he always said, "It is just Nero fiddling when Rome is burning." "That was an excellent discourse," said he one day, after hearing a sermon, "but the meshes were too wide, and the fish would all get through."

On hearing a certain preacher praised as being a fine speaker, he said, "Ay, but has he teeth?" He often quoted a saying of the celebrated divine, Dr. John Owen, to the effect that no preacher was ever successful who had not a certain "tartness," pungent power, in dealing with the conscience. Of those preachers who by a skilful management of the voice make pretence of emotion, and as it were *weep to order*, he said, "They mimic the Holy Ghost: what presumption!" To a minister he said, "Preach hell. Few ministers preach it, and few people believe in it; but it is a *great reality.*" "Some good preachers," he said, "are much too long in their discourses. They put me in mind of a man who, after driving a nail home, keeps hammering at its head till he has broken it and spoilt his own work." He had no patience with *ignorant* lay-preachers, and often said to the young men, "Lads, sink the shaft deeper." On one occasion a man, imagining he had a gift, requested permission to address Mr. Matheson's meeting. This granted, the result was a sad display of ignorance, whereupon our evangelist, tapping him on the shoulder, stopped him, saying, "That'll do, John," quaintly and significantly adding, "Man, don't you know the Shorter Catechism is a splendid book for learners? I would advise you to study it a good while before you speak in public."

He was a good deal tried by the fickleness of friends, and he would often say of such as were not likely to stand in the day of trial, "He is nae to ride the water wi'," adding, "I expect to have no more than two or three *genuine* friends when I come to die." Once, when he was fiercely assailed for the Gospel's sake, a man addressed him in terms of warmest friendship, saying, "Mr. Matheson, I will stand your friend." Matheson, casting a penetrating glance at his new patron took his measure, and replied, "Aye, aye. You will stand by me when I am right; but will you stand by me when I am wrong? When I am right I don't need my friends: I can stand on my own feet then. It's when I am down that I need my friends. Man, will you help me when I am in the mire?"

"When I preached at W——," he was wont to tell by way of illustrating a weak point in the friendship of some, "and gave away my books gratuitously, the people were my warm friends, and used to shake my hand very cordially; but when I stood at a corner with a clothes-basket full of books which I offered at half price, the good people did not recognize me. In fact they had suddenly become star-gazers, and passed by without once seeing me."

On hearing one tell with apparent self-compla-cency of a Christian who had fallen, he said with a tenderness of feeling that made the reproof all the more telling, "Ah, it's him the day, an' me the morn." When shown a calumnious statement made against him in a newspaper, he said joyfully, "Man, I do like a little dirt cast upon me for the dear Master's sake. I think Gabriel would shake hands with me and say, 'I never had such an honor.'" "Suffering persecution for righteousness' sake," he would say, "is far better than a hundred dying testimonies of those who never did or suffered any thing for Jesus." "Mrs. —— died without giving any testimony," said one of whom he stood in doubt. "What of that?" was his reply; "you had the testimony of her Christian life for forty years. If that be not enough to convince you, then hear my dying testi-mony just now:

"'I'm a poor sinner, and nothing at all;
But Jesus Christ is my All in all.'

Do you believe that?"

He knew how to make a ploughshare of an ene-my's sword. "This is no time for preaching," said one angrily to him in a market. "Look here, friend," he replied, "you believe in the Word of God?" "Yes." "Well," said Matheson, "it is written, 'Be instant in season and out of season.' You say this is out of season. Well, we are just doing as we are commanded: we are preaching out of season." "These are men of strong passions," was the sneering remark of another in reference to our evangelist and his fellow-laborers. "Thank God," said Matheson, "we are men of strong passions. He has made us of strong passions that we may be strong in his service." Nothing gave him greater pain than a blow dealt by a fellow-Christian. "An offended child of God gives the keenest blow," he used to say; "he knows a Christian's tenderest part." Yet even in this case he had his answer ready, "Now, just lay your finger on the commandment I have broken, and I will thank you. Which of the ten is it?"

In one place, where for a while he discharged the duties of a pastor, some who were sick complained that he had not paid them a visit. "Did you send for the doctor?" he asked. "Yes." "Why, then, did you not send for me? Is it because you care more for your body than your soul?"

Another in similar circumstances said, "You might have missed me out of church." "You are mistaken," was his reply. "I go to the house of God as a worshipper and a preacher, not as a *detective.*"

When the managers of a congregation among whom he had labored with every token of success for some time intimated to him that his services would be no longer required, as they could secure a preacher for ten shillings a week, he said, "Do

you think you will get the worth of your money?"
To this sarcastic question no answer was given.
"Do as you have a mind," he went on to say; "but
I have a little money at present, and can preach for
nothing. God is blessing my labors here, and I dare
not leave the place. I will take a hall, and preach
there." On hearing all this, the congregation ral-
lied around him. He was requested to remain, and
his meetings were more crowded than ever.

His reproofs were often so sweetened with humor
that no offence was given. Seeing several persons
coming into a meeting too late, he said, "In the
north a minister observing that a certain woman,
though lame and scarcely able to walk, was always
first at church, asked her how she managed to
come so early. 'Sir,' she replied, 'the hert gangs
first, and the feet follow.'" Those who come late, or
for some insufficient reason never come at all, have
been well named "the devil's cripples." Matheson
did not spare such, and sometimes asked if any one
knew how they always grow lame every seventh
day.

One day a gentleman called on him, and inquired
if he knew a preacher who could suitably occupy a
vacant pulpit in a certain large city. After some
conversation, in which the evangelist endeavored
to ascertain his visitor's ideal of a good minister,
Matheson said, "By the bye, do you know Mr. ——,
a preacher somewhere in your neighborhood? How
would he do with you?" "I know him," was the

reply. "We have heard him preach repeatedly, but
he would not do with us at all." "Why so?" "Oh,
he preaches damnation and frightens every body.
This is not the time of day for that sort of thing.
He would never do, sir." At this point the evangelist brought down his fist upon the table with a
tremendous blow, and as if addressing the absent
preacher, exclaimed with his loudest voice, "Bravo!
M——, bravo! my old friend. Thank God, you are
still alive, and faithfully warning sinners of their
danger." Matheson's visitor was astounded, and
remembering he had an engagement at that moment, took up his hat and bade the evangelist good
morning. In this way he stood by his friends, and
this too he did at all hazards, as the following instance will show. A minister preaching in a market being assailed by a man under the influence of
drink, Mr. Matheson interposed, and drawing himself up to his full height said, "If you strike this
man of God it must be through my body." At
the sight of so formidable a barrier, the drunkard
quailed and slunk away.

In the course of his itineracy he once found
himself in a strange, out of the way region with
out a friend, without lodging, and without means.
It was drawing towards night, and he knew not
where to go. Seeing a boy crossing a field, he
called to him, and said, "Are there any godly people here about?" "Na, na," replied the lad, "there
is nae sic fouk in this pairish." "Are there any

believers?" asked the evangelist. "Bleevers!" exclaimed the boy; "I never heerd o' sic things." "Any religious people, then?" "I dinna ken ony o' that kind; I doot they dinna come this road at a'." "Well, then," said the missionary, making a last attempt, "are there any who keep family worship?" "Family worship," replied the lad, with a bewildered look; "fat's that?" The boy, having taken his last stare at the curious stranger, was about to go. Matheson was at his wits' end, when a happy thought struck him. "Stop!" he cried; "are there any hypocrites hereabout?" "Ou, aye," replied the youth, brightening into intelligence; "the fouk say that ——'s wife is the greatest hypocrite in a' the pairish." "Where is her house?" "Yonner by," said the lad, pointing to a house about a mile distant. Having rewarded his guide with a penny, the last he had, he made his way to the dwelling of "the greatest hypocrite in the parish," and knocked at the door as the shades of the night were falling. The door was opened by a tidy, cheerful, middle-aged matron, to whom the stranger thus addressed himself; "Will you receive a prophet in the name of a prophet, and you'll not lose your reward?" She smiled, and bade him welcome. The hospitalities of that Christian home were heaped upon him, and he spent a delightful evening in fellowship. In this way a lasting friendship began, and, what was better, a door of usefulness was opened to him.

Talking one day to his fellow-passengers in a railway train about the concerns of the soul, he was called a hypocrite. On this he took five shillings from his purse, and said to his assailant in the hearing of all the rest, "I'll give you this if you will tell me what a hypocrite is." The man was silent. "You don't know," continued the evangelist; "but I will tell you. A hypocrite is one whose deeds are not consistent with his words and professions. Now I will give you ten shillings if you will point out wherein my actions are inconsistent with my profession." There was no reply, and Matheson proceeded to improve the advantage thus gained by making solemn and pungent remarks with manifest impression on all present.

His practical good sense and ready wit were always at hand to help him. Some were objecting to receiving money for religious purposes from unconverted persons and people of the world. "I have no objections whatever," was his reply. "*God's people spoiled the Egyptians.*"

Sometimes his rebukes were very striking. To a lady, whose life was not in keeping with her light and privileges, he one day said, "It has cost you, madam, more trouble to get thus far on the way to hell than it has cost many to get to heaven." Startled, she exclaimed, "Explain yourself." "Consider," he replied, "how many barriers you have crossed; a mother's prayers, a father's godly life, the remonstrances of conscience, heart-piercing addresses and faithful warnings; and above them all, and in them all, the loving arms of the Saviour. These have stood between you and hell, but you have overleaped every barrier; you have thrust the outstretched hand of mercy aside, that you might pursue the way to death. Tell me, are you now at ease?" The lady burst into tears, and requested him to pray.

"How is it," said another lady jestingly, "that you godly folks have more trials than other people?" "Madam," he replied, "the godly have all *their hell* upon the earth, just as you have all *your heaven* here; but when the redeemed are entering on their eternal happiness, you will be beginning your everlasting misery."

"How can you bear up amidst so many trials?" it was asked of him. "I will answer that question," said he, "in the language of an author I was reading the other day. 'A child of God may be tossed by reason of corruption and temptation on a troubled sea; but that ship shall never be wrecked, whereof Christ is the Pilot, the Scriptures the compass, the promises the tacklings, hope the anchor, faith the cable, the Holy Ghost the winds, and holy affections the sails.' No fear of our bearing up and getting through!"

He constantly endeavored to give the conversation everywhere a spiritual turn; and this he could do in an easy and natural way. A Christian lady having got a sewing machine, he said, "Now I hope that, as the Lord gives you strength, you will use it in sending missionaries to the heathen, or in helping the Lord's work in some way." Calling when very weary at a certain house, the hospitable mistress prepared for him a cup of tea, with which he was a good deal refreshed. "When I get home above," he said, "I will tell Him, 'I was an hungered, and ye fed me.'"

On visiting friends who had removed to a larger house, he said, "Ay, you have got a big house, but I have a mansion up yonder." One asked him if he had ever been wounded while at the Crimea. "No," he said; "but many a time by the enemy of souls." On hearing of a family who were interested in the Lord's work, and counted by the world revival-mad, he said, "Oh, tell them from me to bite every body they meet." Just as he was parting with certain friends at A——, the clock struck the midnight hour, on which he said with great solemnity and power, "The mountains shall depart, and the hills be removed; but my kindness shall not depart from thee, neither shall the covenant of my peace be removed, saith the Lord that hath mercy on thee." As they were about to leave the house of a Christian family where they had been hospitably entertained, his companion made some allusion to the reward promised those who gave a disciple a cup of cold water in the name of a disciple, on which he said in the hearing of all, "Oh, they have the best bargain!" On a similar occasion, as he

and his two companions were going away, he said,
"You may not be aware who your guests are: you
have been entertaining *three kings.*"

One day as he sat in a railway train he sang a
hymn, on which a fellow-traveller said to him, "You
seem a happy man." "Yes," he replied, "I cannot
be but happy; I am safe for time, and safe for eternity." This led to further conversation, with which
the gentleman was so much pleased that he invited
Mr. Matheson to K——, where he resided, to preach
the Gospel there. His happiness was a powerful and
effective sermon. By word, by look, and by deed, he
was constantly testifying to the goodness of his God.
"The Lord has been very, very kind to me," was his
frequent saying, and his cheerfulness was often more
powerful to win than words of persuasive eloquence.
But he did not overlook the other aspect of the Christian's life. "How hard it is to live for *eternity,*" he
would say. "Living above *self* and for God," he
added, "is *real* living for eternity."

It was the custom of our evangelist to hold a meeting for prayer either at noon or in the evening. This
was preparatory to the evangelistic service which he
invariably conducted at the close of the day. Here
he refreshed his own spirit and renewed his strength:
here too the Christians were provoked to love and
good works. An open-air service frequently preceded the meeting within doors. The singing and
praying, the loud voice and bold manner of the lay-
preacher, arrested the attention of the passer-by, and

20

many who had never darkened a church door were thus induced to enter the place of meeting. Scenes of violence were not infrequent on the street, and the preacher received many a blow. At Forfar the roughs began one night to throw stones at the evangelist and his friends. "The devil is got weak now," said Matheson, "when he's throwin' gravel." Turning to his companions, he said, "Cheer on! the enemy is at his worst, and Christ will soon triumph." So it was. The tide turned; and a remarkable work of grace followed.

"You need not go there," said one who deemed preaching Christ on the occasion of "an execution" of no use; "the devil has such power there." "The more need, then," was his reply, "for his being put down." "We won't protect you," said the police at a race-course. "A higher arm than yours will protect me," was his brave but meek reply. After a fierce assault made upon him, a Christian began to express sympathy with him; but he said, "Oh, what about *that?* They *crucified Him.*"

His meetings within doors were conducted in the usual way. His addresses were characterized by great fulness and variety. He could speak to the edifying of saints. With jubilant tones and a cheery pilgrim-like air he often preached from the text, "We are journeying unto the place of which the Lord said, I will give it you: come thou with us, and we will do thee good; for the Lord hath spoken good concerning Israel" (Num. x. 29). With swelling emo-

tions, and in sentences full of the music of his own
joy, he loved to describe the happiness of that people
whose God is the Lord. "Yes," he was wont to say,
"they are happy *when they look back* and remember
the time when Jesus met and drew them to Himself
in wondrous love. Happy *when they look forward*
and see the pillar-cloud guiding them by a right way.
Happy *when they look down* and reflect that they
might have been weeping and wailing in the outer
darkness instead of singing, 'He took me from a fearful pit, and from the miry clay.' And happy *when
they look up* and think of the exceeding and eternal
weight of glory that awaits them. Happy, indeed,
is that people whose God is the Lord."

But his speech was mainly directed to men in their
sins. Some as they advance in their ministry preach
less to sinners and more to saints. The reverse was
true of him. "They say Duncan Matheson is nae
growin'; he is aye preachin' death and judgment,"
were his own words; "but," he added in self-defence,
"these are arrows I have often shot, and I have found
them effectual; why change them?" "The children
of God," said he quaintly, "will waggle through ae
way or anither; but sinners are in danger every moment, and so I keep at them." "Lord, stamp eternity
upon my eyeballs," was his frequent prayer. As the
light of eternity was ever growing more clear and
piercing in his soul, his heart bled with an increasing compassion for the perishing. He was careful
in discriminating between the saved and the lost,

between saint and sinner. He would no more have assumed that all his hearers were true Christians than that all the pebbles on the sea-shore are diamonds, or all the birds in the hedgerows nightingales.

The almost-saved had their sad history and too probable end set forth in the description of a noble ship crossing the wide ocean, surviving many a storm, and then becoming a complete and hopeless wreck at the harbor mouth. "Near the kingdom," he used to say, "is not in it. You may perish with your hand on the latch of heaven's gate."

To the careless, he often said, "There is a question which none in heaven can answer, and none in hell: can you? It is, 'How shall we escape, if we neglect so great salvation?'"

Many a time did the formalist and hollow professor quake as he heard himself described in a discourse from the text, "I saw the wicked buried, who had come and gone from the place of the holy; and they were forgotten in the city where they had so done" (Eccl. ix. 10).

Powerfully and affectionately did he plead with men on Christ's behalf as he spake from the touching words, "Behold, I stand at the door and knock," using homely illustrations of the truth. "A little boy, hearing his father read that passage aloud," he was wont to tell, "rushed away from the window where he was playing, and looking with wondering and eager eyes into his parent's face, said feelingly,

'But, father, did they let Him in?' Friends, you
have heard the knock in some powerful sermon,
some faithful warning, or when your cheeks ran
down with tears and your very heart-strings were
breaking as they lowered the little coffin with your
dear babe into that cold grave. But did you let
Him in? Perhaps you say, 'I fain would, but cannot.' A minister once knocked at the door of a poor,
aged, and lone woman; but he received no answer.
Louder, and louder still, he knocked. At length, as
he kept his ear close to the door, he heard a feeble
voice, saying, 'Who is there?' 'It is I, the minister,' was the reply. 'Ah, sir,' said the woman, 'I
am lying very ill, and cannot rise to let you in; but
if you would come in, just lift the latch and open the
door for yourself.' The good man cheerfully com-
plied, and went in to comfort the dying sufferer
with the consolations of the Gospel. Now, my hearers, you say you cannot open the door yourselves.
I well believe you. But there is a remedy for your
helplessness; ask the Lord Jesus to open the door
for Himself and come in. And He will come in.
Believest thou this? Some of you who once heard
the knock of Christ, hear it not now. Well do I
remember being startled and kept awake by the
boom of the cannon when I went to the Crimea.
After a time, however, I grew accustomed to it, and
could sleep amidst the roar of the artillery. So it is
with many. Jesus knocks at your door in vain.
His knocking does not trouble you now as once it

did. In vain He pleads with you, telling you that
His locks are wet with the dews of night. He is
out in the cold, dark, wet night; but you care not.
He is threatening to depart and leave you to perish;
but you are too drowsy to listen or to care. To-
night He may go away forever. The last knock
will be given. This may be the last one. What
then? oh! what then?"

Regeneration by the Holy Ghost formed a large
and prominent part of his teaching. He had dwelt
long beneath the awful shadow of this great mystery of grace, and he often said, "I have always
been afraid to preach on that text, 'Except a man
be born again, he cannot see the kingdom of God.'"
Yet he continually and most emphatically announced
the necessity and explained the nature of the second
birth. "Who made you a Christian?" he would
ask. "Some are made Christians by their parents,
some by their Sabbath-school teachers, others by
their ministers and pastors, and many are made
Christians by themselves. But man-made Christians cannot enter the kingdom of God. Friend,
were you made a Christian by the Holy Ghost?
They get their salvation from man, not from God.
The sons of God are born 'not of blood, nor of the
will of the flesh, nor of the will of man, but of God.'
'That which is born of the flesh is flesh; and that
which is born of the Spirit is spirit. Marvel not
that I said unto thee, Ye must be born again.'"
This great truth of the Gospel he proclaimed with

no less skill than power, on the one hand avoiding the danger of making it a stumbling-block to the sincere inquirer, and on the other hand taking care that it should not jostle responsibility out of the field, and set men asleep on the damning excuse, " I cannot make myself a new creature; I must wait, and do nothing, till the Spirit comes."

The sovereignty of God in the salvation of man, the sinner's need of the Spirit's grace, the helplessness, folly, and infatuated wickedness of the human heart, were truths written as by a pen of iron and the point of a diamond upon his innermost heart; and he always spoke as he believed. One day a friend referred in conversation to the errors of a low Arminianism that leaves no room and no need for the work of the Holy Spirit or the election of grace. Suddenly stopping, he said, " It won't do, J——; the truth is, you and I would be damned, if it were not for election. But that grips," he added in a decided tone, at the same time clenching his fist. " Yes," he continued, "that is true," and suiting the action to the word, he added, "I know that if I had one foot in heaven, and Christ were saying to me, ' Put in the other,' I would not do it."

Stating clearly the sinner's guilt and wickedness, the evil conscience and the depraved heart, with equal clearness and force he proclaimed the twofold remedy—the blood of Christ and the all-powerful grace of the Holy Ghost. After setting forth the utter ruin of man, it was his manner to say, "Here

is the sinner, and there is 'the blood:' the great
question is, 'How may these two be brought together?' The answer is, 'The Holy Ghost: He
only can do it.'"

The Alpha and Omega of all his addresses,
whether to saints or sinners, was Jesus Christ.
"A full Christ for empty sinners" was ever his
cry. "This man receiveth sinners" was a favorite text, from which he feelingly discoursed of the
love, pity, and tenderness of the Lord Jesus in dealing with sinners. The Saviour whom he loved to
preach was He whose great heart gave way, like the
heart of a little child, when on the mount of Olives
He burst into tears at the sight of the doomed city.
The Redeemer whom he proclaimed was that Holy
One who bore so rare a friendship for publicans and
sinners. The Christ whom he held up to admiration
was the same who took little babes in his arms to
bless them, and received old sinners, like Zaccheus,
into the same bosom, and saved them. He preached
Jesus as able to save to the uttermost; whose arm of
grace reacheth to the lowest depth of man's misery
and the farthest bound of man's wickedness. It was
Christ always; Christ more and more to the last; it
was "Jesus only." His preaching was but an echo
of the announcement made by the heavenly host
on that memorable night when the plains of Bethlehem were aglow with a softer, sweeter light than
the light of moon or stars, and all the woodland
rang with a music that ravished the shepherds'

hearts, and woke the sheep from their gentle slumbers, as those nightingales of another world—the angels—sang, "Glory to God in the highest, on earth peace, good will toward men."

In short, Christ and Him crucified, Jesus risen and exalted to be a Prince, a Saviour, the Lamb of God, Substitute, Surety, Redeemer, the power of God and the wisdom of God to every one that believeth —this was all his theme. And there are tens of thousands who will recall the image of the brave, outspoken, and genial preacher, asking with equal point and feeling the question he never wearied asking, "What think ye of Christ?"

> "How sweet the name of Jesus sounds
>   In a believer's ear!
> It soothes his sorrows, heals his wounds,
>   And drives away his fear.
>
> "It makes the wounded spirit whole,
>   And calms the troubled breast;
> 'Tis manna to the hungry soul,
>   And to the weary rest.
>
> "Jesus! my Shepherd, Guardian, Friend,
>   My Prophet, Priest, and King,
> My Lord, my Life, my Way, my End,
>   Accept the praise I bring."

At an early period of his course as an evangelist, Mr. Matheson was led to follow the practice of meeting with inquirers at the close of every service. "He came to preach at Stirling in 1858," writes the Rev. W. Reid, editor of the *British Herald,* "when two meetings were got up for him, and at the close those who were anxious were requested to remain to be spoken to personally in the pews—a thing unknown before in Scotland. We remember how shy our dear departed friend looked when one said to him, ' Will you speak to those in that pew ? ' He did so with some hesitation; he said nothing about it at the time, but years afterwards he referred to it, and said it was the first time he had seen or done such a thing, 'and I thank God that it was forced upon me, and the neck of the thing was broken, and that I was no longer content to fire at long range, but to come face to face with souls.' He found it, he said, one of the steps by which the Lord prepared him and led him on in his work, and it was no strange thing for him ever afterwards, as long as he lived, to come into personal contact with awakened souls."

Being a true fisher of men, he not only let down the net for a draught, but drew it up again to see if any were caught. Some may be too hasty in searching for results; but even a little impatience of zeal is better than the dozing indolence of those who, under pretence of honoring divine sovereignty, make no inquiry, and cannot so much as tell whether their net has enclosed minnows or monsters. The meeting for directing inquirers was a necessity of the sudden and widespread awakening; and, notwithstanding its occasional abuse or mismanagement, has served important ends in the work of God and the salvation of souls.

Many Christians will remember with gratitude and joy the first time they were brought face to face with a soul grappling with the tremendous realities, *sin, eternity,* and *God.* It forms an epoch in the life of a pastor, or of any Christian. You feel you are in the presence of an immortal spirit in the very crisis of its being. You see the battle, the agony, the portentous despair of a soul wrestling with invisible powers of overwhelming might; and you tremble as you behold the fainting spirit toiling betwixt wisdom and madness to roll back the rising billows of infinite sorrow and ill. You know you are in the presence of the Divine Worker, and you seem to feel upon your own spirit the very breath of the Life-giver as He breathes on the dry bones, and evokes a fairer form than Adam's from poorer, sadder dust than the freshly bedewed soil of Paradise. Wise and patient dealing with inquirers is to a well-instructed believer one of the choicest means of grace.

Not many Christians, however, are qualified for this difficult work. During the period of religious awakening there was more or less patching of old garments and filling old bottles with new wine. The wound was sometimes too slightly healed, and comfort was given where blows were needed. If that old piece of legalism was abandoned, "Go home and read your Bible, and use the means of grace,"

which in effect is to say, "Go and work yourself
into a state of grace," there was a rush to the opposite extreme in a species of bribing simpler ones into
saying they believed, the great question being not
answered, but hushed up. "Only just believe; just
believe." Very good; but what am I to believe?
What is it to believe? How am I to believe? There
is often an anchor in the deep that binds the struggling soul to the shores of sin and death. Not every
Christian can grapple in the depths for the mysterious hinderance that binds the awakening spirit in
unbelief. Some are gifted by the Holy Ghost for
this part of the work.

In dealing with inquirers Mr. Matheson always
took care to discriminate between those who, as he
was wont to say, "had only a scratch" and those
who were deeply wounded. To the former he would
speak a word fitted to deepen conviction and pass
on; to the latter he never failed to preach Christ.
He also found two very different classes who spoke
the same language, both declaring they had no conviction. One of those classes had indeed little or no
conviction of sin, and he dealt with them accordingly. The other class were penetrated with a sense
of sin, but could see nothing in themselves but utter
hardness of heart. These often prove to be the best
cases. He never failed to bring inquirers to the
Word of God and the cross of Christ. His own experience was ever of great use in giving direction
and encouragement. A full, free, and present salva-

tion in the Lord Jesus was held out to every soul.
If they were sinking in deep waters, Jesus was at
hand to help them. If they had no right conviction
of sin, as they said, they had the greater need to
come at once to Christ to receive conviction, pardon,
holiness, and every blessing freely from Him. Christ
is the good Physician, and can deal effectually with
broken hearts and unbroken hearts, hard hearts,
proud hearts, fickle hearts, and all kinds of wicked
hearts. " I will take away the stony heart out of
your flesh, and I will give you an heart of flesh,"
is the gracious and true word of Him who came to
call not the righteous, but sinners to repentance.
"There was once," said our evangelist, "a little bird
chased by a hawk, and in its extremity it took refuge in the bosom of a tender-hearted man. There
it lay, its wings and feathers quivering with fear,
and its little heart throbbing against the bosom of
the good man, whilst the hawk kept hovering over
head, as if saying, 'Deliver up that bird, that I may
devour it.' Now, will that gentle, kind-hearted man
take the poor little creature that puts its trust in
him out of his bosom, and deliver it up to the hawk?
What think ye? Would you do it? No; never.
Well, then, if you flee for refuge into the bosom of
Jesus, who came to seek and to save the lost, do
you think He will deliver you up to your deadly
foe? Never! never! never!"

In dealing with inquirers, his power lay not so
much in the clear, terse way in which he stated the

plan of salvation, as in his homely, genial manner of applying, like a kind and skilful physician, the balm to the wound. Not seldom, when others reasoning out of the Scriptures failed, he would come and try his easy, off-hand method, in which there was profound knowledge of human nature and true Christian wisdom, without any show of either. A young man of talent, now a devoted follower of Jesus, found himself at the close of a meeting in deep distress. "Downcast and sad," he says, "I was stealing away from Mr. Matheson, whom I did not wish to meet. Wonderful love of Jesus! who marks our wayward steps, and still in tenderness and love calls after us, 'Come unto Me,' I was unexpectedly confronted by Mr. M., who introduced me to a minister. Hesitatingly I began, in answer to kind inquiries, to state my case, when Mr. M. laying his hand on my shoulder, said, 'Oh, I know what's wrong wi' James. I know what James is wanting. It was a' settled eighteen hundred years ago; but James is not satisfied with that, he would like something more. Isn't that it now? But that's enough, man. Let that suffice for you.' In this way he held up the finished work of Christ, and relief followed."

Such was the manner of his life and work. It was a life full of toil, weariness, and sorrow; it was also full of truth, and wisdom, and goodness. It was strangely checkered. One day we find him associated with the noblest in the land, who do him honor as a man of original character and apostolic virtue: next day he is out of sight in some obscure village, where he is despised and shunned by all save a faithful few. Now he stands up to speak by the side of the eloquent Guthrie, the Moderator of the General Assembly of the Free Church, who is not ashamed to acknowledge the evangelist and to share in his work. Many days have not elapsed when he is rejected by a little town for whose salvation he had labored with heroic endurance: for his too pointed rebuke of sin he is driven forth amidst a tornado of odium so fierce, that not one of his Christian friends has the courage to stand up and say, "God bless him!" But whether honored here or dishonored there, feasted one day or starved the next, he held on his way with one noble end in view—the salvation of souls. In the midst of the world, with its huge, overbearing materialism, its gorgeous mammon-worship, its fascinating sensuousness, its carnal intoxications, its choice delights of godless pleasure, he saw nothing but *souls*, and spoke only of *eternity*. Men everywhere mad upon their idols he confronted in the name of the invisible God. To the intoxicated worshippers of Time he constantly presented the dread realities of eternity, demanding of them the sacrifice of a delicious, heart-ravishing present, and the acceptance of Christ and everlasting life, or the peril of hell's pains for a refusal. With unconquerable long-suffering he thus held on his way to the end.

CHAPTER IX.

SOME SHEAVES FROM THE HARVEST-FIELD.

"As streams of water in the south,
  Our bondage, Lord, recall :
Who sow in tears, a reaping-time
  Of joy enjoy they shall.

"That man who, bearing precious seed,
  'In going forth doth mourn ;
He doubtless, bringing back his sheaves,
  Rejoicing shall return."

They that wisely and steadfastly set their hearts on winning souls are usually favored with abundant success. They delight themselves in God, and in terms of the promise He gives them the desire of their hearts. For many years Duncan Matheson prayed for a wide-spread revival of true religion. The great awakening at length took place, and he was honored above most men in reaping its fruits. "Give me children, else I die!" was the spirit of all his prayers; and, if facts be of any value, his prayers were abundantly answered.

Several of his spiritual children are already able preachers of the Gospel; some are successful missionaries at home; and some have gone forth to preach among the heathen the unsearchable riches of Christ. A considerable number are useful elders and deacons; others are earnest Sabbath-school teachers and valiant street-preachers; while many more distribute tracts, visit the sick, the outcast, and the perishing. Hundreds are quietly doing that noblest and most difficult kind of Christian work—training up their children in the fear of the Lord. A multitude live to preach the most eloquent of sermons—carrying a cross for Christ; and sing the grandest psalm sung out of heaven—living a holy life. With well-authenticated instances of conversion it would not be difficult to fill a volume. Let us take a few from amongst many.

"I find the fruits of his labors in the various districts which I visit." is the testimony of a venerable servant of the Lord Jesus Christ on his returning from a recent evangelistic tour. "His footprints will long remain fresh and warm all over the North. I spoke to an interesting young sailor in a railway carriage some time ago. He was an Englishman and a warm-hearted Christian. He told me that, years ago, when his ship lay in the harbor of Mac-duff, he went 'to hear a man called Duncan Matheson in the Free Church on a week evening, and the Lord apprehended him.'"

A thoughtless young man at C—— went one night to hear him preach, and came away with an arrow in his conscience; but having promised to attend a ball, he went to the gay assembly in the hope of ridding his mind of anxious thoughts amidst the music and the dance. Not thus was his wound to be healed. In the midst of the dance the thought of eternity seized upon him, and he rushed out to

21

seek Christ in the darkness of the night. He did not seek in vain. The light of the glory of God in the face of Jesus Christ dawned upon his soul. He now abandoned the gaieties of the world, and after a brief career of faith and holiness fell asleep in Jesus.

Another young man, a mason by trade, was awakened, and went frequently to hear Matheson. For a while he could find no rest to his soul. The terrors of the Lord followed him to his work; and when the thought of judgment to come arose in his mind, he would begin to hammer the stones with furious energy. His fellow-workmen were astonished; and when they asked him what ailed him, he made no reply, so entirely was he absorbed in his endeavors to stifle conviction. "The more I hammered," said he, "the worse I grew." Heavier and still heavier fell the blows of the Spirit's hammer, till at length, reduced to self-despair, he dropped into the arms of Jesus and found rest.

On one occasion when he was preaching on the links at Aberdeen, "a gay and godless young man," as he describes himself, was passing by. An arrow guided by the Spirit pierced the conscience of the youth. He was converted and studied for the ministry. Last year he was ordained as a missionary to Madagascar. As the evangelist passed away to his rest, the young missionary stood up amidst the solemn services of his ordination at Aberdeen to tell the audience that the voice of Duncan Matheson

had been the trumpet of God to his ear, calling him
into the fellowship of grace, and the ministry of the
Lord Jesus. The standard had just dropped from
the hands of the brave standard-bearer as he fell;
but bravely was it caught up by his own son in the
faith to be planted on the high places of the field,
where even now scenes of surpassing glory are witnessed in the triumphs of the cross. In the labors
of the foreign missionary it is permitted us to hope
that the voice of the home evangelist will find a
powerful echo among the falling idols of that distant island, and result in gathering a multitude of
the heathen to Christ. Thus not in vain did he sow
beside all waters. The little winged seeds, not visible to every eye, dropping from the branches amidst
the blasts of northern winter are being wafted on the
breeze of providential circumstance to the prepared
soil of the sunny south. "This also cometh from the
Lord of hosts, who is wonderful in counsel, and excellent in working."

At Perth, when special services were in progress,
a young man from Glasgow happened to call at the
house of Mrs. S., where Mr. Matheson was staying.
When the evangelist was informed that Mr. ——
had been at the door, he said, "Perhaps he has been
brought here at this time to be converted and saved.
Let us pray for him." Prayer was offered as follows
(I quote this from the journal of Mrs. S.): "O God,
if Thou hast brought him to this house, to this town,
and to this hall, to save his soul, it will be a won-

derful thing. Do it, Lord, do it." The young man went to the meeting in the hall, was awakened and converted. His own testimony is this: "I was a member of an influential Presbyterian Church, a Sabbath-school teacher, and a tract-distributor, but up to that night I was *a dead soul.* Then I was brought to see I was dead; and then by grace I passed from death unto life through faith in Jesus."

At Kirriemuir a young woman newly awakened was urging her companion to remain to the second meeting, "Never mind," said Mr. Matheson, "let her go her own way; she is determined to perish." This word, accompanied by a look of piercing tenderness, went to the heart of the thoughtless girl. "Yes, yes," she said to herself, "I am going my own way, and that way is to death." The arrow was from the bow of the unerring marksman; and the same invisible hand that shot it drew it out, and healed the wound with the balm of his peace-speaking blood. After two years of a holy life that young believer calmly fell asleep in Jesus.

At Forfar, as was his wont in a strange place, he made the children his friends, and sent them to tell their fathers and mothers to come and hear a stranger preaching. "Mither," said a little boy, "there's a new man come to the toon to preach; gang and hear him." Thinking it strange to be asked by her boy, she resolved though with some reluctance to go. How to conceal from her neighbors her going to a revival meeting was her difficulty. Nicode-

mus went to Jesus under cover of night: this woman took her market-basket on her arm as if she
was going to make the usual daily purchase, and
thus screened herself from the observation and jeers
of her neighbors. Day after day she appeared at
the meeting with the basket. At length she was
brought to the Lord. "Ye'll no need the basket
any more," said the evangelist to her with a significant twinkle of his eye. The basket was laid aside:
she boldly avowed the Saviour, and became signally
useful in bringing others of the same class.

A woman residing in the country, impelled by
curiosity, went to Forfar to hear the lay-preacher.
Deeply impressed, she resolved on taking the fullest
advantage of the meetings, and took lodgings in
the town with the view of attending every service.
The result was her conversion. She went home,
walked with God, testified for Christ, and after
a short time fell asleep in Jesus. She knew the
day of her merciful visitation. Such is the work
of grace.

One day he is standing at a street corner in Perth,
and is singing—

> "Nothing either great or small,
>   Nothing, sinner, no:
> Jesus did it, did it all,
>   Long, long ago."

A young man passing by was arrested by the
words of the hymn, which seemed to convey a new
truth. He listened a moment. A light he had

never seen before dawned upon his heart, and as he stood there on the pavement he became a new creature in Christ Jesus.

"Never shall I forget the first time I had the pleasure of hearing Mr. Matheson," writes a station master on a northern railway. "I was then a stranger to grace and to God. Much against my will I was induced to listen to God's message through him, and for the first time in all my life I was convinced that I was without God, and without hope in the world. His text, 'Escape for thy life,' was brought home to my heart with power and demonstration of the Spirit. I was in due time, thank God, brought out of darkness into His marvellous light, and from the power of Satan unto God. Oh, then, extol the Lord with me, and let us exalt His name together."

Take another—a young man. "I was induced by a friend to go to W—— Free Church on a Sunday afternoon. The preacher was Duncan Matheson. His text was, "Behold, I stand at the door and knock," etc. The word came with power to my soul; so much so that, although very reluctant to give way, I could not refrain from shedding tears. This being noticed by Mr. M. he came and spoke, and invited me to the vestry. I afterwards went to the open-air meeting, where my convictions were deepened. For six weeks I continued in great distress; and all the more that many who appeared not so anxious as I was were obtaining liberty from their burdens. In order to be alone I went in the darkness of night to the hill and knelt to pray, but was often disturbed by the sound of footsteps, as I fancied, but no one appeared. At this time I was looking for a mysterious revelation of the Lord Jesus, with conscious freedom from my burden and for *joy*. I had been urged to receive the Lord Jesus into my heart; and in church I kept calling inwardly faster than tongue could express it, 'Come in, Lord Jesus! come in! come in!' thinking that if I continued long enough the Lord would come in; but all in vain. I went home and threw myself on my knees with the intention of praying till I got the blessing. I continued with strong cries and tears until, as I was afterwards told by the rest in the house, the people in the street were standing to listen. When I thought I was about to obtain deliverance, it was suggested to my mind that by earnest prayer I could get it any time; and, stopping, the Spirit was grieved for a time. I felt I was relapsing, and went again to hear Mr. M. in H—— Free Church, and at the close of the service went with other inquirers into the vestry. Here he addressed us very solemnly, and ended by asking three times, 'Who is for Christ?' My heart responded, 'Me, me.' The moment of my deliverance was come, and the third time the question was put, I sprang to my feet, and exclaimed, 'I'm for Christ!' On second thoughts I was afraid I had committed a great sin; but the words, 'Believe on the Lord

Jesus, and thou shalt be saved,' were open and applied to my heart by the Holy Ghost as they had never been; and I was filled with peace. I ran to my office, but could not work, and went on praying and singing alternately. I felt an unspeakable love to my employer, and thought as he sat beside me I could do any thing for him." Years have passed, and this young man has gone on and prospered, being now an elder in a Free Church, and an indefatigable worker in the vineyard of the Lord.

"I had convictions and the strivings of the Spirit," writes another young man, "from my very infancy. Fears of perishing often possessed my little heart, especially at night, and I endeavored to obtain peace by repeating my prayers. As I grew up, I became reckless and even profane. Happening to be from home on a visit to my friends at M——, I went to hear Mr. Matheson, who was that night in the village. His text was, 'Strive to enter in at the strait gate; for many, I say unto you, will seek to enter in, and shall not be able.' Every word he uttered fell with power upon my heart. Conviction of the truth flashed upon me. I felt as if I were the only one in the church, and that every word was directed to me. I was most miserable. I saw I had been rejecting Christ and trifling with God, all the time He had been seeking to lead me to Himself. Mr. Matheson said that people sought to enter in and were not able, because they would not take Christ as their all. I felt I was doing that.

He spoke also of the Saviour standing by the side
of the broad way, and stretching out his hand to stop
the sinner in his hellward course, and the sinner
pushing aside that gracious hand and hastening on
to destruction. I saw I had been doing so. I never
was in such an agony. It was terrible work now
with me. The church was surrounded with woods,
and oh, how I longed to get out and hide myself in
them! I thought I should wrestle with God until
I found Christ. I felt as if I could have given life
itself to be reconciled to God: I could not bear the
thought of being His enemy any longer. It was
life or death with me; and I felt that I must either
now be saved or plunged into despair. At the close
Mr. Matheson took me by the hand and looked me
in the face, and I burst into tears. We knelt down
and prayed. As I was crying to God, the Lord sent
me deliverance. The light flashed in upon my
mind. Christ must be my all, and none but Christ:
Christ to trust, Christ to love, Christ to obey. It
was no mere feeling, but a clear seeing of the truth.
I saw that Christ received me, and that I was received by God in Him. I was enabled to cast myself entirely upon Him, and receive Him as my all;
and rose from my knees saying, 'Christ for me!
none but Christ for me!' Peace now possessed my
heart, the peace that passeth all understanding. I
felt as if I could not contain it. Mr. Matheson came
forward, and proposed singing the first verses of
the fortieth Psalm, 'I waited for the Lord my God,'

etc. I sang this with all my heart, for I knew I had just been taken up out of the horrible pit and miry clay, and my feet were set upon the Rock. At the door a company of believers joined me, and we were not afraid to awaken the echoes with songs of praise. Next day I spoke to a relative about her soul, and induced her to attend the meeting. This issued in her conversion. Thus the Lord made me instrumental on the first day of my life in Christ in helping to bring a soul to Him. Would that every day since that had been so successful. But amid many vicissitudes of experience, and many short-comings of heart and life, He has kept me till now, and has never permitted me altogether to lose my confidence in Jesus. I have never had a shadow of regret that I chose Christ, and, if I may judge from the past, I never will. And as I witnessed to his name at the first, so I have, though with many shortcomings, done since; and so I trust I will be enabled to do until I am called away to join in the song of the redeemed on high." This young man is a student and a missionary, whose labors have already been blessed in the conversion of sinners in three several spheres in different parts of Scotland.

The case of another young man, now an ordained missionary to the heathen. "Reports of the work of God's Spirit in America and Ireland interested several of us, and we began to meet for reading and prayer. I was specially struck with the earnest joy that the work appeared to create in the hearts of

those who shared in it; and I remember wishing it
should visit ourselves. Mr. Matheson visited our
town, and preached on 'the broad and narrow way.'
Some were impressed; but I felt only the old vague
desire. Next time Mr. M. preached, he said, 'There
are some of us here that can lay our heads peacefully on our pillow to-night, in the assurance that
if we should next awake in eternity we should be
with Christ. Friend, can you?' The question was
· for me, and went like an arrow to my soul. I felt
that that was what I could not do; that I was not
at peace with God; that to me to awake in eternity
would be to awake in hell! The words remained
with me. From that time I set myself earnestly to
seek the one thing needful; but as to the way of
finding it I was as yet quite in error. I thought
there was a vast amount of performance lying to
my hand before I could be accepted of God. Full
pardon seemed to lie beyond great hills and wastes,
which must be crossed with toilsome steps if ever I
was to attain it. All day in school I used to pray,
and when school was over I went home and prayed
through the afternoon. I remember one day that
my 'doing' received a special humiliation. A boy,
younger than myself, provoked me so much that
one of my old sinful expressions rushed out against
him. I was sorely pierced; for then my case seemed
hopeless, and all my past endeavors were nullified.
Mr. M. and others had warned us solemnly against
entertaining any *false ground* of comfort; and that

I might be preserved from this was always a special petition in my cries for pardon. For several weeks I continued to pray and read, but no light seemed to arise. One afternoon, when Mr. M. was preaching, he came upon the expression, 'Coming to Jesus.' 'But,' said he, 'some of you are at a loss to know what coming to Jesus means. I will explain it.' My heart acknowledged its own darkest difficulty; and oh, how eagerly did I listen for the explanation! I thought that now at length I was to learn the way to be saved. But, alas! no. Seeking for something to do, I did not receive the message of the Gospel, that to *look*, to *trust*, was to live. In this state of ignorant legality I continued, though the Gospel of a *present free* forgiveness had been often declared to me, till one afternoon, whose happy date is fixed forever in my memory, I was reading James's 'Anxious Inquirer,' when I came upon these two precious words—'Come unto Me,' etc. (Matt. xi. 28), and, 'Believe on the Lord Jesus Christ," etc. (Acts xvi. 31). Often had I read them before, but never till now did I *realize* them. The blessed Spirit in that hour testified their truth in my heart, and I could not refrain from exclaiming, 'And is this *really all* I have to do? is the work really finished? and have I but to receive it and be saved?' I wondered that I could have read these words so *stupidly* before, they seemed so clear now. Falling on my knees, I thanked God over and over for such a Saviour and so free a salvation. With joyous impatience I ran along to the lodging of a young man who had been one of the first awakened in our company; and when I met him, I told him with an overflowing heart how I saw it all now, and how my heart was filled with peace. That first view of Jesus in His glorious grace can never fade from my recollection. Often since that afternoon has my assurance been clouded; but I have always found, that the only way of peace was to come again, as I did then, in the character of a helpless sinner to an Almighty Saviour. How deeply since that time I have wronged the free love of God only Himself can know; but to the praise of His grace I must declare, that there is all the former efficacy in the blood of Jesus to remove the consciousness of guilt. Nor do I look on sin now with the same regard as once. I can sincerely say, that in my most essential character a complete revolution has been effected by the faith of Jesus, and that now the attainment of likeness to the holy Son of God is my reigning desire. How sweet is the believer's assurance that the sinful heart he now bewails will soon be removed forever. To serve Christ in love, that my soul desires above all other things. To win other hearts for Him, or to hear of others winning them, is my joy of joys. May the passion grow! To Him be all the glory. Amen."

One more instance must suffice; it is that of a young man, now a preacher of the Gospel, and a successful home missionary. "I had heard of the

revival work; and being unhappy, I had serious
thoughts of becoming religious and good. I went
to hear Mr. Matheson. The place of meeting was
crowded, and I could find a seat only near the pulpit. The stranger entered. His manner at once
attracted and rivetted my attention; it was altogether so novel to me. Never till then had I seen
a *man* in the pulpit—only a minister. In his whole
bearing there was such a striking absence of all
stiffness and formality. His prayer touched me:
no introduction, no formal conclusion; it was brief,
pointed, direct. It was so solemn, yet so tender.
Hearing such correspondence with the living God
I was deeply solemnized. The text was Matt. vii.
13. He spoke of the work of grace in other places,
of sinners convinced, of souls saved. I was moved.
But when the hand was pointed towards me in the
first pew, when the eye was fixed on me, when the
appeal was made to me as to the state of my soul,
then the arrow, swift and sharp from the hand of
Jehovah, pierced my heart. I trembled. I saw it
at once, suddenly, clearly—I was lost, lost, lost.
Inquirers were requested to remain. I meant to
do so, but a young man, who was unimpressed,
pushed me out. Another, a working man, said to
me, 'Are you going in?' 'Ye—es,' I replied, and
we went in together. Mr. M. laid his hand tenderly
on my shoulder and spoke to me kindly. His tenderness was too much for me; it touched my miserable heart. I felt that God was in righteousness

against me, and that I had been in sin against God.
The light that gives conviction and condemnation
was shining in on me. I was standing out in painful nakedness and solitariness: I was friendless,
hopeless. The first kind touch, the first kind word,
burst the floodgates of my soul. Giving vent to
my surcharged feelings I burst into tears. They
were the first I had shed for my soul. We were
addressed, and each received a copy of 'The Herald
of Mercy.' But I found no rest. Next night he
preached on Rev. iii. 20. Others were awakened:
many wept: I trembled still the more. Five weeks
of agonizing struggle followed. It was a long pain.
At one time I resolved not to rise from my knees
till I had obtained salvation, but my exhausted
body failed me. Again I vowed and vowed that
if God would only relieve me, I should serve Him
better in the future. It was a long, bitter, agonizing search for peace without reference to atonement
in Christ Jesus, during which there was now and
then pride of conviction and new-gotten religious-
ness. The grace of God through righteousness in
Christ began now to dawn, softly and dimly at first.
Mr. M. returned to preach; and the word was with
power. One evening the peace of God that passeth
all understanding filled my soul. I felt it was the
sunrise of an eternal day. Floods of light fell on
me—light stretching up, far up to the throne of God
—light falling down from His face upon my heart.
'God is light, and in Him is no darkness at all.'

There was no fear, no shadow, no bondage. I was intensely happy. I saw the work finished, the reconciliation already made, and realized my own interest in it. Righteously *in Jesus* I entered into the presence of God; and graciously I was accepted and blessed. I believed in Jesus, believed in God, saw grace righteously and freely offered, and my heart was full of it. Heaven lay about me. Earth afforded no comparison. It was a glorious calm. Old things had passed away. I knew I had entered the kingdom; I was new-born."

The evangelist was not always a savor of life unto life. Incidents of a solemn and affecting character occurred, two or three of which may be here narrated.

One day a woman began to pour contempt on the word of God, and shut her door in order that she might not be disturbed by the voice of the preacher. He spoke to her, and warned her; but in vain. Some time afterward she took ill, and lay dying. Remorse seized her, and in the agony of her spirit she spoke of Matheson, and cried out, "He told me that God would laugh at my calamity, and mock me when my fear came; and it is all true." No light came. She was a terror to all who saw her die. She went into eternity in her despair.

A man of violent passions and avowed hatred to godliness opposed the evangelist with much bitterness. One day he fell a cursing of Duncan Matheson, and died with the oath on his lips.

A young woman heard him preach from the text, "These shall go away into everlasting punishment." Somewhat impressed at the time, she afterwards resisted the Spirit, and returned to vanity. Death came unexpectedly, and knocked at her door. She was unprepared. She remembered the despite she had done to the Spirit of grace, and as she died uttered with a melancholy voice the dreadful words, "These shall go away into everlasting punishment."

Such facts as these are as marginal notes written by the finger of Providence on the borders of revelation. We may not be able to interpret them. None but fools will despise them.

CHAPTER X.

FROM THE FURNACE TO THE SEA OF GLASS MINGLED WITH FIRE.

" Brief life is here our portion;
  Brief sorrow, short-lived care;
  The life that knows no ending,
  The tearless life is there.

"Oh, happy retribution !
  Short toil, eternal rest;
  For mortals, and for sinners,
  A mansion with the blest.

" And now we fight the battle,
  But then shall wear the crown
  Of full and everlasting
  And passionless renown.

22

"But He whom now we trust in
Shall then be seen and known;
And they that know and see Him
Shall have Him for their own."

Towards the close of 1861 Duncan Matheson found himself in floods of trouble, arising from his fearless stand for vital godliness and his faithful reproof of lukewarm religion. Exhausted by gigantic laborers, he sighed for rest, yet held himself ready for new fields of toil, and longed to win fresh trophies for his great Master. He was persecuted, but not forsaken; cast down, but not destroyed. "Come," said he one day to a "companion in tribulation and in the kingdom and patience of Jesus Christ," "come, and let us visit St. Andrew's, and see the place where the old Scottish heroes fought their good fight; it will stir and cheer us, and perhaps God will give us of their martyr spirit." Accordingly they went and saw the place where George Wishart was burned to be a light to Scotland to the end of time; where Knox thundered defiance to Rome, and proved himself a match for mail-clad hosts; and where saintly Rutherford, pattern-witness for the truth not less in his sound teaching and masterly logic than in his rapturous piety and blameless life, labored, and prayed, and suffered, and fell asleep, saying, "Glory, glory dwelleth in Immanuel's land." After they had visited every spot of historic interest, they laid themselves down on the grave of Rutherford, and all alone with their faces on the dust they wept and prayed, praising God for all He has done for Scotland, and entreating for their dear country with many supplications, and tears, another and a complete reformation in the awakening of the churches, and the conversion of all the people in the land. Here too, with the tears dropping from their eyes upon the grass, they consecrated themselves anew to the service and glory of God their Saviour, begging with heartbreaking earnestness for grace to be faithful even unto death. Here too they sang praise. The words of the psalm were joyfully recalled—

> "For sure the Lord will not cast off
> Those that his people be,
> Neither his own inheritance
> Quit and forsake will he :
> But judgment unto righteousness
> Shall yet return again,
> And all shall follow after it
> That are right-hearted men."

As they sang "Rock of ages, cleft for me," they realized at once their security in the great Covenant-Head, and their oneness with redeemed men of every age: and on the spot where saints and martyrs repose so calmly they could sing, "There is rest for the weary" with unwonted joy. Thus they were strengthened for the sore toil and travail that still awaited them.

Some may feel disposed to set this down as sentimentalism. But if fellowship with God and with his saints be sentimentalism, if sympathy with Christ in his blood-baptized cause, and with those that suffered for the love they bore Him be sentimental-ism, if prayers and tears for a lost world that still goeth on in its mad way of cursing and casting out its best friends be sentimentalism, then I say, Heaven send us more of it. Scotchmen are said to have hard heads: but triply hard is the heart of that Scotchman who can drink at the springs of his country's greatness and not be filled as with new wine. The ashes of the martyrs never grow cold; and dull must the Christian spirit be that is not fired with new zeal at the sight of those hallowed spots whence flamed up to heaven and far out upon the world's night Scotland's testimony to Christ, which is our country's truest glory. Happily the echoes of that testimony linger about ten thousand hearths, and come back with strange power on ten times ten thousand hearts; nor will the sweetly solemn reverberations of those martyr-voices die till they merge in the sounds of the last trump.

This incident marked an epoch in the life of our evangelist. Scottish Christianity has been charac-terized by the pre-eminently high and holy place assigned by it to the crown rights of the Lord Jesus as the Church's sole Head and King. Duncan Matheson was thoroughly of that spirit. His mar-tial, loyal, heroic nature must needs love, serve, fight, and suffer for a King. Fondly and unceas-ingly as he preached the atonement of Jesus, and thus recognized the Priest and the one great Sacri-

fice for sin, the chief enthusiasm of his personal
devotion to the Lord, in all the labor and turmoil
of his life, seemed to take rise scarcely so much in
the love he bore his Saviour as in the passionate
loyalty he felt for his King. And this noble affection grew more and more intense to the end of his
life: it was still to the last, "the King! the King!"
When the last campaign was over, and the end drew
near, one of his frequent utterances was, "I am going
to see the King."

After that last and fullest consecration of himself
to God at the grave of Samuel Rutherford, a remarkable change was noticed in him by his more inti-
mate friends. His faith now took a higher flight.
Henceforth he spoke everywhere and always of
"going home." "O how near eternity seems," he
was ever saying: "We'll soon be home." "That
man breathes the very atmosphere of heaven," said
some who met him. When a young man he had
a presentiment that he would not live long: middle
life, he said, would see his sun set. The hope of the
Gospel now taught him to think of the sun rising in
another sphere rather than of its setting in this.
"Heaven will literally be a rest to me," was his frequent saying. In consequence of his incessant,
fatiguing, and often most painful labors, his mind
naturally enough contemplated heaven as a rest.
All the spiritual songs of the coming glory were
now peculiarly sweet to his heart. But the reeling
did not evaporate in mere singing or in the indul

gence of pleasant thoughts. It was in him, as all his beliefs were, a most powerful motive to work for Christ and win souls. "You are hurting yourself," we said to him. "Souls are perishing," was his invariable reply. "But you should take rest." "Nonsense! we'll rest in heaven." Some may think he carried this too far: but he had no idea of what is called "settling in life." A mighty power was working in him. How could he rest? His soul was in the agonies of travail. And till disease struck him down the years that elapsed were one unbroken day of toil for the saving of the lost.

Towards the close of his more active life, although he did not abate one jot of his manly frankness, his uncompromising faithfulness, and his fearless testimony, a mellowing influence was clearly at work in him. His prayers grew more childlike and tender; his addresses, whilst not less searching and faithful, were more deeply solemn, and more tearfully compassionate; and the big heart of the man, like an overflowing well, gushed out in streams of genuine kindness and Christian love.

Little did we imagine, when he stood up on a gloomy November night in 1866, in Hilltown Free Church, where his voice had often been accompanied with more than human power, that we were listening to his last address in Dundee. His text was "Remember Lot's wife." Lot's wife, he said— I here give not his words, but the spirit of them— Lot's wife had many privileges, but she perished.

Lot's wife had a godly husband, but she perished. Lot's wife had often been prayed for, but she perished. Lot's wife had a good example set her, but she perished. Lot's wife had been warned by God, but she perished. Lot's wife saw her danger, but she perished. Lot's wife was led by angels out of Sodom, but she perished. Lot's wife was nearly saved, but she perished. Lot's wife only looked round, and she was damned for that look. She lingered when she should have made haste, and God left her. Mercy drew her, but she grieved Mercy, and Mercy forsook her. Where Mercy left her, Justice found her, and Destruction seized her. She loved Sodom, and would love Sodom, and God gave her her bad love to the full. The Lord took her out of Sodom, but she took Sodom out of Sodom with her. "Let me get a last look at my idol," she said; and she got a *last* look with a vengeance. "She is joined to her idols," said the jealous God: "Let her alone;" and she was let terribly alone: she became a pillar of salt. Sodom was more to her than her daughters, her husband, her soul, or God. In judgment she was wedded to her evil choice: she entered eternity in fellowship with those that suffer the vengeance of eternal fire.

Ah, friends, you see how near being saved you may be, and yet never know salvation. Privileges and means of grace may be yours, and yet you may never enter heaven. You may sit at the Lord's table and sing of salvation, and after all be cast away.

You may feel the strivings of the Spirit, and yet be lost. You may break off from some sins and do many things, and in the end go down to destruction. You may be all but saved, and at last find that from the very gate of heaven there is a path to hell. Anxious inquirer, you are out of Sodom, but not out of danger; you are on the plain, but not in the place of refuge. Flee to Christ. Escape for thy life. Backslider, you are just where Lot's wife was when the devouring fire overtook her. She was looking back; so are you. Remember Lot's wife. "If any man draw back, my soul shall have no pleasure in him" (Heb. x. 38). Procrastinator, you are trifling with your soul and with God. There is no fear of judgment, you think. How do you know? The sin of Lot's wife is your sin: take heed lest her fate be yours. You may die to-night: what then? And if you live, God may give you your own way and let you alone. Let alone, left behind by the merciful God! To be fixed in sin, to be a pillar of salt, a soul encrusted with judicial hardness, as good as damned, how terrible!

> "There is a time, we know not when,
>   A point we know not where,
> That marks the destiny of men
>   To glory or despair.

> "There is a line by us unseen,'
>   That crosses every path ;
> The hidden boundary between
>   God's patience and his wrath."

With heart, voice, and eye overflowing with tenderness, he plead with his hearers to flee to the refuge—to Jesus. The people were deeply moved, and some of them, among the rest a man who is now a zealous office-bearer in a church, have a blessed remembrance of that night, as the time when they entered the ark and for them God shut the door of covenant security in Christ.

In the same month, November, he went to the feeing markets in Aberdeenshire. At Ellon his sufferings were such as he never recovered from. Here, drenched with ceaseless showers, and shivering in fierce hail-blasts of no ordinary violence, he stood all day in the mud, and delivered his last testimony for Christ amidst the din and strife of the fair. "We must not lower the standard," said he, in reference to his trying work. Nor did he lower the standard, for the standard-bearer fell in the very front of the battle. On returning south he revisited Kirriemuir, Alyth, and other places, spending the last night of the year with the Christians in Forfar, whence he writes to his wife:

"Forfar, January 1st, 1867. A happy New Year to you, my dearest M. The Lord bless you very abundantly. As the clock struck the knell of the departing year I was praying for you. My heart was with you all. Ah, my beloved, we may sing, sweetly sing. The Lord hath done great things for us. We may raise our Ebenezer. Now we know not what may be before us this year; but never mind, all will be well. The Lord will break up our way. He will lead us aright. He is our own God. Give each of our pets a New Year kiss from father. I may be able to come and give it myself to them to-morrow. If I am with you by 11 A.M. you will see me; and if not, it will be because of the work. I will try at any rate, but must return at night. We had a blessed time last night. We met at nine, and separated at half-past twelve o'clock. It was very, very solemn. I took the superintendence of the meeting. Very seldom have I seen such a meeting—so much power and evident blessing. A great cry for help comes from many places. I do trust that 1867 will be a year of greater blessing than any before it."

About the middle of January he set out for Orkney; but in consequence of a severe snow-storm, it was only after making extraordinary efforts that he was enabled to reach Aberdeen. There he was arrested by the disease, diabetes, which ultimately carried him to the grave. With the sentence of death in him he returned to Perth, and thence without delay went up to Edinburgh, where he sought advice from the late eminent physician, Sir James Simpson. Little hope of recovery was held out to him; nevertheless, the ruling passion stirred in him, and he addressed a meeting, ill as he was, in the house of Mr. Barbour. On returning home he suddenly grew worse, and in his fevered condition fell into unconsciousness. But whilst reason slept, the gracious heart was all awake, and his talk was constantly of Jesus and souls and eternity. Fancying that he was addressing the students of the New College, Edinburgh, he cried out, "Young men, young men, down with books and up with Christ! Souls are perishing! souls are perishing! Up, and aim at saving sinners." Noble spirit, in thy very wanderings wise and good!

On recovering a measure of strength, he went in April to Limpley Stoke, near Bath, where he sought rest and restoration in the hydropathic establishment. A few of his letters will be read with interest:

"Limpley Stoke, near Bath, 13th April, 1867.

"My Dear Mrs. B——, I cannot tell you how gladdened I was by your kind letter. Away from home, among strangers, sick, one likes to see old friends have not forgotten them. I knew neither you nor Mr. B. would, nor many of the flock to whom I have so often spoken, and to whom if it please God, I hope to speak again—though not this Whit-Sunday—after Turriff market. Markets, I fear, if I should be spared, must be left now to others. My day, I fear, is done with them, and with much rough work besides. It has been a trying time. I cannot tell you all I have passed through for three months, nor recount to you the loving kindness of our God. Oh, how good He has been! How tenderly He has watched over me! How bounteously He has provided for me! I have been treading the banks of the river, and listening to its flow as it rolled along, but all has been peace within. All has been calm, unruffled. I have had no fears, and at the worst was helped to say, "Even so, Father," etc.

" A greater trial than even leaving my beloved wife penniless on a cold world, and children loved with tenderest affection, was the thought of leaving the loved work of bringing souls to Jesus. Away from it—dumb, one sees its greatness, and heaven, hell, God, salvation, eternity, stand out as great realities. I had long battled with the storm, long tried to do something on the field, and God saw fit to put His hand on me even when success in His work was at its highest. We shall know all one day; the web is rapidly weaving, and in glory its finish will be bright, shining in perfect holiness. Hallelujah! I have been six weeks from home. How wondrous the Lord's raising up Mr. J—— M——, of London, to keep me here. He has been as a brother, and I lack nothing, as he is paying all costs. There was no hope of my getting better at home, and I can say it has been good to be here. I cannot tell you exactly how I am. My general health is better, but as yet the disease is apparently not touched. It is greatly kept under, and I am not without hope, in answer to much prayer offered and offering up, I may be so far cured as to be able to preach. It is a strange, mysterious disease, but the Lord can heal it. I am not allowed to preach, read,

or write, though I cannot refrain from sending this
to you. To-day I feel strong. To-morrow I may
be weak. I often think of you all, and am with
you in spirit. May the dew of heaven be on your
beloved husband and his flock. It is a dying scene.
All around this death reigns. Poor, poor England!
Highly favored Scotland! If I could preach I would.
Revival all around this is unknown. My wife left
three days ago for home, going to see Miss M——
on her way. Amidst all her watching, etc., she
has been greatly supported. Give my love to Mr.
B——, Miss F——, and all friends. Pray for me.
I do hope there is room to encourage faith in my
better condition for the last week. I commend you
to the Lord. It is long since we met, going to Aberdeen in the 'Defiance' coach. How many are gone
since! We too shall soon go. Blessed be the Lord,
it is home. There is sweet rest in heaven. God
bless you.

      "Yours in Jesus,   DUNCAN MATHESON."

              TO MRS. J. S.

  "Limpley Stoke, near Bath, 18th April, 1867.

  " MY DEAR FRIEND: Many, many a time I think of
you and of all the S——s of that Ilk. You are often
very near my heart, and the prayer for blessing on
each has often gone up from me here where I am
living, at the back of Horeb.

  " Like an old hulk disabled, I lie passive—no easy
thing for a restless Bedouin like me. I am in a new

school, and if I learn my lessons well I may be able
yet to comfort many and give them a lift Zionward.
Rutherford says: ' Oh, how much I owe to the file
and hammer of the dear Lord Jesus!' Can we not
say the same?

" Tenderly, lovingly, and in a fatherly way, has
the Lord dealt with me. How gently He has held
the cup to my lips! How much of mercy (yea, it's
all mercy) has been mingled with my lot! I have
been standing by the banks of the dark river, and
have listened to its flow, and yet have not been
afraid. I have been on the verge of eternity, and
could sing for joy. Ah, there is no god like *our* God!
no rock like our Rock!

" Right glad was I to meet Mrs. C—— on my way
here. I could scarcely credit it. Short as my interview was, it sent me along more cheerfully. My
heart was much set on coming to see you all; but
the Lord arranged differently. . . It is a strange
and fickle disease, and if I should be ever again as
before, it will be a special forth-putting of divine
power. I long for the loved work of bringing souls
to Jesus. I long to be on the battle-field. I long to
sing over the slain of the Lord, and shout ' victory'
because He has done it. Sometimes I hope I shall.
All is in his hands. The sheep in the wilderness I
feel for. The lambs' bleating goes to my heart. I
pity the *lost*. It is only at times we can realize sin,
salvation, heaven, hell, eternity, as great realities.
How soon shall all have passed here! Life ought to

be an earnest matter, *seeing we have only one.* . .
And now I must close. May all blessing rest on
you and yours. We are under the shadow of His
wings. We are safe in His arms. We move along
the rugged pathway to that land where no sigh is
heard nor sorrow known, where not a cloud darkens
the sky. Ah, we shall soon know about the palms,
harps, crowns of glory! *Forever with the Lord!*
Once again I pray for blessings on you all.

" Ever yours in a loving Lord,
"Duncan Matheson."

TO HIS WIFE.

"Limpley Stoke, May 13th.
"Another morning dawned, my beloved M——,
and another week begun. How they do glide away!
How quickly they run! Soon all will be done, all
will end. The vast eternity lies before. Many in
heaven! many in hell! No day there! no star of
hope! no rest! no rest! no rest! Saved from hell,
we should sing all the way. We should never murmur. Ah, how the thought should still be, 'I shall
never be in devouring fire! I shall never lie down
in everlasting burnings!' As the song of heaven
shall never end, neither shall the wail of hell. May
the Lord save our children! I long to see them in
the ark. They will be brought. Don't let us ever
doubt it for a moment. We had a blessed day yesterday—a sweet word from Mr. T——. The Lord

can restore me fully; but patience must have her perfect work."

"Limpley Stoke, May 15th.
"How few realize the solemnity of eternity! I feel for the people. They are dying, perishing, going to destruction! Oh that God in infinite love would save! I long to be in the field again, but must possess my soul in patience. I am glad I do feel as I do. It's joy to be able to do some little work for God. I cannot express it. My whole system feels as if it partook of joy. If not able to preach, I may for some time be able to get tracts ready, and many things. I hope Lizzie is getting on with her spelling and reading. She will try and be able to read to me the 90th Psalm when I come home. How I do long to see them (the children), and yet the Lord keeps my mind at rest. It has been all love."

Leaving Limpley Stoke in May, he went to Jersey. He is charmed with the scenery, praises God for all he beholds of the divine glory on land and sea, and often wishes his wife were by his side to share his delight. "But we shall see grander sights," he adds: "we shall see the King in His beauty, and the land that is afar off." But the scenery is not the great thing; it is the souls of the perishing. In a certain town he sees the walls covered with placards announcing that Dean this and

Rev. that will lecture on Shakespeare, etc., and his heart bleeds.

From Jersey he proceeds to St. Servan, in Normandy; but the disease has fastened on him, and will not let him go. Not a breath of murmur escapes his lips. He is full of comfort, and often writes to cheer the beloved partner of his life, whose heart droops on his account. Often he breaks out in praise. "Oh praise the Lord, O my soul. How wondrous His love! At times it quite overpowers me. Oh for grace, grace to love His Holy Name! When I think of others I am humbled. Poor —— and his family several times last winter had only meal in the house. He told me so. Oh, how good the Lord is!"

TO MRS. J. S.

"St. Servan, Normandy, France, 27th May, 1867.

"MY DEAR CHRISTIAN FRIEND: Your kind letter reached me at Limpley Stoke. . . . . I congratulate you on the birth of another son. The Lord bless him, and early implant grace, that, if spared, he may be a great blessing. We can take our children to Jesus and not be rejected. They are dear to Him. I like to grasp the promise, 'To thee and to thy seed.' Our charge, our responsibility, is great; but the great burden-bearer will take all. Oh, how He loves! The height, depth, breadth, we cannot fathom. The length we may have some dim idea of, but cannot understand.

23

"I left Limpley some time ago better of my sojourn there. I do feel stronger, but the disease still remains. It seems to have got firmly intrenched; but the Lord can remove it, and no one else. The more I see of doctors, the more do I see they know little of it. As yet its seat is a mystery. Some days I think it is almost gone; and next day I feel great weakness. But all is in a Father's hand, and such a Father too! I would not it were otherwise than He chooses.

"I long to get home, and may in course of a fortnight. My dear wife and children I have not seen for long now. They are well. She longs to meet you all. We shall see if it can be arranged her meeting me at Edinburgh, and both coming on. We shall see as the Lord directs.

"I am all alone in this strange land, unknown to any, and knowing no one. Poor, poor France! You can have no idea of the perfect despotism that reigns. No happy smile seems to light up the people's countenances. There is a restlessness and a yearning after something—they know not what. Alas, alas! no Gospel is preached, no salvation made known, and, so far as can be seen, no souls saved. I often almost weep as I see the masses here rushing on to eternity, not knowing that 'God so loved the world, that He gave his only-begotten Son.' God will not forget the prayers of many a martyred Huguenot. The soil of France was drenched with their blood. The cry, 'How long, Lord, how long,' has gone up

from those beneath the altar. Many a time on entering the churches here, and seeing the mummery
on every side, have I prayed, 'Lord, send thy light
forth and thy truth;' and often have I blessed God
Scotland had a Knox, a Cameron, a Cargill, and a
Peden.

"I was looking to-day at the grave of the great
Chateaubriand, who is buried on a small island off
this place, and asking what now is all the glory he
had? All has perished. Only shall the righteous
be had in everlasting remembrance. Ah! my beloved friend, ours is a glorious hope, ours is a great
reward. What things are in the light of eternity,
and that alone, is worth, and ought to be looked at.
To live for Christ, our motto now, To be with Him
—what shall it be? I do long to go forth again.
Had I been in health, I would have been speaking
to masses with God's blue sky overhead and his
presence realized. Open-air preaching is glorious,
though hard work. I hear from Kirriemuir and Forfar that the converts go well on. Cullen still retains
the blessing. I long to hear of Melrose and Little
Darnick. It will come. Let faith be strengthened.
What God is doing in other places, He can do with
you. My kindest love to your beloved J——, to
Mrs. C——, and all the S——s. Kindly omit no
one. To Mr. and Mrs. B—— and A——, etc., etc.
Now I must finish, as I have a good deal to do. I
send you Psalm cxxi. 6 and Deut. xxxii. 9. We
are marching home. Every march shall yet become

an Elim. He will take the stumbling-blocks out of the way. He will lead and guide. His everlasting arms are around and underneath. He keeps us as the apple of his eye. Hold! is it not enough?

"Ever yours in Christ Jesus,

"DUNCAN MATHESON."

In July he returned to Scotland, and for a while stayed at Bervie, where he set up a daily prayer-meeting. From Bervie he went to Braemar, and from Braemar to Aberdeen, still seeking to recover health and win souls. Health was denied him; souls were given him. From Aberdeen he went to Duff-town, which had been much laid on his heart in prayer. The weak man was strong to bear this burden before the Lord. His prayers were marvellously answered. Here God began to work by him, and several were added to the Lord. At a social meeting held on the evening of the first day of the following year, he delivered an address of extraordinary power, and a considerable number were converted. From Dufftown he retraced his steps to Aberdeen.

His soul is on fire. "I would gladly give all I have," he writes to his wife, "to be once more out preaching Jesus. It is a great and glorious work. I bless God I was called to it. The work done is done for eternity. All other things will soon end. . . . Tell Lizzie I long to hear of her becoming a child of God, a lamb in Christ's fold. Tell her I

long very much. Tell Duncan I wish him to cleave
to Jesus. Tell Mary I long to know she has a new
heart. Tell them I wish them all to be in heaven
with us to praise *forever*. I feel being away from
them, but it is the Lord, and all is well."

In the beginning of 1868 he went to reside for a
few weeks with his Christian friends at Darnlee, in
the south of Scotland. Here again the fire burned.
He could not rest. Gathering together the people
of Darnick, a village in the neighborhood, he indulged once more in the luxury of preaching Christ.
Immediately there was a sound and a stir among
the dry bones. The Spirit of God began to work
gloriously among the dead. The movement, though
confined within the narrow limits of the village and
adjacent country, was a remarkable one: men and
women were brought to the Lord. Happening to
meet him at this time, I asked how he, who was
suffering from a terrible malady, could do so much
work. His reply was characteristic. "Ah!" said
he, "the Lord saw that I was very weak, and just
worked all the more Himself."

In spring he went to Carlsbad, Bohemia, for the
benefit of the waters. On his way to the Continent
he writes from Tunbridge Wells to Miss M——:

"My Dear Friend: Mary has sent me your note
here. I left Perth about ten days ago, and have
been in Hampshire and London. I went to see Major Gibson. He is very ill. I am here for a few
days in a palace. The proprietor, Mr. R——, is a

man of God. I scarcely ever was in a house like it.
'Holiness unto the Lord' is stamped upon it. I am
going to Carlsbad in Austria on Tuesday (D. V.).
The doctors have ordered a trial of its baths, and
God has sent plenty of money to take me. It is a
strange, wandering life, in quest of health. Yet all
is well. I have been rather worse lately. The disease has been very active. All is in the Lord's hands.
I feel leaving all at home. I shall be away about
five weeks. Pray for me that I may be useful, and
if the Lord sees fit, get health for his work. I do
desire greatly to see you. I long for it. Had I not
been going to the Continent I would have come at
once. *All*, ALL, ALL is love. God can do nothing
amiss. All but Mary Jane are well at Perth. We
are kindly treated. We have all things richly to
enjoy. You would wonder what the Lord does for
us. If I come back by London I may get to see
you. Will you not be with us this summer? What
a welcome you will get! I must close, as I have a
good deal to do. There are many changes, but Jesus lives and Jesus reigns. We shall soon be home.
It is a sweet prospect—Home!

"A dear saint of God when dying asked them to
put his simple name on his tombstone, and '*kept*'
under it. We may do the same.

'DUNCAN MATHESON.

Born, ——. Died, ——.

Kept.

J—— McP——.
Born, ——. Died, ——.
Kept.'
"In Jesus, yours,   "Duncan Matheson."

In Carlsbad he found means of distributing some
600 copies of the Word of God. Unable to speak
the language, he would turn up his favorite text,
"God so loved the world," etc., and by gestures and
the use of such terms as he could command he managed to introduce himself and the Gospel to a good
many of the people. By and by they began to know
him, and hail him as a friend. Here he made the
acquaintance of a German Christian, who had charge
of the Bible Depot. An attempt being made by the
burgomaster, instigated by the priest, to stop the
Bible selling and distribution, and the agent being
ordered to leave the house, with the view to his being thrust out of the place altogether, our evangelist took up the case, wrote to a friend in London,
through whose instrumentality the priest's design
was foiled, and the Bible distribution went on as
before. Still panting to be useful, Mr. Matheson
undertook to give instruction to the two Jewish
girls who attended him in his lodgings. His own
children were never forgotten. In all his labors and
wanderings he found time to write little letters to
them. Out of a heap let us take one very much of
a piece with the rest:

TO HIS LITTLE DAUGHTER LIZZIE.

"Carlsbad, 4th May, 1868.

"My own Dear Lizzie: I often think of you, for I love you very much. I often pray for you, for I long to see you safe in Jesus' fold. Many a time when wandering alone in the woods here, I wonder what you are doing, and what kind of a scholar you are getting. You must get on very fast at school, as likely you will one day have to earn your bread through the education you have got. I expect great progress before I return. This is a very beautiful country. The town of Carlsbad is very pleasant, built on both sides of a little river about the size of Bogie at Huntly. The boys and girls are very much like what they are in Perth. I see some with knickerbockers like Duncan's. They have balls, and marbles, and hoops, as the children have in Scotland. But alas! dear Lizzie, they hear not about Jesus as you do. I give some of them copies of the Gospel of John, and if you saw how pleased they are! Some of them begin to know me now, and as I pass smile and take my hand. I love all children; Jesus did so very much. I gave a man a copy of the Gospel, and, poor fellow, he was so grateful, he asked me to come at night and get wine and coffee from him.

"There are a good few Jewish boys and girls here. I feel deeply for them. They hate the very name of Jesus. Oh, my own Lizzie, if you were really converted you would pray for them. We should love the Jews. We got the Bible through the Jews, and

Jesus was born a Jew. Once He was a little boy, running about the streets of Nazareth.

"Would it not be grand if God would send me back to Perth to you all healed? Would I not, as Duncan says, pack up my things, and be off to preach? The waters are very nice, boiling up from the earth. One is very great. I am up every morning long before you now. You must write me a long letter some day. I will try to send a letter to Duncan, and Mary, and George soon. Will you, dear Lizzie, take Jesus to be your Saviour? Oh, do! It would give mother and me more joy than any thing in the world would.

"Your own dear father,

"DUNCAN MATHESON."

TO MISS G.

"Carlsbad, Bohemia, 11th May, 1868.

"MY DEAR MISS G——: How are you all, and especially your dear mother? I do hope you are all well. The larks will be singing sweetly now in S——, and I hope the time of the singing of birds (spiritual) has also come. Thank God for droppings on the parched ground. Thank God for saved ones. The little one shall soon, I trust, become a thousand, and many a sweet flower be planted among your hills that shall bloom and blossom up yonder where the weary rest. Rest is a sweet word. Even a child knows its meaning. My third child Mary is very delicate. One day she came in tired, and in her artless way said, 'Mother, will there be chairs in heaven to sit down on?' Oh, yes, there will be thrones, and crowns, and palms. How we shall make the courts re-echo with the sweet name of Jesus! How we shall shout Hallelujah! Hallelujah! You see, I am far from home in a land of strangers, I know no one. All the time I have been here, I have been the only Englishman. I have met only one Christian, a German Protestant. It is a dark, dark land. No Sabbath here. It is the chief market day. The theatre is open, and almost every shop. The priests have it all their own way. I wish Mr. M—— and others were here one day. After that they would cease tearing the lambs, and speaking against revival. What a terrible doom theirs will be that go to hell from Scotland! Tell W—— to flee for his very life. Were he here he would have no one to tell him. I love W——, and my heart wanders at times from this earthly paradise to the bleak strath. I long to hear glorious tidings from it. I hope M——, 'Greatheart,' has visited you again. God bless him, and give him mighty strength. I was very poorly when I left Scotland. I am drinking the mineral waters, and taking the baths. Thank God, I am feeling a good deal better, but as to whether it may touch the root of the disease remains to be seen. Pray for me. Tell your dear mother to ask healing for the work's sake, if the Lord sees fit. I hope to leave this in three weeks, and may come home by Switzerland.

I enclose this in a letter to Mr. Matheson, London. He will post it for you.

"I feel it sweet to lean on Jesus here. I can speak to Him though I can to no one else. He heareth prayer. My church is the woods alone on the Sabbath day. I have no one to go to. The Lord bless you all. I would like to see you once more. What if my sun is to set at noon? Yet I long to preach Jesus. He *must* reign. He *shall* reign. We shall soon see Him as He is. We shall be like Him.

"Ever yours in Him,
"DUNCAN MATHESON."

The following letter appeared in *The Revival:*

"MY DEAR BROTHER: I am about to leave this land, and I am sorry to do so. Circumstances, however, compel me; and if my work is done in it, I would joyfully say, 'Thy will be done.'

"Since my last, a great door has been opened for the dissemination of the Word of life. I have bought at full price from the Bible Society nearly 600 copies, and scattered them abroad. My main efforts have been directed to the peasantry, as the most hopeful and most needy field. The poverty of many of them is such that they cannot purchase a Bible, and they need it to be brought to their very homes.

"Many a weary mile I have walked, and many a scorching sun has shone upon me. Day after day

I have waited on the highway, some distance from the town, and, accosting the travellers passing along, have made all who could read John iii. 16. I felt God could make one text as effectual as a thousand; and especially that one on which so many have rested their all for eternity. It has undoubtedly been the most interesting work in which I was ever engaged. Many had never seen the Book; and many even did not know its name. This is true of hundreds of thousands, if not millions, in the Austrian empire.

"One day, shortly after my arrival, I gave a copy of John's Gospel to an old man. He took it to his home. In a few days he came to the depot and bought a Bible. Time after time he has come for copies for his neighbors, and now he has become a self-appointed colporteur. Last week the police interfered with him, but he has since got a regular license from a magistrate, and from love to the truth pursues his calling.

"I have had a fine opening amongst the soldiers here in hospital, some of whom had been in Mexico with the unhappy Maximilian. One poor fellow, who has lost his eyesight, asked his comrades what I was doing. On telling him, he said, with a voice choked with emotion as he pointed to his sightless eyeballs, 'No light, no light.'

"One day I came upon an old man sitting by the wayside reading a copy I had given. He smiled on seeing me; and, pointing to heaven, and then to John xiv. 2, repeated with much emphasis, 'In my Father's house are many mansions,' and added, 'Yes, and one for me.'

"It is work needing the greatest caution; for there is the greatest danger of over-driving and attracting notice. One false step might injure for long to come, as, though there is a measure of liberty, yet the priestly power is very great. The work will go rolling along, but not so fast as we may anticipate, or would from our hearts desire.

"To get one Bible into Austria almost baffled me when in the East; and now the Bible Society have an unlimited field, a field the extent of which no one can conceive. Fourteen years ago, 50,000 copies of the Word were sent across the Austrian frontier guarded by dragoons. Now they have returned, and a thousand times more will follow. A bill has lately passed the Hungarian Assembly giving free toleration; and now the colporteur may go from one end to another unmolested. Colportage is the special agency needed. Men of God must be found. The Word must be carried to the cottages of the poor, and the palaces of the rich. Men and money! men and money! The Lord send that with his blessing; for the fields are ripening, and 'the breaker-up' (Micah ii. 13) is going before. Half-hearted efforts will not do. The opening has been made, the prayer of years has been answered, and the responsibility is not realized. Something more is needed than thundering applause at great meetings, when some well-turned sentence is uttered. Something more is needed than singing—

> " ' Were the whole realm of nature mine,
>   That were a present far too small;
> Love so amazing, so divine,
>   Demands my soul, my life, my all.'

"God does not want what we have not to give. The whole realm of nature belongs to Him. He has, however, given money to some, and He expects that his cause shall be supported, and that with liberal hand.

"I have gleaned much information about the Bohemian Protestant Church, and have met with some of its pastors. Looking abroad on Bohemia, you are reminded of Ezekiel's visions. The valley is full of bones, and they are very dry. Can these dry bones live? Yea, Lord, we believe they can. Only breathe, and it is done! Only command, and it shall stand fast! Many of the Protestants live too much on the past. It is well to speak of the sufferings, trials, and triumphs of those who have gone before. It is well to unroll the scroll of martyred lives, and speak with hallowed breath of the names so gloriously written there. But nothing will do in the place of a crucified, living, coming Jesus, and the forth-putting of the Spirit's power.

"Bohemia fills a noble niche in history's page; but as one reads it, how sad the thought, that what faggot and exile could not do a Christless form accomplished! Revival is a thing unknown, and few think of the living power. If they can hold their own, they are satisfied. Efforts for the conversion of others are almost unknown. They have been sadly isolated, and now when they breathe the air of freedom, and the opening is made, no one is ready to enter on it. One said to me yesterday, 'We need evangelists. If God were to raise up a Spurgeon amongst us, the fuel is ready for the kindling.' Only let the cry be heard, 'Bohemia for Christ!' and many would rally round the standard. On its plains the battles of 1866 were fought, which have made a way for the truth never known before.

"I am deeply anxious to get 'The Blood of Jesus.' by Mr. Reid, and a selection of M'Cheyne's sermons, such as I got into Gaelic, translated into the Bohemian language, spoken by three millions. I have so far made arrangements for the translation, and also to have articles taken from the *Herald of Mercy* monthly, and inserted in periodicals published in Prague. Will your readers help with money? It would be but little for some of them to do it altogether. It would be a great privilege. I ask it in the name of Him whose they are, and whom they serve. It may be of infinite consequence having it done soon. Time is passing quickly, and masses are on the march to an eternal hell.

"A gentleman from London has been laboring quietly, and putting the Gospel before many here.

He has great advantages, speaking the German as well as English.

"Farewell, Bohemia! The dark shadows which so long have hung over thee may soon be chased away. A bright morning may soon dawn upon thee. Resurrection-life may be felt in thy scattered hamlets, along thy mountain sides, and in thy crowded cities. I bid thee farewell! and as I do, I breathe out the prayer that God may soon say, 'Arise, shine; for thy light is come, and the glory of the Lord is risen upon thee!'

"Ever yours in Jesus,   DUNCAN MATHESON.

"Carlsbad, Bohemia, June 2, 1868."

After making arrangements with a Bohemian pastor for the translation of Bonar's "Memoir of M'Cheyne," Reid's "Blood of Jesus," and his own "Herald of Mercy," into German, he took his departure from Carlsbad. Passing through Switzerland, he spent a few days at Mannedorf, the scene of Dorothea Trüdel's healing labors, where he was received with the greatest kindness by Pastor Zeller. "All here," he writes, "is love." Ever bent on winning souls, he sought the means of reaching at least one poor heart. A lady, who had lived a gay life, was deeply impressed by his faithful words as he spoke to her of Christ. Hastening home, he reached Perth in a state of utter exhaustion; and it was only too evident to all his friends that the earthly tabernacle was passing rapidly to decay.

At the Perth Conference, in September, 1868, he delivered the following address on co-operation in the work of the Lord:

"We live in stirring times. The old order of things in Church and State is rapidly breaking up, or if not breaking up, great changes are taking place in both.

"A few years ago there was no need of introducing such a subject as this, for evangelists did not occupy the places they now do, and the work which the great God has on the wheels had not then appeared. Whatever may be thought, this subject is a momentous one, and demands instant attention. It is pregnant with infinite results, and affects the destiny of many a soul.

"God has raised up not a few evangelists who go hither and thither. I call the majority of them irregulars, free lances, knowing no church, understanding nothing of parochial divisions, subject to no master but Christ, and, it cannot be denied, wielding a mighty influence on not a few.

"There is much in their freedom of action fitted to help on the work, and also snares which only grace can deliver from. It is likely their numbers will be greatly increased; and if the Lord shall use them as sharp sickles for gathering in souls, surely every Christian will, from the inmost soul, bid them God-speed.

"With such of them as have a single eye in seeking the salvation of the lost (and I think life is nobly spent if spent for this), living ministers can have no difficulty in working. Co-operation with the dead on either side is out of the question; co-operation with the living is to be sought after by every possible means.

"Usually evangelists go to places to which they have been invited by one or more living souls. Their work is to 'PREACH THE GOSPEL.' With all my heart I protest against what I have known—men received with all warmth of simplicity, and quietly leading unsuspecting ones away to their peculiar views, leaving afterwards a leaven of division injurious in its results. Let men be honest. They have a fair field, and the sacred rights of conscience no man has a right to invade. I have preached in many lands, and in this dear land of ours I have proclaimed salvation in its crowded cities, lowly hamlets, by the side of its wimpling burnies, and on its mountain sides, and no one dare charge me with making one proselyte to my views, or spending my time on aught else but the one theme.

"I stand to-day and with my eye fixed on the *lost*, I plead with evangelists to keep at the one thing. With the vision cleared by heaven's lamp, they will see the crowd rushing on to destruction, sporting with death, indifferent to Calvary, laughing on the way to hell. When there are no souls to save, turn to teaching. William Burns, that man of God now in glory, was once asked by a lady many things as to how he felt when preaching to the millions of China. After a pause, and fixing his eye on her—an eye that was always full of pity—he said, 'I never think but of one thing—the LOST and a CHRIST for them!'

"I have been told that it is a sacrifice preaching always to the unsaved. I grant it. We lose much joy in always dwelling about the temple door, and not rising to proclaim higher truths, in which our souls would luxuriate. But if we speak of sacrifices, let us think of the tears wept over Jerusalem, of the sore agony in dark Gethsemane, of the dying love on the cross, and then say if life itself is not worth the giving, if we may but win one jewel for Immanuel's crown.

"Bless God for Scottish caution; but it is often at fault. When an evangelist comes to a place, there ought at first to be a 'trying of the spirits.' Standing on etiquette must be laid aside. Evangelists, if full of power, need not to be patronized. Earnest ministers are not to be ignored. They meet on a common platform. They serve the one Christ.

"Stereotyped modes of action, if need be, must be laid aside, and the ministry of the Spirit must be recognized.

"In my younger days there was a very current advice common amongst the people — '*Bear and forbear.*' There will ever be need of doing both. Essentials must be held by both as with a death-grip; but non-essentials may be scattered to the winds. In one sense neither must act the gentle-

man. Both should toil and sweat as laborers. The
furrows turned up by both should be so joined that
when the seed springs the furrows may be hid under the golden grain ripening for the harvest-home
of heaven.

"I only returned a few days ago from the sea-side.
In my weakness I used to sit and mark the ebbing
and flowing tide. When it was out every inequal-
ity in the shore could be seen, hidden rocks were
laid bare, and the tangle-covered bottom exposed.
When in, all was covered. There was nothing to
be seen but the blue sea—the one great ocean. So,
when the Holy Ghost shall put forth his almighty
power, a subject such as this will not be raised. The
waves of salvation rolling along shall put all out of
sight, as ministers and evangelists—like men rescu-
ing the drowning from a wreck, almost sweating
blood as they do it; or saving the inmates of some
burning home—run with hell pursuing and heaven
beckoning onward, holding up the cross, and in
thrilling tones cry aloud—

    " 'There is life for a look at the crucified One,
      There is life at this moment for thee ;
      Then look, sinner, look unto Him and be saved,
      Unto Him that was nailed to the tree.'

"There is nothing comparable to the loss of a soul.
God, heaven, hell, salvation, are awfully solemn realities. The shadows of eternity are falling on the
path of some of us. They are not dark, but light-
ened by the glory that shines from the better land.

I know not how it may soon be with me. A Father can heal if He pleases. I leave it in His hand. It is sweet to know that we toil only for a little. That sowing in tears, we shall reap in joy. Let us seek the welding heat of heaven. We can only do valiantly as we receive power from on high. That power will not be withheld, and blessing will come. With all the earnestness of a dying man, and with my eye fixed on the judgment-seat, I would affectionately urge all who love the Lord to pray, labor, and live for the lost. Lift up Jesus and 'JESUS ONLY,' for—

> " ' His name forever shall endure:
>   Last like the sun it shall;
>   Men shall be blest in Him, and Bless'd
>   All nations shall Him call.

> " ' And blessed be His glorious name,
>   To all eternity;
>   The whole earth let His glory fill:
>   Amen: so let it be.' "

For the rest of his time he was seldom able to preach. But the ruling passion was strong in him to the last. Although not a murmur escaped his lips, he longed for the old freedom and joy in proclaiming the glad tidings of salvation, and sometimes seemed like the imprisoned lion thrusting himself with a noble violence against the bars of his cage. One day on hearing that three persons had been converted through the instrumentality of his "Herald of Mercy" he said, "I thank God for this;

but after all there is nothing like the living voice for carrying the truth to men's souls." Now and then he indulged in the luxury of preaching, and never at this period without marked results. There was now a marvellous intensity and tenderness in his words. He really poured out his soul in his addresses. It appeared to need more than human obduracy of heart to listen to him without being melted and drawn. In several places sinners were converted at the little meetings.

Now, however, that the living voice was all but hushed did he labor to publish salvation through the press. And the grace and kindness of his Divine Master were strikingly displayed in the remarkable blessing that now rested on his publications. Every week, and sometimes indeed every day, brought him tidings of sinners converted by means of his periodical or special issues. The blessed results of the labor of former years were also constantly and providentially coming to light, and he was both cheered and humbled. "Oh, how good a God He is!" was his frequent exclamation. "Oh! if I were better," he often said, "I would preach Christ more than ever. I would warn men more than ever. I would speak of eternity more than ever."

As he was about to start for the south of England in quest of health, the dying evangelist took up the railway map to examine the route, but forgetting his immediate purpose he began to ponder the spiritual condition of the region, and looking up

said, "These three counties are *dead—utterly dead!*"
Compelled by the inroads of the fatal disease to
avoid the excitement of conversation, he invented
various devices to supply the place of personal dealing with fellow-travellers, or other strangers whom
he happened to meet. Knowing the reluctance of
many to read religious tracts or books, he printed
in large type on little neat cards pointed and solemn truths, with which he sought to awaken the
world's heavy sleepers. For example the following:

"There is
A GOD
Who sees thee!
A MOMENT
Which flies from thee!
AN ETERNITY
Which awaits thee!
A God whom you serve so ill!
A Moment of which you so little profit!
An Eternity you hazard so rashly!
READER,
Where will you spend Eternity?
In Heaven or Hell?
WHICH?"

His was now a new and even more Christ-like
ministry. The ministry of activity, of valor, of exhausting toil, and of heroic perseverance had been
fully accomplished. It was now the ministry of suf-

fering: and holy suffering is most like the ministry
of the Son of God. It is the ministry of the crushed
sandal-tree which yields its perfume to the woodman's axe. The ministry of the alabaster box which
must needs be broken that the aroma of the oint-
ment may fill the house. We saw the breaking of
the box, and the richness of the fragrance tempted
us to ask, Why this waste—why this premature
break-up of that goodly form? We might as well
ask why the angel of the covenant maimed Jacob
just as he obtained victory and blessing. God's
Israels have strange experiences; out of weakness
they are often made strong. It was at this period
he attained his greatest power in prayer. He now
ascended to a summit of faith that few Christians
ever reach. "I have been all night," said he to a
Christian friend, "between Gethsemane and Calvary, between the manger and the cross." Many a
night was now spent on the mount of intercession.
It was not merely the prayer of faith: it was also
the prayer of love. As the glory of love is its dis-
interestedness, so one of the noblest qualities of true
prayer is disinterested love. He seemed to lay his
will alongside of the will of God, and the answer
admitted not of doubt. Often did he rise from his
knees in a flood of tears, but they were tears of joy.
And we have seen a whole assembly moved till
every eye was wet, whilst with child-like simplicity
and holy tenderness he entreated his God—"Lord,
take us to-day to Calvary, and show us afresh thy

pierced hands and feet, thy thorn-crowned brow.
Give us at the cross a new baptism of thy Holy
Spirit. Send us to tell the unsaved that we have
seen the Lord. Make us weep over them, as Thou
didst over Jerusalem. Show us the moving mass
on their march down to the pit. Show us the city:
let us walk its golden streets. We are in it by faith
to-day. Show us its jasper walls, and above all Him
that is its light." Thus he prayed: and it is added
by the narrator, "he wept as he rose from prayer."
Often as he plead for the salvation of Scotland, and
of the whole world, he said, like one of our ancient worthies, "Take long strides, Lord, take long
strides."

The summer of 1869 found him in a dying state.
Many prayers had been offered for his recovery,
but he grew worse. All known remedies had been
employed; for the same generous friends who had
aided him in his numerous schemes of Christian
usefulness, lovingly ministered to him of their substance during his long illness. But all means were
in vain; the disease obedient to the great Master's
will went on in its stern course, till at length every
pin was unfastened, and the tabernacle lay in ruins.
In July of that year he went to Bruar in the Highlands, where he remained till within a fortnight of
his death. Although in a condition of extreme
prostration, he employed much of his time in preparing various matters for the press. "*The Herald
of Mercy*" was got ready for the rest of the year;

and after he was gone it was touching enough to
see his little periodical appear month after month
just as he had prepared it; it was like a voice
speaking out of eternity. He also prepared a little
book entitled "Things Worth Knowing," and papers
called "Good Tidings" and "New Year's Gift," hundreds of thousands of which were printed and put
into circulation. One of these papers, it may be
stated on the authority of a faithful servant of the
Lord Jesus, was instrumental in the conversion of
two persons some three months after the hand of
this unwearying sower of the truth had lost its
cunning in death.

Another instance of blessing on those last labors
appeared in "*The Christian*" of Sept. 15th, 1870:

"H.M.S. *Hibernia*, Malta.—Towards the end of
last year I received a large bundle of tracts, books
and 'New Year's Gifts,' from an unknown donor.
They were addressed to Mr. Hodges, Royal Na-
val Scripture-reader (my predecessor), Soldiers' and
Sailors' Institute, Burmala, Malta, who kindly sent
word that I might distribute them amongst the
men for whom they were intended. This I did as
follows: Hymn-books, Burmala and Valetta Insti-
tutes, books amongst the soldiers and children;
'New Years Gifts' one in each mess of every ship
on the station, some twenty-four vessels; and the
tracts have been given away in various ships, regiments, hospitals, and prisons. Now all these have
not only greatly strengthened my hands during

the past ten months, but a rich manifest blessing has attended their widespread circulation. *The 'New Year's Gifts,' and ' Good Tidings' caused quite a revival of true religion in several quarters.* One remarkable case I will mention. To the reading of a 'New Year's Gift,' one of the crew of the *Bellerophon* owes his direct conversion. This man is a genuine disciple of the Lord; so that if he was the only case of blessing, the person who kindly sent them is richly rewarded. 'That day' will declare all the good done. I ought to mention that, after W—— received the blessing himself, he sent the little messenger home to his aged mother and friends, there to be a further blessing, we trust. I should be very happy to receive another similar bundle ere this year closes, and we will look forward with increasing joy for a greater blessing on them, and to that happy hour when sower and reaper shall rejoice together in our home above. Mr. G. Brown, Sick Bay, Steward H.M.S. *Crocodile,* Portsmouth, will receive any parcels for me, and see them safely delivered.—Charles Brider."

On Sabbath evenings Mr. Matheson addressed a meeting in a room of the house where he lodged. To this meeting he literally crept, so weak was he; and from the last one he was all but carried to his own room. In vain did friends entreat him to spare himself. He knew his time was very short; he several times told his wife he would be removed about the middle of September; and he begged to be indulged in the luxury of preaching Christ once more. These services were deeply impressive, his last text being, "What think ye of Christ?"

As he lay looking out on the hills he said, "Very, very soon these eyes shall be gazing on the everlasting hills. . . . Soon I shall be beholding fairer scenes than those. . . . I shall soon see the King in his beauty, and the land that is very far off."

On September 3d he returned to Perth; and on reaching his house he called his whole family together, that together they might offer thanks for the great goodness of the Lord to him and them. He then calmly set his house in order, not overlooking the most trivial matter. "Give my clothes to the poor," he said to his wife; it was almost the only legacy he had to leave. To his friends at parting he spake words of joy and triumph. To Dr. A. S—— he said, "Resurgam." To Mr. M——, an evangelist, "You are going to speak of the King, but I am going to see Him." To his old Crimean friend, Mr. Hector Macpherson, whose emotion at parting was too strong for even the soldier's firmness, he said, "Do not weep for me: I have only to die once that I may live forever." To another, who found him making arrangements for a series of evangelistic services to be held at Hillhead, near Glasgow, he said, "I should like to die planning revival services." The services then planned by him were in progress at the time of his death: the word

was in demonstration of the Spirit, and a considerable number of persons were converted.

To another friend he said, "I got the victory long
ago—when the Lord first forgave my sins. . . .
You have nothing now to ask for me but that I may
have an abundant entrance."

To Mrs. Sandeman, Springland, he said, "It's all
love—it's all well. *Reality* is the great thing—I
have always sought reality. . . . . . I have
served the Lord for two and twenty years; I have
sought to win souls—it has been my *passion*—and
now I have the fruit of it. One of my spiritual children went the other day as a missionary to China,
and many others of them are preaching the Gospel.
. . . Well, at least you can say you have seen
the vanquished the conqueror."

When alone, he was often heard saying to himself with a quiet jubilance of tone, "Victory!" and
often too, in soft, rapt whispers, "Jesus only!"

From day to day he fed on the good word of
grace. One day it was, "Ye are complete in Him."
Another day it was, "Christ is the end of the law for
righteousness to every one that believeth." Again
it was, "Who his own self bare our sins in his own
body on the tree, that we being dead to sins should
live unto righteousness: by whose stripes ye were
healed." Near his end he triumphed in those words,
"The eternal God is thy refuge, and underneath are
the everlasting arms." Shortly before his departure
he was fiercely assailed by the great adversary.

The conflict was sharp but short, and victory remained with the soldier of the cross. Grasping the
sword of the Spirit, he was enabled to contend till
at length the enemy left the field and returned no
more. Curiously enough, the Scripture by which
he was enabled through grace at this time to overcome was the memorable passage inscribed on his
grand-uncle's tombstone, "They that be wise shall
shine as the brightness of the firmament, and they
that turn many to righteousness as the stars forever and ever!" More than twenty years before he
had knelt upon the grave and consecrated himself
to the service of Jesus, transcribing with prayers
and tears into his innermost heart the words of the
prophet. They had been the helm of his subsequent
career, the guiding star of his extraordinary ministry. To these words his thoughts naturally reverted;
and now when clouds gathered upon the sky, his star
shone calmly down upon him, and he was guided
through the storm. To use his own saying, *he was
now getting what he had gone in for.* There are many
lights in the firmament of the Word; and it may
seem meet to God in his wisdom to guide through
the darkness and the tempest some keen-eyed mar-
iner of faith by a star too remote for your eyes or
mine to discern. "I have not been wise," he said
with unfeigned humility to his wife. "Yet God has
used me in turning many to righteousness, and I
know," he added, with an eye rekindled as the darkness passed away before the light of coming glory

now streaming into his soul, "I know He is true, and I shall be with Him forever."

To his children he spoke of Jesus, and of the chariot coming to take him to glory. He charged them each one to meet him in heaven. To his wife he frequently addressed words of comfort: "You will have your trials," he said, "but the Lord will bear you through them, and the trials will make you shine the brighter." He assured her again and again that the Lord would liberally supply all her and their children's needs. "Mary," said he to her, "I have another text to give you to-day. It is this: 'A Father of the fatherless, and a Judge of the widows, is God in his holy habitation'" (Ps. lxviii. 5.) To his sister he said, "Oh, Jessie, isn't it infinite love that I should not be suffering?" He abounded in thanksgiving, and often asked Mrs. Matheson to assist him in singing praise. Psalms, and hymns, and spiritual songs were the latest efforts of his voice. Two hymns, "Awaiting the Summons," and "Soon to be with Jesus," he frequently repeated; and as they seemed most fitly to express his thoughts and feelings during his last hours, one of them may, in part at least, be given here:

AWAITING THE SUMMONS.

" Away from the wilderness-state
   My spirit would thankfully flee;
And yet in the patience of hope I would wait,
   Till Thou, my Lord, callest for me.

" O why should I tremble or dread
    At whatever may happen around,
While I cling unto Thee, the life-giving Head,
    In whom all true nourishment's found?

" Thou dost not allow me to quail,
    Though keen the blasts oftentimes blow;
For Thou art my refuge, that never can fail,
    Though all things are failing below.

" With a conscience at peace with my God,
    And a heart from anxiety free,
I pray that the rest of my path may be trod
    In happy communion with Thee."

"Mary," he said to his wife, "this room is filled with the heavenly host. Had I strength, how we would sing!" On this he repeated the last three verses of the 72d Psalm in metre, coming back with rapt delight on the last four lines—

" And blessed be His glorious name
    To all eternity !
The whole earth let His glory fill:
    Amen: so let it be !"

He now appeared to be filled with the Spirit of glory and of God; and as if already triumphing amidst the heavenly host, his voice gave out with exultant tones the words of Psalm lxviii. 17—

" God's chariots twenty thousand are,
    Thousands of angels strong;
In's holy place God is, as in
    Mount Sinai them among."

As night came on—the last brief period of darkness to him forever—he said, with characteristic joyfulness of faith, "Light all the lights; and let not

this be a charnel-house." It was to him not death
but life; not sorrow, disaster, or defeat, but joy,
honor, and victory. It was not a time to mourn,
but a festive season; and he would go to the mar-
riage-supper of the Lamb with a garland of praise
in his hand to cast at the feet of the King. It was
in the same jubilance of faith that he often said,
" Be not sorrowful at my burial. Praise God as ye
carry me to my grave. And when you lay me down,
sing—

" ' There is rest for the weary.' "

Yet amidst all this triumph, nothing could be more
striking than the increasing trustfulness with which
he clung to the cross. The scriptures he chiefly
dwelt on were those bearing on the death of Jesus
in the room of sinners. To an evangelist who came
to bid him farewell, he said, with death-like earnestness, "Preach CHRIST." Not long before he had said
to a young minister—one of his own converts—"If
I were to live I would preach *substitution* more than
I have ever done."

His peace was now neither coming nor going, but
flowing on like a river; and he frequently repeated
these lines—

" In peace let me resign my breath,
And thy salvation see;
My sins deserve eternal death,
But Jesus died for me."

He had now but one want—" the coming of the
King." " How is it the King tarries," he said, in a

25

tone of intense longing, "when the chariot-wheels are so very near?" Then he seemed to hearken for a little to the inaudible voice of the King, and after the pause said, "Ah, but He has a purpose in this!" It was said to him,

> "Jesus can make a dying bed
> Feel soft as downy pillows are."

"Yes," he replied; "and He is doing it for me." His suffering was great, but at the worst he said, in his own hopeful way,

> "Beyond the sighing and the weeping
> I shall be soon."

At this time, a few hours before he died, he said that many of his old friends were passing before his mind. His ardently affectionate heart was summoning them up for a last embrace. Mentioning the names of one after another, he said, "Give them my undying love."

Every prayer seemed to be answered and every wish gratified. He longed to see his sister, and she came unexpectedly from Huntly. He desired to see his former pastor and fellow-laborer in the Gospel, Mr. Williamson, and providentially his well-tried friend came in after a long journey. He earnestly desired once more to see the writer of these pages, and it was my privilege to be with him during the last hour of his life. On entering his room I was struck with his appearance. He was singularly elevated, and yet profoundly calm. His intellect possessed all the vigor of his best days; his eye was clear and softly lustrous; his voice had recovered its manliness and power, and his lion-like features seemed to repose in the sense of victory. I saw at a glance that he was on the threshold of glory, for the very light of heaven was on his face. Yet all was so natural and unaffected that I could not help saying to myself, "He is the same man, the very same man, Duncan Matheson and no other." Even a touch of the old humor was there. Taking a few whiffs of a cigar to relieve his mouth of the painful sensations caused by disease, he said, referring to the morbid pietism which his manly spirit had never liked, "If some people saw me at this, they would think it was not very like reading 'Thomas à Kempis.'"

Particularly and tenderly he inquired about the welfare of all his friends. As of old, he asked especially about the work of the Lord, praising God when he was told of prosperity, and saying solemnly in reference to certain who temporized, "Never mind them. 'What is the chaff to the wheat?' saith the Lord." Then he began to tell me that he was resting on the Sin-bearer, at the same time quoting the Scriptures that were yielding his soul peace and rest. He said, "I am weary, and I am waiting. . . . Heaven will literally be a rest to me." He seemed like a man returning from the harvest-field with the last golden sheaf upon his shoulder. Pacing wearily along the stubble in the clear, crisp air of an autumnal evening, suddenly the countenance of the worn-out reaper brightens, and his step is instinctively quickened as his ear catches the first sound of the merry-making and the harvest-home; and all his weariness is forgotten as he anticipates

....   " The shout of them that triumph,
        The song of them that feast."

As he talked of Christ and glory, he said, " It may be a few days yet before I get home, or only a few hours." Perceiving the emotion I could not conceal, he said, with the tear of fond, but manly affection in his eye, " You cannot come with me. You have more work to do, and you must wait a while. . . . . . . Ah! dear Macpherson," he added, with much feeling, as he called to mind the former days, "you and I are like two war-ships "—the old warrior spirit stirred in him to the last—"meeting far out at sea, and one of them is going down in mid-ocean." " Not so," I replied; " rather it is this: one of them is about to enter the haven of peace, while the other is left to toss upon the uncertain deep." Then, as if girding up his loins, he said bravely, "I have cast my five fatherless children upon the Lord, and all shall be well."

His heart now began to stir again with longings to depart, and with the high praises of his God. When we had prayed together, he said in his old familiar way, " Man, I don't get singing enough. I want to sing: will you help me? " I agreed to sing with him the hymn, " Shall we gather at the river?" But before singing he insisted, with that warmth of genuine hospitality that characterized him, on my partaking of refreshment. Just then he was seized with cramp. We seemed to hear a voice saying, "The Master is come, and calleth for thee." Quickly his wife and sister were by his side. "Our friend is in deep waters," said his kind Christian physician whom I ran to fetch. So indeed it was: but his feet were firm upon the rock. The everlasting arms were underneath him. "Lord Jesus, come quickly! Oh, come quickly!" he several times exclaimed. Quickly the Lord Jesus came and took him. Our hymn was not sung. He went to sing by the river: and we were left to weep.

On the 16th day of September, just as the sun was going down, Duncan Matheson disappeared from our view to shine in another sphere. Thus departed a right brave and great-hearted man—the man who above millions had lived for God, the man who above most men had labored for souls and for eternity. "Blessed are the dead that die in the Lord from henceforth: yea, saith the Spirit, that they may rest from their labors: and their works do follow them."

In accordance with his own wish the funeral was a private one. On the 21st September a few friends, not without prayers and praises, and tears and sore pangs of grief, quietly carried him to the new burial place at Scone, and laid him down in a pleasant spot chosen by himself. His friend, the minister of the

Free Church at Scone, having offered prayer by the grave, the company joined in singing, "There is rest for the weary," two of the evangelist's own converts, a preacher and a student, both devoted to the work of the Lord, leading the praise. So we left him there to rest, and truly he sleeps well.

His grave is marked by a plain monument on which is inscribed, as prepared by himself, the following epitaph:

"In Memory
of
DUNCAN MATHESON,
Editor 'Herald of Mercy,'
and
Evangelist.
Born at Huntly, Nov. 22d, 1824.
Born again, Oct. 26, 1846.
Died Sept. 16th, 1869.

"And they that be wise shall shine as the brightness of the firmament: and they that turn many to righteousness as the stars forever and ever (Dan. xii. 3)."

Reader, if you are not in Christ, ponder, I pray you, "the path of your feet." As we part, I will leave the Scottish evangelist at his old post, with his hand pointing you to the way of life. You remember the words of the Lord Jesus in which He describes the wide and strait gates (Matt. vii. 13, 14), and by a few master-strokes portrays the characters, ways, and eternal destinies of the two classes of men, the saved and the lost. This was our evangelist's great burden, and never did he preach on the broad and narrow ways, as we heard him tell, with-

out seeing fruit. The substance of that discourse, so
marvellously owned of God, he printed in a conspicuous form, which he held up everywhere to catch
the eye of travellers to the judgment-seat. Here
then, as we mark the last footprint of this faithful
servant of the Lord, let us erect his finger-post of

THE TWO ROADS.

THE BROAD.	THE NARROW.
Its gate is wide........Matt. vii. 13.	Its gate is strait.......Matt. vii. 14.
Its way is dark........Prov. ii. 13.	Its way is light........John viii. 12.
Its paths are false.....Prov. xiv. 12.	Its paths are truth.....Ps. xxv. 10.
It is crowded by those	It is trod by those who
who forsake God....Isaiah i. 4.	forsake sin.........I Pe. iii.10,11.
who do iniquity.....Isaiah lix. 3.	who do the will of
	God..............Matt. vii. 21.
who serve the devil..John viii. 44.	who serve the Lord
	Christ............Col. iii. 24.
It leads to Misery.....Rom. ii. 9.	It leads to Happiness..Ps. lxiv. 10.
Death ......Rom. vi. 21.	Life..........Matt. vii. 14.
Judgment..Matt. xii. 36.	Eternal Glory.I Peter v. 10.
Its end is HELL, where	Its end is HEAVEN,
there shall be wailing	where there is fulness
and gnashing of teeth.Matt. xiii. 42.	of joy and pleasures
	for evermore........Ps. xvi. 11.

READER,

Mark! On this side you have	And on this side you find
DEATH!	LIFE!
DAMNATION!	SALVATION!
SATAN!	GOD!

Along which of these roads are you hastening!
for in one or the other you most certainly are. Are
you in the way to GOD and HEAVEN? or SATAN and
HELL? A mistake, if continued to the end, will be
fatal. "For what shall it profit a man, if he shall
gain the whole world, and lose his own soul?"
(Mark viii. 36).

Jesus Christ says: "I am the way, the truth, and the life: no man cometh unto the Father, but by Me" (John xiv. 6). "He that believeth on Me hath everlasting life" (John vi. 47). "Him that cometh to Me I will in no wise cast out" (John vi. 37). "I came not to call the righteous, but sinners to repentance" (Mark ii. 17). "The Son of man is come to seek and to save that which was lost" (Luke xix. 10).

WHERE WILL YOU SPEND ETERNITY?

"FOR GOD AND ETERNITY."

SCOTCH BOOKS

AND

SCOTTISH AUTHORS.

PUBLISHED BY

ROBERT CARTER AND BROTHERS, NEW YORK.

KER (REV. JOHN) DAY DAWN AND RAIN 2 00
LEIGHTON'S COMPLETE WORKS 3 00
McCHEYNE'S WORKS 3 00
McCOSH'S DIVINE GOVERNMENT 2 50
——————— TYPICAL FORMS 2 50
——————— INTUITIONS OF MIND 3 00
——————— DEFENCE OF TRUTH 3 00
——————— CHRISTIANITY AND POSITIVISM 1 75
——————— LOGIC 1 50
———————SCOTTISH PHILOSOPHY 4 00

MACDUFF'S WORKS.

Morning and Night Watches .	$0 50	Sunsets on the Hebrew Mountains. 12mo	$1 50
Words and Mind of Jesus . .	0 50	The Prophet of Fire. 12mo .	1 50
Footsteps of St. Paul. 12mo .	1 50	Shepherd and his Flock. 12mo	1 50
Family Prayers. 16mo . . .	1 25	Memories of Olivet. 12mo. .	2 00
Memories of Gennesaret . .	1 50	Noontide at Sychar. 16mo. .	1 50
Memories of Bethany. 16mo.	1 00	Memories of Patmos. 12mo .	2 00
Bow in the Cloud. 18mo . .	0 50	St. Paul in Rome. 16mo . .	1 25
Story of Bethlehem. 16mo .	1 00	Tales of Warrior Judges . . .	1 00
Hart and Water Brooks . . .	1 00	Comfort Ye, Comfort Ye. . .	1 50
Gates of Prayer	1 00	Healing Waters	1 25
Grapes of Eshcol. 16mo . .	1 00		

MACLEOD (DR. NORMAN) HIGHLAND PARISH 1 25
MILLER'S (HUGH) WORKS. 10 vols 15 00
——————— ——————— LIFE BY BAYNE. 2 vols 3 00
PATERSON ON THE SHORTER CATECHISM 0 75
POLLOCK'S COURSE OF TIME 1 25
REID (JOHN) VOICES OF THE SOUL 1 75
RUTHERFORD'S LETTERS . . . · 2 50
SCOTIA'S BARDS, ILLUSTRATED 4 50
WILSON'S LIGHTS AND SHADOWS OF SCOTTISH LIFE . . 1 00
YOUNG (JOHN) THE CHRIST OF HISTORY 1 25

530 BROADWAY, NEW YORK
October, 1875.

ROBERT CARTER & BROTHERS'

NEW BOOKS.

FORTY YEARS IN THE TURKISH EMPIRE.

Memoirs of Rev. William Goodell, late Missionary at Constantinople.
By E. D. G. PRIME, D.D. $2.50.

AUTOBIOGRAPHY AND MEMOIR OF THOMAS GUTHRIE, D.D. 2 vols. 12mo. $4.00.

"It is told in the chattiest, simplest, most unaffected way imaginable, and the pages are full of quaint, racy anecdotes, recounted in the most characteristic manner." — *London Daily News.*

THE WORKS OF THOMAS GUTHRIE, D.D.

9 vols. In a box. $13.50. (The vols. are sold separately.)

HUGH MILLER'S WORKS. 10 vols. 12mo. $15.00.

FOOTPRINTS OF CREATOR . . $1.50	FIRST IMPRESSIONS OF ENGLAND $1.50
OLD RED SANDSTONE . . . 1.50	POPULAR GEOLOGY 1.50
SCHOOLS AND SCHOOLMASTERS 1.50	TALES AND SKETCHES . . . 1.50
TESTIMONY OF THE ROCKS . . 1.50	ESSAYS 1.50
CRUISE OF THE BETSEY . . . 1.50	HEADSHIP OF CHRIST 1.50

LIFE AND LETTERS. 2 vols. $3.00.

D'AUBIGNÉ'S HISTORY OF THE REFORMATION IN THE TIME OF CALVIN. Vol. 6. $2.00.

By the Author of

"THE WIDE WIDE WORLD."

1. THE LITTLE CAMP ON EAGLE HILL. **$1.25**
2. WILLOW BROOK. $1.25.
3. SCEPTRES AND CROWNS. $1.25.
4. THE FLAG OF TRUCE. $1.25.
5. BREAD AND ORANGES. $1.25.
6. THE RAPIDS OF NIAGARA. **$1.25.**

THE SAY AND DO SERIES, *comprising the above 6 vols.*
In a box. $7.50.

By the same Author.

THE STORY OF SMALL BEGIN- NINGS. 4 vols. In a box . . $5 00	HOUSE OF ISRAEL **$1.50**
WALKS FROM EDEN 1.50	THE OLD HELMET. 2.25
	MELBOURNE HOUSE 2 00

By her Sister.

THE STAR OUT OF JACOB . . $1.50	HYMNS OF THE CHURCH MILI-
LITTLE JACK'S FOUR LESSONS . 0.60	TANT $1.5
STORIES OF VINEGAR HILL.	ELLEN MONTGOMERY'S BOOK-
6 vols. 3.00	SHELF. 5 vols. 5.00

BRENTFORD PARSONAGE.   By the author of
"Win and Wear." 16mo. $1.25.

Uniform, by the same Author.

WHO WON? **$1.25**
MABEL HAZARD'S THOROUGHFARE 1.25
DOORS OUTWARD 1.25

By the same Author.

WIN AND WEAR SERIES. 6 vols. $7.50	LEDGESIDE SERIES. 6 vols. . . **$7.50**
THE GREEN MOUNTAIN SERIES.	BUTTERFLY'S FLIGHTS. 3 vols. 2.25
5 vols. 6.00	

IMOGEN. A Tale. By EMILY SARAH HOLT. **$1.50.**

By the same Author.

ISOULT BARRY. 12mo . . . $1.50	ASHCLIFFE HALL. 16mo . . **$1.25**
ROBIN TREMAYNE. 12mo . . 1.50	VERENA. 12mo 1.50
THE WELL IN THE DESERT 1.25	THE WHITE ROSE OF LANGLEY 1.50

.

ELSIE'S SANTA CLAUS. By Miss JOANNA H.
MATHEWS, author of the "Bessie Books." $1.25.

MISS ASHTON'S GIRLS. By Miss JOANNA H.
MATHEWS. 6 vols. In a box. $7.50.

FANNY'S BIRTHDAY GIFT . . $1.25	ELEANOR'S VISIT $1.25
THE NEW SCHOLARS 1.25	MABEL WALTON'S EXPERIMENT 1.25
ROSALIE'S PET 1.25	ELSIE'S SANTA CLAUS . . . 1.25

By the same Author.

THE BESSIE BOOKS. 6 vols. . $7.50	LITTLE SUNBEAMS. 6 vols.. . $6.00
THE FLOWERETS. 6 vols. . . 3.60	KITTY AND LULU BOOKS. 6 vols. 5.00

By Julia A. Mathews.

GOLDEN LADDER SERIES. 6 vols. $3.00	DARE TO DO RIGHT SERIES.
DRAYTON HALL SERIES. 6 vols. 4.50	5 vols.. . . . . $5.50

COULYNG CASTLE; or, A Knight of the Older
Days. By AGNES GIBERNE. 16mo. $1.50.

By the same Author.

AIMÉE: A Tale of James II. . $1.50	THE CURATE'S HOME. . . . $1.25
DAY STAR; or, Gospel Stories 1.25	FLOSS SILVERTHORN 1.25

THE ODD ONE. By Mrs. A. M. MITCHELL PAYNE.
16mo. $1.25.

FRED AND JEANIE: How they learned about God.
By JENNIE M. DRINKWATER. 16mo. $1.25.

CHRISTIAN THEOLOGY FOR THE PEOPLE.
By WILLIS LORD, D.D., LL.D. 8vo. $4.00.

CHRISTIANITY AND SCIENCE. A Series of
Lectures, by Rev. A. P. PEABODY, D.D., of Harvard College. $1.75.

MIND AND WORDS OF JESUS, FAITHFUL
PROMISER, AND MORNING AND NIGHT WATCHES
By J. R. MACDUFF, D.D. All in one vol. Red Line Edition. Hand
somely bound in gilt cloth, gilt edges. $1.50.

THE SCOTTISH PHILOSOPHY. Biographical,
Expository, Critical. By JAMES McCOSH, LL.D., President of
Princeton College. 8vo. $4.00.

By the same Author.

THE METHOD OF DIVINE GOV-		LOGIC $1.50
ERNMENT $2.50		CHRISTIANITY AND POSITIVISM 1.75
TYPICAL FORMS 2.50		ROYAL LAW OF LOVE. Paper. 0.25
THE INTUITIONS OF THE MIND 3.00		REPLY TO TYNDALL 0.50
DEFENCE OF FUNDAMENTAL		
TRUTH 3.00		

THE PILGRIM'S PROGRESS. Twenty full-page
Pictures. Handsomely bound in cloth. 4to, gilt and black. $2.00.

NURSES FOR THE NEEDY. By L. N. R. $1.25.

THE GOLDEN CHAIN. By MISS MARSH. $0.90.

FOUR YEARS IN ASHANTEE. By RAMSEYER
and KUHNE. $1.75.

TWELVE MONTHS IN MADAGASCAR. By
Dr. MULLENS. With Map. $1.75.

LITTLE BROTHERS AND SISTERS. By MAR-
SHALL. 16mo. $1.25.

New A. L. O. E. Books.

AN EDEN IN ENGLAND. 16mo, $1.25 ; 18mo,
75 cents.

FAIRY FRISKET. 75 cents.

THE LITTLE MAID. 75 cents.

THE SPANISH CAVALIER. 75 cents.

ALICE NEVILLE AND RIVERSDALE. By C. P
BOWEN 4 Illustrations. $1.25.

THE SUFFERING SAVIOUR. By F. W. KRUM-
MACHER. $1.50.

THE WORKS OF JAMES HAMILTON, D.D.

Comprising : —

ROYAL PREACHER.	GREAT BIOGRAPHY.
MOUNT OF OLIVES.	HARP ON THE WILLOWS.
PEARL OF PARABLES.	LAKE OF GALILEE.
LAMP AND LANTERN.	EMBLEMS FROM EDEN.

LIFE IN EARNEST.

In 4 handsome uniform 16mo volumes. $5.00.

NATURE AND THE BIBLE. By J. W. DAWSON,
LL.D., Principal of McGill University, Montreal, Canada. With 10
full-page Illustrations. $1.75.

ALL ABOUT JESUS. By the Rev. ALEXANDER
DICKSON. 12mo. $2.00.

THE SHADOWED HOME, and the Light Beyond.
By the Rev. E. H. BICKERSTETH, author of "Yesterday, To-day, and
Forever." $1.50.

EARTH'S MORNING; or, Thoughts on Genesis.
By the Rev. HORATIUS BONAR, D.D. $2.00.

THE RENT VEIL. By Dr. BONAR. $1.25.

FOLLOW THE LAMB; or, Counsels to Converts.
By Dr. BONAR. 40 cents.

*CARTERS' 50–VOLUME S. S. LIBRARY.
No. 2. Net, $20.00.

These fifty choice volumes for the Sabbath School Library, or the home circle,
are printed on good paper, and very neatly bound in fine light-brown cloth. They
contain an aggregate of 12,350 pages, and are put up in a wooden case.

Also, still in stock,

*CARTERS' CHEAP SABBATH–SCHOOL LI-
BRARY. **No. 1.** 50 vols. in neat cloth. In a wooden case. Net,
$20.00.

DR. WILLIAMS ON THE LORD'S PRAYER.
$1.25.

DR. WILLIAMS ON RELIGIOUS PROGRESS.
$1.25.

TIM'S LITTLE MOTHER. By Punot. Illustrated.
$1.25.

FROGGY'S LITTLE BROTHER.　By Brenda.
Ilustrated.　16mo.　$1.25.

THE WONDER CASE. By the Rev. R. Newton,
D.D.　Containing:—

Bible Wonders $1.25	Leaves from Tree of Life . $1.25
Nature's Wonders 1.25	Rills from Fountain . . . 1.25
Jewish Tabernacle 1.25	Giants and Wonders . . . 1.25

6 *vols.　In a box.　$7.50.*

THE JEWEL CASE. By the Same. 6 vols. In a
box.　$7.50.

GOLDEN APPLES; or, Fair Words for the Young.
By the Rev. Edgar Woods. 16mo.　$1.00.

A LAWYER ABROAD.　By Henry Day, Esq.
12 full-page Illustrations.　$2.00.

THE PERIOD OF THE REFORMATION, — 1517
to 1648.　By Prof. Ludwig Häusser.　Crown 8vo.　$2.50.

⁕SONGS OF THE SOUL.　Gathered out of many
Lands and Ages.　By S. I. Prime, D.D.　Elegantly printed on super-
fine paper, and sumptuously bound in Turkey morocco, $9.00; cloth,
gilt, $5.00.

THE ARGUMENT OF THE BOOK OF JOB
UNFOLDED　By Prof. William Henry Green, D D.　12mo
$1.75.